Praise for
The Nesting

"A taut, scary thriller that winds the suspense so tightly you can barely breathe. I was rooting for the heroine all the way to the terrifying conclusion. This one will definitely keep you up at night."

— Simone St. James, *New York Times* bestselling author of *The Sun Down Motel*

"Norwegian fjords and folktales are beautifully evoked in this vivid and compelling novel."

— Rosamund Lupton, *New York Times* bestselling author of *Sister*

"An original and haunting thriller, filled with secrets, ghosts, and Norse folktales, *The Nesting* is an evocative and chilling tale that will keep you guessing and is best read with the lights on."

— Alice Feeney, *New York Times* bestselling author of *Sometimes I Lie*

"A gorgeous, atmospheric book that chilled me to the bone. The perfect escape book into the deep woods of Norway, where nothing is as it seems. C. J. Cooke just became one of my favorite authors."

— Samantha Downing, *USA Today* bestselling author of *My Lovely Wife*

"A thrilling blend of lore and suspense, *The Nesting* is a gripping, deliciously tense page-turner that will give you chills."

— Rachel Harrison, author of *The Return*

"Nordic folklore, snowy landscapes, and an ever-turning screw of tension—a fun, Gothic treat."

— Kirsty Logan, author of *The Gracekeepers*

"Chilling, totally engrossing, and full of intrigue. The pages just whizzed by."

—Katherine May, author of *Wintering*

"*The Nesting* is at once a taut psychological thriller, an eerie Nordic fable, and a thoughtful meditation on stewardship—not only of children but of friendship, of truth, and of the natural world we take for granted at our peril. Ms. Cooke tells her story with a spare, elegant prose that betrays a poet's ear and also a poet's discipline. The language is beautiful but effortlessly so, pushing the story forward in two deftly handled timelines. The characters are heartbreakingly three-dimensional yet tell us only what we need to know when we need to know it. This is my favorite kind of book—a quick read with a long echo."

—Christopher Buehlman, author of *Those Across the River*

the nesting

c. j. cooke

BERKLEY · NEW YORK

BERKLEY
An imprint of Penguin Random House LLC
penguinrandomhouse.com

Copyright © 2020 by C. J. Cooke
Readers Guide copyright © 2020 by C. J. Cooke
Penguin Random House supports copyright. Copyright fuels creativity, encourages
diverse voices, promotes free speech, and creates a vibrant culture. Thank you for buying
an authorized edition of this book and for complying with copyright laws by not reproducing,
scanning, or distributing any part of it in any form without permission. You are supporting
writers and allowing Penguin Random House to continue to publish books for every reader.

BERKLEY and the BERKLEY & B colophon are registered trademarks of
Penguin Random House LLC.

LIBRARY OF CONGRESS CATALOGING-IN-PUBLICATION DATA

Names: Jess-Cooke, Carolyn, 1978– author.
Title: The nesting / C.J. Cooke.
Description: First Edition. | New York: Berkley, 2020.
Identifiers: LCCN 2020011330 (print) | LCCN 2020011331 (ebook) |
ISBN 9780593197660 (trade paperback) | ISBN 9780593197677 (ebook)
Subjects: GSAFD: Horror fiction.
Classification: LCC PR6110.E78 N47 2020 (print) | LCC PR6110.E78 (ebook) |
DDC 823/.92—dc23
LC record available at https://lccn.loc.gov/2020011330
LC ebook record available at https://lccn.loc.gov/2020011331

First Edition: September 2020

Printed in the United States of America
10 9 8 7 6 5 4 3 2 1

Cover image © Lee Avison / Trevillion
Cover design by Sarah Oberrender

This is a work of fiction. Names, characters, places, and incidents either are the product
of the author's imagination or are used fictitiously, and any resemblance to actual persons,
living or dead, business establishments, events, or locales is entirely coincidental.

For
Jared
&
Phoenix

the nesting

prologue

Aurelia sprints through the dark forest, her white nightdress billowing like a cloud, her strides long and swift across the carpet of bark and brambles. She tries not to think too much about how the towering silver birches resemble skeletons, moonlight transforming the silvery trunks into endless prison bars and the weeping sky soaking her to the bone.

Her breaths come in quick, frantic gasps, her lungs ache, and her feet bleed, but he is tearing after her and he will do much, much worse to her than the forest, or the thing in the house. He will hurt the babies, Gaia and Coco, and she will do absolutely anything to protect them. She has to draw him away from them, as far as she can. For good, this time.

So she powers downhill, her heart trying to climb into her mouth and her mind churning like a river wheel, though she knows there is no way she can outrun him for long, and there is no one to call in the wilderness that spreads for miles on end all around.

She takes the trail toward the cliff, where a drop of two hundred feet connects the south end of a sapphire fjord to muscular granite. Her mind splits into two voices, one that tells her yes, this is the only way, the only option, and the other that shouts at her to turn back, it's crazy, utterly crazy.

She reaches the cliff edge sooner than she'd anticipated. Her toes feel the rush of icy air at the end of the path and she has to wrap her arms around an oak tree to stop herself from tumbling off the end.

She can hear the thud of his feet fifty feet behind. She has only seconds to decide. The risk is enormous. It isn't the thought of dying that brings a sob to her throat. It's the girls. Gaia and Coco. Growing up without her.

She sees them in her mind, two bright angels. Even when she feels him grow closer, she holds on to that vision and imagines reaching out to them, taking their hands.

Come on, Mumma! Hold on tight!

With a snarl he lunges at her, and quickly she darts out of his way, letting him plunge headlong toward the edge of the cliff, where there is nothing but night separating rock and water, life and certain death.

But his shoulder collides with hers, and although she reaches out to take her daughters' hands, her feet lift and she falls down, down into the endless dark.

Once upon a time there was a river who, like all rivers, knew exactly where she wished to go. Some people willed her to change her course, and when she did not bend to their will, they began to tear her apart, pebble by pebble, stone by stone.

Of course, the river won in the end, and returned to her route with a wet sigh of relief, running the length of her spine against the familiar gray rocks and stretching luxuriantly against the grooves of earth she had known for centuries.

And she made sure that the people paid dearly for their foolishness.

from P. Johansen's
Book of Remembered Norse Folk Tales, 1999
(trans. A. Faraday)

1

endless dark

M eg was the one who found me slumped against the bathroom wall with red pouring out of my arms. I could make out what she was saying, though it sounded like we were under water. *Oh no, oh no. Lexi! What the hell have you done, Lexi?*

She crouched in front of me and I wanted to tell her not to because she was going to ruin her lovely yellow skirt by kneeling in my blood. Also there was glass on the floor from the mirror I'd smashed and I'd feel awful if she cut herself.

She grabbed some towels, wrapped them around my arms, and started to cry when she couldn't tie them tight enough. Have you ever tried to tie a knot in a towel? Really difficult, it turns out.

Meg dialed 999 on her phone. By this stage I was swooping in and out of consciousness—I'd taken a fistful of paracetamol, just in case—and I could no longer decipher between reality and hallucination, which is always fine by me as long as neither is threatening. They must have hoiked me down the stairs and into the ambulance, but I don't remember any of that. I woke up in the hospital a few hours later, puking my guts up. I've no idea what they gave me, but it was efficient in wringing me out. They stitched me up, masked the cuts with padded dressings.

Meg came back the next day and brought me lunch in a brown paper bag and looked tearful when I said I couldn't touch it. David came and I immediately felt guilty again for being a burden on him. He said, "I had to use annual leave to come see you. What happened? Why are you here, Lex?"

I had no answer. I wondered if he'd had to clean up the blood. David was always squeamish.

A doctor came along, stood beside my bed with his hands in his pockets.

"Lexi, before we send you home we need to be sure you won't do this again. We need you to sign a form saying that you have no more plans to harm yourself."

He produced a form. I signed it. I took the bus home.

On the phone my mother said that I was always an attention seeker. I read somewhere that those who get under our skin are our best teachers, and while it sticks in me to call my mother a teacher of any kind, I'll say that her comment inadvertently sparked an epiphany, because even as she moved on to give me a blow-by-blow account of that morning's *Jerry Springer*, I realized that she was part of the reason I'd tried to top myself. And secondly, I realized that if I was to stay alive, I should probably stop speaking to her altogether.

I lost my job. I was working as an administrator at a care home and took a month off to recover. I didn't get a medical note, so they sacked me. It was probably illegal, but the thing with illness, mental or otherwise, is that it tends to annihilate your capacity for argument. At the time I was spending twenty-three hours a day in bed. For the first few weeks I mostly slept, though I had such psychedelic nightmares that it wasn't exactly restful. Dreams about my childhood, about my mother telling me she wished I'd never been born. Dreams of being shipped out to strangers while she "sorted herself out."

David didn't say much to me during this time. He went out to work every morning, sent me a text at lunchtime, and then came home at dinnertime with a ready meal or takeout. I didn't eat much. He'd sit in bed beside me marking homework assignments while I tried to follow *Game of Thrones*. When the cuts healed I started sleeping less, and the fear set in again. I asked David if I could go to work with him and he looked at me like I'd suggested he get a full body wax.

"Come to work with me? What for?"

I didn't want to say I was lonely at home. "Because I'm lonely at home."

"Go back to work, then."

"They sacked me, remember?"

"Can't you just look for a new job?"

"I could sit in the staff room and read."

"You can't do that . . ."

"Why not?"

"It would be weird, Lexi. You know it would."

"Maybe the janitor's cupboard."

"The what?"

"Don't schools still have those? Mine did."

"Look, I'll FaceTime you."

He didn't FaceTime me.

I went to the public library, but it was too loud. People were staring and it felt like being branded with hot irons. The books were full of stories that shouted at me and I worried they might fly off the shelves and hit me. Difficult to explain these kinds of things when a librarian is leaning over you asking why you're hyperventilating on the floor.

So I went home, opened my laptop, and started to write. I wrote and wrote and wrote. It was like the story was being dictated to me. It was about a twenty-eight-year-old woman who had a nightmarish childhood due to her mother passing her around to strangers who did terrible things to her, and the girl grew up to be an inventor and made millions and learned self-respect. Note the feminist angle. It was set in Norway. After my doomed trip to the public library, I realized I'd somehow managed to check out some novels, all of them whodunits set in bleak Nordic landscapes. Scandi noir. After I finished reading them I thought, *That's what my book is.* I tweaked a few details and lo, a Scandi noir it became.

I knew David was going to break up with me. We'd been together eight years and the last six had been fairly rough going. He was like the Arctic. Impenetrable, cold, rugged. I used to find those qualities attractive. Or rather, I remembered the look on my mother's face when she met him. She was all timid, couldn't get her words out. He was middle class, which is a bit like saying he was from Middle-earth, wielding a sword that turned blue at the prospect of charging orcs. My mother finds middle-class people—or in other words, anyone with a mortgage—intimidating.

That was reason enough for me to move in with him.

Being dumped went far worse than I'd expected. I hadn't really considered that the flat was technically David's and that if we broke up I might end up homeless, but there it was. He came home and looked like he'd had a few drinks, and he said:

"I can't do this anymore, Lexi. I can't take it. You're too much."

I looked at what he was wearing—since when had he started wearing a shirt and tie?—and said, "Too much of what?"

"Too much of *you*. We need to split. I'm sorry."

We hugged. It seemed very amicable. I felt a small amount of pride in what ego I had left that here I was facing the first big milestone of adulthood—namely, the death of my first long-term relationship—and yet I was still managing to say things like "no, no, you're right, it's better that we stay friends, that's the main thing" instead of falling apart. I felt very fond of him right then, because at least he looked like he regretted us parting ways.

But the next morning, he was back to being the Arctic personified.

"When are you moving out?" he said, avoiding eye contact as he did his tie. Navy blue with white stripes. Very corporate.

I looked around at all my stuff strewn across the bedroom floor and spewing out of the chest of drawers. I had barely enough strength to make it to the toilet and back, never mind pack eight years' worth of crap and organize a removal company. And a new home.

"When do you *want* me to move out?" I asked.

"By next week, if that's all right," he said, and I nodded as though this was a perfectly reasonable request. Note: I'd never done Breaking Up before, not when it involved moving out of my home. And I was on a daily 100 mg dose of an antipsychotic that occasionally made the bread bin initiate a conversation.

Next week came. I got dressed. Jeans, white T-shirt, bottle-green cardi, and a laser-cut necklace that spelled out *protagonist* in glossy black Helvetica. I filled a bag with some random items I thought I might need—a tin opener, clean socks, the toaster—and made a packed lunch.

I had forty-one pounds and fifty-nine pence in my bank account. I eyed my wardrobe, full of clothes, shoes, and Christmas presents, with trepidation. You might as well have asked me to dredge up the *Titanic* as ask me to find a way to pack all of it up. It didn't occur to me to ask anyone for help. I'd put everyone through enough. I'd ruined Meg's yellow skirt and traumatized that poor librarian.

So I took my packed lunch and bag and closed the door of the flat behind me, leaving my key on the table.

When I went outside it was raining. I didn't have an umbrella.

I had a coat, but no hood. This felt symbolic of my life up until that point. *She had a coat, but lo, it had no hood.*

I reached into my pocket in case I should find an unused poo bag from walking Mrs. Hughes's springer spaniel with which to shield my head against the downpour. No poo bag, but I did find David's prepaid rail pass. I'd found it in the hall and meant to give it to him, but the thought had trickled out of my head like a ribbon falling out of a ponytail.

At Newcastle I took a train headed to Birmingham New Street with lots of stops in between. I had no idea where I was going, and it didn't matter, because the train was moving, and it was a mild comfort to be headed *somewhere* when my entire life had come to a complete stop. Plus, I was dry, and my arms ached from hoiking around the Tefal four-slice stainless steel toaster that David had bought me for my last birthday.

The train was full of commuters. As ever I picked up on the cues of people's lives—accounts spreadsheets, text messages flashing up on screens with evening plans and reminders to pick up milk, phone conversations about a colleague or a sick aunt. I started to have those thoughts again, the ones that had persuaded me that I was already dead so it wouldn't be a big deal if I committed suicide. It would be a relief, and everyone would benefit from it. I started to cry. No one paid any heed until my shoulders started bobbing up and down, and then a group of women gathered around me like hens and asked me what was wrong. I told them I'd broken up with my boyfriend.

"Dear, oh, dear," one of them said, and another said, "Well, if you ask me, he sounds like a Grade A cockwomble," and they hugged me to their fleshy bosoms.

The train stopped at Durham. The hens told me I was pretty and young and didn't need a man, and then they got off the train. I dabbed my eyes and kept my gaze fixed on the cathedral, on its sharp spires jabbing the bellies of clouds. Cars threaded through the streets and a smudge of kids played in a back garden. I envied them their central heating and washing machines, the comfortable beds that they'd be able to climb into at the end of the day. I had none of that now, and I had the sensation of being a tiny boat cut loose and drifting rapidly along a thrashing river with a waterfall thundering in the distance. To make matters worse, it occurred to me that I'd left my medication in David's flat. I found my mobile phone in my bra and rang his number, but it didn't connect. He had blocked me.

Panic started to stir in me like a thousand manic butterflies. What was I going to do? Where would I go?

I would end it.

That's what I would do.

Properly, this time.

My own reflection came into view in the glass, and I jumped, thinking at first that a woman had somehow materialized on the other side of the window. But no, it was me. I barely recognized myself. It had been ages since I looked in a mirror—I deliberately avoided this because I hated myself so much—but there I was, looking back at myself.

My reflection had a surprising look of grit. She didn't look nearly as awful as I felt. She was thin, yes, and her outgrown bob was messy, and she had dark circles under her eyes, but she looked like someone I'd like to talk to. Someone who would listen and not wait until it was their turn to offer an opinion.

My reflection said, *You're writing a book, remember? If you die, the book won't get finished.*

I remembered I'd promised myself that I'd finish writing this damn book. This untitled Scandi noir that was unfolding quite nicely, unlike my miserable life. I owed it to that book—to the little girl in the story, Alexa, who suffered so much—to tell the world her story.

2

hauled in by the throat

NOW

The train filled with new passengers and started to pull out of Durham station. A couple of younger women sat in the seats in front with their backs to me, continuing a loud conversation about a job that one of them was applying for.

"But, Sophie, do you *really* want to go to Norway?" the one in the blue top said.

My ears pricked up. Norway? My novel was set in Norway. Oslo, to be precise. All the other Scandi noir novels I'd read were set there, and the murderously-hostile-but-dramatic Nordic landscape felt very much like the inside of my brain. So in a way, although I'd never been to Norway, the place felt intriguingly familiar.

"Well, not really," Sophie said, "but Lucia's starting school and Philippa said she'll only need me during the summer holidays. And that's not enough, is it?"

"Couldn't you just get another job during the school term?" Sophie's friend countered. "And then nanny for Philippa during the summer hols?"

"I've got my application all ready," Sophie said, flipping open her laptop and turning it to her friend. "All I have to do is click send."

I could see it through the gap between the seats. I leaned forward and saw the white page of a PDF with boxes requesting information about previous employment and a large white section where Sophie had written a statement—in Comic Sans—about why she wanted the job. A sentence began, *The well-being of children is my number one priority,* but I couldn't make out the rest of it. Just then Sophie's friend flicked her long black hair over one shoulder, obscuring my view.

"How long is it for?" Sophie's friend whined.

Sophie mumbled a reply, but I didn't hear, though her friend gasped.

"You can't go to Norway for that long!" she said, horrified. "That's *ages.*"

"I know," Sophie said sadly, "but it's a great job. Really well paid. All food and board taken care of, super gorgeous locale. They want someone to start right away . . ."

Now I was *really* interested. Free food and accommodation in Norway? Well paid? I could feel myself being drawn in—no, *hauled* in, by the throat—and there was a tingling sensation all over my body that I hadn't experienced in a long, long time. Kind of like falling in love, only without the certainty that it's going to end in tears and vile accusations.

When I was little, Mrs. Corbett—my year four teacher, who didn't get under my skin but who showered me with love and the kind of smiles that made me stand a little taller—told me about *serendipity.* A happy accident, she said, orchestrated by the universe. She said we were all made of star dust—which I thought was gross at the time—so the oldest parts of our being would recognize when something was serendipitous. I told her that when

I met her I had a big shiver all over, and she crouched down and said, "That is *exactly* what serendipity feels like, Lexi, sweetheart. Exactly that."

"You *can't* go!" Sophie's friend hissed. "Look, I wasn't going to say anything for another week or so, but . . . I'm pregnant!"

Sophie gave a squeal and wrapped her arms around her friend. "Oh. My. Word. *What?!*"

Her friend was sniffling and giggling now and I rose a little higher in my seat to catch sight of the laptop screen for the job details.

"When are you due?" Sophie said, hugging her friend and rubbing her back.

"February. I *need* you here, Soph. I was counting on you helping me out, especially since I've got this project to deliver by bloody Christmas. I wanted you to be my doula. Please? Look, whatever this job pays, I'll double it."

Sophie considered. "All right," she said, smiling. "Oh, blimey, a *baby,* Seren?"

Seren. Like serendipity.

It was as though the universe was pointing a gigantic, God-like finger from parting clouds right at me, and a Charlton Heston voice was booming, *This job is meant for you, Lexi Ellis.*

I had to get the details of that job. Not just the details—I had to get Sophie's statement, her CV, and her references. After all, she was the one with the experience in nannying, not me. In one wild moment of crystalline clarity, I knew what I would have to do in order to get the job—I would have to pretend I was Sophie.

"I'm going to get some lunch," Sophie announced. "Are you hungry? Well, you will be, won't you? Now that you're eating for two!"

Her friend—Seren—deliberated. I'd pulled out my phone by this point, hell-bent on getting a screenshot of the laptop screen before she put it away, but Seren was blocking my view, and just as she rose up out of her seat she closed the laptop lid. My heart sank.

Thanks, Universe. Thanks for toying with me.

"Hold up," Seren called after Sophie. "I'm coming."

Sophie glanced back at her bag and laptop, a worried look on her face. She was tall and slender, long auburn hair to her waist, and a belly top revealing a slender midriff. To my horror, she caught my eye.

"Would you mind?" she began, and I stared back at her, cow-eyed. "Would you mind watching my stuff while we head to the buffet carriage?"

"Oh," I said, finding sudden composure. "Not at all."

She flashed an appreciative smile. "Thanks."

The two of them headed off down the carriage chatting loudly, and I breathed a sigh of relief. I glanced around to check no one was looking before reaching an arm through the gap in the seat and lifting the lid of the laptop. It was probably password pro-tected. Damn. Quickly I flipped it open and the screen whitened. To my relief, the PDF of the job application was there, right in front of me, and so I thrust my phone forward and took picture after picture of the screen. I scrolled up and down on the keypad, no longer really seeing what I was taking photos of, but snapping hastily at everything and anything to make sure I got it all.

"Thank you so much!"

Sophie's voice sounded, sending a javelin of fear right through me, and I sat back in my seat, sweat streaming down my back and my heart clanging in my chest. As Sophie and Seren tucked into their croissants and coffees I scrolled through my phone and zoomed in on the images I'd taken. Some were blurry, most were lopsided, but it didn't matter. I'd got what I needed.

My name was now Sophie Hallerton and I had a brief CV detailing my nannying experience, an e-mail address for a reference, and a saccharine statement in florid prose about my passion for looking after children. In other words, I was *set*.

I set up an e-mail account. Sophiehallerton1088@gmail.com. I downloaded the form and copied out the answers and Sophie's responses. If there was one thing I was good at, or at least something I used to do all day long in my last job, it was completing forms and setting up e-mail accounts. Finally, I sent off the application from my new e-mail address.

As the train pulled into Birmingham New Street three hours later, my phone bleeped with an e-mail.

> To: sophiehallerton1088@gmail.com
> From: maren.larsen@tfarchitecture.net
>
> Subject: Re: job application
>
> Dear Sophie:
>
> Many thanks for your application for the position of Nanny.
>
> We would like to invite you to interview for this role as soon as possible.
>
> Would you be available to meet with myself and Mr. Faraday next Wednesday at 1 p.m.? The address is: 313 Rowan Gardens, London, NW3 5TD.
>
> We will contact the person(s) you have listed as employment references in the meantime, if that's OK?
>
> Kind regards,
> Maren Larsen

My heart leaped. I felt sick and excited at the same time, exactly the same feeling I had when I jumped off the top diving board at the swimming pool, or went on the Ferris wheel with the creaky carriages.

To: maren.larsen@tfarchitecture.net
From: sophiehallerton1088@gmail.com

Subject: Re: Re: job application

Hi, Maren,

Thank you for your e-mail.

Yes, I'd be delighted to attend this interview.

Kind regards,
Sophie Hallerton

A reply swooped back within seconds—wonderful, see you then—and I leaned back in my seat, my nerves pinging with excitement and adrenaline. Sophie and Seren sat in front of me sucking croissant flakes from their fingers and discussing baby names and birth plans, the job application long forgotten.

Next Wednesday was exactly a week away. The rail pass expired at midnight that day, though David could easily cancel it before then once he worked out it was missing. If he did, I didn't have enough money to buy another ticket. Come to think of it, I hadn't enough money to book a place to stay until then.

Using the last of my phone's battery, I dialed Meg.

3

a place to stay

NOW

M eg didn't answer her phone.
I sat on the train, watching the platform fill up with people making their way to the exit. I tried Meg again, and again.

"Aren't you getting off, miss?" a train conductor asked from the aisle.

"Oh. Yes," I said, trying not to be "weird and twitchy," as David had often accused me of being. I hoisted up my bag and saw him eyeing the contents. I stepped onto the platform and headed for the exit. Outside I spotted a café, and in a series of highly focused nonweird and nontwitchy movements, I ordered a coffee and parked myself at a table.

What happened next wasn't ideal. First, my phone battery died, then the waitress came and told me they were closing in ten minutes. I realized with shock that it was almost six o'clock in the evening. This is the thing with depression, and particularly with antipsychotics—your internal clock goes AWOL, as does your libido, hunger, balance, focus, sense of humor, and short-term memory. So I wandered around trying to forage for a phone charger, then caved and got back on the train to Newcastle, which was now full of drunk, red-faced blokes shouting about a football match. I found a seat as far away from them as possible and curled up in a ball, hoping they wouldn't shout at me, which they did. And then, at York, the train broke down. Signal failure. We had to get off, were promised we'd be refunded. It was freezing cold, the platform was swarming with aggressive football fans, and I had nowhere to go.

I approached one of the police officers who had serendipitously appeared on the platform.

"Excuse me," I said, and in my mind I was poised to tell them a story about losing my purse, and could they point me in the direction of a hostel? My mouth, however, had other ideas. "I'm homeless and I've nowhere to go and two months ago I tried to kill myself so will you help me please I'm so lonely," my mouth said, and I started to cry.

Within a minute I was being asked to get into the police car, and within ten minutes I was standing outside a women's refuge.

The refuge had a big common area with sofas and a hand-painted mural of a forest across three walls, and a kitchen for us to eat together. The dorms were all full of women and children, but the lady in charge said I could spend the night on a sofa.

I ended up spending the week there. It felt nice, like a little community of bruised, terrified, and addicted women. Jill ran the place with a team of volunteers. Jill was large and had bright red hair piled on top of her head and she always wore a black vest top with a swishy black skirt with purple Dr. Martens. There was a massive garden out the back with deck chairs, and Jill told me every day to sit out there and "clear my mind." A doctor visited and I told her I needed a refill prescription of the medicine I'd been on. She frowned and suggested I try a lower dose of something that was apparently "less taxing" on the brain. Another woman—

a volunteer at a charity shop—came around with clothes, which was great as I literally had only the clothes on my back. I picked out a black trouser suit with a white shirt for my interview, and she found me some sensible shoes.

Wednesday came and I got on the train to London for the interview. I was super nervous, but Jill put some makeup on me and insisted that I look at myself in the mirror. I was surprised. My eyes always looked sallow, but she'd blotted out the dark circles with concealer and added mascara and a flick of kohl just above my eyelashes. A dab of bronzer made me look healthy, and on my lips she dabbed a demure coral lipstick that apparently made my eyes "pop." I found this to be a rather distressing mental image, so Jill clarified: "It means your lovely brown eyes look like melted chocolate. OK?" Melted chocolate can only ever be a pleasant thing.

I also washed my hair for the first time in weeks—months, maybe—and she used a hair dryer and scorching-hot tongs to bring it to life.

"There you are, my lovely," she said, spritzing my hair with something called "gunk." "Just like Kim Kardashian, you are."

I'd expected the interview to be in some big, space-agey skyscraper, but instead the taxi dropped me outside a beautiful mansion in leafy Hampstead—close to the Freud Museum, as it happens. I'd often wondered if lying on a couch talking about my problems—or rather, my mother—would have done a better job of fixing me than medication, but then I figured that slathering myself in snake oil or burying a potato at the root of an oak tree on a full moon would have done a better job of fixing me than medication, so the answer was probably a resounding yes.

I walked up the garden path and pressed the buzzer outside the red door, which had a crescent of stained glass in every color.

A heavyset woman with cropped platinum-blonde hair opened the door. She looked like she was midfifties, with a handsome face and an intelligent, penetrating look about her.

"I'm here for the interview?" I said softly. "I'm Lex— Sophie. My name is Sophie Hallerton."

Damn. I'll never remember to keep that one up. Sophie. I'm Sophie. Sophie. Sophie. Sophie.

"Maren," the woman said, holding out a hand. I shook it. "Do come in."

It became clear that the house wasn't an architecture firm but a family home, with rustic wooden floors, sage-green walls dotted with family photographs, an old rocking horse, and a glass cabinet filled with pictures and cute ornaments in the spacious hallway. A staircase swept upward, where a children's program was playing on a TV. Maren gestured for me to follow her through the hallway toward a large kitchen, which was a mixture of high-end design and country charm. An open-brick chimney breast was filled with a silver range cooker; in the center of the room was an island with six white barstools and an arrangement of baby-pink peonies. To my left, a pretty garden was visible through French doors: a weeping willow, a pond. The marble surfaces were pristine, but I could make out children's drawings stuck to the doors of a double fridge freezer standing at the far end of the room. Whoever lived here clearly cared a lot about their family.

"Can I get you anything to drink?" Maren said, and I noticed a hint of an accent. Clipped, European. "Tea? Coffee?"

"Just . . . a glass of water," I said. She took a glass from a cupboard and filled it at the fridge freezer's water dispenser, then got one for herself.

"Thanks," I said.

She gestured for me to take a seat at the kitchen island and did the same. This wasn't how I expected the interview to go. I noticed she was wearing a floaty navy tunic with white linen trousers, and I suddenly felt overdressed.

"Thank you very much for your application," she said. "We were very impressed by your experience. This is clearly a vocation for you."

It took me a moment to deduce that this was a question. I nodded and gave what I hoped was a relaxed, vocational smile.

"Oh, *yes*," I said. "Definitely a vocation."

"Wonderful that you have a nursing degree."

"Oh," I said. "Er, yes. I thought it might . . . come in handy one day."

"And a certificate in vegan cookery!"

I blinked. Was that on Sophie's CV? I couldn't remember. "Vegan cookery is something I'm very . . . vocational . . . about."

"Fantastic!" she said, clapping her hands together. "I'm not vegan myself, though I am partial to red lentil tagine."

"Oh, yes," I said, unconvincingly. "Me, too . . ."

"Of course, Mr. Faraday is vegan," she interjected, "and he intends his girls to be vegan, too." I gave a nervous laugh. Why hadn't I noticed the bit about being a *vegan chef*? Maren glanced at her watch. "Speaking of which . . . Mr. Faraday will be joining us shortly, but first I wanted to chat to you about . . . one or two matters that you should be aware of."

She gave me a meaningful smile, and I felt acutely aware, now that I was here, that I hadn't read the job description. It was a nannying job, and I'd assumed that meant looking after some children, or in other words lots of reading and painting and trips to the park. You see, I used to babysit regularly—albeit for my mum's friends who were either too unconscious or preoccupied with partying to care for their kids—and I'd toyed with the idea of training to become a primary school teacher. None of my babysitting involved vegan cookery, however, or indeed anything that a nursing degree might find a use for, with the exception of the time little Bobby Fitzmaurice cracked his head open on a bong. Duct tape and toilet roll sorted him right out.

"Mrs. Faraday—Aurelia—sadly passed away a few months ago," Maren said slowly. "Naturally the children are still getting used to the situation . . . Gaia in particular, given that she's a little older . . . and we are trying everything to make life as easy as possible . . ."

"I'm very sorry," I said, the gravity of her words reaching me like physical blows.

"Gaia and Coco have a nanny here," Maren continued, "but sadly she is unable to join us in Norway during the build."

I felt a huge amount of relief at the mention of the children's names. This was another detail I'd overlooked. Gaia and Coco. What pretty names. It would have been disastrous if I hadn't known their names. Poor girls, to have lost their mother so young.

"The build?" I asked.

"Tom and Aurelia bought land in Norway. They intended to build a holiday home, but during the construction period, Aurelia . . . passed." I saw her pale eyes moisten, and I realized she must have been close to this woman. I'd spotted a photo on top of the glass cabinet in the hallway of a woman with long, wheat-blonde hair grinning at the camera with an arm wrapped around a little girl of about four. Was that Aurelia? It must be.

"Aurelia adored her girls," Maren continued in a sad voice. "They meant *everything* to her. Part of the reason for the summer home was so that she could cultivate *friluftsliv*—"

"Oh, *friluftsliv*," I said, because of course.

"—which is the Norwegian itch for the outdoors," Maren explained. "Aurelia wished to give her daughters the kind of summers that she had enjoyed as a child, always out in nature, and connect them to their heritage . . ." She wanted to say more but suddenly couldn't, her words winnowed by grief. She reached into her pocket for a tissue and dabbed her eyes. "And now," she said in a stronger voice, clearing her throat, "the build must recommence, but Tom is anxious to be on-site for its duration and requires the children and nanny to be with him. I'm Tom's housekeeper, and I'll also be there." She stuffed the hankie up her sleeve and turned to me with shining eyes, the memory of Aurelia evidently filed away in her mind so that normal service could resume.

"The job will require you to be with the children on-site on a full-time basis," she said, "at least until March. Is that a problem?" Her eyes searched my fingers for any sign of a ring. "No . . . partner who'll want you home for Christmas?"

"Oh," I said. "No. Quite the opposite, in fact."

She frowned at that, but something in her mind told her that this was the answer she wanted and she moved on. "Well, your reference was *glowing*, of course. Tom only sent the application pack to a selection of trusted associates—we don't use recruitment agencies or anything like that—so we were delighted when Verity championed you."

She was beaming now, and my face contorted into a rictus grin while my mind did somersaults. *Verity?*

"Oh, Verity," I said lightly. "She's . . . that's so kind . . ."

Maren batted her hand in the air as though I was being modest, not clueless. "Of *course* she championed you. And after the thing in Belgium . . ."

I gave a nervous giggle and eyed the door. *What thing in Belgium?* I wanted to shriek. It was abundantly, sharply clear now that I was way out of my depth. It was wrong to lie to a family who'd lost their mother. It was wrong to parade as something I wasn't, despite how desperate I was. I placed a foot on the floor and lifted my hips off the chair, preparing myself to sprint the hell out of there.

"Hello?" a man's voice called. I looked up and saw a figure in the French doors, silhouetted by celestial afternoon sunlight that was swelling in the garden. A tall, lean man in a smart navy polo shirt and chinos, dark, tousled hair flecked with silver, and a hint of beard. A slightly more upmarket, skinnier Colin Farrell, with rimless glasses and overlapping front teeth. He marched across the room toward me and extended a hand. A gold wedding band flashed in the light. "Tom Faraday," he said, grinning. "You must be Sophie. A pleasure to meet you."

"A pleasure to meet you, too," I said.

He raised his eyebrows. "Is that a Geordie accent?"

I hesitated. "Yes?"

He glanced at Maren. "Spend a lot of time in the north, did you?"

"I . . . looked after a child from the north," my mouth said, while my brain tried to keep up. "She was homesick and so I adopted her accent to make her . . . less homesick." Phew. My excuse seemed to make sense. But I would have to curb my accent. Now that I thought about it, Sophie didn't sound particularly northern.

A warm smile. "Well, that's very kind of you. How long have you been nannying?"

"Ten years," I blurted out. *Lies, lies, lies,* said my brain.

I was sure Maren would launch into questions about the specifics of this—*who* did I nanny, and where—but she merely smiled and said, "And if you had to describe your nannying *style,* what would you say?"

I tried to make up another lie, but a squeak came out. My bladder was actually threatening to explode right there on the floor.

I stood up. "Sorry," I said. "But is there a loo I could use?"

"Certainly," Tom said, spinning around to his left. "Straight ahead, past the fridge. Oh, on second thought, best not, as it's still blocked. Kids and their toys . . . Use the one upstairs. Second door on the left."

"Thanks."

I headed quickly upstairs and locked the toilet door behind me, then sat down with my head between my knees and groaned. What was I doing? *What. Was. I. Doing?*

I spent a few moments taking deep breaths and planning my next moves. I would go back downstairs and tell them that I was very sorry but I couldn't do it after all. My friend was pregnant—or Sophie's friend was pregnant—and I had to be around for her. Or Plan B: I'd tiptoe back down the stairs, open the front door, and run the hell out of there.

I was still weighing up Plan A and Plan B when I opened the door to find a small child staring up at me. She had white-blonde hair tied back in a loose plait, a pink gingham dress with a strap hanging off one shoulder, both arms behind her back. Round green eyes shone through turquoise spectacles, and I noticed that someone had drawn pictures all over her hands and bare legs in red felt-tip. She surveyed me curiously.

"Are you my new nanny?" she said.

"I'm . . . I'm Sophie," I said.

It sickened me to lie to a child, I swear, but I could hear Tom's footsteps on the stairs.

"I'm Gaia," she said. "I'm six. How old are you?"

"I'm twenty-eight."

"My mumma's in heaven," she said.

This was a sucker punch to my heart. "I'm so sorry," I said.

"This is my teddy," she said, producing an old teddy from behind her back with floppy limbs, a tweed waistcoat, and a missing eye. "He's not feeling very well today."

It was clear that there would be no sprinting out the front door, so I crouched down in front of her and said, "What's your teddy's name?"

"Louis."

"And why's Louis not feeling very well?"

"He's just feeling a bit sad. And he has a sore tummy."

"Ah," Tom said, reaching the top of the stairs. "I see you've met Gaia and Louis." He winked at Gaia. "How are you doing, pudding?"

"Daddy!" She ran to him with her arms out, wrapping them around his legs and burying her face in his thigh. "Is this my new nanny?" she said, glancing back at me.

Tom scooped her up and grinned at me. "Well, that depends."

"On what?"

"Shall we introduce Sophie to Coco?"

Tom gestured for me to follow him into one of the bedrooms and I opened my mouth to say something along the lines of *I have to go now*, but somehow I found myself in the sweetest child's bedroom I'd ever seen, more a mini apartment than a bedroom, with thick cream carpet, powder-blue velvet curtains, and peachblossom walls, a crescent moon made out of twinkling LED lights, a miniature hot-air balloon as a chandelier, and enough toys to fill a crèche, including a plush, twelve-foot toy giraffe. The name *Coco* was hand-painted in fancy gold lettering across a wall, and when I looked over the white sleigh cot I saw a little girl in a Babygro hanging on to the bars, her legs wobbling as she looked up and threw me a wet smile.

"I'm Ellen," a voice said. "How do you do?"

I hadn't noticed the woman in a long green dress sitting by the crib. She was cross-legged, her arms held out in that absent-minded way I'd seen mothers do when their babies were learning to walk. The nanny who Maren mentioned before. The one who couldn't go to Norway.

"Sophie," I said, uneasily. Coco let go of the bars and plopped down on her bottom, then turned around and started to crawl. Tom bent down and scooped her up. Blonde, downy curls around her neck, like a little duckling, the same wide green eyes as Gaia. She was adorable.

"And this is Coco," Tom said, planting a kiss on her cheek.

I was struck by how young Coco was, particularly since her mother had passed away.

"She's nine months old," Tom told me; it was as though he was thinking the same thing. He seemed lost in thought for a moment, then pulled himself together. I can tell when people do that. "She's just learning to crawl," he said then, his voice slightly loud. "And she can say Dada. Say Dada, Coco. Da-da."

Coco smiled wetly at him. "Ma-ma," she said. "Ma-ma. Ma-ma."

The room was suddenly charged with emotion, and I felt my lies pressing down on me like lead weights. But just then, Coco reached out to me, both her hands open wide. Tom passed her to me and I took her, feeling the lovely warmth of her in my arms. I swear, I've never been remotely maternal or gooey over other people's kids—quite the opposite, especially during the drool stage—but there was something different about Coco and Gaia. Or maybe I just related to their loss.

It was clear that Coco had an interest in my hair—she grabbed on to it and yanked it hard, and even when Tom stepped forward to undo her grip she did it again and laughed hysterically. I pulled a face and she clapped her hands together and laughed again. I pulled another face and she squealed in delight.

"Shall I let you spend some time with the girls?" Tom asked me. "Ellen can fill you in on their routines."

The urge to run out of there screaming was starting to wane. I was on surer territory now, especially since I felt so comfortable around Gaia and Coco. It almost felt like I'd known them much longer than three minutes.

Serendipity. That's what it felt like.

Tom left me and Ellen to chat while Gaia and Coco played in the nursery. Ellen told me she'd worked for Tom for just two and a half months, but she was getting married and couldn't go to

Norway. I could see she'd been torn about this and it was clear she loved the girls.

"So you didn't know their mother?" I said, calculating the length of time Ellen said she'd been in the post and the length of time it had been since Aurelia died.

Ellen shook her head. "No. It's clear that they were devastated, though they're so young that it takes a long time to process something like that, losing your mother . . ." She paused briefly. "It was one of the reasons Tom wanted me to nanny for him, while he tried to keep his business going and get his head around it all. I've had child counseling training, you see." She glanced over at Gaia, who was playing with an enormous dollhouse. "They're doing much, much better now, though Gaia still asks questions. Just so you know, if she asks what happened, the party line is: *Mummy had an accident and is in heaven.*"

I nodded, though the phrasing made me unsettled. "An accident?" I said cautiously.

Ellen dropped her gaze to the floor. "Suicide," she said in a low voice. "Terrible, isn't it? What would drive someone to do something like that?"

The scabs on my arms began to itch beneath my sleeves. "Yes," I said after a long pause. "Terrible."

I left an hour later, both exhilarated and disgusted with myself. There was no way I could take the job, absolutely *no freaking way*. I'd be lying to a family who had been utterly devastated by an unthinkable tragedy.

But on the other hand, I wanted to be a part of their lives.

I wanted to go to Norway, yes, and I wanted a home and a chance to write my book and turn my life around. But Gaia and Coco were sweet, precious girls who had lost their mother to something I knew better than I knew myself, and beneath the usual thrumming cacophony of self-hatred in my head was a quiet but insistent whisper that maybe—just maybe—I could actually make a difference.

It's up to you, Universe, I thought. *Que será, será, okeydokey?*

On the train back to York, an e-mail arrived in my in-box.

To: sophiehallerton1088@gmail.com
From: tom.faraday@tfarchitecture.net

Subject: nanny

Dear Sophie,

Can you start on Monday?

Warmly,
Tom

4

the nanny

NOW

I could not believe it.

I had to scroll up and down a few times to make sure there was no *P.S. Just kidding, loser!* at the bottom of the e-mail. I even zoomed in on the e-mail address to make sure it was from *that* Tom, the same Tom with the crinkly gray eyes behind rimless glasses, the same Tom whose sadness had swirled around the room when his baby girl said "Ma-ma," and then I had to say the e-mail out loud to check that I wasn't getting the wrong end of the stick—"Can you start on Monday?" really *did* mean "We're offering you the job," didn't it?

I clapped my hand to my mouth and gave a little scream. I thought I'd come across a little too wired-to-the-moon, especially when Maren was asking all the questions about my nursing degree and vegan cookery.

Speaking of which, I had five days to learn everything I could about veganism, and I figured I ought to brush up on some first aid . . . When I managed to get my hand to stop shaking I e-mailed back and said I'd be *delighted* to accept the job, and a reply came back shortly after saying that *he* was delighted, too, and that details of the flight I'd need to book to Norway would follow shortly after from Maren, as well as money to pay for it.

I could hardly keep still in my seat. It was as if every emotion in existence had come blasting into the train carriage in a torrent, drenching me and leaving me gasping for air. I always did feel things a little stronger than the next person, but usually it was Bad Feelings that I felt strongly, and I'd basically gone through life like a dandelion clock, blown to smithereens over and over by an endless series of misfortunes that gusted into my life. But now—*now*—things seemed to be actually working out, and while it wasn't a feeling to which I was accustomed, it was the best high ever.

A woman sat in the seat opposite staring at her phone with a frown, and I desperately wanted to reach across the table and shake her by the shoulders, screaming, *I've got somewhere to live! Isn't that great?* And I wanted to shout about how I felt this was *meant to be*, that those little girls needed me in their lives and that the book I was writing was going to basically write itself, now that I was going to live in Norway surrounded by moody fjords and sinister, abandoned fishing villages.

Then I started to weep. I felt staggered by relief. Shortly after that, paranoia kicked in. A tiny voice in my head that sounded exactly like Eartha Kitt whispered, *But what about when they find out you're not Sophie Hallerton?* But to that voice I said, *Shut up, shut up!* and when the woman across from me looked up sharply I realized I'd said this out loud.

I pulled out my phone and dialed Meg's number. I was on complete autopilot, and it was only when she answered that I realized with a jolt that I'd not spoken to her since she came to see me in the hospital. Also, she answered with a distracted "Yeah?," as though she was expecting someone else to be on the other end of the line and I worried I might be disturbing her.

"Meg? It's me, Lexi. You're not going to *believe* what I'm going to tell—"

"Where are you?" she demanded, and I glanced out the window in case we were near something that indicated my location. Still just fields, sheep, and wind turbines.

"I'm not exactly sure. I'm on a train . . ."

"Right, but where have you *been*? I've . . . I've been calling you *loads* . . ."

I told her about the women's refuge and the interview in Hampstead, about how I'd used David's rail pass to get there and was in fact using it now, though I wasn't quite sure where I was headed. I covered the handset with my fingertips and hissed at the woman opposite, who was starting to look considerably nervous.

"Where is this train headed?" I asked her.

She cleared her throat. "Inverness?"

I reported this back to Meg. "Anyway, I'm moving to Norway on Monday, but I've nowhere to stay until then so I wondered if I can stay with you? And maybe you can lend me some clothes? I'll be gone until March and I legit have one set of clothes."

A long pause on the other end of the line. "Do you mean . . . you're coming tonight?"

"Is that OK? I'll see if I can get off somewhere near Newcastle. If not, I'll get a train back from Inverness . . . Can you pick me up from the station?"

"Yes," Meg said, strangely emphatic. "Yes, absolutely. Just . . . text me whenever you get in, yeah?"

"OK, but it might be really late . . ."

"That's *fine*. See you when you get in."

"OK."

"Oh, and, Lexi?"

"Yeah?"

"I'm so glad you're safe."

There was a weird, motherly tone to her voice. I hung up and frowned at the phone, then the woman opposite. "What was all that about?" I asked her, and she gave a nervous shake of her head in response. "I mean, I don't have a single missed call from Meg. I don't think she's rung me *once* all week. Why would she lie to me?"

The woman muttered a reply, but I was too caught up in my own thoughts to really hear it. I'd known Meg for over ten years. We'd gone to college together, both of us cajoled into getting a diploma in business studies when the creative writing course turned out to be full. Meg wrote micro horror stories in biro, usually on people's skin, a precedent for her current job as a tattoo artist. We were always close, and sometimes I confided in her when I felt down.

"She sounds . . . very nice," the woman said, and I agreed. Meg was the closest thing to a soul mate I'd ever had. I'd miss her when I went to Norway.

The train pulled in to Newcastle a couple of hours later. I called Meg, and ten minutes later she was on the platform, waving her arm in the air. I noticed how dressed up she was, in a cerulean swing dress with white polka dots, her pink hair swept up in a chignon speared with a peacock feather. She pulled me into a tight hug, and then we walked to her car.

Meg's flat was in the Avenues in Gateshead, close to Saltwell Park. When we pulled up I noticed a To Let sign outside. I asked her about it, but she didn't answer. She made me dinner—a fry sandwich, a banana, and a cup of tea—while I told her all about the interview, about Tom and Gaia and Coco, and about my novel. She didn't say anything. I noticed she'd had a new tattoo done. A big fox on her left biceps in thick black ink.

"I have a favor to ask," I said finally, when she didn't respond the way I thought she might. "Obviously I'm a bit skint just now, so I can't afford to get my mail redirected, and David has blocked my number. Could you possibly nip round every month or so and pick up my post 'til I get back?"

She looked winded.

"What's wrong?" I said.

She sat down at the table and clasped her hands, so that the letters on her knuckles read *LHOAVTEE*.

"Look, I'm just going to say it," she said, lowering her eyes. "I'm . . . David and I . . ."

"David and you *what*?"

I felt like I was in a meeting with my manager, about to be given a Verbal Warning. She was wearing pea-green eyeshadow and navy lipstick. I always admired how Meg could pull off color like that.

"You've been pretty hard to deal with, Lex," she said tersely. "Canceling plans at the last minute, not responding to text messages . . . You've never even paid me back that forty quid I lent you."

"When was this?" I asked, flustered. "Forty quid?"

"And you lost my Zara dress."

"I . . ." The Zara dress flashed into my mind. Meg was a champion at finding amazing dresses. This one was an elegant chiffon number that I'd borrowed a couple of years ago when David and I went to York. I'd left it at the hotel and they'd never sent it on. I'd offered to buy her a replacement on eBay, but she said not to worry about it.

"I didn't mean to lose your Zara dress, Meg. You know I didn't."

She rolled her eyes and leaned back in her seat as if I'd told a barefaced lie. "You see? It's always about *you*, Lexi. You're so wrapped up in your own stuff that you never consider what other people are going through."

The room seemed to be breathing and I felt a migraine coming on. Did she pick me up just to give me a bollocking?

"I'm sorry," I said meekly, and she started to say more about something else I'd done, but then she clapped her hands to her eyes and started to cry.

"Meg . . . ?"

She lifted her hands off her face, her makeup streaked all down it.

"I know I'm a complete tit at the best of times," I said. "But . . . I'm sensing this really isn't about your Zara dress or the money I borrowed."

She looked down at her lap.

"Look," she said. "David and I . . . We're moving in together."

"OK," I said gently.

She rubbed her nose. "And I know this sounds like I'm a bad friend, but it wasn't planned. We just . . . I didn't intend for everything to happen like this. OK?"

"OK."

"I'm going to make it up to you," she said, reaching over to a box of tissues on the worktop and dabbing her eyes. "I'm going to go over to his flat tomorrow and pack up a suitcase of your things for you to take to Norway."

I wondered if I should mention that David insisted on separating our food with named labels, even after eight years of living together, that he snored like a tractor was passing through the bedroom, or that he liked to cut his toenails with one foot raised on the dinner table, usually while I was eating. Maybe she already knew this.

"Here," she said, sliding a silver door key across the table. "There's milk and bread and eggs in the fridge. I'll bring some ham and carrots tomorrow night."

I tried to imagine a meal made of ham and carrots, but she interrupted my thoughts to ask if I'd left anything at David's that I needed. My mind turned to the wall clock in the spare bedroom in the shape of a jam jar, my rattan bookcase, and my framed Frida Kahlo print, but Meg disagreed that these were crucial items for a seven-month trip to Norway.

"Where are you going?" I asked when she got up.

"I'm staying at David's," she said in a thin voice, looking away. "You can stay here. I'll bring your stuff and take you to the airport on Monday. OK?"

Oddly enough, I wasn't perturbed at all by the thought of my best friend shacking up with my long-term partner a mere fortnight after we'd broken up. I was more concerned—amused, even—by the thought of Meg discovering that he liked to spend weekends holed up in the spare bedroom with violent video games and a bag of weed, or his weird thing about digging half an inch of wax out of each ear, only to leave a ceremonious row of used cotton buds lined up along the sink instead of chucking them in the bin.

That night, it is safe to say I had the best sleep I'd had for months.

The next day Meg turned up with ham and carrots and a large suitcase of clothes I'd forgotten I even had. I was pleased to find that I now had seven tops, all with long sleeves to cover the ugly gashes along each of my forearms. The skin between my wrists and elbows was still raw and puckered, and the scars resembled the botched job I made once of repairing the hem of an old quilt. I didn't want Gaia or Coco to see that. Plus, my cuts still hurt like hell and sleeves meant I could wear padded dressings without anyone asking awkward questions.

Meg had also packed some of my old makeup—she must have really dug through my gear to find that—and an old bottle of Body Shop perfume, deodorant, some earrings, underwear, towels, a hairbrush, painkillers, a pretty pair of white leather sandals I'd never worn, my best dress, some of my favorite books, and—

luckiest of all—my laptop charger. I was stoked. She'd really put a lot of thought into what I'd need.

"I'm going to take the rest of your things to the charity shop, OK?" she said. "It would be weird, moving in with Dave and having all your stuff around."

Mum phoned while we were driving to the airport. I hadn't spoken to her in weeks and she was eager to share with me the latest plot developments in *EastEnders*, but I knew I had to be firm. I took a deep breath, recalled the epiphany I'd had, and said, "Mum, I'm going on holiday for a while, and I won't be able to talk to you. So I love you, but for now I'm saying . . . *au revoir*."

"Holiday?" she spat out on the other end of the line. "Where do you think you're off to, eh?"

"I don't *think* I'm off anywhere," I said curtly. "I'm headed to Norway, as it happens, and for quite some time."

"*Norway?*"

She started to shout and swear then, a fiery, threat-filled tirade that circled the question of who was going to acquire cannabis for her if I wasn't around, and though I was sorely tempted to share the news about the end of my relationship and subsequent homelessness, I simply said, "You have David's number, Mother dear. Ask him for weed *yourself*."

I said good-bye to Meg, checked my suitcase, and took my seat on the plane. I'd been booked in first class, which meant that I was served an amazing meal of rump steak, garlic potatoes, and tenderstem broccoli, followed by sticky toffee pudding with banana ice cream. I'd even put on mascara and lipstick, and wore a smart white blouse with skinny jeans and white sandals, and when the other people in first class spoke to me they didn't look wary or full of pity. I felt almost *happy*, excited instead of skewered by fear, like I could hold a conversation with someone without apologizing for my general crapness.

In short, I felt like I was a different person entirely.

And I *was* a different person. As I stepped off the plane at Ålesund and headed into the terminal, a woman was holding up a piece of white card with my name spelled out in red capitals:

SOPHIE HALLERTON

5

building a nest

THEN

Aurelia sits up in bed and glances woozily at the contraption to her right.

The crib.

There's a noise coming from it that sounds like an alarm, but something at the back of her mind tells her she can't just reach out and press a button to quieten it down. The room is strange, an arrangement of garish antique dressers and a monstrous wardrobe and that hideous purple wallpaper with a pattern that resembles moths fluttering against the sky at dusk . . . Slowly, the foreign shapes and smells shift into familiarity.

She moves her legs carefully to the edge of the bed and leans forward to check on the soft, mewling bundle of her daughter, her peachy cheeks and rose-petal eyelids dotted with milk spots, a tuft of blonde downy hair springing up from the crown of her head. As always, her tightly bunched fists are held at the sides of her head, and she is wrapped caterpillar-like in a turmeric-yellow hand-knit blanket gifted from a client.

Aurelia watches as Coco drifts back to sleep, then leans forward to ensure the blanket is safely tucked under the mattress. The movement seems to cause her internal organs to slide around the spacious room of her abdomen, and she recalls with a shudder Coco's quick birth back in London just four weeks earlier.

She'd been at her Preschool Singing Time group with Gaia when the cramps started, but there were yet a couple of weeks to go before her due date. Gaia had had to be poked and prodded out of the cozy nest of Aurelia's womb twenty days after she was supposed to be in the world, and even then it took another seventy-one hours before she begrudgingly emerged, her angry shouts of protest bouncing off the walls of the hospital room. No, it was too early for these cramps to be anything more than Braxton-Hicks, she'd thought, as the group sat in a circle and began to sing "Row, Row, Row Your Boat." The midwife said false contractions were more common with subsequent children because the body had to work harder, running around after one child while growing another.

She asked the group leader for a cushion to make the hard floor more comfortable to sit on, but it didn't work, and when she could no longer sing for pain she stood up and took Gaia quietly by the hand to their car.

She drove home, intent on having a restorative nap with Gaia to ease the cramps, but they grew worse with alarming speed, so that by the time she pulled up into their driveway in Hampstead she couldn't make it out of the car.

"What's wrong, Mumma?" Gaia asked, unclipping herself and clambering through to the front passenger seat. She placed her hands on Aurelia's belly and looked at her mother with concern. "Is it the baby? Is she coming?"

Aurelia tried to answer, but just then a contraction was building to an almighty peak, rearing like a tidal wave of fire, prying her jaws open and flowing out of her mouth in one long, agonizing holler. Her waters broke in a terrific gush between her legs and around the foot pedals, and in the ecstasy of the gap between that contraction and the next she found her mobile phone and dialed for an ambulance. It came five minutes later, and the team that raced up the driveway found Gaia standing by the car, hand on hip.

"I can see my sister's head!" she yelled. "Come quick!"

A noise makes her glance up. Tom is standing in the doorway, a broad smile across his face, his arms folded and his head cocked in curiosity. She is breastfeeding Coco. She can't remember lifting her out of the crib and putting her to her left breast—the one that always produces more milk—but Coco is feeding nicely, and surprisingly it doesn't hurt.

Tom takes a couple of steps across the room and kneels down in front of her.

"I thought you'd be busy with Clive," she says, wondering what time it is. "Are you done for the day?"

He doesn't answer, but presses his hands into the mattress on either side of her, leaning in to kiss her. She pecks him back, but when he makes to kiss her more passionately the baby struggles, Tom's weight pushing her into Aurelia's chest.

"Tom," she says, pressing a hand against his shoulder to ease him away. "You'll hurt the baby."

But he persists. He straightens his legs and raises his hips, his mouth hard against hers, his tongue searching. She turns her head away in rejection. She is feeding their child, for heaven's sake, can't he see that?

He raises himself to his full height, his eyes blazing. What is wrong with him? She has a urinary tract infection that has knocked her for six, and she is still bleeding. He knows this. But it seems only his needs matter.

Suddenly, without any warning, he swings his arm back and cracks her across the face with all his might. She reels, gasps. Her cheek burns and her eyes brim with tears. She stares up at the horrible, cruel expression on his face and dissolves into tears.

"Tom! Why did you do that?"

She sits up with a gasp, her heart racing, and looks down into the emptiness of her arms. Where is the baby?

A low cry tells her Coco is in her crib, and slowly she realizes that she was dreaming, thank God, it was just a dream. Tom didn't hit her. She dreamed it, and it's over now.

With shaking hands she reaches down the side of the bed and pulls out the red, leather-bound diary with *AF* inscribed in gold lettering. The diary that Tom bought her, and in which she records her dreams, as per the midwife's instructions. *We want to keep an eye on you,* the midwife said. *We need to make sure you're well inside* and *out.*

She writes the date and the dream.

> *Tom smacked me across the face when I wouldn't have sex with him????*

She stares at the words on the page and wonders whether she should score them out.

The baby's cries get louder, insistent. "There, there, baby girl," she coos softly to Coco, lifting her out of the crib and relishing that moment when, as always, Coco rolls her shoulders and bottom back in a big stretch, before sensing the proximity of a nipple and widening her mouth like a bird, searching for it. A spear of pain chases right up through the nipple to Aurelia's shoulder, collarbone, and all the way back down to her knees. She groans at the sharp scorch of it as the baby latches on and suckles.

Her heart continues to race and her mind reels with images from the dream. The look on his face when she rejected him. The crack of his hand against her cheek.

Later, she'll tell him about the dream in wounded tones and he'll hold her close, kiss the exact spot on her cheek where the pseudomemory still stings. "Did you eat some cheese before going to bed?" he'll laugh.

Coco releases the nipple and sinks back to sleep in Aurelia's arms, satisfied. Aurelia's breast feels smaller, emptied, and she fastens her bra before lifting Coco to her chest and rubbing her back. Unlike Gaia, Coco tends to wind really well, bringing up a healthy belch within a few seconds that tells Aurelia she's ready to be settled back into the crib.

But Aurelia cannot sleep. She rises, her head swampy and her body aching, to check on Gaia in her room next door. She sees a foot hanging out of the side of the duvet, a mass of blonde curls, and decides to let her sleep on.

Aurelia pads along the wooden floor of the old house, but it has all the foreign dimensions of a hotel and she makes a dreadful creak that she is certain will wake both children. Mercifully, neither stirs. She heads downstairs to the large kitchen swimming in morning sunlight.

The house may yet feel strange, but that is to be expected—she's only been here eight days, and with a brand-new baby, and this is not to be their home in any case. This six-bedroom traditional red-painted wooden lodge, named Granhus, Norwegian for "Spruce House," and constructed in the nineteenth century, will be properly restored after their high-concept summer home is built close by. *That* will be their summer home, and Granhus will become Tom's Norwegian office for his architecture firm. Or a holiday rental. Or both. It's big enough for both. Either way, he promised that it wouldn't be their base. She found it creepy when they bought it, and she finds it creepy now.

From the window by the sink she can see fields whitened with fresh snow all the way to the horizon, where serrated, snow-dusted mountains soar into the clouds. It's almost Christmas. From the window by the table, the garden sweeps down to a cliff, an ancient forest of towering pine trees gathered on the site of the new building. Beyond that, she can just make out a belt of deep blue—the fjord.

"We'll get a boat," Tom had said when they came to view this plot of land. "We'll take day trips up the fjord. Maybe sail all the way to Ålesund, have high tea, then turn around and head back home for supper."

Ålesund is where her father spent his childhood and where her grandparents lived. They're buried there now, along with aunts and uncles and cousins she never met. It's a charming port town on Norway's west coast, and she has fond memories as a child walking around the colorful art nouveau quarter.

"Come and see what I've found in the shed."

The sound of Tom's voice makes her drop the mug she is holding and it shatters across the floor in a dozen pieces. He rushes forward to gather up the pieces with a dustpan before she steps on them in her bare feet.

"Are you all right?" he says, laughing. "Didn't mean to scare you."

She recovers, smiles, though her heart is racing. She can still feel the burn of her cheek from where dream-Tom slapped her. The crack in her heart.

"I found this massive thing in the shed," he says, before she can mention the dream. He tips shards of mug into the bin. "Do you want to come and see?"

She raises her eyes to the ceiling. "What about the girls?"

"It'll only take a minute," he says.

She slips on her padded coat and a pair of Tom's wellies and traipses after him out the back door toward the old woodshed at the rear of the house. It's barely eight in the morning and the forest is carpeted in snow, but it's unseasonably mild, sunlight picking its way through the towering pine trees all around the house.

"Be *very* careful," Tom says as he approaches the door to the shed. He holds out a hand and she wonders for a moment if a wolf or lynx has got trapped inside. No. He'd have locked her in the house with the girls if that were the case, and taken down a shotgun. She watches, nervous and excited, as he digs his mobile phone out of his back pocket, switches on the flashlight, and shines it inside the shed.

She follows after and watches the light as he shines it toward the ceiling.

"There," he whispers, grinning. "Isn't that incredible?"

At first she thinks she's looking at a ceiling lamp, a kind of Frank Gehry–esque ceiling lamp, cone-ish in shape, about the size of a medicine ball and patterned with art deco swirls in peach and mauve. With horror, she realizes what it is, and takes a step back in case its inhabitants wake and come seething out in a frenzy.

"Hornets!" she hisses at Tom, grabbing on to his arm.

"Wasps, most likely," he whispers back, not taking his eyes off the cone.

"I'll call pest control," she says, inching backward, not daring to tear her eyes away from it.

"Shame," Tom says.

She looks at him as if he's gone mad, so he explains. "Well, it's beautiful, isn't it? A perfect papier-mâché cone made by thousands of tiny creatures." To her horror, he reaches up to trace it dreamily with his fingertips. "It's a work of natural art, the texture of papyrus. Like finding something from an ancient world."

"You won't be saying that if they sting you," she says.

Back in the house, she hangs up the phone, relieved that pest control will come imminently to destroy the nest. Tom is still banging on about how *they've* intruded on the wasps' territory, Anthropocene this, biodiversity that. She'd forgotten how much of

Norway feels off-limits to humans. "Haven't the wasps merely done what we're attempting to do?" Tom says, lightly but fully serious. "They just created a home for their babies."

Vile that the nest should take the shape of a womb, she thinks. With a shudder she imagines a baby inside, its head lowered into the cone.

She turns back to the window to drink in the view of the fjord, or rather the bits of blue she can make out through the woodland. She can't imagine why the previous owners of this place didn't cut down the trees that obscure such an amazing vista. If just a handful of trees were removed she'd be able to see all the green pleats of the valley crimping on forever and that navy ribbon of fjord stretching to the city.

She tells this to Tom, who frowns. "They're pretty ancient, those trees," he says.

"*All* trees are ancient, Tom. And it's not like there's a shortage of trees around here. You could use the wood for the new house, surely."

"You mean 'Basecamp.'" He announces the house's name with air quotes.

She laughs. *Basecamp.* She'd have preferred something along the lines of *Villa Faraday* or *The Tree House*, but whatever. Tom says "Basecamp" captures the sense of family adventure they're embarking on, so Basecamp it is.

"Basecamp," she deadpans, and Tom grins.

"I'll cut down those trees tomorrow. Happy?"

"Ecstatic."

It is nighttime. Coco is lying against Aurelia's left shoulder and Gaia is curled up beside her in the armchair as she reads from her father's old journal of Norse folklore, as told to him as a child by his parents and grandparents. The yellowing, crumpling transcriptions with inkblots are much too delicate now for handling, and they're in Norwegian. Some years ago she began the painstaking process of translating and digitizing the book into an English PDF file that she reads on her iPad to Gaia. Many are simply too macabre for a six-year-old, but there is a selection of tales that are entertaining and that provide a good source of education about Gaia's heritage. Gaia loves the tale about the raven who raises two sparrows in her nest when her own eggs are stolen. She particularly loves the one about the man who changes into a wolf when his sadness gets the better of him, and always squeals at the tale of the bear who tries to catch a fish that turns out to be a whale that swallows the bear whole—a metaphor, Aurelia thinks, for biting off more than you can chew.

"Can you read the one about the lady who was friends with the big deer?"

"Yes, of course," Aurelia says, swiping to the beginning of the PDF.

"Here it is," she says. "'Grete and the Elk.'"

Once upon a time there was a woman called Grete who had two daughters. All day long Grete did the work of women, but at night she would stand by the door and dream about sailing across the ocean, or diving to its depths, or even soaring to the moon.

One night, whilst she was standing by her door eating a bowl of riskrem ("riskrem is a kind of porridge," she tells Gaia), she heard a noise in the woods, the sound of shaking branches and twigs snapping underfoot. Her dog began to growl, and fear seized her so that she shut the door with trembling hands. But when she peered through the window she saw an enormous elk sniffing at the latch. The next night the same thing happened, and the night after, but on the fourth night she decided to hold her nerve and see what the elk wanted.

The elk was a magnificent creature with a majestic crown of antlers that glinted in the moonlight. Grete was afraid of being run through by them, but as the elk stopped a little way away from her she sensed that it did not mean her harm. Her dog rushed toward the elk, barking and warning it off, but the elk merely looked down at it, and eventually the dog quietened and seemed to accept the elk.

"What do you want?" Grete asked the elk. It took one step closer, then another, and she noticed its eyes peering at the remains of the riskrem she had just been eating a moment before. Gently she held up the bowl and the elk ate from it.

The next night Grete made two bowls of riskrem and the elk visited and ate. This visit became a regular habit, and Grete found that she spent her days doing the work of women anticipating its visits with happiness. The elk listened to her more than her husband or children, and she'd noticed it would often seem to respond with little grunts or huffs that sounded as though it understood every word she spoke.

But then Grete became ill. Her oldest girl fetched the doctor, who told her nothing more could be done—she would have to stay in bed, where she would eventually die.

Grete asked for her daughters to put a bowl of riskrem by the front door each night. At first they asked why, but after the first night they understood. After three nights, Grete was wakened by the tap-tap-tap of hooves across the floorboards. She was astonished and joyful to see her elk walking through her home, where it came to rest at her bedside. She reached out to stroke his velvety muzzle and told him many tales, to which he nodded and grunted in response.

It is said that, even when Grete passed away, her elk would often visit the house, and her children would wake oftentimes to find muddy hoofprints along the floorboards, for the elk had come to watch over them.

Aurelia has read this story to Gaia many times, always taking care to lighten her tone at the parts concerning death, but still she has questions: "What's 'the work of women,' Mumma? Was the elk her best friend? Wouldn't his antlers have damaged the walls when he came into the house? What does 'die' mean?"

"Will *you* die, Mumma?" Gaia asks, falling serious.

"Not for a very, very, *very* long time."

The wrinkle in Gaia's brow softens. When Aurelia tucks her into her bed the questions about death continue, and she makes a mental note not to read that story again.

But in just ten and a half weeks' time, she will be dead.

6

a home or a nest

NOW

I'm Sophie," I said to the woman holding the sign. "Sophie Hallerton."

The name rolled off my tongue as though it was always meant to be. It sounded sophisticated, and I could well imagine my mother's face screwing up upon hearing someone refer to me as Sophie Hallerton.

The woman grinned and stretched out a hand. "Derry Boydon," she said in a London accent. Strange—I'd expected her to be Norwegian. She was short with sleek black hair and large blue eyes that put me in mind of a cat. "This is my husband, Clive," she said, turning to the man standing next to her.

"How do you do?" he said, holding out a hand. "I'm Tom's business partner. Tom's a bit tied up today and I've to drop Derry off in the city anyway, so here we are."

Clive insisted on fetching my bag from the carousel and taking my handbag off my shoulder while Derry pinned me with her huge blue eyes and some very intense small talk.

"Is this your first time in Norway?"

I nodded.

"It's a *wonderful* place," she said. "You're going to have so much fun."

"I hope so."

"What are you talking about?" Clive interjected. "She's here to nanny, not sightsee."

"Ignore him," Derry said as he hoisted my suitcase into the boot of their car, a flashy Mercedes SUV with heated leather seats that smelled overwhelmingly of pine. "When I'm back *I'll* take you sightseeing. I'm sure Gaia and Coco will relish the chance to get out of the house."

I strained to take in my surroundings from the backseat. It looked like England, with the addition of snowcapped mountains and a smooth, navy-blue lake in the distance. Everything was very blue and very spiky. So in other words, nothing like England.

"Not a lake," Clive said when I pointed at it. "That's a fjord. Grytafjorden, if I'm not mistaken."

"Oh," I said. "What's the difference between a fjord and a lake?"

He gave me a look in the rearview mirror as if I'd just asked where babies come from. "The fjords were made by glaciers over a number of ice ages and then filled with seawater. They always connect with the sea."

Derry told me more about the region, and about Norway more broadly: how the country was world-leading in its environmental ethics, that it was the first country to introduce paid paternity leave, and that it once knighted a penguin.

"It sounds like an amazing place," I observed.

"Bloody expensive," Clive countered. "Especially if you decide to build a house out here. My advice on that is—don't."

"Noted," I said, and he laughed.

I guessed that Clive was in his mid to late forties, a little older than Derry. He wore a gold signet ring on his pinky, and a navy suit. Orange hair graying at the sides, pale skin, expressive blue eyes, thickly set. He had that same air about him that Tom and most of the people in first class on the plane had—confidence. I wondered how he got that confidence, and how I could get it. Maybe it was just the posh accent. I opened my mouth to ask where he was from, but just then he said: "So you're a nanny? Been doing that a long time, have you?"

I nodded stiffly. "For . . . a while, yes."

"My niece is nannying over in Spain at the moment. Or 'au pairing,'" he said, making exaggerated air quotes with his fingers, "which means she gets paid nothing to run around after three kids under the age of five all day. A so-called 'cultural experience.'" More air quotes. He threw me an isn't-that-ridiculous smile. I tried to match it and failed epically.

"Still, *you've* got a great guy as an employer," he said. "Tom's great. Really, he is. And you'll have met the girls? Little Gaia and Coco."

"Yes. They're really special . . ."

He nodded. "Yes. It's such a shame . . ." he said, throwing a strange look at Derry.

"Such a shame," she agreed.

I presumed they were talking about the death of the girls' mother, Aurelia, but just then we pulled up at a sign that seemed to indicate that one of the lanes across the bridge was closed and the traffic was slowing to a halt, so I wasn't quite sure whether he was referring to the dead mother or the traffic. We sat in silence for a few moments, indicating to merge, until someone let us in and we pulled off.

"So . . . you're Tom's business partner?" I asked Clive, wondering why that meant he should be in Norway, or picking me up from the airport.

"We run the company together," he said. "Architecture. I'm not sure how much he's told you about the build . . ."

"Not a lot, actually. It's a summer house, isn't it?"

"Indeed. He and Aurelia acquired the site last year. There's an old lodge on the land, just behind the woods. That's where everyone is staying at the moment. By everyone, I mean you, Tom, the children, Maren, the housekeeper—I gather you've met her already?"

I nodded. The blonde woman who interviewed me at Tom's house in Hampstead.

"Occasionally Derry and I pop over and stay for a weekend to project manage, or kick the contractors up the backside, in layman's terms."

This news made me feel uneasy. I don't exactly know what I was expecting, but certainly not a household filled with watchful, confident adults.

"The build's important," Clive continued in a somber voice, "because regardless of what Tom tells you or anyone else, this house is not *just* his family holiday home. It's also a kind of showstopper of a piece for the company. It's our calling card, if you like. The centerpiece of our portfolio. And this one's ten times better than the first house."

"First house?" I asked.

"Oh, blimey," Derry said, in a voice that sounded like there was a whole backstory I wasn't aware of.

"Yes, well . . ." Clive said, clearing his throat. "There was a house before this one, but . . ."

"They built it on a river," Derry said, as though building on a river was a big nope. "Basecamp, it was called."

"I'm sure Tom will be *very* glad to fill you in on Basecamp," Clive added loudly, keen to move on. "Aurelia's Nest is going to be the ticket."

"Aurelia's Nest?" I asked.

"The name of the *new* house," Derry explained.

"Prior to this we've focused mostly on commercial design," Clive said, "but once we've built Aurelia's Nest we'll attract more clients engaging with high-end residential design. And right now, that's where the money is."

I nodded as if I followed any of this. "And . . . how long do you think it'll take? The . . . build, I mean?"

Clive became very sullen then and I worried I'd hit a nerve. "Unfortunately a project as ambitious in scope as this one requires a lot of red tape. That's before the construction, which is fairly precarious. Basecamp was built over a river, which in hindsight was a very bad idea, and we've all since learned from our mistakes. Now Tom is taking zero chances. Aurelia's Nest is being built on the side of a cliff."

"Beg pardon?" I said in a mousy voice. "Did you say . . . ?"

"Right?" Derry said, turning all the way around. "A house on the side of a two-hundred-foot sheer drop!"

I looked from Derry to Clive with abject terror.

"Trying to find a team of builders who'll do their job while hanging off a sheer drop has proved . . . challenging, shall we say?" Clive said. "Impossible, that's another word. This is why Tom and I work well together, you see. He's the risk-taking artist and I'm . . ."

"The sane one?" I offered.

Clive liked that. He threw me a smile in the mirror. "Something like that."

"Still, it'll look terrific when it's finished," Derry added.

"Very modest, aren't you?" Clive added, and I must have looked confused because Derry explained. "Tom has asked me to do all the interiors. I run an interior design company. *That's* why it's going to look fabulous."

"You mentioned an old lodge," I said. I was suddenly glad that I'd be staying in the lodge. A nice, safe lodge.

"A lodge, yes?"

"What'll happen to the lodge once the new house . . . the one hanging off the edge of a cliff . . . is completed?"

"Ah. Well, Tom wants to restore it," Clive said. "But between you and me, I think the place is past it. Lots of damp and draft . . . Derry can't stand it. Can you, darling?"

Derry shook her head. "It needs tearing down, made into a nice pasture. A vegetable patch, or something along those lines." She threw me a look of grave concern. "You'll know what I mean when you get there."

We dropped Derry off outside a ferry port, where she said she was getting a ferry to Trondheim to work on a new college. She gathered her bags before getting out and flashed me a smile. "So sorry I'm heading off just as you're arriving," she said. "But I'll be back in a few weeks. Good luck!"

We pulled off the motorway and took a road that gradually got narrower and less road-like by the mile. In more positive terms, the scenery got more and more intense, to the point where Clive rolled down the windows and encouraged me to stick my head out instead of pressing my nose against the glass in awe.

It was like *Lord of the Rings*, *Harry Potter*, and *Game of Thrones* all wrapped up and multiplied by a trillion. The road climbed steadily up the side of a shark-fin mountain range, so that we were driving along a stone ridge looking down over a fjord with postcard-blue water. A white dot moving through the middle of it turned out to be a cruise boat, but the water was so still that the boat looked like it was a zip being pulled up a sheet of turquoise velvet. On the other side of the gorge were black zigzags of rock speckled with snow, rich green fields, and gushing waterfalls crowned with rainbows. The clouds were so dramatic that I couldn't decide where to look—the sky or the fjord—so I spent most of the journey with my neck craned out the window, nodding up and down.

"Impressive, isn't it?" Clive said. "That's Hjørundfjord," he said.

"Hjørund," I repeated. I had the sense that Clive enjoyed knowing things and telling them to others. But I didn't mind. I would remember Hjørundfjord for the rest of my life.

A red house came into view at the end of a long path through a forest of enormous fir trees. It looked like something straight out of a fairy tale, with a pitched black roof, a white-framed gable end, and a cute round window set against the pillar-box red, ivy trailing up one side, and a name, *GRANHUS*, spelled out in wood-carved letters above the front door. A dozen ravens circled the chimneys, their large wings fanned out like black sails. Beyond the house was a dense patch of hard hats carrying iron girders through the woods.

Suddenly some of the men came running up the hill toward us, looking back and waving their arms at Clive as though something had happened. Clive jumped out of the car. I wasn't sure whether to stay put or follow. Overthinking this decision entirely, I slowly got out of the car and decided I'd tell him I needed the loo if he asked why I'd followed.

Six men—clearly Norwegian, given that I couldn't understand a word they were saying—were all frantically shouting at Clive and pointing back at the patch of trees down the hill. It was clear Clive couldn't understand them either, because he held up his hands and shouted, "I can't understand any of you! English, please!"

One of the men stuck his hands at either side of his head, the palms facing forward and his fingers splayed.

"Moose?" Clive said, and the man nodded.

"*Big* moose."

A few seconds later, we saw it—this huge, dark brown creature with a staggering set of antlers on his head, around five or six feet wide. The moose was both gigantic and irate. It walked slowly toward a wooden frame and butted it with its antlers.

Standing on a rock I could make out a handful of men near the moose, all of them with their hands up in surrender. One of them was waving something, evidently trying to get the thing to back away, but with the effect of making it more pissed off. Clive seemed to think the waving thing was a great idea, though, because he pulled off his jacket and started flapping it above his head, shouting and yelling.

Suddenly a huge gunshot sounded, a terrific, echoing blast that made me jump. I spun around and saw a man at the back door of the red house holding a large rifle with smoke coming out of it. Tom. A sound of hooves on the ground signaled the animal's departure, and all the men clapped and cheered.

Tom walked down the steps toward me, one hand holding the rifle, the other extended toward me. "Sophie," he said, beaming. "So glad you could make it."

I smiled nervously and shook his hand. "You scared off the moose," I observed.

He nodded, just casually reloading a long silver bullet into the chamber of his enormous rifle. "Sorry about that. He's been a bit of a nuisance these last few days. I'm hoping that was enough to see him off for a while."

Clive came marching back up the hill, grinning. "You missed," he said to Tom.

"I wasn't aiming for him," Tom answered, gesturing for me to come inside.

"Pity," Clive panted, mopping his brow. "I heard moose tastes delicious."

Inside the red house, or Granhus, as it appeared to be named, Gaia raced up to me in the kitchen and wrapped her arms around my knees as though we were long-lost friends.

"Sophie!" she yelled. "I've missed you so much!"

"You have?" I said. I wanted her to say it again. I don't think anyone had ever said that to me before.

I told her I had a present for her, and she got so excited I fretted I'd built her up for something like a scooter, or maybe a pony. I presented her with the little pair of tweed trousers I'd made from one of Meg's cushion covers for Gaia's teddy bear, Louis. "To go with his waistcoat," I said, and she gave a squeal of delight.

"He'll *love* them!" she shouted. "Come and see your bedroom!"

Maren appeared then, telling Gaia to wait just a minute. She asked if my journey was a pleasant one, and would I like a cup of tea?

"Yes, please," I said. I didn't, but yes seemed the right answer. I sat down at the table opposite Gaia, who was introducing Louis to his trousers and chiding him for not wearing any beforehand. *It's naughty, Louis. And you could get a chill.* I could hear Tom outside, pacing up and down and chatting to someone on his mobile phone. The kitchen had old Shaker-style turquoise cabinets, red bunting, and the most incredible views framed by each of the three windows. Maren poured me a cup of tea and explained the moose intrusion, though I'd seen it all firsthand.

"They keep coming because they think the river is here," she said. "This is the problem when you mess with nature. The animals of this place have been drinking from that river for hundreds of years, maybe thousands. And now it's gone."

"Gone?" I said.

She grimaced. "Tom built a dam. He meant it to divert the river, but then it bled into the ground. Turned the whole site into a marsh. And now the elk are going crazy. I won't be surprised if I come down one morning and find one drinking from the tap."

She gave a rueful laugh.

I tried to laugh along. *Great.* She rinsed some mugs, turned back to Gaia. "Shall we show Sophie the rest of the house?"

——

We'll start at the top and work our way down, shall we?" Maren said, leading me up an incredibly narrow set of stairs. Maren's ample hips blocked out the light ahead of me, rubbing either side of the wood paneling. She led me to the attic, a long room with six feet or so of headroom and bookended by two porthole windows.

"Mostly storage up here," she explained, batting away a moth. "But we keep a bed here in case we have guests."

The next level down had a bathroom and three bedrooms, all with whitewashed floorboards that creaked whichever way I stepped. I noticed framed black-and-white photographs on the walls of the hallway, ghostly, moody images of the tall, narrow trees I'd seen on the way to the house. Maren saw me admiring them but kept us moving.

"These bedrooms belong to me and Tom, and Clive and Derry have what used to be the children's." She turned and smiled politely. "Yours is downstairs, and we've moved Gaia's and Coco's bedrooms there, too."

She took us back downstairs and along a narrow hallway behind the kitchen, where a recent extension created a modern living room with a bookcase, sofa, and armchairs, then a small office, and a long playroom kitted out with tables, whiteboards, play mats, sand tubs, and endless cabinets and cupboards filled with every toy under the sun.

"This is your room," she said, opening the door to the last bedroom at the corner of the house. It was smaller than the other bedrooms, but I loved it. A single iron-posted bed with a cozy red quilt ran alongside a window overlooking the woods. A modest wardrobe at the foot of it, a chest of drawers, a bedside table, and a lamp. A door adjacent to the bed led to a bathroom with a shower cubicle, sink, and toilet.

"Perfect," I told her, and she looked relieved. I sat down on the bed, testing out the mattress. Good and firm. Perhaps I'd have a nap, then do a spot of writing. The view from my window was exactly what I needed to get going.

"Good," Maren said, clasping her hands. She glanced at her watch. "Would you like half an hour to freshen up?"

She seemed to pick up on the fact that I was utterly clueless as to what she meant.

"The baby's nap ends in thirty-five minutes," she said. "She'll need a half hour of flash cards, then reading time, dinnertime, and songs for bed. And Gaia, too, obviously."

"Obviously," I said, and she smiled, satisfied that I knew what I was doing. Which of course I didn't.

"Oh, before I forget," she said, sliding a folded piece of paper from an invisible pocket in her skirt. "This might be helpful."

I unfolded it. A spreadsheet mapping out each day from 6:00 a.m. until 7:30 p.m., with activities such as "slime time," "messy play," and "hidden music" all signaling exactly how I was to spend each hour. *Slime time?* Mercifully Sundays were blanked out as a "Daddy and Daughters Day!," though I noted the asterisk at the bottom of the page: *Occasionally you will be required to work on these days.*

"That's just Coco's schedule," Maren said, lest I grew too comfortable with the thought of only working eighty hours a week.

"Obviously," I said, wearing my finest rictus grin.

"As you know, Gaia is homeschooled," she said. "Her schooling coordinates with Coco's naps, totaling three hours a day, with the exception of her Norwegian lessons."

"Norwegian lessons?" I said nervously. Becoming fluent enough to teach Norwegian in a few hours might be a stretch, even for someone as desperate as I was.

"I teach Gaia Norwegian," Maren said. "The rest of the schooling lies with you. Tom favors the Montessori method. I was led to believe that wouldn't be a problem?"

"Oh, *no* problem!" I said, too loudly. "Montessori is my middle name!"

"Excellent," she said, stepping toward the bedroom door. "Well, I'll see you in approximately twenty-eight minutes."

"Great!" I said, giving an actual thumbs-up.

Twenty-eight minutes. I hoped with all my hoping cells that this place had broadband. I was going to have to do some serious googling. What was it called again? The Tesserati method?

"One last thing," Maren said, stepping back inside the room. "Tom's accountant flagged that the standing order for payment of your salary has been set up to someone called Lexi Ellis?"

I froze. My heart shot into my mouth and I tried not to look like I was going to puke. "Erm, yes," I stammered. "It's my . . . business name."

"Oh. Right," she said. "Well, so long as it's the correct account . . . Just be sure to let us know if you don't receive payment at the end of the month. Oh, and another thing."

I thought I was going to black out. I watched, rigid with terror, as she pulled the door behind her in case anyone else heard. She'd found out, I knew it. She was about to yell and scream at me. *You're an imposter! A cuckoo!*

I deserved it. I deserved it all.

"The basement," she said in a low voice. "It's a no-go area."

"Basement?"

She nodded, then looked upset; her hands started to wring of their own accord. "It was . . . it was Aurelia's room. Tom has insisted that we're *not* to go in. So, even if you hear something down there, please remember to stay out."

"Oh. Of course."

"Wonderful." She visibly exhaled away the sadness triggered by the mention of Aurelia. Then, with a finger in the air: "See you in twenty-*six* minutes!"

I held up my own index finger. "See you then!"

She shut the door, and I sat down heavily on the bed, crumpled by relief. And when my heart stopped trying to punch its way through my rib cage I wondered if I'd heard her right, or if the new drugs I was on were every bit as brain-mangling as the last set.

Even if you hear something down there, please stay out.

Hear something?

What the hell was in that basement?

7

are you going to die?

My memories of that first month are pretty hazy. Suffice it to say that looking after two Tasmanian devils single-handedly and without any forewarning of their talent for finding sharp objects and scaling dangerous heights faster than lightning, or of their need for constant enraptured attention, was a baptism by boiling lava.

I spent a good part of the time seeking out ways to escape, and had I not been so leached of energy I might well have attempted to swim up the fjord all the way back to the airport. Caring for a ten-month-old was like trying to lasso a hurricane. I began to perceive parents as heroic but very deranged masochists. For the first three weeks "Daddy and Daughters Day" did not happen, and the sacred promise of rest that I'd clung to all week popped like a leftover party balloon. Lack of sleep turned me into a cloud that wafted around after Gaia and Coco, whose combined energy could power South America for years to come.

But wait—I'm getting ahead of myself. Back to the beginning. To the moment I entered the seventh circle of hell.

Stepping into my role as nanny felt like entering the Roman

Colosseum to face a gladiator armed with flails and scourges. I was quite literally just off the plane and expected to have had a bit of time to adjust to my surroundings. Well, I guess I had some time—*twenty-six minutes!*—which was enough to put on some deodorant, stare at the mad schedule Maren had given me for Gaia and Coco, and do some frantic googling.

Messy play: Developing cognitive and fine motor skills through the medium of a bag of flour thrown liberally around the room.

Slime time: Literally involving slime, which I'd possibly have to make using shaving foam and contact lens fluid, before encouraging the kids to slime each other.

Montessori: "Child-centered intellectual exploration merely guided by a teacher." I had a vague sense of what that meant. I figured that "intellectual exploration" likely meant reading and collecting leaves and pine cones, and I thought back to the time I'd taken little Matty Barris to the local park while his mum slept off a hangover on our kitchen floor. We'd gathered up all the beer cans around the slides and spent the afternoon making a beer-can sculpture. He cut his hands a few times and I filched a few syringes out of the cans before Matty got to them, but our end product was Tate Modern–worthy, if I do say so myself.

At three o'clock I ventured along the hallway to the nursery, where I was supposed to find Coco emerging from her nap. At the far end of the cot I could see her little blonde head, damp with sweat, and a chubby arm wrapped around a comfort blanket. A pacifier was wedged in her mouth and she sucked at it rhythmically, like a real-life Maggie Simpson.

I sat down in the green rocking chair by the window and glanced at the clock. A minute past three. Hadn't Maren said Coco was meant to wake up at three o'clock? Should I wake her? I waited another five minutes. Finally, Maren appeared in the doorway, her hands clasped and a tight smile on her face.

"Everything all right?" she said, and I nodded.

"I think . . . she's still sleeping."

Maren pursed her lips—I noticed she did this when there was a job to be done, and one that ought to be done by someone other than her and she wanted to remind them of their responsibility—and clapped her hands. Coco jolted awake at the sharp, sudden sound in the peaceful room. Her eyes flicked open and she sat upright with a loud gasp. After a few moments she burst into tears, scared and still half-asleep. I glanced at Maren, who raised her eyebrows in a way that signaled I was to sort out the crying.

I reached down into the cot and lifted Coco out. She was heaving long, bitter sobs, the kind that suggested she was none too pleased about being wrenched from the deepest of slumbers. She felt warm and surprisingly heavy in my arms, and I bounced her for a bit to calm her down, but as she began to wake up she focused her eyes on me and fell silent. *Good,* I thought. *See? I've always had a way with babies.* But just then, as she took in the sight of me, this weirdo she didn't know from Adam, she burst into fresh howls and squirmed, trying to wriggle out of my arms.

"Now, now, Coco," Maren chided, grabbing her and setting her on her hip rather roughly. "This is Sophie, your new nanny. *She's* the one who looks after you." Then, tapping her foot: "Shall we bring Coco to find Gaia? I expect she'll be waiting for you."

Maren led Coco and me back to the playroom, where she showed me a cupboard stacked neatly with paint pots, sheets of card, wooden animals, train sets, books, and—oddly—kitchen utensils, such as whisks, pans, sponges, and wooden spoons.

"You'll find no princesses or Barbie dolls in here," Maren said. "Aurelia was against such things."

"I like her already," I said, and she flinched.

Gaia raced into the room then, pulling chairs and a small table from a corner of the room and setting it up with a crayon holder and sheets of paper.

"Now, now," Maren said, wagging her finger at Gaia. "I'm afraid drawing time isn't until five o'clock. Right now is flash card time."

I saw Gaia's face fall. "She loves drawing," Maren said, in a tone that suggested drawing was on a par with skinning dead rodents. "Here are the flash cards." She handed me what resembled a large-scale set of playing cards featuring frogs and umbrellas. Then, her work done: "Have an enjoyable afternoon. Dinner is at five thirty."

I felt a sense of relief when she left. I turned back to see that Gaia was already in the middle of a drawing, hands splayed on either side of the page and her face so low it was almost touching it. Her teddy—Louis—was sitting on the seat beside her, and every so often she'd look down at him, as though to check he hadn't leaped off and run somewhere. I sat in the chair opposite with Coco on my lap and held up one of the flash cards to Coco. This one featured a large letter *R* in both upper- and lowercase, with a cartoon rainbow.

"See, Coco?" I said. "*R* for *rainbow*." Blimey, I was doing pretty damn well. I was responding to the name "Sophie" without batting an eyelid, and my accent was legit BBC Radio 4. Nannying was going to be a piece of cake.

Coco gave me a cross look. I lifted another card. *S* for *snake*. She reached out and grabbed the flash card, shoved it in her mouth, and chewed off a corner. Without looking up, Gaia said, "Coco hates flash cards."

"Does she?" I muttered, trying to retrieve the chewed piece of card from Coco's mouth. When she chomped down on the end of my index finger I gave a loud "Fu-uh!," stopping just in time before the whole word came out, and she looked at me with alarm before bursting into a loud laugh.

"Say that again," Gaia said. "She likes it."

"Say what again?" I said. "Fu-uh?"

Coco laughed again, louder.

"Best not," I said.

"Fuh!" Gaia said to Coco, sending her into fits of laughter. "FUH!"

I glanced at the door, waiting for Maren to emerge with a concerned look on her face. I found the appropriate flash card and held it up to Coco. "*Fuh* for *fox*. See?"

"Here," Gaia said, thrusting a picture at me. "It's for you."

I tried to make sense of the heavily colored shapes on the page. A rainbow, I could make that out, and beneath it five hollow-eyed figures that appeared to be walking on stilts whilst holding hands.

"That's you," she said, pointing at one. "And that's me, that's Coco, and the small one is Louis."

"Who's this?" I asked, pointing at the tallest of the figures.

"That's Mumma," Gaia said. "She's holding your hand because she wants you to take care of me."

"Is she?" I said, swallowing hard, and before I could change the subject Gaia fixed her jade-green eyes on me and leaned close to whisper in my ear. "Mumma *told* me that she wants you to take care of me."

"How did she tell you that?" I asked.

Gaia looked puzzled. "Mumma tells me lots of things," she said, shrugging.

I wasn't quite sure what to make of this. She took a fresh page and started on another drawing, which started as two large circles that she proceeded to fill in completely with black felt-tip.

"Look, Coco," I said cheerfully. "Balloons."

"No, not balloons," Gaia said flatly. She added a mouth with bared teeth beneath them. "It's the Sad Lady. See?"

"Who?"

"She lives in our basement. And she doesn't have eyes, just holes."

"O . . . K . . ."

I tried to push this comment to the recesses of my mind. The basement. Holes for eyes. Not a weird thing at all for a six-year-old to say. Maybe she'd had a similar warning from Maren. *Don't go near the basement!* Such a warning would fire anyone's imagination. Or maybe Gaia was just predisposed to a Gothic temperament. I had been a weird kid, too, I reasoned. Long before my mother's dysfunctionality rearranged the wiring of my brain I was the Wednesday Addams of every playgroup, a collector of dead insects, precociously obsessed with winding up any overly smiley adult with whom I came into contact by telling them that Satan was my father, or replying to their benign, who's-a-pretty-girl questions by deadpanning, "I eat souls."

Happily, Gaia moved on to relatively chirpier subject matter rainbows, which she transformed into gravestones—and finally we read the flash cards, or rather *I* read the flash cards while Coco devised a game of speed-crawling out of the room and up the stairs. When four o'clock came I consulted the schedule: it was time for "splash and scoop," though I had no idea what that was.

"It's when we fill the tub with water and splash it," Gaia said, her expression joyless. I looked around for the tub in question, but just then she brightened and said: "Could we do something else?"

"Certainly," I said.

Gaia pushed her glasses up her nose, shuffled off her chair, and lifted Louis. "He likes his trousers," she said, rubbing the hem of them between her finger and thumb. "They're a bit scratchy, but he likes the pattern."

"Thank you," I said. "I can make him another pair, if he likes?"

She smiled, and next thing I knew she was walking behind me and playing with my hair. Coco—who was gnawing on a crayon at this point—gawped up at her sister as she ran her fingers through my hair like a comb.

"I like your hair," Gaia said. "Why is it so black?"

I was learning fast that six-year-olds were masters of the Abstract Question. It was better to respond with truth, or at least a version of it. "Well," I said. "My biological father was from Spain. Possibly." The full truth was that I had been conceived while my mother was on her one and only sojourn out of the cosmopolitan wonderland that is Sunderland on a hen-do in Majorca. A few weeks after that she began to feel sick, and for four or five months thereafter she numbed the sickness with weed. "That's how I became a weed addict!" she used to muse fondly. "Little did I know I was up the duff! If I'd known, I'd have had an abortion! Lucky you, eh, Lexi?"

My father could have been one of any number of men she encountered on that trip, none of whom she could recall clearly. What *was* clear was that I inherited nothing of my mother's clammy English pallor, and the olive-skinned, brown-eyed, and black-haired coloring that I did inherit served only to invite a wide range of soul-crushing xenophobic taunts that would be hurled at me in the playground, in the street, and occasionally in my own home.

Of course, I didn't tell any of this to Gaia.

"What does 'biological' mean?" she asked.

"It means my real daddy. So, your daddy is your real daddy, isn't he?"

She nodded.

"I never knew who my real daddy was."

She cocked her head. "Why?"

I opened my mouth, then closed it. There was simply no safe way to answer that question.

"Why don't we play a game?"

"Shall we play hairdressers?" She started running her fingers through my hair again. "I *love* your hair. When I grow up I'm going to have black hair just like yours."

"That's very sweet of you, Gaia."

"I can do your makeup, too."

I started to tell her to stop, but just then the sensation of having my hair played with was so soothing that my willpower rolled over like a dog wanting its belly rubbed and before I knew it I was allowing both of them to twist my hair into dreadlocked braids and draw all over my face.

Maren entered the kitchen right as Coco decided she'd had enough of my attempts to feed her soggy pasta and broccoli—this was all I could cook, vegan-wise, for a good three weeks—and picked up the bowl, plopping both the bowl and its contents on her head like a hat. Maren stood next to me, looking over the scene with her mouth open. It was then that I realized I hadn't removed the face paints that Gaia and Coco had slathered all over my face during our makeup session, nor had I fixed the bird's nest they'd made of my hair. Also, Coco's nappy had exploded—I had forgotten that babies need to be changed regularly—and whilst I had been frantically attempting to change her, Gaia had applied the face paints to her own face. She'd gone for a Halloween look, covering her face entirely in orange and applying white circles around both eyes.

"Sophie?" Maren whispered. There was a whole paragraph inside that word.

But before I could answer, Gaia shouted: "We had so much *fun!*"

"Ya-ya!" Coco shouted, the bowl still atop her head, and clapped her hands. "Ya-ya!"

Tom came in then, his phone pressed to his ear like a prosthetic. His mud-caked wellies left a trail of leaves and dirt behind him. He told the caller he'd speak to them later and approached the girls, kissing both on the cheek. "Lots of role-playing, I see."

I hooked on to this. "Yes, yes, we were *role-playing.*"

Gaia perked up, absorbing this new narrative. "She's Upsy Daisy from *In the Night Garden.*"

"Is she?" Tom said. Like me, I don't think he had the foggiest who Upsy Daisy was. "And who are you meant to be, Gaia? An Oompa Loompa?"

"No, Daddy," Gaia said. "I'm a Halloween pumpkin."

"Oh," he said. "A Halloween pumpkin with glasses."

She whipped her little spectacles from her face self-consciously, only to return them once she realized she couldn't see anything without them.

Just then, Tom's phone rang, and he was out the door again, tramping pine needles and clods of earth in his wake.

Bath time was straightforward enough—though I did end up wearing the contents of the bath, thanks to Coco's love of splashing—and by the time bedtime rolled around I felt like I'd been hit by a tractor. Fifteen storybooks and much cajoling, singing, and bribing later, and both girls finally drifted off to sleep.

I felt like I deserved a medal.

It was a relief to get to my own room, my own space, where I wouldn't be required to glue my eyeballs to Coco in anticipation of the moment she'd find a shard of broken glass to chew on or a window to hurl herself out of, and where I wouldn't have to answer Gaia's infinite stream of brain-melting questions, such as why the moon was called the moon and if people could still poo in heaven.

I took off my clothes and put on my pajamas—it was only half past eight, but I was dog-tired—then headed to the bathroom to use the toilet and brush my teeth. Right as I was sitting on the toilet, the door creaked open. I gave a jump of fright and called out, "Who's there?"

A small hand appeared around the door, and I recognized it as belonging to Gaia.

"Can I come in?" she said from behind the door.

"I'm . . . I'm on the loo," I said, clutching on to my pajama bottoms. "Are you all right?"

"If I promise to close my eyes can I sit with you?"

I was thrown by the question. "Sit with me? You mean, on the toilet seat?"

"On your lap," she said. "Mumma always let me sit on her lap when she was on the toilet."

Before I could answer, Gaia made her way through the door and climbed onto my knee, right as I hoisted my pajamas up around my waist. She said nothing, but simply sat there, as if my knee was exactly where she ought to be sitting. Then she said quietly: "I don't like my bed."

"Oh," I said. "Is it uncomfortable?"

She shook her head.

"Is it . . . cold?"

She shook her head.

"Are there worms in it?"

She looked up, confused. "Why would worms be in my bed?"

"Well, what's wrong with your bed, then?"

Another world-weary sigh. "It's too empty."

"Maybe it needs more teddies in it," I offered. "Let's go and find some, shall we?"

And I took her by the hand and led her to her bedroom, settled her into bed with an army of soft toys, then went back to my own bed. Within minutes I was asleep, but at half past two Gaia's shrieks ripped through the house. I staggered quickly to her room, expecting to find it full of bats or giant spiders, and when I found neither I tried to console Gaia with a glass of water. She held my hand in a viselike grip, and when I woke again—once more to the sound of screaming—I was on the wooden floor beside Gaia's bed huddled beneath a blanket. Again, I settled her to sleep by stroking her face and holding her hand, and this time she said, "I love you, Mumma," between tear-stricken gasps. I was exhausted, but my heart broke for her.

This went on every night, with a side order of Coco waking every couple of hours. Coco didn't shriek, though. She was sturdier than Gaia, in both build and temperament, her shining round cheeks always lifted in a gleeful smile. She was quite a heartening child to be around. At night, she babbled and bounced in her cot until I deduced that a warm bottle of milk persuaded her to lie down and quietly mull over the idea of sleep.

One night, when I'd put Gaia back into her bed for the millionth time and fallen asleep beside her, I was woken not by screaming but by a question.

"Sophie?"

"Hmm? What?"

"Are you going to die?"

"What?"

"Are you going to die?"

"*Die?* Uh, no, Gaia. Not at the moment. I'm too tired."

"What about tomorrow?"

"Why are you so worried about me dying, Gaia?"

She was sitting up in bed, her hair a fuzzy cloud and her glasses askew on her face. Her pajamas—navy with a snowdrop print— were buttoned wrongly, and Louis was sitting at her feet. She bounced my question around her mind.

"Mumma died," she said softly, and my heart expanded to the size of a football pitch. I wrapped my arm around her.

"I know she did. I'm so, so sorry. I bet she loved you lots and lots."

I thought of what Ellen had said about their mother. Suicide. How awful. *The party line is that Mummy had an accident.* How long, I wondered, could they really expect to keep up that pretense? Gaia was a very perceptive child, visibly possessed of that firstborn curse of wisdom beyond her years. If her mum died by suicide there would have been signs. Gaia would have known something was wrong.

Gaia buried her face in my side and wrapped her arms and legs around me so tightly I thought I would be left with bruises. She caught one of the scars on my right arm with her wrist and I yelped in pain.

"What's wrong?" she whispered, panicked.

"Nothing," I said, though my arm was in a white-hot kind of agony. "All better now."

"Don't leave," she whispered. "Please, Sophie. Please don't die?"

"I won't," I said. "I promise."

"Pinky promise?"

"What?"

She held out her little finger. "Pinky promise. You have to use your pinky. Like this."

She demonstrated what I needed to do by hooking her pinky around mine.

And as I lay there in the darkness with Gaia clamped to me like a warm, snoring limpet, I felt a stab of guilt for the dozens of times I'd looked out the window of the playroom at the woods and the fjord beyond and regretted what I'd signed up for. I'd even thought about running away. It wasn't that I thought the girls weren't sweet or that the landscape wasn't mesmeric—I just felt so completely out of my depth.

And yet it seemed I was the only one vaguely interested in

looking after Gaia and Coco. Already I had a sense that the other adults around them—Tom, Clive, and Maren—were fairly clueless in their own ways. After all, they'd hired *me* as a nanny, and while Tom was full of promises to sit and have dinner with us, or to read Gaia a bedtime story, he was perpetually distracted. He worked from dawn until dusk on the build, wafting into the house at odd moments to snatch a cup of coffee or a cigarette from the packet I noticed he kept hidden behind the toaster, before wafting back into the gloom of the forest like a ghost. He didn't appear to eat. Clive was fairly absent, too, but then he was only Tom's business partner, and nothing to do with Gaia and Coco. I had forgotten he was staying at the house until I caught sight of him in the hall one morning. We exchanged a pleasant hello and he went on his way.

Maren spent most of the time doing housework and ironing everything to within an inch of its life. I can still see her now at the ironing board amidst clouds of steam, sawing back and forth across curtains, towels, and table runners until they succumbed and became as flat as she desired. For all her effort, though, I have to say she wasn't much of a housekeeper. Black mold crept along windowpanes, caterpillars of dust slept snug atop picture frames, and the girls' washing was regularly stuffed into their drawers instead of being folded and laid neatly flat. I figured Maren's strengths lay in baking bread, which she did every morning, filling the house with mouthwatering smells. She also spent an hour a day barking Norwegian nouns at Gaia.

Why bring Gaia and Coco out here at all? I wondered. There was nothing for them to do beyond the dour realms of the creepy red house: no parks or play areas, no trampoline or dodgy wooden swing in the garden. Just past the trees toward the cliff, men in work clothes and hard hats shouted and drilled all day long.

Granhus was noisy, too, with pipes that groaned anytime you turned on a tap or flushed the toilet, and a strange high-pitched wail that drifted from the bowels of the house. "Old air vents," Maren said dismissively, but it was loud and sounded very much like the yowl of a cat, or a baby crying. Granhus was bracketed by thick woods inhabited by wolves, bears, and probably witches, and a towering cliff that overlooked the fjord. At night, when the girls were finally asleep, I'd tiptoe outside to look at the silhouetted forest, the shimmering fjord, and the galaxies that jeweled the sky. The woods became conscious with owls, foxes, bats. Moonlight fell on elaborate spiderwebs and glinting demon eyes hiding in the shrubs.

It was at once mesmerizing and slasher-movie sinister.

The wildlife seemed determined to get inside. Mice and spiders roamed so freely that Gaia began to name them, and often the mice wouldn't even budge when I stumbled upon them in the larder—they'd stare me out until I swiped at them with a broom. Day and night, enormous black birds—crows, or maybe ravens, but on steroids—circled the house, predator-like, as though they were just waiting for the moment when they might swoop down and peck us all to death.

By far the strangest thing was the morning I woke to find muddy hoofprints—like two devil horns—on the floor of my bedroom. They came all the way through the hallway right up to my bed. Actual hoofprints. I touched the mud with my fingertips to make sure I wasn't seeing things. The prints stopped by the side of my bed, as though a moose had crept into the house at night and then stood over me as I slept.

When Gaia held on to me that night, and as I watched her sleep, I knew it wouldn't be fair to leave her. The reason she woke screaming every night was clear to me—she was missing her mother in a way that she could barely understand, and a hot, surging undertow of confusion and grief coursed through her so strongly I could almost feel it in my arms.

That night, I held her until morning. And she didn't scream at all.

8

the river

Tom wishes he hadn't agreed to this. The land, and therefore the river, belongs to him, and despite a nerve shredding visit from a stern surveyor earlier in the week, he is free to build their house as planned. Well, he's free to build once full planning consent is granted, but the paperwork has been filed, the plans have been drawn, and Clive is drafting contracts for the construction team. In the meantime, he is trying to figure out how to divert the river so that they can build on the section of land that offers the best view of the fjord. Aurelia's correct—the part of the cliff that noses outward over emerald-green hills and plunging valleys all the way to Ålesund is by far the best spot for their house. Better yet, he won't have to cut down any more trees if he builds here, as the site is in a clearing—but he *will* have to sort out the minor problem of the river that winds all the way down the hill and over the cliff into the fjord.

"I can't do it," the engineer says. Mr. Ragnar Saltvedt, recommended by the head of the construction team that has agreed in principle to build Basecamp. A big square-shaped man with an acne-scarred face and shaggy brown hair.

Tom looks from the river to Ragnar. "I'm afraid I don't understand. You can't do it or you won't do it?"

"Both," Ragnar says with a grimace. He looks down at the small lick of water that trickles weakly over the stones in the groove of land that acts as a riverbed. "You have no permit from the environment agency."

Tom shifts his feet. He hadn't thought he'd need approval for something like this. "The what?"

"The Norwegian Environment Agency. They have to check the threats posed to the river from alteration."

"Threats?" Tom says, folding his arms. "What kind of threats?"

"The river runs into the fjord; the fjord runs into the sea. The alteration might cause harmful substances to suddenly enter the ocean. We have big problems with sea lice in the fjords just now because of people like you. Wild salmon numbers falling. Genetic mixing. Big problem." Tom bristles at *people like you.* "Wildlife will use this river as their water supply," Ragnar continues, stepping to the other side of the river. "Wolves, bears, elk. They might be affected. One river we worked on had sixty-five different species using it on a daily basis. Sixty-five."

"I've not spotted anything using the river," Tom says, knowing as soon as he's said it how petulant this sounds.

"They'll be using it at night," Ragnar says. "If you set up a night camera you'll be surprised. Ecosystems are very sensitive to human interference."

"How long does it take to get a permit from the environment agency?" Tom asks.

"Very big backlog. Problems with overdevelopment, you see. Lots of people like you building houses just now. I'd say . . . six or seven months."

Tom can't conceal his dismay. He thanks Ragnar for his time, says he'll be in touch. Lies. Even as the man is getting into his car he's thinking of how to do the job himself. He hasn't got six or seven months. And the river is hardly Niagara Falls.

He relays this news to Aurelia, who is disappointed. Such is the dejection in her face that he tells her not to worry. He'll do it himself.

The next morning he pulls on his wellies, thermal gloves, and Gore-Tex jacket and takes a spade, a flask of tea, and a wheelbarrow of concrete blocks to begin damming the river. It's a mild, silvery morning, a white scarf of mist draped over the hills, the sun a splash of orange against mother-of-pearl sky. There are cataracted slabs of ice here and there, some of them several inches thick, but for the most part the river runs fresh and clean through the trough of pebbled earth carved out over millennia. The insistent movement of the river is startling, even touching, among so much stillness—the land's vibrant pulse. No signs of any salmon, or fish of any kind. It'll do no harm to divert it.

He sets about digging a new riverbed at a right angle from the river, trailing his spade all the way through the earth to the cliff. It takes him several hours. By the time he's done he can barely lift his arms. But then the river begins to siphon off into its new bed, and he holds his breath, worried that it'll suddenly seep into the earth. But as he begins to lay the stones across its old path the new river blooms like a strange new flower.

He gives a loud whoop of joy to see the river taking hold in the land, funneling away, undefeated, brilliant in its new life. He wonders if this is how women feel when they've given birth: a sense of awe at something that now lives because of you.

He sits on a tree stump to pour a cup of tea from his flask, triumphant and starving. How stupid not to accept Aurelia's offer of a slice of lemon cake this morning; he is ravenous. The light is already fading. Even so he can make out the red blur of Granhus through the trees. Why on earth did the original owners build the house so far back from the cliff? Why not build it where the view is best? They would have to have moved the river, he thinks. As Ragnar said, the river's probably been here for hundreds of years. He figures that the builders of that old house had had the same dilemma he faces now. To move the river or leave it be.

He finishes his tea, rinses out the cup in the water, and then gives in to a boyish temptation to drink from his new river. He removes a glove and scoops a hand in, both knees in the snow, brings the water to his lips. It tastes beautifully cold and fresh. He should think about connecting the river to their water supply.

When he lowers his hand again beneath the surface he finds he can't withdraw it. His hand is suddenly held in the water, clasped, held tight. Not trapped under a rock, not caught somehow on a network of twigs—gripped by the water itself from the wrist down. It's as though it's encased in steel, not water. His fingers move pitifully against the stones on the riverbed. Maybe his wedding ring has caught on a bindweed. He clasps his right hand around his left wrist and pulls, but his hand doesn't shift. It feels as though his wrist is lanced tightly by the surface, sucked down by an invisible force.

He wonders whether he should laugh or call out for help. Just then, something catches his eye—a reflection on the river's surface, illuminated by the moon.

Someone is here to help.

A glance at the reflection reveals the dark shape of a woman, confirmed by the roundness of hips and slender shoulders, her head bowed down at him. He turns sharply to where she's standing, three feet or so to his right, but there's no one there. Just the trees towering above him and the cold eye of the moon. Was it an animal he saw? A bear? He is helpless, trapped, and something is with him. No. He's sure it was a woman.

"Hello?" he calls. "Help, please!"

Just then, whatever caught his hand lets go, and with a yelp he falls backward, flat on his back into the snow, grasping his wet hand as though he expects it to have been severed at the wrist.

He approaches Maren whilst she's still unpacking from her journey. Like Tom, Maren has traveled from London not by plane but by car and ferry, and is naturally exhausted. He should leave her to relax and settle in, but he's deeply unnerved by his experience at the river.

He taps on the living room door, steps inside when she looks up. Closes it behind him.

"Maren, did anyone happen to call by today? A woman?"

She looks confused. "A woman? I don't think so." She starts to explain that she only arrived last night and may have been preoccupied. He cuts her off.

"It's just . . . I saw someone up the hill. A woman. I wondered if perhaps she'd called to the house."

Maren pulls a face that tells him no, a woman didn't call. He already knew that. Something about the woman he saw—the strangeness of her appearance, and its timing, right as his hand was caught in the river—tells him she wasn't a passerby or a visitor. He already knows that nobody just passes by this way, at least not on foot. It's dangerous, liminal terrain—almost on the cusp of another world, the realm of the impossible. And even if someone *did* call at the house they would have no reason to be on the hill where he was.

But still, logic dictates that she *was* there, and therefore there has to be a reason.

"Come, sit down," Maren says, moving a pile of folded laundry from the chair next to her. He sits down reluctantly, awkward at having to ask his housekeeper for advice. But somehow she's the only one he trusts to answer the questions that pound his brain.

He sits down. He looks awkward, like a child who has done something wrong and is compelled to confess before punishment is meted; she searches for the cause of this. Perhaps the new baby isn't sleeping. Or Aurelia isn't coping out here. Well, Maren *did* think it was a bad idea, bringing a new baby out into this hostile wilderness, but nobody heeds her advice.

She waits, patiently, for him to find the words.

"I had an unusual encounter today," he says slowly. He tells her in broken sentences the sequence of events—the creation of the new riverbed, the tea, his longing for lemon cake. He stammers when he describes what happened to his hand, offering possibilities for the water's grip even as he explains it. Maren strains to read between the lines. She asks questions. What did it feel like? Did he find any weeds caught beneath his wedding ring? Had the water perhaps frozen solid? Did a fish seize his hand, or an eel?

When he exhausts her own suggestions and mentions the reflection of the woman behind him and her sudden disappearance, Maren falls silent. She has heard of water trolls in Norway, usually referred to as *nøkken*. They were called nymphs in other parts of the world, nix, or water sprites—malicious and mischievous beings from another world, though they had been known to help and even save humans. When she was a child in Finnmark people talked about them as though they were real as the family dog. Her father always left some of his catch at the shoreline for the *nøkken*, to ensure a plentiful haul next time. She never saw any, but she didn't question their existence, though she hasn't thought about them for years.

Tom loathes himself for not yet having found a rational explanation for the water's grip on his hand or the presence of the woman. He's tried to tell himself that the reflection was a tree, or a cloud, though he can't deny what he saw, if only for a split second. It's as though that image is branded now on his memory—a dark figure right there in the woods with him. As for the river, he's already sent an awkward e-mail to a professor in environmental science at Cambridge, asking in a roundabout way if it would be possible for a river to seize and hold an object.

He admits this to Maren.

"And what did he say?"

"The reply was . . . unsatisfactory."

She nods. "My father used to tell me tales of the Sami who lived in our village before we did. They knew that Mother Nature was our ruler, and that we had to be careful not to abuse our privileges."

Tom scowls. "Privileges?"

"The *nøkken* act on behalf of Mother Nature. They punish humans who overstep the mark. They might make shallow pools deepen and drown people who abuse nature. I've heard of crops that turned poisonous when the earth was not given proper stewardship."

Tom looks away, angered by Maren's tangent into Norse folklore, of all things. There has to be a logical, scientific basis for what happened. He tells himself it was likely due to a combination of the cold, hunger, fatigue, and poor light. His muscles contracted after all that heavy lifting. He gets up to leave.

"What did she look like?" Maren asks. "The woman you saw."

"Oh, I don't think I saw anyone. Just the light playing tricks."

She doesn't seem convinced. "Are you sure? Because—"

"Thank you, Maren," he says, rising and striding toward the door.

"Perhaps you'll rethink your plans to divert the river?" Maren offers, but he doesn't answer. As he reaches for the door handle his wrist tingles as though to remind him of the water's grasp, cold and insistent as an iron cuff.

9

is there something you're not telling me?

And lo, it came to pass that "Daddy and Daughters Day" finally arrived, and lo, there was much rejoicing in the land.

Tom *was* going to take the girls, Maren had announced the night before, and I had fantasized about how I was going to indulge in those blissful twenty-four hours.

I would sleep until the bed and I became one entity.

I would bask in the luxury of eating without a small angry human flinging pasta at me. No one would climb into my bed in the middle of the night and pee in it—what bliss!

But above all, I would *write*.

My book—now titled *A House in the Woods*, featuring a creepy red house just outside Oslo where Alexa is held hostage—hadn't increased in word count since I arrived in Norway. I'd attempted to chip away at it during the evenings, but it turns out that caring for children all day long mulches your brain. I spent one memorable evening repeatedly misspelling the word *if*, and when I'd eventually squeezed out a whole chapter my laptop crashed, and the entire effort was digested by my hard drive, gone forevermore.

I was put off even attempting to write for a few weeks. But now, today, I would make real, actual progress on my book. I would brainstorm and plan out the chapters, with deadlines and milestones to ensure I kept on track. After all, the first month had gone in a blink. The trees were starting to redden, the cliffs above the fjord a shimmering collar of ruby and gold. The temperature had dropped. If I wasn't careful I'd wind up finishing my time here without a book to show for it.

Finally, Tom took the girls out. There was a lurching moment where I thought the day would be canceled, as both girls cried bitterly for me, which I found touching until Tom looked like he was about to give in and cancel his plans. I whispered in Gaia's ear that I'd let her do whatever she wanted the next day. Little schemer that she is, she bargained with me.

"Screen time," she hissed at me. "Two hours of Netflix."

I nodded. "Deal."

Gaia gave a small, demonic smile. Then, in a loud voice, an about-face: "Come on, Coco. We *love* spending the day with Daddy, don't we? It's going to be *so* much fun."

Tom looked happily surprised. Coco seemed to follow Gaia's lead, for she fell silent and allowed Tom to strap her into the baby carrier that he hoisted onto his back. I almost asked him where he was headed, given that the area outside the house was a construction site, but I held back in case he decided to quit his plans altogether.

When the door finally closed I stood for a moment, bathing in the silence. No squealing. No stomping of feet or sound of something smashing to the ground in a million pieces. Bliss.

I headed back to my room, climbed back into bed, and flipped open my laptop.

"Sophie?"

I looked up to find Maren standing in the doorway to my room.

"Might I have a quick word?"

My heart sank. This didn't sound good at all.

"Yes, of course."

She came in and shut the door, then clasped her hands and smiled.

"I thought we might have a review of your tenure," she said. Tenure? I couldn't even pretend to understand what this meant. "How are you finding the job?"

"Fine," I said with an innocent, so-glad-you-asked smile. I hoped that this would be enough to make her leave.

"Fine?" she said, cocking her head. She kept darting her eyes around the room in a way that made me wonder if she suspected I had someone else in here with me. An errant builder hiding under my bed, perhaps. "How is Gaia's education going? Hmm? Because I noticed you hadn't filled in the logbook."

"Logbook?"

This was the first I'd heard of a logbook. I felt my cheeks burn and my voice was thinned by guilt. Her eyes flicked across the room, and I suddenly interpreted the whole scenario—the question about the logbook was a trap. She already knew I was lying about who I was. And I surprised myself, because despite how completely and utterly wrung out I was, I didn't want to leave. I loved those girls, and I loved being part of a family, albeit a grief-stricken, distracted one. I felt needed, or *necessary*. And in any case, I'd be homeless again if they kicked me out.

"Maybe I'm using the wrong term," Maren said, suddenly doubting herself. "It's the . . . uh . . . learning folder. Learning journey booklet."

"OK," I said slowly, flooded with relief. She really *was* asking about the logbook. I played along with her confusion, trying to mask my confusion at the existence of some sort of logbook by pretending I was wrong-footed by its correct translation.

Maren flapped her hands, flustered by not being able to access the correct English term. "Perhaps this is why you didn't fill it in?" she said. "You mistook it for something else. Only I had expected to find it full of photographs of Gaia's progress. Her writing samples, reading log, and so on."

"Could you show me the logbook?" I asked gently. She nodded and turned on her heel toward the playroom. I followed, my heart leaping about in terror like a caffeinated frog, and watched as she rooted in a drawer for the logbook. When a few minutes passed with no sign of the book, I said: "Isn't it there?"

She looked flustered now, her sleeves rolled up and her lips pursed. "Perhaps it is in the office," she said. "I will check."

"Was there anything else?" I said sweetly.

She smoothed a strand of blonde hair back into place. "Yes, there was, as it happens," she said. "I wanted to ask about your cooking. You recall I expressly stated that Tom wishes the girls to be raised vegan."

"I've been making vegan meals."

I had been meticulous about checking out the food stores. There wasn't exactly a Tesco around the corner, and Maren had mentioned she went shopping once a month, but happily the huge chest freezer was well stocked with frozen vegetables, bread, cakes, yogurts, and vegan mince, chicken, and even bacon (soya-based stuff that tasted pretty decent). In the larder sat row upon row of hand-labeled jars of jams, nut butters, preserved fruits, and cartons of almond milk, and along the floor sat great sacks of dried rice, pulses, flour, potatoes, and a thousand different kinds of dried beans. We certainly wouldn't starve.

Maren sighed, and again I felt my cheeks flush and my heart stammer, as if I'd done something terribly wrong.

"Is there something you're not telling me, Sophie?" she said then.

I lifted my gaze to her searching blue eyes. It was hanging in the air, her suspicion of me, her eyes perceiving every inch of my terrible lie as though it was smeared ten inches thick across my face.

"I'm not vegan," I heard myself say. "I've . . . renounced veganism."

Her eyebrows shot up.

"I'm not convinced veganism is . . . nutritionally adequate," I continued, or rather my mouth continued. "Studies have shown . . ."

I was glad Maren cut in then, one hand held up as if to say she'd heard *all* about "studies," because I had no idea what kind of studies I was about to refer to. "Yes, yes," she said. "And frankly, I agree. But Tom has . . . Look, *I* don't mind if you give Gaia honey."

"Honey?" I said, incredulous. Nothing I'd read mentioned honey as a carnivorous food. There were three thousand, four hundred and sixty-eight jars of it in the pantry, all from local sources and with intriguing flavors, like clover and acacia. Lavender was Gaia's favorite.

"I know, I know," Maren said wearily. "Frankly I'd say honey is perfectly vegan. But Tom doesn't agree with some of the practices of beekeeping now, so he'd rather we avoided honey altogether."

I reassured her that of course I would abide by Tom's wishes going forward, but I could sense she didn't trust me, and I wondered what I'd done to create a bad impression. And then I realized, and when I did I could barely speak for sheer, ground-opening horror: the window opposite threw back my reflection, a reflection that showed I had rolled up my sleeves and revealed to Maren the long red scars all over my forearms. The cuts had healed and the swelling had gone down, but they were still visible, stark signatures of what I'd done in David's bathroom. Like a child caught with her hand in the biscuit tin I immediately and not at all subtly swiped both arms behind my back, and although Maren continued chatting about free-range milk, wondering aloud whether goat's milk could qualify as vegan, there was a moment, wide as the universe, of silence. That silence told me she had seen the scars and knew exactly what they were. Moreover, she knew that those scars did not tally with my counterfeit identity. Sophie Hallerton was not the sort of person who would inflict such injuries on herself. And after all, who would want someone capable of injuring themselves so badly looking after their children—young children whose own mother had recently committed suicide?

I can't remember what Maren said after that, but I think I mumbled a promise about avoiding honey before heading back to my room, climbing into bed, and crying beneath the covers. I was crying not simply because I was sure the game was up but because I had been reminded that the difference between Lexi Ellis and Sophie Hallerton was a vast gulf that could be measured in light-years. Perhaps my mother had always been right. I didn't deserve to be here. That was a fact. I was a fraud, a trickster.

That night, a storm broke across the cliff. Rain thick as embroidery swept across the forest, drumming the roof of the house and worming its way through the slates, dripping into the attic. Purple lightning whipped across the skies in tremendous arcs. I was worried that the house would collapse or that the roof might cave in, but when I heard Maren race upstairs with a mop and bucket I was suddenly seized with an idea. I remembered I had used one of Sophie's references. What was her name? Verity? What if she'd e-mailed the real Sophie to check up on how she was getting on? She would doubtless have e-mailed Maren straightaway once she found out that Sophie had never actually interviewed for the job.

Quickly I tiptoed to the office, where I knew Maren had been working before the rain started. Tom was in his studio at his enormous easel, the floorboards creaking every time he shifted in his seat. I went into the office and pulled the door slightly shut, then turned on the computer. It was still logged into Maren's user account.

I found the e-mail icon and clicked on it, and immediately Maren's in-box was on the screen. Ninety-four unread messages. Many of them in relation to the project management of the build, some of them urgent. More than half were more than three days old. Why hadn't Maren checked them? Wasn't she employed to do the housework *and* admin? I remembered then a comment she'd made about being a Luddite—obviously she wasn't keen on admin that involved technology.

I scrolled down. Some from Tom, a dozen from his accountant with red exclamation marks. But there was one e-mail, right at the bottom of the list, that made me freeze. The subject was "Application for Nanny Position." The sender was Sophie Hallerton.

To: maren.larsen@tfarchitecture.net
From: sophiealicehallerton87@hotmail.co.uk

Subject: Application for Nanny Position

Dear Maren,

I am writing to apply for the nanny position advertised a few weeks ago—I do hope that I'm not too late and that you're still accepting applications!

I have extensive experience working with children in a variety of capacities, and I am available immediately to accompany them to Norway. I have attached my cover letter and CV here and look forward to hearing more if the position is still available.

My very best,
Sophie Hallerton

I could not believe what I was reading. *Sophie had actually applied for the job.* What had happened to her pregnant friend? Maybe she had lost the baby. Poor Seren.

Whatever the cause of Sophie's change of heart, I had to act fast. I blocked her e-mail from Maren's account.

Quickly I trawled through Maren's older messages until I located a message from Verity Porter. I quickly scanned the glowing reference she had sent before blocking her e-mail as well. In all likelihood, both Verity and Sophie had more than one e-mail account. Perhaps Sophie would follow up with a second e-mail to check whether Maren had received her e-mail. Damn. Quickly I unblocked her again, typed out a hasty reply from Maren's account (Dear Sophie, I'm afraid the position has been filled, but thank you for thinking of us. Best wishes, Maren), then deleted the message from the Sent folder and reblocked Sophie's.

Even then, I knew that this was no prevention against being caught. In fact, by replying to Sophie I had possibly made things worse . . .

Lexi.

I looked up, startled by a whispering that sounded distinctly like my real name. Two syllables whispered hoarsely by someone close by. All the hairs on my arms stood on end.

I stepped lightly to the doorframe and peeked out into the dark corridor. No sign of Gaia, or Maren. But then a movement in the kitchen caught my eye.

It was dark, but as my eyes adjusted I saw the outline of a figure by the sink. A woman. I saw immediately that it wasn't Maren—she was shorter and seemed to have long dark hair in a kind of loose, wet ponytail. Did Tom have female builders working on the site? I didn't recall seeing any, and in any case she wasn't exactly dressed for construction work—she was barefoot and wore a long gray dress, and even though I only flashed a look at her I deduced that she was wet. Like, soaking wet, as if she'd been caught in the rain. But she wasn't doing anything, wasn't grabbing a tea towel to dry her hair—she was just standing there, her back to me, hands by her sides.

"Hello?" I called. No answer. "Can I help you?"

I took a few steps into the kitchen and flicked on the light. And then I jumped.

The woman was nowhere to be seen. Fear pinioned me to the spot. How had she managed to walk out the door in just a few seconds? My heart was racing. I glanced at the door, then walked nervously toward it, checking the handle. Locked. I felt my breathing grow labored with a mixture of confusion and fear. I *had* seen her, hadn't I? She had stood right there, by the window, dripping wet.

"Sophie?"

I flung around to see Maren approaching, her face crumpled in confusion.

"There was . . . a woman . . ." I stammered.

"A woman?"

I nodded like Tigger. "Yes. She was standing here."

Maren glanced into the office. The light of the computer screen shone on her face and she turned back to me.

"What were you doing in here?" she said archly, and this time her suspicion was naked, angry.

I walked toward her, still babbling about a woman. Somewhere in the house a child's wail sounded. Coco.

"This," I said, picking up a purple pacifier I had just spotted on the floor. A moment of adrenaline-fueled genius. "Coco's favorite pacifier. She'll be needing this tonight, I think."

"Right," Maren said, narrowing her eyes. We both knew what happened when Coco was without her favorite pacifier at night.

My heart close to bursting like a piñata through my rib cage, I walked quickly to Coco's room before Maren's gaze burned a hole through my back. Coco woke up with a desperate howl, groping around the bedclothes.

"Here you are, darling," I said, slipping the pacifier into her mouth.

I sat for a long while in the chair beside her crib, my heart still pounding from what I'd seen and heard in the kitchen. I had heard someone whisper my name. A woman. And I had *seen* her—I remembered that there had been a trail of soil: proof that she had been there. And quickly I thought back to the morning I had woken to find large hoofprints in my room, leading to my bed. If it wasn't weird enough to find actual hoofprints in the house, indicating that a creature had come in while I was sleeping and had stood over my bed, weirder still was the absence of a second set of prints from where the creature turned around and left. It hardly went out through the window. So why just one set?

After that night, I became more vigilant. Instead of writing in the evenings, I studied YouTube videos and Pinterest boards on all kinds of early learning activities. I learned all about the milestones Coco should be reaching, and how to deliver a Montessori education through drawing and play. I never found any logbook, but I made one out of a notebook and kept detailed notes about the girls' development. And every time I went near the kitchen I dived for the light switch lest some weird woman should be standing at the window. When I read to the girls, I read aloud in my new southern accent. *How now brown cow.* I was beginning to sound, look, and even smell like someone else. Like Sophie Hallerton.

I couldn't prevent the truth from coming out entirely, but I could certainly do my best to stall it as long as I could. Gaia and

Coco laughed more, slept better. I found some old sandbags in the nursery and stitched them to the corners of a quilt to form a weighted blanket, which had the effect of enabling Gaia to sleep in her own bed—and without screaming—for the first time. This earned me a lot of brownie points with Tom.

But when I spoke with Maren, I saw it in her face: suspicion.

10

the hole you left

NOW

Don't go too far," he calls to Gaia.

She skips into the trees. "OK, Daddy, I won't."

He promised the girls a picnic in the woods—a bear's picnic, which sounds much more ominous now that they're in actual bear territory—and so he lays out a groundsheet in a dry part of the clearing and sets Coco down on a seat pad while he unpacks his flask of tea and pasta salad, along with a box of sandwiches and blueberry muffins for the girls. There's no rational explanation for why this most banal of tasks—pouring the tea into a sippy cup for Coco, peeling the edges off Gaia's sandwich so she doesn't complain about it later—should suddenly have him in tears, but there it is. He weeps silently as he prepares lunch, glad that Gaia isn't here to ask him why he's crying. *Is it because of Mumma?* Yes, he thinks. Yes. I'm crying because the river has been restored to life and yet my wife remains dead. Why couldn't it be the other way round?

The raw reality of Aurelia's death is a maw he steps into again and again. All her clothes, perfumes, soaps, and shoes are still in her closet, untouched. Books she read, notebooks holding her writing. He keeps her phone charged, watches videos of her. Listens to her voice recordings, compulsively checks her Instagram account for updates, and each time he sees that the account has stalled at that last haunting image of fir trees whitened with snow, his heart lurches. She is dead—actually, stunningly, dead. How can that be?

He keeps looking for a map of some kind to navigate this alien terrain, help him find a way out of the nightmare. Grief is made of trapdoors, each moment plunging you into a memory. That his wife is dead is one thing; that she died in such a harrowing, inexplicable manner is another. That phone call. *We've found a body part. We suspect it belonged to Aurelia.* And then, the morning he had to drive to a morgue alone and identify her body. No, not her body—a carcass. Bloated, broken, and waxy from time in the water, picked at by animals before a farmer found her.

The ground still shifts beneath his feet when he thinks about it. And yet he hasn't told anyone about how she was found. Not her family, not his. How could he speak of such a thing? How could he ever begin to scale such horror with mere words?

As he sits in the woods he recognizes the impulse that rises up in him as he scans the trees, the unquestionable certainty that any second now, Aurelia will walk through the clearing with her camera in one hand and a handful of pine cones for the baby in the other. She'll be smiling, her faced flushed with whatever new scene she's managed to snatch with her lens. The sun will rest on her blonde hair, which trails behind her in gold waves.

Instead, the small figure of Gaia reappears then through a prism of trunks, running toward him with something cupped in her hands, and the re-realization that his wife is dead, that the sweet, innocent girl bouncing toward him will grow up without her mother, rains down on him like a shower of burning oil.

"Look, Daddy! Look!"

In a moment she is there, breathless from the run and excitement, and he sees what she has found: a baby bird, about three inches long, fuzzy-headed, eyes bulging out of livid red skin, legs hooked like claws.

"Is she dead, Daddy?" Gaia says, panicked.

She allows him to scoop the nestling gently from her hands into his own warm palms, where he inspects it closely. One tiny eye creaks open.

"No," he tells Gaia. "Not dead at all. Where did you find it?"

She turns and points in the direction of the woods. "By that tree."

"On the ground?"

She nods. Coco seizes fistfuls of his sweater to haul herself to a standing position, then reaches over to pluck the bird from his grasp.

"No, Coco!" Gaia yells. He tries to jerk his palm away from Coco, but she manages to plant her hand heavily on its head, prying a small but distinctive "cheep" from its mouth.

"Did she hurt it, Daddy?" Gaia says, her eyes glistening with tears, and before he can reassure her she throws a fierce look at her sister. "*Naughty* Coco!"

"Ma-ma-ma," Coco answers happily.

"It's still moving," he says, turning toward a shaft of bright sunlight to inspect the bird more closely. "He looks very tired. I expect his mum will be looking for him."

Both he and Gaia raise their eyes to the canopy above, as though a mother bird will appear, searching for her lost chick. When no such bird appears, they turn their eyes back to the helpless creature in his palms, which is now opening and closing its beak as though making an effort to talk.

"We should get her something to drink," Gaia offers. "And perhaps some food. I can look for worms. Should I look for worms, Daddy?"

He tells her instead to take him to where she found the bird in the first place. With one arm he scoops up Coco onto his hip, then trudges across the crisp carpet of leaves and twigs after Gaia, who meticulously retraces her steps to the precise location where she found the baby bird at the foot of a towering pine tree.

"I think I can see a nest!" Gaia announces, craning her head so far back she almost falls over. "Up there, Daddy! I think its mummy is there, too."

That the nest is there at all, much less with mother bird in situ awaiting the safe return of her lost chick, is unlikely. But Tom plays along, sharply aware that the bird's rescue is accruing symbolic weight with each passing second, as though the crack in the planet caused by Aurelia's death can be mended by returning this bird to its own family, its own mother. No matter how much he believes that he is able to accept this most terrible of losses, he cannot undo the sensation of being mightily off-kilter, at once accelerated and freeze-framed, and he recognizes the sudden burst of longing in his daughter for things to be put right. For restoration.

Tom glances down at the bird in his hand. It is barely moving. His heart is heavy, but he registers that Gaia is silently pleading with him to revive the nestling and return it to its mother. He catches himself right as he's about to say something about how the mother bird will likely reject the bird anyway, given that it's now bathed in his scent, but even as he opens his mouth he knows that such information will wound Gaia. For her the world is still a place where tragedy can be outdone by triumph. Where sorrow can be quenched by noble acts, and the long shadow of death can be outshone by love's light. He is duty bound to protect the world in which Gaia lives, this world of untarnished hope and unicorns, for as long as he can.

"Let's take this fella into the house," he says. "Get him some water."

Inside, Gaia sets about sourcing a cardboard box, which she lines with a cashmere scarf, a Ping-Pong ball in case the nestling needs a toy, a Peppa Pig figurine, and a piece of Christmas tinsel.

"What's the tinsel for?" Tom asks.

"Decoration," Gaia replies earnestly. "To make her bed pretty."

"What's Peppa Pig for?"

"In case Dora gets lonely."

"Dora?"

"That's what I've named her."

"Ah," he says. "After the cartoon." He thinks about the endless reruns of *Dora the Explorer*, and the map song that has to be the worst earworm of all time.

"No, Daddy," Gaia says, offended. "Not after Dora the Explorer! After Dora Carrington. The surrealist painter, remember?"

"Oh. OK."

He bites back the argument that the bird most definitely is *not* Gaia's new pet, and they don't even know if it's a boy bird or a girl bird.

"Can you keep her in your bedroom, Daddy?" Gaia says suddenly. "I can't keep her in my bedroom."

"No, no," Tom says, distracted. He's trying to google instructions on feeding a nestling, but Gaia is suddenly tugging on his sleeve, relentlessly trying to get his attention. "Daddy, Daddy, Daddy. I can't keep her in my bedroom, Daddy."

"Stop it," he says, jerking away. As always, the stab of guilt when he sees her face fall. He pulls her into a hug. "Sorry, pudding. Why can't you keep her in your bedroom? Wait, of course you're not keeping her in your bedroom . . ."

"She has to stay in *your* bedroom, Daddy, because the Sad Lady doesn't like your bedroom . . ."

His head hurts. What is she saying?

". . . She only likes my bedroom, Daddy, but she'll scare Dora, I know she will."

"What are you talking about? What lady? Do you mean Maren?"

She stares up at him solemnly and shakes her head.

"Sophie?"

"*No*, Daddy. The Sad Lady doesn't have a name."

He frowns. "Right. So, what does she look like?"

"I don't know because I don't have my glasses on in bed. I don't think she has any eyes."

"Blimey."

"She frightens me, Daddy."

"Sweetheart, I know you're sad about Mummy. I know you're really, really sad."

Gaia nods and sniffs.

He notices her teddy, Louis, on the table nearby. "How's Louis feeling these days?"

She turns and looks at the teddy, then picks him up and straightens the trousers he's wearing. Tom doesn't remember the teddy having trousers before.

"Louis is scared."

"OK. Do you want to ask Louis why he's scared?"

"I don't need to ask him, I already know."

"Why, then?"

She considers this. "Well, he's a little bit excited that we found Dora, but he's worried in case she dies because that would be sad . . ."

His attention turns back to the bird. Of course, the bird. It'll make her feel better if they somehow keep it going.

". . . and Louis doesn't like the Sad Lady either and he's scared of her, too."

He sighs. "OK, what Sad Lady? Who is she?"

"I don't know," she says quietly. "She sometimes comes into the house at night and she looks very sad. She makes me very scared because she just comes into my room and stands at the window. I think she's a ghost."

He recalls Gaia's night terrors. "OK. These are *dreams*, sweetheart."

"They're not dreams, Daddy . . ."

"Maybe we can have you move rooms or something?"

She shrugs, disheartened that he won't listen. "I don't know."

He straightens. A small feeling of pride at having achieved something. "And now, we need to feed this little bird. We need dog kibble, boiled eggs, and sugar water."

"What's dog kibble?" she asks, her attention moving back to the little bird that needs her love just to survive.

"Dog kibble is food for dogs."

"We don't have a dog, Daddy."

"Right." For the thousandth time he regrets that they picked a site so far from civilization. Amazon doesn't even deliver out here, and Tom has to collect mail from a tiny shop that only opens twice a week in a village ten miles across terrain that he's sure is annihilating the suspension on their Mercedes with every trip.

"Let's try the egg yolks and water, shall we?" he offers at last.

"We have eggs?" Gaia asks brightly. She had a sneaky egg once at a friend's house and it was delicious.

Tom doesn't respond. The eggs belong to Maren—gifted from a farmer on the other side of the fjord—but he's sure she can manage without one on this occasion. "We'll get dog kibble later this afternoon, OK?"

"Will that be too late?" Gaia asks. He tells her no, it'll be fine, and proceeds to rifle through the cupboards for a cappuccino cup in which to hold the egg. His movements are too clumsy and he sends a glass toppling to the floor, where it shatters. Gaia screams and Coco laughs. He finds a small dish, but in his haste to retrieve it from the cupboard he sends a mug to the floor. Another almighty crash, ceramic on tile. The mug is one of Aurelia's, and even as he glances down and spies the duck-egg-blue fragments rearranged like a modernist sculpture, he recalls taking her that very mug, filled with steaming-hot tea, whilst she nursed Coco in bed. He feels tears of anger prick his eyes. He wants to punch something.

"Is everything all right?" a voice asks.

He twists from his stooped position over the glass—he's picking up shards with his bare hands before Coco can plant one of her knees or palms on them—to see a girl in the doorway. Sophie, the nanny. She looks disheveled, her black hair sticking out like that bloke from the Cure and a purple bra strap visible from where her nightie has slipped down one shoulder. He wonders if he should ask her about this Sad Lady nonsense. She'll be able to explain it.

But in the handful of seconds that he's been distracted, Coco has padded across to the shattered mug and glass, and Sophie lunges forward, scooping her up right as Coco makes for a jagged shard of glass sitting up from the floor like a stalagmite.

"Oh, no, you don't, my lovely," Sophie tells Coco, who wriggles and squirms to be down, as though hell-bent on finding anything with which she might injure herself. *Like Aurelia,* he thinks, and his mood spirals into shame.

"Come on, girls," Sophie tells Coco and Gaia. "Let's go play while Daddy sorts out that mess."

"Are you sure?" he asks Sophie. It's Sunday. It's her day off, and suddenly it strikes him that the reason she looks so . . . untethered is because she's catching up on sleep. It's how Aurelia started to look on weekends. *Go back to bed,* he'd tell her, and she'd give him a look of deep gratitude before returning to their bedroom and staying there until evening.

"Yep," Sophie says, throwing him a smile. A yawn catches her by surprise.

"But Dora," Gaia says, and she proceeds to tell Sophie all about the nestling they found, and how she desperately needs water and dog food, and please can Sophie save her, please, please?

Tom fetches the vacuum cleaner when he concedes that they mustn't own a dustpan and brush and sucks up the broken glass and mug while Sophie and Gaia endeavor to revive Dora. A chorus of squeals and claps indicates that the bird has taken a few sips. Gaia is crying, Sophie hugs her tightly, and a great wave of gratitude rolls over him.

"I'll get dressed," he hears Sophie tell Gaia. "And we'll go find Dora's mum. Deal?"

Gaia nods, swiping tears from her cheeks. "Deal."

An odd indignity warms him, and before he can exert any self-control he's striding toward Sophie and murmuring that the mother bird will likely reject its nestling, given that it's been handled by humans. "Look, I think it's kinder if we just tell Gaia the truth," he says. "It's going to die whatever we do."

"Oh, no," Sophie says. "That's just an old wives' tale. The rejected-because-of-human-smell thing." She smiles to show she's not interested in proving him wrong but that the possibility of the nestling being restored to the nest—and thus, pleasing Gaia infinitely—is in their mutual interests.

He grimaces, looks away. He doesn't like being wrong.

Later, when he overhears Gaia's happy chatter from the playroom, relief catches him by surprise.

On his desk, a photograph of Aurelia smiles back. She has her arms wrapped around a tree, her hair sweeping away from her, and that smile, her beautiful smile that deflected from so much darkness and turmoil, beaming out of the frame like the North Star. He can hear her voice, clear as a bell.

Oh, Tom, she says sadly. *Why did you do it, Tom?*

11

the felling

THEN

It's been a month since Aurelia first arrived at the site. She's grown used to Granhus, and the finishing touches Tom has added in the form of new sofas, books, and a toy room have made it homey. He had the old boiler fixed so she can have hot baths every night if she wants to, and the Aga is actually brilliant—it really does heat the whole house, even a place as big and as drafty as Granhus.

Still, she hasn't felt right since Coco was born. No, not since then—since she came to this wild place on the edge of the cliff. She WhatsApps her friends back home often—miserable out here, send gin 😞—and is more serious than they think. If she was back in London, meeting up with Dulcie and Saffy and their new babies, or at her mother's house in Oxford, being fussed over and ordered to take long hot baths every night (*It soothes the soul, darling*), maybe she wouldn't feel as . . . hollow. As though the world is black and white, devoid of smell, taste, and texture.

And then there are the weird dreams she keeps having.

She looks at herself in the long mirror in the corner of the bedroom. She's still in her nightdress, her blonde hair wild and tangled, her face bare. When did she last wear makeup, or proper clothes? She can't remember.

Tom keeps asking if she's all right, and the answer's always the same: *Of course I am. We're building our dream home! It's amazing.* And she smiles, and portrays herself as she usually is: happy, focused, full of plans. But something has changed. She can feel a darkness settling inside her bones, a fog veiling her thoughts. The midwife would say it's postnatal depression, but she's sure it's not. She has had low days like everyone else, but this is something completely new, beyond the scope of her new-baby, new-house situation. When did it happen? She glances outside at the untrammeled view of the fjord, and the answer crystallizes: it was when Tom cut down the trees.

She recalls the morning when she'd stood, right in this very spot, holding a mug of tea in one hand and Coco in her other arm, looking down at Tom felling the first tree. A big gnarled thing with a hollow in the middle, like a mouth, two branches crooked out at either side like arms. A storybook tree. The trunk was six feet wide. Hours later, Tom emerged drenched in sweat and exhausted, as though he'd had to box the tree down with his bare hands. He held up a jar of the sap: so dark it resembled blood. "The king of the forest is conquered," he'd said with a grin.

That was when the darkness had seeped into her. She knew she'd been wrong to ask him to cut down the tree. Everything feels so different here, as though they're no longer on the earth but in some other place—an in-between. Time, light, and even the elements are expanded and contracted here, so different they require different names. She feels the boundary between her own self and the land has been ruptured. That she is *affected* by the forest, the fjord, the wildlife. No, not just affected—occasionally possessed by the spirit of the place. She touches her hand to the glass of the mirror and gives a wry laugh. If anyone heard her thoughts they'd think she'd gone mad. Possessed! Still, the felling of the tree feels like a death, like slaughter. She feels physically pained by it.

Tom reassured her that he'd put the wood to good use. He Skyped Derry, who began to draw up plans for bespoke kitchen units, a dining table, a hand-carved bed for Coco. It reassured her a little that the tree would not be wasted. But when she'd gone outside there were at least a dozen nests on the ground, some still with broken eggshells inside. A steady trail of insects ribboned away from the branches. Squirrels and other creatures she didn't even recognize darted on the ground, as though they, too, had been displaced. The roots of the tree looked like human veins ripped from flesh.

She tries to remember what Tom said. "There are a *million* other trees for them to go to, Aurelia. Don't be so sensitive."

He'd said it gently, pulled her close, and kissed her forehead. More to the point, he was right. She's just adjusting, that's what this is. They're both such city slickers that they didn't even think to find out about garbage disposal. It's not like the council is going to be sending out a weekly bin collection.

She checks that the baby is still asleep in the crib beside her bed before opening the last box to be unpacked. There, right at the bottom, are her cameras. A digital Nikon SLR and a Leica M6 with a few dozen films. She's not used the Leica in ages as it's crazy difficult to get film developed. She remembers burning her fingertips on the acidic chemical fluid in the college darkroom as a teenager, then taking Polaroid selfies back in the nineties and being amazed when, in a minute or so, a photographic souvenir of whatever wild night out she was enjoying with uni friends could be captured on a slim card. How things have changed. Somehow taking photographs on her phone feels like a little bit of the magic is lost.

She thumbs the beautiful Leica, holds it up to her eye. Already she feels a bit better, the darkness shifting a little. This movement tugs her instantly to a thousand other times and places that she's held a camera to her eye: in Namibia, photographing tribeswomen naked to the waist, their babies held at the hip and their dreadlocked hair matted with mud; at Downing Street, photographing the prime minister addressing the nation after the vote for Brexit; and in a small, overlit studio, photographing a celebrity who had been giving the interview of her life, and whose face was still raw and swollen from crying. Moments that defined her more than they defined the subject on the other side of the lens.

"Aurelia?" Tom calls from the kitchen. The door slams behind him. She glances at the baby in the basket before making to answer, but he's already stomping up the stairs. She sighs. It sounds as though he didn't get permission for the build after all. Something's gone wrong at the last minute. A conservation query. An issue about the architectural drawings. Weeks of paperwork for nothing.

"What happened?" she says when he enters the bedroom. "What went wrong?"

He sits down on the bed, unsheathes a thick wad of paper from an envelope, and thrusts it at her.

"What's this?" she asks, panicked.

"It's the contract for the build."

"We got consent?"

He nods. She throws her arms in the air and gives a shriek of joy, making Coco jolt briefly awake. Aurelia straddles Tom and throws her arms around him, kissing his face.

They kiss, chaste pecks at first, then deep, passionate kisses that feel to Tom as new as the day they fell in love. It has been thirty-nine days since they made love. He feels all thirty-nine days and eleven hours grinding on him like a stone. When she pulls away he wants to plead with her not to stop but remembers the last time he did that, and the look of disappointment and—strangely enough—hurt on her face. *I have an infection, Tom. You make me feel like I can't so much as look at you without you begging me for sex.* So he lies back on the bed with her on top of him and summons every ounce of his courage not to plead with her.

She plucks up the contract. "Wow, this is long."

"Thirty-six pages."

"Blimey. That's a lot of pages just to say yes."

"It's a complicated yes."

She looks down at him. He doesn't meet her gaze. It must be something awful.

"They've insisted that I install a mechanical ventilation system."

She laughs. "That's it? What about the river? No issues with you diverting it?"

"I don't think you understand . . ."

She turns back to the contract, trying to make sense of all the legal mumbo jumbo. "And they were fine with the house being on stilts?"

"Pilings, my love, pilings. Not stilts . . ."

"Pilings, then. They were OK with it?"

He nods. She seems appeased by this. Good. She gives up on the document and leans over him, pressing her breasts against his chest and her mouth against his. It takes all his willpower not to rip her clothes off. He should get a medal, he thinks.

She rolls off him and lies beside him, basking in the victory that is contained in all thirty-six pages of the contract. Their house is going to be real. Their dream house. It's incredible, a dream come true. Her mood soars, but Tom is returning to the reason why he looked so glum earlier. He's complaining, whingeing. She wants him to shut the hell up. They've just won governmental consent to build their dream home here in Norway, for heaven's sake. What is there to complain about?

". . . and the issue I have with that is that it's completely unnecessary. It's a tick-box requirement. We're in *Norway*, above a *fjord*. We have the best air quality in the world."

She rolls over onto her side, cupping her abdomen as it slides to the mattress. "I'm still not following . . ."

He explains that a mechanical air ventilation system will require energy. He's been insistent on the house being completely eco-friendly, off-grid, producing more energy than it consumes, *blah blah blah*. She yawns and does her Kegels, thinking about fittings for the new bathroom as she clenches the hammocked muscles of her pelvic floor.

"More than three-quarters of the land on earth—"

"—has been modified by humans. Yeah, I *know*, Tom. You've mentioned it a few thousand times before."

"I'm just saying. I'm not being a pain in the arse . . ."

"You are, Tom. You are."

"All right, but it's about . . . look, if I just abandon my principles and overlook what really matters despite being an architect and, you know, *aware* of how we're destroying the planet, then what hope is there for the next generation, huh? For Gaia and Coco?"

She stops clenching, a little out of breath. "Isn't diverting a river modifying the land?"

"Aurelia, you asked me to change the course of the river. You picked the spot where we would build . . ."

"I know I did . . ."

"The river's still going to be there. It'll just . . . bend a little. So it becomes part of the aesthetics of the house." He's stumped by her calling him out like this. Frustrated, even. He hadn't wanted to touch the river. He's invested in making this house as eco-friendly as possible. "You're saying you *didn't* want me to divert the river?"

She sighs. "All I'm saying is I really don't think installing a mechanical ventilation system in a house is going to melt the ice caps . . ."

His face lights up. "You see? That's what *everyone* thinks. 'Oh, it doesn't matter if I chuck this plastic bottle out, there's already a whole island of plastic bottles in the Indian Ocean,' or 'Sod going vegan, a burger never hurt anyone.'"

She laughs. He joins her. They laugh for different reasons.

After a moment or two she touches his cheek.

"It's going to be out of this world," she says. "We're so lucky to be able to do this." She kisses him deeply, holds his face close. He feels his fingers reach for the buttons of her shirt.

"You know I'm leaving for Oslo tonight," he says, his brain flagging a last resort for sex. "I'll be gone for a week."

But she doesn't answer. Something has appeared in the fringes of her vision by the bedroom door, a shape. A woman with her head bowed, wearing a long dress.

"What's wrong?" he says, following her gaze to the doorway.

Aurelia rises to her feet sharply. "Someone was here."

"Who? Who was here?"

Aurelia raises her hand to her head. She looks upset. "I could have sworn I just saw . . ."

He gets to his feet, studies the space that Aurelia is staring at. The doorway. "What? What did you see?"

She gives a deep sigh, presses her palms against her eyes for a few moments. "Nothing," she says finally. "Just a trick of the light."

Sex is out of the question now. He strains to find a way to bring it back into the realm of possibility, but he can see she's unsettled. "Are you sure you'll be all right here with the girls?" he says.

She swivels her green eyes back to him and forces a smile. "I'm sure."

"You could come, you know."

"A hotel in the city in winter is the last place I want to take a newborn. But I'll miss you. Come back early if you can."

"Of course I will."

He kisses her again, and this time she doesn't pull away.

Tom has been gone two days. The house is quiet and still, and Maren has restored a sense of order to the place. Aurelia settles the girls into their beds, but the process takes longer than it does back home: both Coco and especially Gaia are unsettled by the change in their environment. Gaia doesn't like the house, well-stocked playroom notwithstanding. "It's scary, Mumma," she says, turning to look at the window, where a full moon is silhouetting the huge willow tree that sits right next to the house. By day, the tree is beautiful, a kind of tree-waterfall hybrid, but at night the leaves that drape from its branches resemble tentacles, or witchy fingers. She rises from the bed and tugs the curtains closer to block out the view.

"There," she tells Gaia. "Nothing to be afraid of. See?"

She sits beside Gaia and strokes her forehead to calm her, but just then Aurelia stiffens.

"What's wrong, Mumma?" Gaia murmurs when she feels her mother straighten, primed to get up.

Aurelia shushes her. Her instincts home in on the source of the sound. A low human voice, or perhaps the low growl of an animal. A bear, perhaps. She knows the sound came from the basement. This makes no sense. How could she possibly hear such a low sound from two levels down? And yet she did.

All the hairs on Aurelia's arms stand on end.

"Stay here," Aurelia whispers to her, rising to inspect the noise.

"Where are you going, Mumma?" Gaia says, swinging her legs over the side to follow her.

"Stay *here*," Aurelia says again, in a voice that fixes Gaia to the bed. Seeing Gaia's face, she softens. "You stay in bed, sweetheart, OK?"

"But *why* . . . ?"

She sighs. "Look, I think I heard a noise downstairs. I'm just going to check it out, OK?" She forces a smile, but Gaia recognizes that strained, false look immediately and her worry doubles in size. She wiggles back down under the covers and tries hard not to cry.

Aurelia heads downstairs. No sign of Maren anywhere. She likes to take a walk once a day. She must be out. She pats the pocket of her cardigan to ensure her mobile phone is at hand. Before she reaches the bottom stair she takes out the phone to check she's got a signal—yes—then freezes as she hears the sound again.

Aurelia.

A voice. It said her name.

It came from the basement.

Quickly she taps her phone and calls Tom. He can't do anything from where he is, at least not physically, but if it's an intruder she wants him to know about it. No answer. Damn him. He *never* answers his phone when there's a genuine emergency—she thinks back ruefully to when she was in labor with Coco—but mysteriously manages to answer clients, cold callers, and wrong numbers on the first ring.

She wraps her fingers around the handle of the basement door. Her heart is pounding furiously. Upstairs she can hear the drumming of little feet along creaking floorboards. Gaia, terrified for her mother and straining to listen out for her.

She opens the door as quietly as she can. A blast of cold, damp air. She holds her breath and leans into the stillness. No sound, yet her instincts are ringing like bells, telling her that someone—or something—is down there. And they are requesting her presence. She places a foot on the first stair. The walls are raw stone, the darkness impenetrable.

She tries Tom's number again, and while it rings she calls out, "Hello?"

Something shifts. She senses it immediately—she's been heard. Whoever is down there *heard* her. She thinks back to the figure she saw in the doorway of their bedroom earlier in the week. A woman. It could have been a man. She's not sure. But she saw *someone*.

The silence changes quality, and the knowledge of it sends a shiver all over her body.

"Hello? Aurelia, you OK?"

Tom's on the line. She presses the phone to her ear. "I'm in the basement," she says in a low voice.

"Why are you in the basement?"

"I'm just at the door. I think someone's down here."

"Someone?"

"I heard . . . noises."

"Shut the basement door right now and go back inside the house. I'm calling the police."

She draws a breath. "Tom, the police are *miles* away. By the time they get here, Basecamp will be built and decorated."

She holds the phone away from her ear and listens hard to the darkness. Her instincts tell her that whatever was down there has gone. She frowns. How could it be *gone*? But her heartbeat slows and the tightness in her throat eases, and she tells Tom to stay on the line as she investigates. She uses the flashlight on her phone to illuminate her path, then finds a cord at the bottom step, which she pulls, flooding the place with light.

"Anything there?" Tom asks on speakerphone.

She looks around. No one is here. Still, she studies the space as though a trace of whoever was here might appear. It's a smaller room than she expected, and no sign of any external entrance. A solid stone room with no windows or exits of any kind. Dusty spiderwebs everywhere. A sour, chemical smell.

"I'm checking the cupboards, Tom," she says loudly, to alert Tom and any intruders that she's doing so. But they reveal nothing, and suddenly she feels stupid. The sound is gone and no one is here. How peculiar.

"Are you sure?" Tom says, worried now. "Those old houses can have hidden doors. Check carefully."

"I can see an air vent," she says, glancing at a small square opening high up in a corner. "Perhaps that was the source of the sound."

"You think so?" Tom asks. "I guess that would explain it."

Her instincts tell her no, that wasn't the source of the sound, but they also say she's no longer in any danger, and so she moves toward the benches to uncover whatever is hidden beneath the old beige tarpaulin, turning her head as she shakes off a fur of dust.

"Tom," she says with a laugh. "You will never guess what the basement is."

"A crypt?"

"It's a darkroom!"

She laughs again, looking over the equipment she's uncovered. A webby cupboard reveals a set of baths and barrels of chemical fluid. Tweezers, a red light that works, even a box of paper. It has been years since she used a darkroom, but already her mind is flipping through the process, anticipating the magic of witnessing a blank sheet revealing its hidden photograph in the clear fluid, like a secret coming to light.

"See?" Tom says. "I told you the house was meant for us. This is a sign."

She laughs with relief and hangs up. Then she stands in the space that holds whatever uttered her name, listening with all her senses. Nothing.

It is possible that she was just paranoid. And yet she knows what she heard.

12

this is a sign

NOW

S ophie! Sophie, look!"
I looked down into the shoebox. The baby bird that Gaia had found—Dora, she'd named her—was waddling around and pecking at the tinsel as though it was a ball of worms.

"She's alive!" Gaia laughed. "And she's so gorgeous!"

Gorgeous was the very *last* thing Dora was, but I was relieved and not a little surprised that she hadn't kicked the bucket. In fact, she was pretty spritely, going at the tinsel with all the gusto of a little raptor. She was still hideous, bless her. Ninety percent beak. Less a bird than a beak with a growth of red skin daubed in black fur, like mold.

"She must be hungry," Gaia observed. "Shall I get her some of the food we made?"

"Yes," I said. "Oh, and, Gaia?" I lifted a finger meaningfully to my lips, indicating to her our promise—she wasn't to tell her father that we were looking after the bird. We'd gone out into the forest to try to find Dora's nest, but it was a bit like trying to find which tree a pine needle had come from—there were hundreds of nests in the tree branches, like clots. Some abandoned, some with little heads bobbing around, and the risk we ran in putting Dora in a nest that wasn't hers was giving her to other nestlings to be eaten alive. Not a pleasant fate. So I relented and told Gaia we'd bring Dora into the house and try again the next day. But then it had rained, and Dora seemed to be eating the weird mixture we'd made for her out of egg yolks and mashed-up nuts. She'd ruined the cashmere scarf lining the box by pooing all over it.

I reached in and removed the tinsel. Dora seemed upset by this, cheeping her discontent. "We should get her some twigs," I told Gaia. "Maybe some leaves. Make her a proper nest."

"What about her toys?" Gaia said sadly, straightening a toppled PJ Masks figurine.

"The problem with baby birds is that they don't know how to use a toilet," I said, sounding very wise. "So Dora will probably continue to poo all over the toys, which isn't very hygienic. At least we can just replace leaves and twigs every time she goes to the bathroom."

"Let's go now and get some," Gaia said eagerly.

I glanced over at Coco, who was pulling herself to her feet by the playroom table and using the chairs to steady herself as she took careful sidesteps, babbling happily to herself. It wouldn't be long until she started walking. "We can't go now, Gaia."

"Why not?"

I consulted the laminated schedule pinned to the board opposite. "Because it's almost time for spellings . . . I mean, phonograms."

Gaia rolled her eyes. "Show me the card," she deadpanned.

We were on *ir*. Gaia looked at it.

"Girl fir stir dirt first skirt *bird*—ha!" she said. "Can we go now?"

"You have to be able to write them, too," I said. Another eye roll. She marched over to a chair, plonked down, and started writing. A few moments later she held up a sheet with all the words written correctly.

"*Now* can we go?"

"OK," I said, quite astonished that she'd managed to get all the spellings correct. I was no expert on childhood development, but I'd have put good money on Gaia being some kind of miniature genius.

I put the girls in their rain suits and wellies—it had rained for three days solid—and we headed outside with a bucket to gather "forest treasure" with which to refurnish Dora's bedroom. The ravens were back, an army of black sails circling the house and piercing the air with their angry cawing.

Outside we kept to the thickest part of the forest, where the dense branches of fir trees funneled the sheeting rain to a drizzle. Gaia jumped in every puddle she could find, holding tightly on to my hand as she stomped in the muddy water with a squeal of glee. Far from gathering up whatever foliage she could find, Gaia selected her items carefully, inspecting each twig and tossing whatever specimen failed to live up to her requirements. When I finally begged her to let us return to the house—a good hour later—her basket contained only a few sticks, a handful of pine needles, and some pretty red leaves.

"Come on, Gaia," I called when she lagged behind. I was carrying Coco now and simultaneously wrestling a twig out of her mouth. Coco liked to experience the world, twigs included, through her teeth. When Gaia remained rooted to the spot, staring down at a patch on the ground, I finally begged her to hurry up. I was tired and freezing cold on account of possessing only a woefully inadequate jacket and boots. I was on the verge of offering her unlimited Netflix time when she looked up and shouted:

"No! You need to come and see!"

I reluctantly turned back and squelched across the muddy forest floor toward her.

"What is it?" I said wearily. She was still staring down at something by her feet. My vision was blurry on account of the heavy rain, but all I could make out was mud and branches.

"An elk has been here," Gaia explained. She looked around as though expecting to see whatever had left the prints nearby. I squinted down and the print came into view: two devil horns imprinted in black mud and filling quickly with rain. I recognized the print, too—it looked identical to the marks I'd spotted on my bedroom floor.

"Let's go inside," I told Gaia, tugging her away, but she kept glancing back across the trees, hoping to see the elk.

"How did you know an elk left the prints?" I asked Gaia as we shook off our coats.

"I've seen one," she said. "Mummy taught me how to spot its prints. Come, I'll show you."

I followed her into the hallway, where she stopped and pointed up to the wall.

"There," she said.

Up until this point I hadn't paid much attention to the photographs on the walls of the house. They were dreamlike, at once old-fashioned and modern. It took me almost two months to identify Gaia in several of them, because she was just a detail in an otherwise wide frame. In one of the photos, a line of trees appeared as odd black shapes against a white sky, and in the darkness of the lower part of the frame I saw a blurred image. It was Gaia, running, or spinning with her arms held out.

The picture she showed me, though, revealed something I hadn't noticed before—the faint outline of an elk among the narrow birch trees on the other side of the house, close to the cliff. It was indeed a huge creature, with antlers that towered high above its head—more branches than antlers. Its face was turned to the camera, as though it had heard the click of the shutter from all that distance.

Another picture turned out to be a close-up and not a land-scape shot—it was a close-up of a snow globe, and there was a quarter of a face in the right side of the frame. A woman's face. I guessed it must have been Aurelia's face, and that Gaia had taken the photograph. Still, she'd framed it. I found myself paying more and more attention to that photograph, deliberately taking the long way to the kitchen in order to pass it. I was curious about Aurelia. I think I was curious not just because she was the mother of the two girls I was falling in love with but because somehow she had passed through that door that I had only knocked on. The door of suicide. We both understood something of the grim path that leads to that door, but Aurelia had had so much more to lose than I had. She must have known it, too. She had a beautiful fam-ily, a stunning home in London, and then this dream home out here in Norway. The photographs were a little out there for my taste, but she was clearly a talented woman. Talented, rich, sur-rounded by people who loved her.

Why would she kill herself?

And as though she could read the thoughts turning over in my head like pages, Gaia started to bring up her mother more often. It was less of the "Mummy's gone to heaven" kind of statements and more about her Mummy running away.

"Your mummy didn't run away," I told her gently one night, as I was settling her into bed. A farcical move, really, when we both knew she'd be creeping back into my bed a handful of minutes afterward. "Your mummy is in heaven, my darling. And heaven is *very* comfy. Like a big soft bed made of clouds, with unicorns and rainbows and long summer days."

She took off her glasses and set them on the nightstand. "No," she said, rubbing the worry doll I'd made her out of an old table-cloth with one hand and clutching her teddy Louis in the other. "I saw her. Do you think she went to find the elk?"

She started telling me about how she'd left a bowl of porridge out, but it didn't work and Mummy might have found her friend again.

I hadn't a clue what she was talking about.

"Mumma ran away." She pouted. "I didn't have my glasses on, but I saw her . . ."

This was new information. "OK," I said. "When did Mummy run away?"

"It was the last time I saw her," she said in a small voice. "I saw her running from the house."

"Which house?"

"*This* house. She ran outside."

"Maybe she had to go help your dad with something."

An emphatic shaking of the head, her chin swinging from shoulder to shoulder. "She saw something."

"What did she see?"

"I think she had to go swimming."

"Swimming?"

"In the fjord. Derry went swimming, too."

None of it made any sense, but I could see Gaia was growing frustrated so I changed the subject. "All right, my lovely," I said in my finest Mary Poppins voice. "Enough about bad dreams. That's what your worry doll is for, OK? She absorbs all your bad thoughts and fears like a sponge, leaving you to dream sweet . . ."

"I *did* see Mumma," she said in a firm voice, way older than her six and a half years. She held me in a fixed stare for a handful of seconds, before turning over and laying her head on the pillow.

I placed a hand on her shoulder. "Good night," I said. Usually she'd reply, but tonight she didn't. And I felt guilty.

I went to my room and waited for Gaia to come creeping in, but she didn't. I flipped open my laptop and tried to add to my story, but the protagonist, Alexa, stood in the proscenium of my mind's eye, her face pulled into a tight sulk and her arms folded. One foot tapping. *You should have let Gaia speak.*

I sat watching the rain for a long time, feeling rather blue and surprisingly lonely. My own memories were starting to dredge up like rusty shipwrecks inhabited by sharks and killer squid. I got up and headed to the kitchen, intent on fixing Coco a bottle of milk for the inevitable midnight cry of "Ya-ya!"

But on returning to bed, bottle of milk in hand, I heard a noise. A moan, or a sort of low cry. At first I thought it was Coco, bang on schedule, demanding her milk.

I walked quickly along the hallway to the stairs. The door at the end of the hall was ajar. By this point I knew the inside of the house intimately, from the yellowing skirting boards to which floorboards creaked and where gangs of spiders liked to hang out, and I happened to know for a fact that this door was always locked. Fiercely, unremittingly locked. The door led to the Basement, that unspoken hinterland into which I was forbidden to venture.

A chilly breeze washed over me, a breeze that was belching from the depths of the basement. A sour odor permeated the air. My mind spun to the cause of such a weird smell. A torture chamber. Or a vat of chemicals for storing dead bodies. *Stop it*, I told my brain. *It's probably just used for storage, like every normal cellar. Maybe someone's giving the place a clean. That'll be the reason for the smell, not formaldehyde or decomposing corpses.*

Maren or Tom would be down there, scrubbing their completely innocent, corpse-free basement with eco-friendly liquids. But just then, I heard another sound that came from the basement, and immediately two thoughts laced together: Gaia had risen from her bed and followed me. And she had gone down into the basement.

I opened the door and stepped into the darkness. I reached for the light switch and flicked on a single, naked bulb that revealed steps to nothingness.

"Gaia?" I hissed. "Gaia, are you down there? Come up, please?"

No answer. I turned and glanced behind me, fearful of getting another write-up in Maren's Book of Wrong.

"Gaia?" I called in the direction of her room. If she was there she would answer. But I was met with silence.

I glanced down into the gloom, seeking out the familiar shape of Gaia at the bottom of the stairs, but there was nothing. "Gaia?" I called again, and this time there was a distant whimper, and in an instant I feared she'd tripped and fallen down those horrible concrete steps. The sort that you'd really *not* want to fall down, as you'd be left with a broken rib or two. So I quickly took to the steps, but I was only halfway down when the lights suddenly went out. A second later, the door slammed shut. I froze. I was in pitch darkness and barefoot.

"Gaia, are you down here?" I said. I tried to listen into the silence, but all I could hear was the rush of blood in my ears.

A moment later, a voice.

NO.

A hoarse voice.

Not Gaia's voice.

I froze in the dark, every muscle in my body flooded with terror, my eyes searching out any chink of light to reveal who had spoken. As I turned I felt something grab me, a hand clutching the breast pocket on my shirt. I screamed and lurched backward, stumbling and tripping up the stairs to the door. I reached it and turned the handle, but it was shut tight. I pounded my fists against the door. "Help!" I shouted. "There's someone down here!"

After what seemed like an eternity but was probably about three and a half seconds, the door opened. I stumbled and fell on my knees, vomiting all over the feet of the person standing in front of me.

Tom. He stared down at me in disgust.

"What's happened?" a woman's voice said. I recognized it as Derry's voice, the woman who'd picked me up at the airport.

I felt like a rag doll as she and Clive lowered me into a chair in the kitchen. I saw Tom check the basement door thoroughly before coming in to join us. His face was flushed. I'd crossed a line. I'd gone into the Verboten Basement *and* puked all over his designer shoes. I was probably going to be fired. But I was so weak and terrified that I didn't care.

Clive put the kettle on and made small talk about air pressure and seasonal affective disorder and wouldn't it be great if a Chinese takeaway was nearby. Derry took a mop and bucket out to the hallway, and I remembered with stinging embarrassment that I'd vomited out there. When she returned she sat down with me and rubbed my back. I was shaking like a leaf in gale-force winds. Tom paced up and down the kitchen and a few minutes later Gaia appeared in the doorway. I saw her eyeing me with concern. The little minx. I wondered if she'd been responsible for the door closing, locking me in that horrible, haunted basement. No wonder Maren had told me to stay out. This was clearly not the first time someone had encountered whatever lived down there.

"Go to bed!" Tom roared suddenly, and I saw Gaia stiffen with fright before racing off down the hallway. I wished I had the strength to comfort her. When Clive poured me a cup of steaming-hot tea I gulped it back, trying to restore my calm, but in fact I only managed to burn my mouth.

"Should we call a doctor?" Clive asked Derry.

She looked at me carefully. "Did you fall?" she asked. I shook my head but could say nothing more. My mind was churning and churning with the voice I'd heard and the feeling of something grabbing me, pulling my nightie so hard I thought it would rip. I had read *Jane Eyre*. Maybe Tom's dead wife was being kept in the basement. He definitely had an air of Rochester about him.

"Why were you down there?" Tom barked, thrusting me out of my memories of high school English, and I jumped.

"Tom . . ." Clive said.

"I . . ." I said. "I . . ."

Derry rubbed my back. "You're shaking! Can we get another blanket?"

Someone threw a duvet around me, which actually worked—it felt like a big hug, and I squeezed my eyes shut and concentrated on my breathing. After a few minutes I explained in a weak voice about coming to the kitchen for a bottle for Coco and how the door was open and I worried that Gaia might be down there.

"Rubbish," Tom said. "The door hardly opened itself."

"Tom . . ." Clive said again.

"So the basement door was just . . . open?" Derry said, and I nodded again.

"It's been locked for months," Tom countered, folding his arms.

"It's an old house, mate," Clive said.

"Maren?" Tom called. "Maren, are you upstairs?"

"Did you have a fall?" Derry asked me.

"No," I said. "The light went out, so I couldn't see." I went to mention the thing that spoke and grabbed me, but decided I'd be best skipping that part. "And then . . . then I tried to open the door, but it was locked . . ."

"I thought you said the door was open," Tom said, glowering.

"It shut behind me," I said. "It . . . slammed shut . . ."

"Who closed it, then?" Clive asked.

"Maren must have been down there," Tom said, pacing and

running his hands through his hair. I couldn't quite work out why he was so furious. "Maren! Come down here, *please!*"

"It doesn't matter *who* shut the bloody door," Derry shouted. "The wind probably caught it. Let's get poor Sophie to bed."

She rubbed my back again. "Thanks," I managed to say as I rose to my feet, glad of the opportunity to head to my room and hide under the covers. Nothing they had said or done had diminished what I knew had happened—something was in that basement.

Maren was suddenly there, her hair damp and askew and her cardigan inside out as though she'd emerged from the shower and hastily thrown on whatever clothes came to hand. She looked from me to Tom, who remained furious.

"Why were you in the basement?" he roared at her. "I've said it a hundred times. *Nobody* goes in the basement!"

Maren took this in without answering. Her eyes fell on me and widened in horror. "Are you all right?" she asked me. I nodded and gave a thumbs-up, grateful that she cared enough to ask.

"Answer me!" Tom thundered. "Why were you down there?"

Maren looked too shocked to speak. Her eyes trailed across our faces, embarrassed. Tom was giving her a complete dressing-down for no good reason. He continued ranting.

". . . and when you blatantly disregard these simple rules it makes me feel like I just can't trust you, do you understand? I've trusted you with my house, my business . . ."

"Mate," Clive said, putting his hand on Tom's shoulder. "We get the point. Can we drop it now?"

Tom shoved off Clive's hand. I saw Derry stiffen, as though braced for a fight, and at the same time Clive lifted up both hands in surrender.

Maren straightened, having found her voice at last. "I can well understand why you're upset, Tom," she said. "And I'm not sure why the basement was opened. I was in the bath at the time it appears that Sophie accessed it." She swiveled her eyes toward me, and my cheeks burned. I shouldn't have gone inside. She had warned me. But I had thought Gaia was down there. I had heard a noise.

Tom had his hands on his hips, his head lowered. I was beginning to stop shaking, my breath slowing, and I saw Clive give Derry an unreadable look. Maren shifted from foot to foot, visibly wondering if this was the right time to leave, but Tom wasn't done with whatever ax he had to grind.

"I don't appreciate lies," he said in a low voice, stepping toward her and looking her straight in the face. "Though you know that perfectly well, don't you, Maren?" This time I saw her flinch, as though expecting to be struck. "Don't let it happen again. Understood?"

"Understood," Maren said in a hoarse voice.

Tom turned his back to her. A few seconds later she slid out of the room, and everyone breathed again.

"Perhaps you'll join us for breakfast, Sophie?" Derry said. "I'm making a full English."

I glanced at Tom, who rolled his eyes. Derry gave a wry smirk.

"Tom knows perfectly well we're both carnivores," Derry said with an eye roll. "Perhaps I can tempt you?"

"A full English sounds great," I said, stupidly, causing Tom to raise his eyebrows in surprise. I couldn't think fast enough to counter this statement so I mumbled, "G'night," and headed to my room.

would you return

NOW

I climbed into bed and pulled the covers over my head. I was disappointed that both Gaia and Coru were all tuckered out in their rooms. There was no chance of me sleeping, and I was still very queasy. Hideous thoughts stampeded around my brain like wildebeests. Maybe I was actually going out of my mind.

I cowered beneath the covers for a long time, until the voices along the corridor died down and the noises in the woods began to stir. When the floorboards outside my room creaked, I whispered, "Come in, Gaia. It's all right."

"Not Gaia," a voice answered back. I looked up and saw Maren standing in the doorway, still in her slippers and inside-out cardi, holding a glass of something. She raised it.

"You want to join me?" she asked meaningfully.

I eyed her nervously, unsure I'd heard her correctly. "Join you . . . for a drink?"

"You don't drink?"

Maren mysteriously turned to walk away, glancing over her

shoulder in a manner that suggested I was to follow. My stomach dropped into my socks, then from there to the core of the earth. She was on to me.

I tried not to be sick with fear as I followed Maren upstairs to her room, which was lit by a table lamp and a cobwebbed chandelier, its light dimmed low as candles. A small TV monitor played a Norwegian game show. A large sleigh bed occupied the middle of the room, and by the bay window an armchair was turned to a small table, upon which sat a chessboard, a crystal bottle of something alcoholic, and an ashtray unspooling a thread of smoke from a cigarette.

"Have a seat," she said, gesturing at the chair on the other side of the table on which a pile of laundry had been abandoned.

I lifted the laundry and looked from left to right for a place to dump it. Maren made no suggestions but settled into the armchair opposite and offered me a drink. I said yes without asking what it was. Finally I placed the laundry on the bed beside the other items that had been dumped there—a bag of wool and knitting needles, a mirror, and a box of Christmas decorations—and sat down.

"Smoke?" Maren said, a fresh cigarette bouncing between her lips. I shook my head nervously.

"Mead," she said, when I tried the drink she'd poured. "Dates back to Viking times."

I coughed and set down the drink. I wanted this all to be over and done with. *Just say you know I'm not Sophie.* But she merely sucked on her cigarette and smiled, enjoying my torment. "I'm sorry about earlier," I started to say. "Honestly, I didn't go in the basement to snoop . . ."

She waved away my comment. "When the workday is over I prefer not to think about any of it." Suspicion still dancing in her eyes. I looked away and wrung my hands beneath the table. She pulled the stopper out of the crystal bottle and topped up my glass. "To help you sleep," she said. "Even if you don't like the taste it'll make you sleep like a baby."

I didn't argue, though it crossed my mind that perhaps there was something more than alcohol in that bottle. I waited until she poured her own glass.

"*Skål*," she said. I raised my drink with a trembling hand and we toasted.

"So," she said, tapping her cigarette into the ashtray on the table, and I braced myself for what was to come. *How does it feel, preying on the trust of orphans?*

"How are things?" she said. A gentle opener before the inevitable quartering.

"Things are *great*," I said, much too cheerfully in a bid to steer the mood. I had this mad notion that perhaps I could distract her from her purpose. "Um . . . we're working on Gaia's phonic blends and high-frequency words. And next week we're starting our mini-beasts project . . ."

Maren tilted her head. "I don't mean the schooling. How are things with *you*?"

I lowered my eyes. "I feel . . . terrible, actually . . ."

"Terrible?" she said. "Oh, this is my fault."

I opened my mouth to respond but found I couldn't.

"You haven't had a chance to see Norway. Next time you have a day off you must travel. You drive, don't you?"

"Um . . ."

"I'll let you use my car. You can reach Ålesund in ninety minutes. Spend the day sightseeing. Lots to see. I'll write down some places."

I muttered a "thank you" and wrung my hands. What was going on? She knew I was a liar, an imposter, and she was going to hand me over to the police.

"Look," she said finally, and I took a deep breath, preparing myself. This was it. Game over.

"I saw your scars." She lifted her hand and pointed at my fore-arms, the cigarette between her fingers looping smoky circles in the air. "Tell me about them."

Instantly I tightened my arms across myself, as though I could erase the scars entirely. My heart was hammering, and the relief at not being caught out in the way I'd expected was soon replaced by nausea at her understanding what my scars were. The silence stretched out across the space-time continuum. Maren was still staring and smoking, waiting for my answer.

"It was a suicide attempt," I said.

"Why did you do it?" Maren asked. I flinched. To say it aloud would for sure unravel my identity as Sophie Hallerton.

"Did you leave a note?"

"No," I said, and she exhaled another cloud. Who would I have left the note to? Who would have cared enough to read it?

"But you meant to do it, yes?"

I nodded.

"Aurelia left a note." She sighed reflectively. "I think she was a lonely sort of person. There are people like that. Surrounded by friends but still smothered in a sense of aloneness. I never thought . . ."

To my horror, she started to cry. I sat for a moment, spasming with indecision, until she said, "She was more than a . . ."

"Woman?" I said, stupidly.

Maren looked puzzled. "Employer. I meant, she was more than my employer. She became a friend. And this is why I ask about your scars, you see. Because I still don't understand *what happened*. I've been depressed. We all have. But I still don't . . . Aurelia wasn't . . ." She struggled to find the right words. "I don't believe she killed herself."

"Does Tom think that, too?" I said.

"I don't know," she said, wiping tears from her cheeks. "I guess it's just still hard to accept. You see, this is the dreadful thing about *this* kind of death. And particularly Aurelia's death."

I wasn't sure what she meant by that, and I must have shown it all over my face, because with a sigh, she offered an explanation.

"We didn't find her body until a week after she disappeared. They found her hand first." I gave a gasp. She swiped fresh tears from her face and blew her nose loudly on a handkerchief.

"She'd been in the water a week. Lots of animals around here, as you already know. So she wasn't . . . intact."

Intact. I gave an involuntary shiver.

"How did she . . ." I began, but couldn't say the next two words. *Do it.*

Maren poured herself another drink, refilled my glass. "Aurelia drowned. In the fjord. Wrote a note, walked out into the night, and jumped off the cliff." I gave another gasp. Maren's eyes turned to the window, where we both knew the cliff sat beyond the trees that shivered in the dark.

"I knew something was wrong," she said, her voice beginning to break. "I *knew*. But of course, you never suspect someone is actually going to kill themself. Suicide happens to other people. Not the people you love."

I winced at this. Nobody cared about me. Maybe that's why I deserved it. But then, this logic didn't apply to Aurelia—everybody seemed to love her. Even her housekeeper.

"You must have liked Aurelia very much," I said carefully.

She swirled those words around her brain. "Aurelia was a wonderful person. I grew protective of her."

"Protective?" I asked, thinking of how snippy Maren was with the girls. I tried to imagine her in a different capacity to the woman I only ever saw wrestling an ancient vacuum cleaner around the rooms, or swearing in Norwegian at the Aga.

"The problem with being a housekeeper is . . . you see things. I knew this when I took the job, of course. Family life is often . . . fractious, and messy. Being in someone else's home means being in their lives. You don't just keep the house; you keep the family, with all of its stains and grime. It requires a certain amount of emotional distance. You have to prevent yourself from being drawn in." She drained her glass. I savored the word *family*. *Family life*. "I'm afraid I was never good at following rules," she continued, blowing a thick cloud of smoke to the side, "and even worse at preventing myself from being drawn in. Aurelia was the sort of woman who . . . what's the expression? Wore her heart on her shirt?"

"On her sleeve," I said, uselessly tugging at my sleeve.

"She confided in me near the end. She told me she was hallucinating. Seeing and hearing things that weren't there. It was distressing her very much. She felt she was failing as a mother, as a wife."

The word *hallucinating* made me shiver. My own hallucinations were not pleasant. In fact, they were terrifying. Memories might come charging out of the walls with the force of a tornado. Not wispy fragments of remembrance at all, but real, blood-and-flesh incarnations with the power to knock me to the ground. Hallucinations could also transform ordinary objects into talking characters, but whereas a talking candelabra in a Disney movie was cute, I found that these kinds of hallucinations were the most terrifying. Your brain knows full well that a laundry basket that's singing isn't actually singing, except it is. And at any moment you might be having a natter with your boyfriend about *Strictly* or *X Factor* and the yucca plant on the coffee table will announce—in a thick Spanish accent, no less—that you don't deserve to live.

I hadn't expected the hallucinations to follow me here. Deep down, I knew I didn't really come to Norway to write a book, or because I was homeless—those were superficial reasons. The deeper reason was that I was running away from my life in England, from talking toasters and swearing cutlery drawers. But then I'd seen a woman in the kitchen here, standing by the window, and I'd heard a voice in the basement. *No,* it said. And I'd felt something grab me. My hallucinations hadn't just followed me—they were gathering strength.

"What sort of things did Aurelia see?" I asked carefully.

Maren finished off her cigarette with a sigh, scratching her temple with a thumbnail. "She said she'd seen animals in the house. An elk, I think. It's not completely unlikely that she *did* see an elk, a real one, but she was so freaked out by the fact that she might be losing her mind . . . I think she wasn't sleeping very much. She wasn't the sort of woman to heed limitations. Even her own. Still, what *I* saw gave me cause for concern."

"You hallucinated, too?" I said, stupidly.

"Hallucinate?" She gave a wry laugh. "No, no. I mean, what I saw in the household. Between Aurelia and . . ." She trailed off again.

"Tom?" I asked, only mouthing his name. She stared at me for a moment, and I suddenly panicked in case I'd misjudged the conversation entirely.

"I'm sorry," I said. "It's not my place . . ."

She set down her glass, leaned both elbows on the table, and stared me in the eye. "Nobody can fathom why he came back here to continue the build. Aurelia's friends, even Tom's own family."

"Why?" I said.

She leaned even closer. "Let me ask you a question," she said, sliding her eyes to one of the portraits on the wall of a doleful woman with wide green eyes and long flaxen hair. As she struggled to find the words for her question, I wondered what she was going to ask me. Was it a proposition? A confession?

"If someone *you* loved committed suicide, would you return to the exact spot that they died and build a house on it?"

I give this some thought. It did seem in poor taste, even callous, that Tom would do such a thing. I thought back to how angry he had been earlier when he discovered I'd been in the basement. I had pegged him for a placid sort of guy, but the outburst was unnerving—he had actually looked like he might strike Maren. And yet she hadn't had anything to do with the basement door.

"Have you heard what the workers have said?" she said, lighting another cigarette.

I shook my head. *Workers?* She meant the builders.

"They're scared by this place. Many believe it is haunted. And for Tom to return here only months after she died and build a family home on the very site of her death . . ." Her eyes drifted away from me, suddenly filled with fear.

I opened my mouth to mention what had happened in the basement. The voice. The hand grabbing me. *No,* I told myself. *Don't mention it.*

"You might call it superstition," Maren continued. "In Norway, we call it . . ."

"Distasteful?" I offered.

"Egregious," she countered through a mouthful of smoke.

"Do you think he is just in shock?" I said. "I mean, it's a pretty awful thing to experience. The death of his wife, I mean. Maybe he wants to remember her here . . ."

"He's been manipulated," she said, in a way that suggested I had missed her meaning entirely. "Tom is not an evil man. Stupid, yes. But to come back *willingly* would have been egregious, even wicked. He was persuaded."

"By who?" I said.

She ignored me. "When the first house was destroyed, he was furious. I mean, of course. I would be. A lot of money to lose because of a storm."

I was struggling to keep up. "What first house?" I said. "Do you mean their home in London?"

"Basecamp," she said. "The house they built before this new one."

She rose from her seat woozily and gestured for me to follow her across the room to the hallway. Maren staggered forward, both hands against the walls of the hallway to steady herself. Fear zipped down my spine like someone had chucked a pint of cold water down the back of my shirt. What if Tom found us creeping about the house in the dead of night? Maren had the grace of a rhino on stilettos. She took to the stairs, lumbering down toward the kitchen. No, not the kitchen—Tom's office. I followed her inside as she flicked on the light.

She reached for something on top of a filing cabinet in the corner. She hefted it down, almost dropping it. I reached out and helped her lower it to the floor.

"This was Basecamp," she explained. I could make out that the model—a beautiful 3D-printed model—replicated the woods and the cliff, with a piece of shiny blue plastic for the fjord and a painted strip of blue for the river. A ladder seemed to stretch down from the house along the rock face to the bottom of the fjord, where a small beach was marked out with smooth plastic.

"They'd pretty much finished it, too. Aurelia loved it. Basecamp was *her* house. Tom wanted something more—what does he say? Oh, yes, *innovative*. Aurelia had wanted a more traditional Norwegian wooden house that sat on top of the cliff overlooking the fjord, so that's what they built."

"And what happened?"

Maren sighed. "Tom diverted the river, and when a storm hit, the river wrecked the foundations. They had to start all over again."

She glanced at the wooden easel, on which sat a large, hand-drawn charcoal sketch of what looked like a pod hanging off the side of something. It was only when I made out the trees that I realized the right-angled shape was meant to be the cliff, and that the pod was a structure that was half in, half outside the rock face.

"That's the new house," she said, seeing that I was questioning the pod structure. "I know what you're thinking. *What kind of a house is that?* Well, if you take your first idea of what a house is, then toss it into a blender with some fairy dust and a handful of crazy, you get this. He even calls it 'Aurelia's Nest.'"

"That's unfortunate," I said, my thoughts cartwheeling to "the Eagle's Nest," Hitler's gaffe in the Bavarian Alps, and *One Flew Over the Cuckoo's Nest*, where Jack Nicholson gets lobotomized. Evidently Tom had overlooked the less salubrious connotations of the word *nest*.

"Or perhaps he knew very well what he was doing when he called it that."

Maren laughed, and I realized I'd said this aloud. I widened my eyes and pressed a finger to my lips, telling her to keep quiet in case she woke Tom. Or the girls. She nodded, chastised, and fell silent.

"It seems . . . dangerous," I observed in a low voice.

"It's more than dangerous," she said, her blonde eyebrows raised. "Building a family home right where his wife died? Right after the first house was destroyed?" She glanced again at the model of Basecamp. "Many people said the storm was a punishment."

"A punishment?"

She turned solemn as a winter morning in Glasgow. "Mother Nature wasn't happy that he built Basecamp where he did. *She* destroyed that house. He should have taken the hint. But he didn't, and Aurelia died. But even now he's pressing on, too stubborn to see . . ." She shook her head and gave a deep sob.

"You mean, Aurelia's death was a punishment for the house?" I asked carefully. Surely I hadn't heard her correctly?

"Everything in nature is connected," she said with a sigh. "He stopped up that river to build Basecamp. So foolish. It's not just *one* river, it's the whole forest. The whole *region*. Countless animals and plants . . . the fjord . . ."

She moved to place the scale model back where she'd found it, and my eyes fell on a photograph of Tom, Aurelia, and the two girls. It was a happy photograph, placed on his desk. He looked very different in that photograph from the man who had thundered at Maren.

"Tom doesn't realize what he's done," she said gravely as she followed my gaze to the photograph.

"Maren," I said carefully, "I need to ask you something."

She swiveled her eyes to me.

"You said Tom was manipulated into coming back here. Who manipulated him?"

But she'd already turned back to the model of the first house, and when she spoke it seemed as though she'd forgotten I was there and was addressing someone else. "It is madness, all of it. Who brings *children* out to a place like this, with the cliff and the forest and the beasts? Who builds a house right where their wife died just a few months earlier?"

14

she who is missed most

Gaia sits up in bed. It's dark outside. Slowly she works out that she's in her room. There's a figure lying beside her on the floor, huddled beneath a blanket. A long strand of hair spills out from the top of the blanket across the floorboards. Gaia catches her breath. It's Mumma. Her heart glows in her chest. *You came back!* She knew she would, eventually. Mumma always comes back. Mumma doesn't leave, not forever. Mumma is always there because she loves Gaia with all her heart and she is back now for good.

She taps Mumma on the shoulder. "Mumma? Wake up. Wake up!" Mumma doesn't stir. She must be really tired. Maybe Gaia should just let her be. Mumma is often tired.

Gaia sits for a few moments in her bed, her hands playing with each other in excitement. The objects in the room are a smudge because her glasses are on the nightstand, but she doesn't mind because Mumma is here and she wants to scream with excitement. She has so many drawings she wants to show her. If she'd known Mumma was coming today she would have painted a big banner saying *MUMMA WE MISSED YOU WELCOME HOME* with rainbows and Viking ships, because she remembers how excited Mumma got that time they went to the Viking museum in Oslo. Well, she'd thought Mumma was actually sad, because she cried, but later she explained that she was just so overcome at the sight of a real Viking ship that she cried, because sometimes grown-ups cry instead of dancing when they're excited. Gaia hasn't danced in a long time, but she feels like it now. Her body is beginning to bounce in the bed and her arms want to move, like they're filled with beans or lots of tiny balloons.

Finally she gets up and walks to the dresser where Louis sits, looking on. She hopes her movement will gently wake Mumma, and even if it doesn't she'll feel better once she can tell Louis that Mumma is back now. He'll be relieved, and maybe even surprised, because he said Mumma was never coming back.

But when she picks up Louis she notices he looks really weird. Not happy at all at the sight of Mumma.

"What's wrong, Louis?" she asks crossly, because how dare he not smile and laugh and say how amazing it is. She remembers how she felt when Coco came—excited at first, but quickly disappointed because Coco was so boring *and* she got all of Mumma's cuddles and attention. "It's not like that, Louis," she tries to reassure him, but quickly she notices his face—he looks stunned.

"What's the matter?" she whispers, but he won't look at her. In fact, he's squirming in her hand like she does when she needs the toilet. She follows his gaze to Mumma, but when she turns around Mumma is no longer on the floor but on her feet.

She is standing there, both hands by her sides, her feet in a puddle of water. The water is coming from her dress, which is soaking wet. She sees the drips dotting the puddle. It's not Mumma but the Sad Lady, and as she lifts her head a little the moonlight reaches the features of her face and Gaia opens her mouth to scream because she looks like a monster and her eyes are missing and in their place are two endless holes that reach to the bottom of every grave right down to the bottom of the earth.

the bottom of the earth

NOW

I felt anxious after the conversation with Maren about Tom. She'd hinted that Tom's return to the very site where Aurelia killed herself less than a year earlier was indicative of some sinister character flaw. My relationship history had proven that I was rather wanting in the Character Judgment department, but I'd discerned that Tom was a Still Waters kind of guy. That is to say, most of the time he was an affable, tea-drinking middle-class architect, but occasionally he'd have a meltdown over the slightest thing—an offhand remark, a piece of wood cut a centimeter too thick, a missing pencil—and hurl a torrent of abuse at everyone in sight until the error was corrected. His face would turn red, veins would bulge in his neck, and sometimes he'd punch the doors in frustration.

Even Gaia seemed a little nervous around him. She seemed more nervous in general, now that I think about it, and her drawings got more Gothic. The same horrific figure with big black holes for eyes, drawn over and over.

But now that Derry was back, I felt safe. She was super buff.

Her arms looked like stockings filled with melons and she had the thighs of a racehorse. She rose at five each morning to clamber down the ladder that ran down the cliff to run ten miles along the fjord. While I was shuffling like Igor after Coco around the playroom at dawn, yawning into my fist and counting the seconds until I could grab a coffee, Derry was bounding back into the house, sweaty as a farm horse and lithe as a pipe cleaner, the sound of the Prodigy's "Firestarter" pumping out of the earbuds around her neck as she stretched out her piriformis. Even last thing at night she was still radiant with inexplicable jubilation, her smile so broad that you could see both rows of teeth all the way back to her shining white molars.

At first, I kind of hated Derry and all her bead-wearing, namaste-ing, "life is a journey" balderdash. But her particular brand of guru-level Inner Peace was magnetic, and soon I found myself practicing her smile in the mirror. It hurt my face. I suspected I might pull a muscle in my neck. Even when I decided that Derry must be on crack—because nobody is *that* happy just because it's another day—her indefatigable elation crept into my attitude, and I started finding myself attempting to think happy thoughts. I even printed out and laminated some quotes about positivity for the playroom.

"What are these?" Gaia asked when I Blu-Tacked them to the whiteboard.

"'Happiness is when what you think, what you say, and what you do are in harmony,'" I read aloud.

"What?" she spat.

"Mahatma Gandhi said that," I said. "Do you know who he is, Gaia?"

Her scowl deepened into unveiled disgust. "What's wrong with you?" she said, looking me up and down. And then she walked away.

One day, Derry invited me to accompany her on her morning run.

"Sorry," I said, stifling a yawn. "I have to be up for the girls."

"Don't they wake at six thirty?" she said. "We can be back well before that. I usually leave at five, but we can leave even earlier . . ."

It was the tail end of November. Midwinter in Norway meant that a cataracted sun cast a resentful smattering of oblique light for approximately twenty minutes each day before giving up the ghost and tagging in Blackest Night. Even Tom had started to talk about investing in SAD lamps for Gaia and Coco, who were even grumpier than usual. An unexpected bonus of the pervasive gloom was that Coco had started sleeping through the night, and occasionally she slept in past seven. Relatively speaking, the supernal bliss of eight hours' sleep *should* have gifted me with the energy levels of a gazelle, but I'd found that the decrease in sunlight exposure felt like lead being pumped directly into my veins. The slightest effort plundered my energy stores. I was clearly designed for the bounteous rays of Apollo, and I began to loathe Tom for choosing Norway as the locale for his summer home instead of, say, California.

"We don't even have to run," Derry offered. "We can . . . *jog* . . ."

"I'm afraid I'm not much of a jogger . . ." I said. In the hours before dawn, I reckoned I would barely be able to crawl.

"Walk, then?" she said, her voice breaking at the word *walk*. She had these big deep-set eyes, Frodo blue, that seemed capable of removing my willpower. A perfect nose, perfect teeth. Seven tattoos in a line down her spine—chakra symbols, she'd said, to "focus her energy centers." "Oh, come on, Sophie! I promise you'll *love* it!"

"You won't love it," Clive grumped from behind his phone. "You'll have a minor heart attack while Derry does thirty-mile laps. Or you'll wreck your knee cartilage like I have. Don't let her suck you in."

"I . . ." I said.

"Oh, Clive," Derry laughed, waving her hand at him. "Honestly, he needs his heart chakra massaged *big*-time. Say you'll come jogging with me, Sophie. Or walking, whatever. Please?"

Before I could answer she had lowered herself down, balancing her weight on her palms, with both legs impossibly straightened out to one side, hovering a few inches above the floor.

"What are you doing?" Clive said.

"Astavakrasana," she panted, wobbling slightly.

"I thought you were going for a walk with Sophie?"

"Tomorrow morning," she said, throwing me a wink. And lo, it was decided.

I didn't have any running shoes so Derry loaned me a pair. "Luckily we're both a size six," she whispered, her words transforming to icicles right in front of me. It was four thirty, pitch-black, and freezing cold. I slipped on the trainers, pulled on my woolen hat and gloves, and crossed myself.

The air was so cold that it seemed to be gnawing my face. Derry immediately began pumping her arms as she walked and encouraged me to copy her, which I did, assuming this was to prevent frostbite setting in. I had expected us to head toward the cliff, but instead she ventured away from the house toward the thickest part of the forest.

"Don't worry," she said when I started to whimper. "I know these woods really well. There's actually a path that cuts right to the road."

But how will we see it? I wanted to say, given that the forest was so dense that the light of the moon and stars was almost blocked out. Derry fumbled in her pocket for something, then strapped a headlamp to her forehead. The garish white light fell on a number of creatures ahead of us, who immediately scattered into the bushes.

"Let there be light!" Derry said, laughing and strutting onward. I marveled at how unafraid she was, how *awake* she was. Given how cold and miserable it was, I had half expected her to suggest we turn back for another hour's sleep, but she simply powered on through the forest, oblivious to the squelch of soggy leaves underfoot and the bats whirling overhead. We walked through the trees and, although Derry chatted amiably, I responded with *mm-hmm*s, focused on keeping my mouth closed in case I inadvertently swallowed a spider or, worse, a bat.

And then, in a matter of minutes, we were on flat tarmac, the road that swept past Granhus and the forest and ran above the fjord. The view ahead was dazzling, and Derry turned to survey my face with glee.

"See?" she said, turning back to look over the fjord, which was a glistening purple necklace running across a nape of silvery rock. We could see sky clearly now, and it was sequined with white stars. I actually gasped. I had never seen a sky like it. Back home, the night sky was flat and mud brown, with maybe a star or two managing to peek through the city smog.

"Look at you!" Derry laughed, laying a hand on my arm. "You look like you're going to cry!" She took a deep breath through her nostrils and planted her hands on her hips, stretching from side to side. "I don't blame you. This is exactly why I come out here every morning. By eight o'clock the landscape is *completely* different. Cars, tractors, boats . . ." She lifted her head to the sky. "And this time of year is ideal for catching sight of the northern lights. I've not seen them yet, but maybe we'll get lucky."

We walked side by side downhill along the grass verge of the road, which narrowed to a ridge close to the side of the cliff. Below us were terraces of fields and trees. On the other side of the fjord a white waterfall feathered down the cliff.

"So tell me about yourself," Derry said, clearly walking slower than she'd like. "What brought you all the way out here?"

I tried not to show I was panting for breath, woefully unfit. "I, uh, I'm a nanny. I applied for the job . . ."

She gave a high-pitched laugh. "I know that, silly. You're based in London, I take it?"

I tried to think. Was Sophie based in London? "Uh, I nannied for Verity for some time in London, but before that I was in Durham." Phew. I'd actually remembered some crucial elements of Sophie's CV. But I needed to steer the conversation away from me—or Sophie—to something less likely to get me unmasked.

"You'll have heard about the tragic backstory, then," Derry said, glancing at me. "Aurelia. Awful. How are the girls taking it? I'll expect you've had to deal with some tears."

I thought about Gaia waking in the night, shrieking. About Maren, and how sad she'd looked when she asked me about my own suicide attempt. "Yes. It's so sad." Then, feeling brave: "Did you know Aurelia well?"

A sigh. "I thought I did. You don't really ever know someone fully, do you? She was a wonderful woman. Beautiful, rich, successful . . . I'm so pleased you're taking care of those wonderful girls of hers. They've lost so much. Well, you can imagine," she said, and I made sure to nod deeply to show I most definitely could. "And Tom was such a good husband. It was all for her, the house he's building. But . . . I suppose she had demons."

I thought back to the conversation with Maren. "I guess you never know what goes on behind closed doors."

"What do you mean?" she replied, quick as a flash.

I needed to be careful how I answered this. She was friends with Tom, and anything I said against him was probably going to filter back. "Oh, it's just a general observation," I said, backpedaling as smoothly as a drunk clown on a unicycle. "You never really know someone. People can be struggling with their own issues behind what appears to be a perfectly wonderful life."

"True," she conceded.

"So what brings *you* out here, then?" I asked, giving the subject of Aurelia a wide berth. For the past few weeks Derry had seemed to just hang out at Granhus, her days carved up by a hectic schedule of yoga and meditation.

"You mean, why would I come somewhere that has no cafés, restaurants, or yoga studios?" she replied with a laugh, marching a few steps ahead. "Well, I'm freelance, so I'm pretty much able to take my work anywhere I please."

"You're a writer?" I asked. I'd seen her spend a number of afternoons scribbling into a notebook.

"I'm a designer," she said. "But I do write now and then. Just as a hobby. I wrote a screenplay last year."

"Wow. A screenplay," I said. "That's incredible."

"Thanks," she said, beaming. "I'd like to attempt a novel, but it seems too . . . Oh, I don't know. I went on one of those week-long courses last summer. You know, where you stay with other writers in a big house and have lessons by published writers during the day?"

"Oh, yes," I said, though I'd never heard of such a thing.

"Golly, it was *terrific.*"

"Golly," I replied, because I wanted to try the word out, and I was sure Sophie was also the sort of person who said things like "golly."

"But I still haven't managed to publish anything." Derry clocked my look of interest. "Do *you* write?"

I gave a sheepish smile. "I'm about halfway through a novel. About fifty thousand words in. It's complete rubbish."

Her eyes widened. "Fifty thousand? I think I managed twenty thousand on the novel I tried before I gave up. I just ran out of steam . . ."

"Maybe we can critique each other's work," I said. This was uncharacteristically bold of me, and I said it slightly under my breath, so that if she kicked back on the idea I could pretend I'd said something about the scenery, or put the suggestion down to lack of oxygen reaching my brain.

But Derry had the hearing of a bat. "Definitely!" she said. "Golly, what a terrific idea! I've been plowing away in my free time at this new project, but it keeps wandering off into weird tangents. It's a bit naughty of me, actually. I *ought* to be running my business, but writing becomes addictive, doesn't it?"

A memory of her and Clive picking me up from the airport returned—she'd mentioned that she ran a business in design. "You work in interior design, isn't that right?" I said.

"Yes," she said, in a voice that sounded like she hated the very idea of it.

"You don't enjoy it?"

"Oh, it's all right," she said. "I'm glad to help out Tom with the interiors for this new house. But generally speaking I'm a bit . . . bored."

"What would you prefer to do?" I asked, thinking back to my days as an admin assistant. I would have preferred to get paid to design an office instead of working *in* one, but I sensed that Derry had never had to work in admin, or indeed any job that paid eight pounds an hour.

"I don't know," she said with a dramatic sigh. "I'm forty this year. I fancy doing something different." She stopped and put her hands on her hips, though she didn't gasp for breath like I did.

"The original plan was to have a baby," she said then, her voice tinged with sadness. A hand pressed against her flat stomach. "It didn't work out as planned. Five rounds of IVF, two miscarriages . . ." She turned away, suddenly upset. "Sorry," she said, wiping her eyes. "I'm a total oversharer."

I stepped closer. "I'm sorry to hear that," I said. She pulled a tissue from an inside pocket and blew her nose loudly.

"Clive and I desperately wanted to start a family. We waited, of course, until we'd traveled and got the house we wanted. I had it all planned out. Two children, two years apart. A boy and a girl. They were going to be called Hugo and Genevieve. I even had the nurseries designed in my head." She sighed. "But then it all came to nothing. We even looked into adoption, but . . ." She shook her head ruefully, and I didn't press.

"Clive had this magical idea that I could design the inside of Tom and Aurelia's new house," she continued, changing the subject. "So that's ostensibly why I'm spending so much time here, though of course the place is nowhere near finished yet. Still, I don't mind. And now that I've discovered I've got a fellow writer here, I might just stay a bit longer."

"I'd love that," I said, and her smile widened.

After twenty minutes Derry suggested we turn back, and although my muscles wanted to tear themselves out of my flesh and thank her personally, I found myself realizing that I was enjoying myself. The cold wind playing in my hair, the sunrise progressing through shades of copper, transforming the fjord to liquid gold. I enjoyed Derry's company, too, and I even began to feel like I could relax in her presence. Something about her manner made me realize that, despite her obvious wealth and social standing, she was still human. She wasn't better than me at all. She just had more money. And more confidence.

"Can I ask you something?" I said before thinking it through.

"Sure."

I took a breath. "Do *you* think Aurelia committed suicide?"

She did a double take, and I closed my eyes, wincing at my own stupidity. I shouldn't have asked. I knew I shouldn't.

"I'm sorry," I said. "I really shouldn't have asked that."

She smiled. "But you did ask it. Has Gaia said something?"

"Gaia? Not about suicide. I don't think we're meant to say . . ."

She pulled her face into a sensible pout. "No, no. Of course."

"I suppose I just . . . Well, I was talking to Maren, and she said . . ."

"Maren," she said in a grim voice.

"She . . . well, she . . ."

"What did Maren say?" Derry pressed, her voice rising in pitch and volume, and I felt my capacity to lie shrivel up as though she'd jabbed me with a syringe filled with truth serum.

"She told me that she didn't think Aurelia killed herself," I blabbed.

"What?"

"She said Mother Nature was punishing Tom for building on a river and that's why she died."

Derry reacted to this divulgence, her face frozen in a look of horror. But then, she laughed. A head-right-back, mouth-wide-open laugh. A nervous titter escaped my own lips. I rarely made people laugh, but yes, there was something hilarious about what I'd just said.

"Oh, that's brilliant," Derry said, dabbing her eyes. "Maren is just so . . . bonkers. I'd like to see what Tom makes of that theory."

"I imagine he'd be very upset," I observed.

Derry became thoughtful. "Maren was very taken with Aurelia," she said, frowning. "It was a bit . . . concerning." She put a hand on my arm, warningly. "And she hates Tom. He's only keeping her on out of duty, but I'm worried."

"Worried about what?" I said.

She bit back a reply, and visibly replaced it with something more tactful. "You do know Maren isn't actually a housekeeper, don't you?"

"Well, to be honest, that explains quite a bit . . ."

She leaned even closer. "She *was* an artist. Apparently a very talented one. Exhibitions and what have you. But somehow she stopped painting and started cleaning for Aurelia."

I went to ask how a talented artist ended up scrubbing toilets for a living, but Derry cut in before I had a chance.

"Then things started to go missing. Belongings of Aurelia's."

I processed this, thinking back to Tom's cruel comment to her. *I don't appreciate lies.*

"Tom found them in Maren's room," she continued. "Small things, really. A pair of earrings, some of her photographs. As you can well imagine, he hit the bloody roof. Maren became obsessed with Aurelia, but Aurelia felt sorry for her. She was always so softhearted . . . She persuaded Tom to keep her on. Maren's devious—"

"I don't think she's devious," I said before I had thought it through, and Derry stopped walking and stared at me with an expression I couldn't fathom.

"Sophie, Sophie, Sophie," she said with a sympathetic shake of her head.

"What?"

She bit something back. Then, placing a hand on my arm and fixing me with those big blue eyes: "For my money, I'd say Maren locked you in that basement. Did you know Tom had called her earlier that evening to say we might not make it back that night?"

I drew a breath. "No?"

She gave a grim, I'm-sorry-to-say-so nod. "As far as Maren knew, *nobody* was coming. It was just going to be you, her, and the kids in the house."

I felt my legs give. *I would have been stuck in that basement all night.*

"Anyway," Derry said breezily, turning to nod at Granhus, which was now visible through the trees. "I'm here now. We can look out for each other, can't we?"

the cliff and the forest and the beasts

THEN

Aurelia keeps her distance as Gaia plays in the forest. The snow is thick, the kind that turns the conifer trees into cottony white triangles and makes terrific snowmen. She and Gaia have had a fun morning building a family of snowmen, with carrot noses, pebble eyes, and twigs for arms and hair. Coco is still asleep in the baby sling, her little bobble hat slipping down over her eyes as she lolls against Aurelia's left shoulder. Aurelia presses her camera to her eye and surveys the world through her lens. The trees are so tall that she can only capture their powdery white skirts and the virgin snow, foam-smooth, that sweeps across the forest floor. She leans close to a crooked branch adorned with a triangular prism of snow. *Click*. Gaia has discarded her fleece hat and rolled up the sleeves of her snowsuit to do cartwheels in the snow. "Watch me, Mumma!" *Click*. Aurelia crouches down to inspect something on the ground. A deep, clean imprint in the snow. *Click*.

"Mumma, you weren't watching. I did a *perfect* cartwheel."

Gaia approaches her and stares at the spot on the ground. Two crescent moon shapes facing each other. "That's an elk print, sweetheart," she says, drawing a breath.

Gaia cranes her face up at her mother. "Elk?"

Aurelia feels her heart quicken. "Yes. Remember the pictures we looked at?"

Gaia remembers. "It looks *very* big, Mumma. Maren said that elk used to drink out of our river."

"It's not *our* river, darling . . ."

"But Daddy said it is. It's our river."

A chill runs through Aurelia unexpectedly. She's vulnerable out here in the woods. The trees provide excellent insulation, muffling shouts. She pats her pocket and finds her mobile phone there. Good.

"Let's go back inside now," she says.

"Aren't you taking pictures?"

"Yes, but I'm almost out of film."

"Can you take one last one of me? I promise I won't pose."

Aurelia grins. "All right. One more."

Gaia races off—a little too far for Aurelia's liking—and hides in the forest. With the exception of Coco, Aurelia is completely alone in a grove of towering trees, about forty feet tall and snow-clotted, and creamy clouds overhead make it almost impossible to discern where trees end and sky begins. She is in a womb of white, an impossible room of winter.

She can no longer hear Gaia. She is spellbound. The visual and acoustic qualities of snow remove you entirely from the rest of the world, from time itself. She can hear her own breaths, the crunch of the snow underfoot, the rub of the camera strap against her wrist. She feels watched, a distinct sensation of someone or something observing her carefully. When she looks up she swears the scene has changed. Did . . . did the trees move forward? She stares at the row of trees ahead of her, then behind. She could swear they've closed in around her. She tries to laugh off the thought, but it's creepy here. As though the forest has intentions. The fir trees loom over her like gods.

She shivers, holds her breath, listening hard for the sound of Gaia's voice singing to herself as she cartwheels through the trees.

"Gaia?" Her voice is thin with fear.

No answer.

"Gaia, where are you?"

She stumbles forward through the heavy branches, her flailing arms knocking clods of snow on top of her and a startled Coco. She is blinded by snow, her mouth full of it, her feet losing purchase on the ground. She swipes at her eyes and coughs hard.

"Gaia!"

"I'm here."

Aurelia squints ahead. Her vision is still blurry, and for a moment the scene ahead is like something in a snow globe. Silvery sunlight spears through the clearing, illuminating the small figure of Gaia from behind. Relief makes her knees buckle, wrings the air from her lungs.

As she staggers forward and clutches Gaia tightly to her, the feeling of her daughter's skin against her hands, the knowledge that she is safe, restores the forest from a ghostly, watchful presence to mere woodland. She laughs and cups Gaia's face.

"I'm sorry, Mumma," Gaia says, observing the fear in her mother's face. "I didn't mean to worry you."

"It's OK, darling. We're together now."

In the house, Aurelia glances repeatedly at the trees through the window, in case they happen to inch closer again, as they did outside. Satisfied that they've stayed put, she feeds a sleepy Coco in the playroom before settling her into the Moses basket. Derry comes downstairs, yawning and rubbing her eyes. She and Clive arrived late last night. They'd spent Christmas in Sydney and are completely jet-lagged.

"Go back to bed," Aurelia laughs when Derry settles in the chair opposite. Derry is *never* tired. Aurelia finds it irritating, to be honest. Derry's one of those people who can function quite happily on four hours' sleep. Aurelia has never been like that. Even in her pre-baby days she needed a good eight hours to be at her best. Sleep, she's learning, is both an area of competitiveness and a luxury. She's learned not to complain about exhaustion in front of Derry, whose utter befuddlement about the concept of being even slightly knackered is tiring in itself.

"I can't go back to bed," Derry says through another yawn. "I'll make it worse if I sleep now. I have to push through until bedtime."

"Now you know how I feel most of the time," Aurelia can't help herself from saying.

Derry deduces her meaning, looks from Coco to her. "I don't know how you do it," she says, round-eyed with seriousness.

Aurelia adores Derry for precisely four seconds. This second expedition into the wilderness of motherhood reminds her that the job comes without any validation. Everyone's out to *advise* you, or point out that something you're doing is wrong, or even life-threatening. No one *praises* you—unless you're a father, in which case it seems you only have to look at the baby for people to hail you as some kind of Woke Hero. A father who changes a nappy is a god. A mother who continues to breastfeed through mastitis and hemorrhoids and a third-degree tear is just a mother. Still, she hates that she feels the need for praise. Has she really become that weak?

"Come *on*, Mumma," Gaia says, pulling at her arm. "Let's go do the photos."

Coco slides off the nipple, still half-asleep. "Shhh," Aurelia tells Gaia. "We need to wait until Maren's back from getting the shopping so she can look after Coco."

Derry's ears prick up. "I can look after the baby if you like?"

"Really?" Aurelia says, her mood lifting.

"And Gaia," Derry says. Gaia's face drops. Aurelia fastens up her bra quickly and passes over the sleepy bundle to Derry.

"You're a natural," Aurelia tells her, and it is Derry's turn to beam. For a moment Aurelia feels grateful for Derry. They've known each other since before Gaia was born, and when they met she believed they would become friends, maybe even as close as Tom and Clive. After all, they're similar, at least on the surface— both freelance creatives, both descended of Welsh stock, both shop at John Lewis, Toast, and Estée Lauder, listen to Sia and Sigur Rós, favor pinot noir. Both studied at Russell Group universities and are roughly the same age—they can remember cassette tapes, rotary dial telephones, and sticking posters of Keanu Reeves circa *Bill and Ted* to their bedroom walls. Even so, they've never managed to forge a particularly strong friendship. Something about Derry rubs Aurelia the wrong way and she's spent time trying to put her finger on it, without success. Perhaps deep down she envies Derry her child-free, well-rested existence, and this is what has fundamentally prevented an otherwise beautiful friendship from blossoming. Aurelia rarely sees many of her tribe because they're all so busy dealing with teething, weaning, or infected children. Besides Maren, Derry's the only woman she sees much of here in Norway. Maybe now they're making progress toward a friendship. After all, Derry is here for a good while this time. It would be wrong not to take advantage of female companionship.

Or at the very least, the offer of a moment's peace.

Gaia watches her mumma tiptoe out of the room to the dark-room. She looks at the coloring-in book and pack of crayons her mumma has placed in her lap to occupy her, then at Derry, who is holding baby Coco and staring at Gaia with a strange expression. It's strange because it's neither a cross nor a happy expression. If Gaia had to draw her face she'd do a straight line for Derry's mouth and big circles for her eyes, which are pinned on her.

"Aren't you supposed to be drawing?" Derry asks at last.

Stung by Derry's tone, Gaia plucks a blue crayon from the pack and starts to shade in the ocean of a cartoonish pirate scene. When she dares lift her eyes a little in Derry's direction she sees she is staring at baby Coco with that same look on her face. The way she holds Coco is funny, too. She doesn't touch her—just has Coco laid on her lap like she's a book, or a cushion. Most people stroke Coco's cheeks, or hold her tiny hands.

"Do you like your baby sister?" Derry says.

Gaia nods, and instantly her tummy flutters. She told a *lie*. She tries to tell herself that actually she didn't tell a lie because she didn't speak, but even so she feels bad. But it feels wrong to say that no, she doesn't like her baby sister. That seems mean, even though it's the truth.

"I hated my sister," Derry says then, and Gaia lifts her eyes to her, shocked. "She was mean to me. She'd pinch herself and tell Mum that I did it until I put tacks in her shoes. She didn't pinch herself again after that."

Gaia's mouth falls open. She has no idea what to say, though it's an odd kind of relief to know that she isn't the only person in the world who dislikes her own sister.

In the basement Aurelia flicks off the garish overhead lights and turns on the red safelight that, mercifully, is still working. She gets to work quickly, worried that Derry might fall asleep with the baby on her lap.

She slides the negative strip under the small square eye of the enlarger and opens the aperture on to the sheet of A4 developer paper. Then she uses the tweezers to dip the paper into the first tub of liquid, then the second. In college she would use her fingers on account of a lack of funds to buy tweezers—she got used to burning her fingertips off in the acid—and she often did this same process in the pitch dark, and without a timer. Even now, she counts the seconds in her head. *One, two, three, four . . .* She holds her breath. This is a holy moment, the closest she has come to prayer and worship—bringing the past to life on a blank page. Coaxing it there, and fixing it so that it doesn't become over- or underexposed, both of which would inform the eye that it's a poor simulacrum and not the true past. Get the image right and the photograph hooks you back to the moment it captures with all its sensory context—smells, sounds, even the mood of the day.

But when she glances down at the finished image, she's confused. The image is obscured by a word drawn in capitals, as though on a windowpane, or perhaps in the wet sheen of the film:

MUST

She can't make any sense of what she's seeing, or why she should be seeing it. Her thoughts race to work out how the image could have absorbed these letters. Sometimes an overexposure will cause cloudlike shadows and shapes to appear, but this is a word scrawled over the image of Gaia spinning in the snow, her head tilted to the sky.

With shaking hands she pins the sheet to the line to let it dry. After all, she's looking at the paper in the strange red glow of the safelight, not daylight—perhaps when she takes the photograph upstairs she'll see something else entirely.

She struggles to keep her breath steady. Sweat beads her forehead and crawls along her collarbone as she dips another sheet into the fluid. She counts, stares hard at the edges blackening into formation, then gasps when another word appears.

YOU

In the haze of the safelight she stares at the letters on the print, so startled and sickened by the absolute dearth of reasons why an image of Gaia upside down in midcartwheel should be obscured entirely by these three large letters. What does it mean, "you"?

She glances up at the stairs leading to the house, listening out for Coco's cries. Nothing. One more. She'll do one more print and then she'll take them all up to the light to get a better view.

LEAVE

She pins the print to the line, no longer wanting to hold it in her hands. The word shouts from the page. When she turns on the main overhead light, bleaching the room in a cold white glare, there's a second where she's convinced the words will be gone. But there they are, now a chilling triptych swaying on the line:

YOU MUST LEAVE

It is morning. Aurelia sits up in bed and looks over at the crib. Coco is laid flat, her head turned to one side, her lips puckered in deep sleep. Aurelia has barely slept. After the discovery of the weird words on her photographs last night she rushed upstairs to Derry—who mercifully still had Coco on her lap—and showed her the prints. Derry admired them, said she saw no words, no letters at all . . . And when Aurelia looked again she saw that the prints were merely images.

"But . . . they had words on them," she stammered, holding the prints to the light, and began to explain what she'd seen and why she was so flustered.

"What happened?" Maren asked, returning with the shopping, and Aurelia thrust the prints at her, to see if she would confirm what Derry had said, that the words had disappeared.

"I see only some trees and Gaia dancing," she said. Aurelia sank into a chair, equal parts relieved and baffled. Most of all, she felt tearful.

The fuss stirred Coco. Derry stood up and rocked her, which silenced Coco, at least for a few moments. Maren sat next to Aurelia and fixed her with a stern look.

"Tell me what happened," she said. In a low voice, Aurelia did her best to explain—the basement, the red light, the three photographs that revealed the words *you must leave* in large, hand-drawn letters. They must have been drawn in the wet film, she explained, but that was impossible. And who would do such a thing? And how had the letters disappeared? Had she imagined it?

She expected Maren to tell her she needed more sleep, that this was all in her mind.

Instead, Maren said, "Is this the first time this has happened?"

Aurelia went to say yes, then paused. "I felt like someone was watching me today. In the forest. I know it sounds paranoid . . ."

"It doesn't sound paranoid," Maren said gently. "Did you see who was watching you?"

Aurelia bit her lip. "The trees." She squeezed her eyes shut. She sounded ridiculous. She *was* ridiculous. She needed more sleep, more vitamin D. More wine. Definitely more wine.

"Did it feel threatening?" Maren persisted, and Aurelia nodded. She reached for her eyes, cautious that Gaia and Derry might not see that she had started to cry.

"Some people are susceptible to it," Maren said with a sigh. "Others not so much. I think you might be the first type."

Aurelia straightened. "Susceptible to what?"

"If you are susceptible, it can make you feel afraid," Maren continued. "My father told us that sometimes it can bring out people's dark sides, their baser selves. Make them act in cruel ways."

"*What* can bring out people's dark sides?" Aurelia said, utterly confused.

Maren pursed her lips thoughtfully. "Well, people nowadays regard nature in very romantic terms, like it's something out of a Wordsworth poem." She shook her head. "What they don't realize is that nature has been around much longer than humans. We don't understand it, not really."

Aurelia felt more confused than ever. Her head pounded. She looked down at the photographs in her hands. Had she *really* seen words there? Maybe it was a trick of the light.

"The truth is," Maren continued, "nature always protects itself by whatever means possible."

Aurelia had endless questions now, but Gaia had already bounded over, a new drawing in her hand.

"Look, Mumma!" she said. "I've drawn your photograph with *color*! I'm doing cartwheels!"

"That's beautiful, darling," Aurelia said, appraising the sketch absentmindedly. She turned to Maren to ask her questions, but then Coco woke, and the moment was gone.

Later, right when she was about to say good night and head off to bed, Derry earned her sympathy. They were talking about Tom and Clive, about the build and how amazing the new house was going to be.

"How do you get Tom to stay interested?" Derry asked in a careful tone, with a pause before "stay interested." Aurelia had to think about what she meant. *Interested in what? His job? Exercise? What?*

Derry folded her arms and glanced away. "Men just seem born to roam, don't they?"

"I suppose each man is different," Aurelia answered, equally vague. She knew if she said she actually trusted Tom and had never once thought about how to keep him interested—this wasn't the 1950s, after all—the conversation would shut down. "How do you keep Clive . . . interested?" She broached the question gently, aware that this line of conversation was perhaps Derry's way of reaching out for help of some kind. She was patently troubled by something.

"I don't think I do," Derry said, smiling and looking away. "I'm hoping a baby does the trick."

And with that, Aurelia felt her heart at once go out to Derry and plummet for her. Using a baby to keep a man was the oldest listing in the book of Things That Don't Actually Work.

But she didn't say this. Instead, she poured them both a glass of nonalcoholic pinot noir and said, "I'll drink to that."

A knock at the kitchen door makes her jump. She turns and sees a figure through the glass who she recognizes faintly as one of the men working on the build. Erik, she recalls, the main contractor whose team was carrying out the physical work of the build. She likes Erik. He's a man in his fifties with those enormous builder's hands, white shaggy hair, and pale, sad eyes. In fact, before he'd even mentioned the recent passing of Siv, his wife of thirty years, she'd sensed a great sadness about him. Breast cancer. She'd noticed how his chin trembled when he spoke of it, unable to contain it, to process it. A man still staggered by loss. All that grief and love on display, raw as an open wound.

She opens the door. "Hi, Erik," she says brightly. He suddenly looks embarrassed and she remembers with horror that she's just been breastfeeding Coco. Her shirt is only halfway buttoned, revealing a deep cleavage but mercifully not the full veined breast, and she hastily fixes herself as Erik darts his eyes away, first to the ground, then to the teenager standing next to him.

"This is my son, Dag," he says.

Aurelia finishes fastening the rest of her shirt buttons with one hand and extends the other to Dag. He's a pimpled, black-haired version of his father, maybe seventeen or eighteen years old. Tall, slender, the same pale eyes and bee-stung lips. He offers a smile and a surprisingly firm handshake. "How d-d-do you do?" he stammers shyly.

"Dag is finishing high school," Erik says, his accent less refined than his son's—Dag has immersed himself for the last four years in English-speaking TV shows. "I spoke to Tom about this, maybe he didn't mention it . . ."

He trails off. She cocks her head, trying to recall.

"I'm c-commencing my studies at the S-School of Architecture and Design in Oslo next fall," Dag says, before sliding his eyes to his father to fill in the rest.

"I had wondered if . . . maybe you and Tom would be OK with Dag volunteering on the site," Erik says cautiously. "It's a good idea for a trainee architect to get some experience, you know? Maybe he can help with the build . . ."

Aurelia frowns. She is still foggy-headed, words and meaning melting together. She forgets things often now. Just the other day she could not for the life of her remember what a kettle was called. She'd referred to it as the "silver thingy that boils water," which made Tom laugh until tears pricked his eyes. At least she can serve *some* purpose, she thinks, other than producing milk.

"What sort of experience?" she asks. "Oh, and I'm sorry. Where are my manners? Would you both like to come in? I could put the kettle on."

Kettle, kettle, kettle, she thinks, pounding the word mentally on her mind like the keys of a typewriter etching some gray-matter memory bank. She'll master sleep deprivation and its brain-numbing effects if it's the last thing she does. At sundown her mood tends to slide off a cliff, that's the only problem. No real way to master that, more's the pity, and then there are her dreams. Or nightmares. The boundary between sleep and wakefulness is frightfully porous.

The men shuffle into the kitchen in their boots and heavy jackets, the sight of them in this unfamiliar setting making for a moment of discomfort. She has brought them inside the bosses' territory, made them cross a line, and she punctures the unease with bright, rambling chatter that draws a squeal from Coco's bedroom. Damn. She's woken up the baby, wrecked the fine work put into getting her to sleep by overenthusiastically greeting these men. They remain standing, shifting from foot to foot as they look over the messy kitchen, the cup of the breast pump still dripping with yellow milk, and Tom appears in the doorway. Coco is in his arms trying to latch on to his nose. He surveys the scene of Erik and the boy and his wife with her shirt buttoned up wrong with perplexity.

"Hello, Erik," he says.

"Tom," Erik says, blushing deeply. He begins to inch back to the door, keen to get outside, his natural habitat. Aurelia offers them a seat at the dining table, but her voice is drowned out just then by Coco, who senses her mother and wails loudly for her to come close and hold her.

"What was all that about?" Tom asks once the men have darted out the door. He hands the baby to Aurelia, who holds Coco to her shoulder and rubs her back, kissing her little forehead.

"That was Erik and his son, Dag," she says. "He wants Dag to shadow you."

"He wants him to *what*?"

"Shadow you. Like work experience. He wants to be an architect."

Tom gives a rueful laugh. She watches as he strides across the kitchen to unhook his overcoat.

"He just wants some tips, Tom. A bit of mentoring, that's all."

She reminds him that Erik is newly widowed, points out that Dag looks like a nice boy. Has a place at the Oslo School of Architecture, is proud of how much she can recall from the conversation. See? She's not losing her mind. Not completely, anyway. So much depends on sleep, it turns out. Tom is rubbing his face and sliding on his boots. "I don't have the time, Aurelia," he says, perhaps more crossly than he intended. He stops, looks up. "I'm not into . . . all that."

"Into what?"

He rolls his eyes. "I work best on my own. If I'd wanted to *teach* architecture I'd have gone into bloody academia."

"No one's asking you to teach."

"Maybe they're not," he says. "But that's what it'll turn into. You're always saying I work too much. That I put my work before you and the girls—"

"Tom . . ."

There's a tone in his voice that she doesn't like. He's angrier these days than she's ever seen him. Is it exhaustion? Probably, but she's worried it's to do with Coco. Sometimes she actually fears he might hurt her in a moment of frustration. She's so little, so fragile, and his anger makes him seem capable of things she would never say aloud. It was only a few weeks ago that he lay in bed behind her, his hands cradling the smooth roundness of her belly to feel each kick. He laughed each time he felt it. He positioned himself between her legs and spoke into her navel, mimicking the voice of an astronaut: "Earth to baby Coco, this is Earth calling baby Coco. Are you happy today, darling? One kick for yes, two for no."

His slide into simmering fury has coincided with Coco's entrance into the world, she thinks, kissing Coco's soft, warm head. He wasn't like this when Gaia was born. Tired, yes, but happy. Not angry. In fact, in all their years together she's never known him to be prone to anger.

Or maybe it's just the build. He's frustrated by it. She's watching him being ground down by it. And as for feeling he's capable of hurting the baby—well, her maternal instincts are on overdrive. Still, it's unnerving, the feeling that she would choose either one of her girls over him in a heartbeat. Maybe he can sense that, just as she can sense his anger.

He turns at the door, his face dark.

"It would mean a lot to Erik if you helped Dag," she says softly. "No one's asking you to give up your time. It's just the gesture."

A short smile, no eye contact. "Try to get some rest."

She returns to the playroom, where Gaia is drawing at her desk.

"I wrote you a letter, Mumma," Gaia says, holding a piece of paper aloft. "Would you like me to read it to you?"

"Oh, yes, darling. Please do." Aurelia settles back slowly into the nursing chair while unbuttoning her shirt. No sooner has she unclipped her bra strap than Coco has lurched forward and clamped herself to the breast, suckling hungrily. Aurelia's toes curl and she closes her eyes tightly against the pain, which quickly subsides.

Gaia stands in front of her, her posture straight, the letter held with both hands like an epistle.

"'Dear Mumma,'" she reads. "'I love when you spend time with me and I would like a pony, please. Can you send Coco back now as she is very noisy. Love, Gaia. Kiss, kiss, hug.'"

Aurelia grins. "That's a lovely letter," she says, puckering her lips for a kiss, which Gaia offers willingly. Aurelia cups Gaia's cheek fondly. "I love spending time with you, too. Though I think Daddy would object if we got a pony."

"What about the part about Coco?"

"You want me to send Coco back?" She gives a chuckle and looks down at her, smoothing the soft striations of downy blonde on her little head. "Oh, I think we should keep her. Don't you?"

"No, I don't," Gaia says in earnest. "We need to send her *back*."

"Oh. Why?" Aurelia says, a little shocked by this development. Gaia had been very keen on her role as Big Sister all throughout the pregnancy. Even so, Aurelia had been mindful to buy children's picture books about the adjustments required by a new baby, countering jealousy and so on. She thought she'd sliced up her waking hours—of which there are more than she can feasibly cope with—into neat proportions, ensuring Gaia got all the attention she needed. This letter, however, suggests Aurelia got the balance wrong somewhere along the line.

"She's too small," Gaia says. "And she's too noisy."

"I see," Aurelia says. "You've certainly got a point there."

Gaia nods and looks fretfully at Coco, reaching out to stroke her head. "I mean, she *is* quite cute, even though she's bald. And she wakes a lot during the night, doesn't she, Mumma?"

"She does," Aurelia says.

"And that makes you very tired."

Aurelia stifles a yawn with the back of her hand. "Yes."

"*And* she's boring. The other day I showed her my Peppa Pig toys and . . . well, guess what?"

"What?"

"She didn't even look at them. She's got no interest in toys *whatsoever*."

Aurelia lifts Coco against her chest and rubs her back, smiling.

Poor Gaia. She looks crushingly disappointed, and quickly Aurelia reads the situation, and what she must do. "Come here, my love."

Gaia looks downcast. She watches glumly, suddenly on the verge of tears, as her mother places her sleeping sister back into her basket like the kind of occasionally screaming statuette that she really is. When Aurelia lies down on the floor, placing a cushion beneath her head and resting both hands on her still-rounded belly, Gaia is puzzled.

"What are you doing?"

"Role-play. We're going to pretend that I'm a newborn baby and you're the mum."

Gaia's eyes widen. She relishes this game, reaching at once for her nurse outfit and administering all kinds of ointments and bandages, before remembering that her mumma did none of this for baby Coco.

"OK," she tells Aurelia a few minutes in. "Your name is Dora."

"Good choice," Aurelia affirms.

"Shush. You can't speak, remember?"

Aurelia obediently folds her lips inward.

"And now, baby Dora, it's time to drink your milk."

She fashions a bottle out of a jam jar and holds it to her mother's lips for a few seconds. "Now it's time to play."

Aurelia doesn't move. Gaia stares.

"Dora can't play," Aurelia whispers, cupping her hands against her mouth. "She's just been born so she can't walk yet. And she has to sleep for about twenty hours a day."

"Oh," Gaia says. "How long is twenty hours?"

"A *very* long time."

"Well, in that case, can I read you a story, baby Dora?"

Aurelia smiles. Gaia pulls out a book she knows back to front and sits down beside her, legs crossed, before patiently reading the story and pointing at the pictures. She asks questions to which

Aurelia does not respond, then catches herself. "Ah, yes, you're just a baby, Dora. You can't talk yet. That's OK. It just means you're a good listener."

Gaia finishes the story and moves on to another, and then another, settling into her role as mother by parroting what Aurelia often says to both her daughters. *There, sweetheart. Do you need another blankie? You're so special to me. I love you. I'll take care of you.*

Aurelia can hear Coco begin to move in her wicker basket, the familiar snuffling and grunting sounds that signal she's not settling. Aurelia knows she will need to get off the floor and tend to her, most likely pick her up and cuddle her, but she's so tired, and the floor is surprisingly comfortable, especially with the numerous blankets and Sherpa throws that Gaia has sourced from the blanket box and placed upon her. She wishes she could sleep, have a little nap. She wills Coco to settle, just for five more minutes, but she's starting to cry.

"What are you doing?" a voice says.

"Shush, Daddy," Gaia says, and Aurelia spots Tom's boots in the doorway. "Mumma is my baby. She's very sleepy."

Coco's cries grow frantic, desperate, that urgent shrill tremble signaling that she needs to be picked up. Tom crosses the room and lifts her out of the basket. Aurelia could applaud him for it. This is what love is, she thinks. Not flowers, not romantic notes. There is simply no gesture of love that comes close to the act of tending to Coco and allowing Aurelia to stay on the floor underneath all these warm blankets, the aches of her body lessening as she gives in to the urge to lie flat and still.

Coco is still crying from the other side of the room. Tom is pacing with her, bouncing her lightly against his shoulder and rubbing her back, humming something. Gaia is reading another story, and Aurelia is so comfortable. She would give anything for even ten minutes' sleep. Pay any amount of money, do any amount of work, just to sleep. But Coco's cries have changed gear. They're urgent, higher in pitch. Aurelia opens her eyes and looks over at Tom.

What she sees makes her sit upright with a hand clapped to her mouth. Tom is holding the baby in the air above his face. In the corner beside him is a woman facing the wall. She is dripping wet, as if she has crawled out of the fjord, her clothes old and bedraggled. Aurelia opens her mouth to ask what she's doing here, but Tom's face is bright with fury, a vein in his temple pulsing as he begins to shout.

"Shut up, you little bitch! Shut *up!*"

Coco's mouth is wide open in a prolonged wail, tears streaming down her face and her legs wheeling frantically in the air. And then he shakes her. His hands squeeze Coco's sides and he shakes her like a doll, and Aurelia cannot get to her feet fast enough to stop him from shaking her three, four, five times, her head bobbing dangerously.

Aurelia is on her feet, the room spins and sways as she lurches toward him, and with a yell he half drops, half throws Coco to the ground. The woman in the corner doesn't move. Aurelia holds her arms out to catch her, but she trips on something—a toy tractor or a pram, she's not sure—and falls, and even before she reaches the ground she knows she can't reach Coco.

Coco hits the ground a moment before Aurelia reaches her and is still.

She finds herself on the floor, gasping for air, on her elbows in a half crawl. Gaia is standing over her. Somewhere in the distance is the sound of crying. She scans the room for Coco, but she isn't there, and neither is Tom or the woman. In a great rush she realizes that Coco is still in the basket, and the air around her ionizes with the slow knowledge that she fell asleep again, that she was dreaming, that the terrible thing that happened didn't happen.

Her heart is still pounding in her throat and her shirt is soaked with sweat. "Are you OK?" Gaia asks timidly. She watches as her mother pulls herself to her feet with all the stiffness of a skeleton stepping out of its grave and lumbers toward Coco, scooping her gently out of the basket.

"Is everything all right?" a voice says from the doorway. Aurelia screams, an involuntary reaction to the sight of Tom. She is trembling, crying, and when he tries to take Coco from her, she pulls away from him, holding the baby as though she's just been attacked.

"Aurelia?" he says, reaching out to her a second time, but she doesn't respond. He looks down at Gaia as though she might reveal the cause of her mother's hysteria. But Gaia merely stares up at him, her eyes wide, seeing the gulf widening between her parents, and her mother fragmenting like a scattered jigsaw.

Aurelia keeps her distance from Tom, as though he's radioactive or clutching a live grenade, and paces unevenly by the window, which is beginning to blister with rain. Six months ago they stood in this very room, emptied of its contents and blooming with fungi. They looked out at the view of the woods and endless sky and glittering fjord. *Let's buy it,* Aurelia said. *It's perfect.* And so he did.

"Aurelia?" he tries again, summoning all his patience. "What's going on?"

When she doesn't answer he feels a flush of rage. His own words boil in his throat. Just like his father. Finally she turns to answer, but he has already walked out of the room, slamming the door so hard behind him that the wood cracks in protest.

words that boil, wounds that burn

NOW

What do you mean, 'rumors'?" Tom asks, angling his head up at Clive.

"Look, I know what you're going to say—"

"No, you don't," Tom throws back. "You haven't a clue what I'm going to say."

Clive stares at his friend. Lately he'd like nothing more than to punch him in the face. Always so defensive, always so quick to turn things into an argument. Working with Tom these days is like trying to be a bloody contortionist, twisting himself into knots over every little setback that arises with this never-ending build just to get Tom to do what is required. Clive sucks air in through his nostrils and chooses his words carefully.

"The construction team have *concerns*," he says.

"What about?" Tom gives him a flat stare. "I've paid them up front. What the hell do they have to be concerned about?"

This is news to Clive. He swallows hard. *Paid them up front.* Tom will sink this business if he continues running it like a toddler.

"They're concerned about some rumors that have grown out of the situation with the first house," Clive says in measured tones. "The river—"

"Don't talk to me about the bloody river," Tom snaps. His decision to redirect that river almost ruined him. And after all that effort, the river is back now, burbling away through the trees as it has done since the last ice age.

Clive looks over Tom's face—the man looks haggard. His face is drawn. He's not eating. His eyes are sunken behind his glasses, all the light gone. His hair has more flashes of white than ever before.

"Clive," Tom says flatly. All the friendliness has gone from his voice. Clive wonders if Tom's next move is to suggest he go home, step down from the company. "What rumors?"

Clive feels bad, shifts from foot to foot. He hates saying it aloud. "They're a suspicious bunch, this lot. Some of the men say the site is haunted."

Tom grins. Hilarious. He leans back in his chair and folds his arms. Haunted? Magic.

"Go on," he says brightly, suddenly warmed by having to prod Clive to tell him this kind of news.

"They're scared, Tom. That moose has been on the site six times now."

"Elk," Tom corrects. "Moose is the American term."

"Will you just listen? It keeps wrecking things. It's a big animal."

"I know," Tom groans. This was the other outcome of the river fiasco: apparently every animal in Norway drank out of that damn river, and when he redirected it they all got confused. Or pissed off. The latter is more likely, given that the moose/elk keeps coming to the site and wrecking things. "We'll get pest control out again."

Clive double-takes. "Pest control? Tom, it's a *moose*. Pest control won't touch it. Anyway, it's not just that. The build itself is no picnic. Things keep going missing."

Tom frowns. "What do you mean, missing? Is someone stealing the equipment?"

"We're not sure. A couple of things have ended up in the fjord." He fixes Tom in a stare. "No one knows how they got there."

Tom leans forward, his lips curled into a sneer. "They're building on the side of a cliff, you idiot. The wind could have caught them . . ."

You idiot. Clive bites back a sharp retort, grits his teeth. "They didn't fall off the side of the cliff. They'd have shattered if that were the case. Someone . . . or something . . . had to have carried the stuff down the cliff and placed them in the fjord. And we're not talking about hammers or small objects, here. The big sheets of glass you ordered for the front façade. Slates. Tiles. These are heavy, highly breakable objects. Removed from the site and found in the water. Do you realize what I'm saying?"

He says this last bit as though he's talking to a three-year-old. Tom gives him a thousand-yard stare.

"They think the site is haunted. I'm serious. It's concerning."

"It's very concerning," Tom mumbles. "It's concerning that we've contracted people who believe in ghosts."

"And there's another rumor," Clive adds in a low voice. He'll need a stiff drink after this conversation. He rubs his chin. "I think this particular rumor has some truth in it."

"What's that?"

"That we're running out of money."

Tom doesn't answer. They both know this is only partly true. The real truth is that they ran out of money some time ago.

"We need an injection of cash," Clive says.

"Who doesn't?"

"Tom. I need you to be serious for a second."

Tom gives him a hard look. Clive feels a fresh ripple of anger. He wants to scream in Tom's face. *This doesn't just affect you,* he wants to yell. *This is my income, my life. If you go under, you take me with you!*

"I hate to ask this . . ." Clive says.

"Just ask it."

"All right." He sighs, deeply uncomfortable. "Was there any . . . insurance money?"

Tom stares at him blankly for a few seconds. "Insurance money?"

Clive studies the pattern on the tablecloth. "From Aurelia's death."

"For crying out loud!" Tom spits, reeling as though he's been stabbed.

"I'm only asking," Clive says, but he can't look at Tom, and good thing, too, because Tom has a mind to reach across the kitchen table and throttle him.

Clive leans forward. "Do you think I *want* to ask about this? Do you not think I'm waking up every night in a cold sweat, wondering how we're going to pay for this house? And the irony is, it's not even *my* house! It's yours!"

Tom is pricked by guilt. He knows he has been reckless. He hadn't really thought about how it was affecting Clive and Derry. He hadn't really cared, until now. "I'm *sick* with worry," Clive continues, a little tearful. He bites back a sob. "Derry wants to do one last round of IVF and I can barely afford to pay the gas bill, never mind fork out fifteen grand or whatever it costs now." Then, shifting tack and wiping his eyes: "We need to strategize. Make a plan. Did you look over the spreadsheets I sent you?"

Tom shakes his head. Of course he didn't.

Clive sighs deeply. "We've got to pay the glass company by Tuesday. We don't have anywhere near enough to cover the bill, and there isn't time to get another bank loan." He pauses, hoping this sinks into Tom's thick head. "I'm going to put it all on my personal credit card. Just . . . don't tell Derry, all right?"

Tom takes this in. "Don't be stupid."

"Well, what else do you propose? Unless you see a bank anywhere that we can rob? We've begged and borrowed from every possible source as it is." A pause. "Unless . . ."

"Unless?"

Clive clicks his tongue against his teeth. "I just had a thought . . . Perhaps you could persuade your father to dip into his pockets again. One last time."

Tom recalls with a distinctly physical pain—a stabbing sensation just beneath his ribs—the last time he spoke with his father. It was the only time in his life he asked the man for money. Basecamp, the house that he had designed and built just a few hundred feet from where he sits, now lies in ruins after a horrific thunderstorm laid waste to the site. Lightning of biblical proportions. The river that Tom diverted had dispersed, and the rainfall made it swell, ruining the foundations of the house. Luckily, Granhus was shielded by the trees, losing no more than a few slates and panes of glass. Basecamp collapsed into mud.

And if that wasn't enough, they still had to pay for the materials. They had to pay a contractor to come and clear up the mess. Clive acted quickly, bled the company dry to pay the invoices. But the workers' salaries—they needed to be paid. Men had to feed their families, and they couldn't wait until a business loan was approved. Tom picked up the phone, called his mother.

"What's Dad's number?"

She gave it to him. Warned him. *Be careful what you ask.*

The conversation with his father was the first in several years. He had done the honorable thing when Gaia was born—rang his parents to inform them they were grandparents. His brother, Edward, would have a child with his new girlfriend, Beatrice, a year or so afterward, but for now this was a new thing, his parents becoming grandparents. Gaia was their first grandchild. When Tom had called his mother to inform her that Aurelia was pregnant, she'd drawn breath and murmured, "Let us hope it's a boy. Your father will want to continue the Faraday name." It had taken a few months to swallow that down, and he hated himself for the way his heart—just for a moment—sank when the sonographer declared they were having a girl.

"That's amazing," Aurelia had said, a tear sliding down her cheek. "A little girl, Tom. Our little girl."

Nonetheless, he had gritted his teeth and steeled himself for another unbearably tactless comment when he called home shortly after Gaia was born. His father answered, and Tom was horrified to find himself breaking down as he spoke.

"Dad? I'm a father. Aurelia . . . we have a little girl. We've named her Gaia Rose Faraday."

His father had cleared his throat and said, "Jolly good." There was a long pause, during which Tom covered the mouthpiece of the phone and wept. Then: "Shall I pass you on to your mother?"

Ten words in as many years. Ten words in response to the most important moment of Tom's life. Still, he felt warmed by the tone of his father's voice, and nobody could say that the conversation hadn't gone well, relatively speaking. But when he called his father in the aftermath of Basecamp to ask for a loan, he should have known better.

"How much?" his father demanded.

"I need two hundred and seventy thousand by Friday," Tom said. He made to mention it was to pay salaries, but thought better of it. He knew what his father would say to that.

"And will you be paying interest?"

Tom felt his fists clench. "If you wish."

"I see. And shall we make this arrangement—this *loan*, as you say—via solicitors or would you be agreeable to signing something electronically?"

"E-mail's fine," Tom said stiffly. Even after all this time, his father's approach to parenthood never failed to incur the most abject disappointment.

"All right," his father said wearily. "I'll send a contract through this evening. I presume your mother has your current e-mail?"

Tom nodded at the phone. He'd had the same e-mail address for a decade by then, not that his father knew that.

"Once I receive the signed counterpart I'll have my accountant organize a transfer. Agreed?"

"Agreed."

And with that, he hung up. An hour later, the e-mail pinged into his in-box. His palms sweaty, Tom opened the contract. His father had decided upon a loan period of twenty-four months with an interest rate of ten point four percent. *Ten point four percent.* The point four cracked him up. This from a man who had millions in numerous bank accounts, who barely spent any time at all with his two sons while they were growing up. Nannies, boarding schools, forgotten birthdays . . . And Tom could have applied for a loan at half that rate with a repayment period of up to a decade. It took every ounce of self-control not to shoot back an e-mail telling his father to shove the money right up his arse.

But he had no alternative.

And now, even though his father has not reneged an inch on that tyrannical arrangement, not even when he learned that Aurelia had died, Tom is calling home once more.

"Dad," he says, feeling nothing, feeling everything. "I need money. I'll pay whatever interest rate you want."

———

Clive is appeased and the workers are paid. The company is injected with forty thousand pounds, but it isn't enough to stop half the construction team from walking off-site. The next Monday morning Clive stands at the edge of the cliff, looking over abandoned girders and sheets of glass, sucking on a cigarette. The stress has made him take up smoking again. He's frustrated beyond words, but he can't half blame the poor guys for leaving the job. These sheets of glass weigh five hundred pounds each. They're massive—fifteen feet by twelve—and therefore not easily shifted. All six sheets were found two-hundred-odd feet below here, right at the bottom of the cliff in the tidal waters of the fjord. The guys had looked everywhere for these vanished glass walls. Clive has hefted them himself—not alone, obviously; it took six men to move them off the helicopter that delivered them—and has a keen knowledge of their weight. For them to wind up in the fjord is mysterious. For them to wind up in the fjord *unbroken*, completely undamaged, is downright supernatural. Add this supernatural mystery to the other weird things about the build—the storm, the moose, the voices the crew say they've heard, rumors about the site being haunted—and he has a mind to tell Derry they're getting the next flight home.

But then, that would be defeatist. There's yet a small voice in his head that says this build, *this* house, could turn everything around. Put the company on the map. Enable him to get what he wants. Finally.

Tom has consoled himself about the loss of so many workers by zipping himself into work clothes and absorbing several construction roles. There are still six men on-site, and two of them he knows pretty well. One of them is Dag. He has warmed to Dag considerably over the last while, not least because of how industrious and intelligent Dag has proven himself to be, but also because Aurelia urged Tom to take Dag on. Dag is a kind of link back to her, a remnant of a time that floods Tom with warmth. And so, when Tom claps eyes on him now, he feels something return to his limbs, an old energy that reconnects him to the world.

"How's it going, mate?" Tom asks, planting a hand on Dag's shoulder.

"Pretty g-g-good, mate," Dag says with a grin, and he pulls off a glove and wipes sweat off his forehead. Tom notices that Dag's T-shirt is soaked with sweat. It's barely above freezing. Tom is wearing a thermal vest beneath his work clothes and gloves lined with sheepskin. He looks over the steel framework and grins. For the last three weeks Dag has been painstakingly drilling through the cliff face to insert the thirty-millimeter-wide, twenty-foot-long iron rods that will secure the lower level of the house to the cliff.

"How many more do you have to do?" Tom asks.

"Seven," Dag says, and Tom does a quick calculation in his head. Two days per rod. He frowns. Another fortnight just to secure the foundations is longer than he'd like.

Dag clocks the frown. "M-m-maybe if I get some more men to work with me we can cut that time right down," he says quickly. "Dad spoke with a new t-team yesterday. They just finished up a p-project in Stavanger. It's likely they won't have . . . won't have heard about . . ." He trails off, lowers his eyes. Tom feels as though he's been punched in the gut. "I mean . . ." Dag begins again, trying to sweep the inference out of the air. *He meant the ghost,* Tom thinks, his guts churning and his blood boiling. His disgust at his own team of construction workers downing tools and abandoning their jobs because of a rumor—a rumor about a *haunted site*, no less—has hardened to fury. What is this, he thinks, the sixteenth bloody century? Norway isn't some rednecked, backwoods country. It's a place of intelligent, progressive thinkers and pioneers, not superstitious morons.

But of course, that's not why they've abandoned their jobs, he realizes. Clive hasn't paid them. That's the real reason.

"Possibly," Tom says in reply to Dag's stammered suggestion of a new crew, a team who won't be subject to the wiles of spooky tales about ghosts haunting the site of their death. Or maybe it's more than that, he thinks, looking out over the fjord. He's standing directly over the spot where Aurelia fell to her death. *Where she jumped.* As he looks down he spots a trickle of water snaking through the leaves and spilling over the edge of the cliff. The resurrected river, returning to its destination.

"Ahoy there," a voice calls, and both Tom and Dag lean back from the platform strapped to the side of the cliff and look up where, a hundred feet away, an arm waves down. It's Erik.

"Hey, D-Dad," Dag calls up. "Are you c-coming down?"

"Send up the platform," Erik calls.

Tom and Dag tug the pulley to hoist the wooden platform upward, and in a few minutes Erik is there, trying not to show how out of breath he is. He's carrying a lunchbox and a flask and hands them both to Dag, who flushes with embarrassment—he doesn't like Tom seeing that he's a kid whose dad brings him lunch.

"How're you getting on?" Erik says, grinning as he scans the scene. He slaps the rock with a large hand, pleased with the progress, pleased with his son. "Excellent work," he tells Dag, then Tom. "He's done well, yes?"

"*Very* well," Tom says. He's pleased not only with Dag's dedication and the progress of the project, but with the fact that these two men have remained loyal to him. They could have bowed to the pressure posed by their colleagues, made their apologies, which he would have accepted. But, when all the others left, Dag and Erik were two of only eight men who remained tied to the project, and he senses their investment in the project stretches beyond Dag's ambitions. Even so, he's glad he heeded Aurelia when she urged him to take Dag under his wing. Had he gone with his own feelings on the matter, it is certain both men would not be here, and the project would have stalled.

Later, once sheeting rain has made further progress impossible and he has insisted that Dag and Erik join him for a drink in the kitchen—how he wishes sometimes a pub was nearby; note to self: *always* make sure a project site has a local pub—he recalls the moment when he met Dag, and he almost didn't agree to allow him on the site. After all, getting consent for the build was hard enough. It took months, and a lot more money than he'd expected. The insurance costs for each additional man on-site were a burden.

"It was my wife who said I ought to get my head out of my ass and start being more of a people person," he says, "And I'm grateful for that." He raises his glass. "Here's to gratitude. And wise counsel."

Erik nods, chinks his glass. Dag follows suit, though isn't quite sure of the tone of the conversation. Is Tom saying he had planned *not* to mentor him?

When Dag gets up to use the facilities, Erik leans in close.

"How are your daughters?" he asks. "Gaia, no? Coco? That's their names?"

His eyes flick over a photograph of the two girls on a shelf behind Tom. Beautiful girls. So little.

Tom studies his fingernails. "They're fine," he says. "I have a nanny. She cares for them. And a housekeeper."

Erik leans in. "I don't mean are they getting food on the table and clean clothes," he says, raising his eyebrows. "I mean, how *are* they? Without their mother? Only gone a matter of months. It must be hard. For you as well."

Tom's throat is burning now. He swallows back the anger that has shot into him and nods.

"It is hard," he says softly. "They miss their mother very much."

"And you?" Erik says, with kindness in his voice.

Tom rubs his eyes. He'd prefer not to talk about this, not to open up. His mother still e-mails quotes from Marcus Aurelius, and occasionally his brother will text asking after the build. Few people ask him how he *is*.

"I'm fine," he says.

Erik says nothing. It's a crap answer to give to anyone, let alone another widower. That's what he is, he remembers. A widower. The term changes nothing.

"I don't know how I am," he says. "Grateful? Yes. I'm grateful." Erik looks confused, so Tom elucidates. "I have two beautiful girls. And I had ten years with the most incredible woman I have ever met. Or ever will meet." He picks up his glass of vodka and drains it to steady the wobble in his voice.

"If I can give a word of advice," Erik says gravely.

Oh, please, yes, Tom thinks. *Definitely give me advice, I can think of nothing I'd like more.*

"Don't work too hard," Erik says. Tom waits. Was that the advice? Or was there something in between that he missed? He blinks. Yes, he realizes. That was the advice.

"Don't work too hard," he repeats, trying to pluck the meaning out of those words.

"When Siv died," Erik says, his voice breaking, "I threw myself into work. It was my savior. But then one night I had too much time on my hands and . . . it all hit me. Everything I'd avoided. All the grief in one go." He shakes his head, fixing his pale eyes on Tom. "I keep a gun in my bottom drawer. I took it out that night. I had one bullet. And I almost used it." He leaves a long pause for that to sink in. "Those precious girls of yours need you to be OK."

A warm smile. "And *you* need you to be OK. So . . . don't work too hard. Take the time to recover. OK?"

"OK," Tom says, and he smiles to indicate he has taken it all to heart, that he is absorbing the counsel of wise words offered by a man who has walked the path he is on, the path of burning coals and searing flesh. But he lets the words roll off him, discarding them.

Without work, he will drown.

18

the attic

Now, lean forward and put *all* your weight on your palms. That's it. A little more. Feet off the ground."

I was in crow pose—or bakasana—which means I had both hands planted on the floorboards of Derry's bedroom, my legs bent at the knees and my feet kicking up behind me a foot or so off the ground. It sounds weird because it *is* weird, especially if you have the biceps of an office worker, which is to say—none.

"Hurrah!" Derry said, clapping. A second later I keeled forward and landed flat on my face.

"Whoopsadaisy," Derry laughed, helping me upright. "Well done. Why don't we try some of the easier asanas? Legs outstretched, like this."

I tried to copy her on my mat—one of Derry's—but as I raised my arms in the air my sleeves started to roll down. Derry had insisted on loaning me yoga pants—("green, the color of the heart chakra!")—and a top, but I had panicked a little at this. The sleeves had very loose cuffs, and I *definitely* did not want Derry seeing my scars.

I clutched the hems of the sleeves with my fingers and held them tightly.

"Fingers spread wide," Derry encouraged. "Right inside the center of your palms is a circle of energy. Let it flow, Sophie. Let the energy *dance*."

I tried this, but immediately the sleeves began to slide down my arms. I stood upright, embarrassed. "I think I've . . . hurt my shoulder," I lied.

Derry gave me a look of concern. She pressed her palms and feet together and bowed deeply. "Namaste."

I began to roll up the mat, but she stopped me. "Let me massage your shoulders."

She pressed down on either side of my neck with startling strength. "Wow, yes. There we go. A truckload of tension right there in your rhomboid minor. You must be in agony. Lie down for me, please."

Still clutching my sleeves, I lay down as bidden, stomach flat on the mat with my head turned to the side, like roadkill. Derry knelt over me and pushed and prodded at my shoulders.

"You have trigger points right down to your shoulder blades, my love. You must feel unsupported in some area of your life. Is that true?"

"Maybe," I said vaguely.

"Golly. Lots of heat coming from this one in particular. Interesting. It's connected to the root chakra."

She was pushing on a muscle I didn't know I had, right at the base of my neck. "Is that a good thing?" I grunted, trying not to scream.

"The root chakra is your foundation. It's where you keep all your childhood stuff, your family issues, boundaries, and survival instincts. Your deepest fears. I sense this chakra is very blocked." She paused. "May I ask a personal question?"

Mercifully she stopped pushing at the muscle and allowed me to sit upright. "Yes?"

She opened her mouth, thought carefully, then abandoned her original question. "Your novel . . . is it biographical?"

"You mean, is it based on my life?" By which she meant *autobiographical*, but never mind.

"Yes."

I nodded.

"I thought so. You mentioned about Alexa not knowing who her father is. That she wondered sometimes where he was . . . from."

I nodded again, feeling my cheeks flush. *From.* Such a small word, just four letters to hook someone's whole identity on to. So many kids could start a new school and never be questioned about where they were from, which was rarely asked out of kindness. Even the ones with a different accent could slide into the ecosystem of the schoolyard without much bother. I had a northern accent, but because I looked different, I was treated like an outsider.

For as long as I can remember I've crafted origin stories last thing at night, vivid fantasies of being reunited with my father— devastatingly handsome, rich, and full of pride in me—and living out my days with a group of loving family members who embraced me as their own. But deep down, I knew this would never come true.

I told a shorter version of this to Derry, who I could tell didn't really relate. "In that case," she said, pursing her lips, "I understand even more why your root chakra is blocked."

"How do I . . . unblock my root chakra?" I asked. Words I never thought I'd say.

"I want you to do some visualizing," she said. "Every morning, before you look after the girls, I'd like you to visualize a bright ball of sunshine right at the base of your spine whilst chanting 'lam' to yourself."

She also told me to use affirmations—"Repeat 'I am safe and secure' twenty times a day, out loud." I figured this might draw surprised looks from anyone in earshot, but Derry was very persuasive.

With that, she bowed deeply, and I returned to my room.

It had been a week since that first morning walk with Derry, and I was slowly being molded into a kind of Derry disciple. When the early-morning start occasionally proved too much for me prior to an exhausting day as Coco's Zimmer frame—she was now attempting to walk—Derry had invited me to join her "sunset practice" of yoga, or her "hour of spiritual awakening," as she called it, which involved ringing a little bell, lighting candles, and lots of breathing and bowing. To my surprise, I was starting to look forward to it.

I had noticed that Maren didn't like my developing friendship with Derry one little bit, and she definitely didn't like Derry. I had put Maren's absence during the day down to the busy life of a housekeeper, but more and more I was detecting that the housework simply wasn't being done. Gaia's Norwegian lessons didn't happen either, not that Gaia minded. I'll hold my hands up and say that I had my own demons of slovenliness to battle with. When I was recovering from my suicide attempt the flat virtually fell apart and I didn't care. But there seemed to be something odd, even pointed, about Maren's strike. The kitchen floor remained covered in dirt from all the muddy feet that came back and forth for cups of tea. The laundry towered in the bathroom and dishes accumulated beside the sink. The usual groan of the vacuum cleaner was no more. Even the curtains stayed drawn in the living room.

I soon worked out that Maren was spending a lot of time in the attic. One night I crept up there to see what could possibly be holding her attention. The attic was as dusty and forlorn as I'd last seen it, but there was a distinct smell of smoke in the place. After a bit of snooping, I found the cause—a half-empty box of cigars beneath the guest bed. That wasn't nearly as interesting as the box placed next to it. With a hammering heart, I opened it to find a stack of photographs, letters, and newspaper cuttings. At first, I thought all of them were of the same person—Aurelia. There were snapshots of Aurelia and Tom on family outings, indicated by the presence of backpacks, flasks, and photo-bombing sheep; there were even notes apparently written from Aurelia to Maren:

> *Maren dearest, could you be a star and drop off the*
> *dry cleaning today?? Love you incredibly, A xxx*

There were many ways that one could take "love you incredibly," but my immediate thought was that it was a figure of speech. There were a couple of photos of Aurelia and Maren, too, back in the house at Hampstead at Gaia's third birthday party. Aurelia had her arm across Maren's shoulders. There were also some objects in the box. A bracelet, a large round button, a small ceramic penguin figurine, and a half-used L'Oréal lipstick. I looked down at them in my hand, certain they were Aurelia's. I remembered Derry telling me about Maren stealing from Aurelia. If Tom found these he'd hit the roof. Maybe even throw her out.

Was Maren spending all day long up here, smoking cigars and looking through these mementos of Aurelia? I knew she was pretty sad about Aurelia dying, but it hadn't struck me at all that she might be grieving. Derry's words came back to me: *Maren became obsessed with Aurelia.* But then, right at the bottom of the box, I saw the newspaper clippings and the photographs, and my curiosity deepened. The newspaper clippings were in a language I couldn't read, but which I guessed to be Norwegian from the handful of nouns I recognized from Gaia's Norwegian spelling books. They were dated from the 1980s and seemed to be all about some girl named Ingrid who, spookily enough, looked *exactly* like Aurelia. Same hair, same small nose, same eyes. Only the mouth and chin gave her away. There was an old Polaroid image there, too, of Ingrid. Ingrid Olsen. She looked like she was in her late teens or early twenties, and she was sitting at a campfire in a pair of jeans and strappy vest top, her head tilted to one side and her long blonde hair sweeping to the side. In another photograph, Aurelia held the same pose. They must have been related.

I had no idea why Maren would be spending all day long staring at these images, nor why she had them in the first place.

A noise downstairs told me it was time to put the box back underneath the bed, but as I scrambled to get everything back in the same order as I'd found it, I came across a newspaper article that sent chills up my spine: Ingrid had been murdered. I couldn't read a word of the text, but the pictures said it all, the same image of Ingrid, smiling up in pixelated black-and-white alongside a man in handcuffs being led from a court. Another image of a detective addressing reporters.

With a sinking feeling in my gut—Derry would say that my sacral chakra was misaligned—I put everything back carefully and approached the attic stairs. To my horror, Maren was standing at the foot of them, staring up at me with a cold, suspicious expression.

"What are you doing?" she said in a tight voice.

"I . . ." I said. "I came to see if you were all right." Partially true.

Her face softened. "Oh. Well, I'm fine. Thank you."

I climbed down the stairs and turned to her. "I noticed you hadn't been doing any housework," my mouth said, while my brain informed me I was stupid. "I thought maybe you'd hurt yourself and was going to offer to help." *Thanks, brain.*

"Oh." She was taken aback by that. She clasped her hands and glanced, I noticed, in the direction of Derry's room. "That's very kind. I've just . . . felt a little down lately." Her eyes fell on my forearms. "You'll know what that feels like."

"Yes, I do," I said, overly sympathetic.

"I meant to ask," she said then. "Coco's birthday party. What did you have in mind?"

I stared blankly. *What did I have in mind?* I had all but forgotten that she was turning a year old in a matter of days, and completely overlooked the fact that this may require a birthday celebration of some sort. It had been some time since I celebrated my own birthday, and the last birthday party I could remember attending was Meg's. There was a large bonfire, a druid pop band, and we all had to come dressed as pagan gods. I didn't think this kind of thing would sit all that well with Tom.

Maren was still staring expectantly. "Well . . ." I said, straining to think what a child's birthday party might involve. I'd never exactly had one of my own, at least not one that didn't involve adults getting drunk on cheap cider, fighting in the street, and getting arrested by the police. I couldn't quite imagine Tom going for that sort of party either. "We could . . . get some . . . balloons?" I said. This prompted a nod. Good. "And . . . a cake?"

"Very good," Maren said. "Shall we go tomorrow?"

Another stupid stare. "Go? Go where?"

She looked puzzled. "To Ålesund. Coco's birthday is on Friday."

"Ah, yes," I said. "Yes, let's . . . go to Ålesund."

It was the first time I'd taken the girls out for the day, and to be honest I was quite excited. Also I was clueless about what we should pack, so I brought everything—bottles, almond milk, sandwiches, three changes of clothing for both girls, nappies, two different pushchairs, and a spare bag filled with toys—and we all piled into Maren's Volvo.

It was astonishing how much the landscape had changed since

I first arrived in Norway. I mean, everything was still there—I don't mean that an earthquake had happened or anything—but the seasons transformed the landscape entirely. The emerald-green cliffs with gushing white waterfalls and a turquoise fjord I'd seen back in August were now dark brown, with snow dribbling down the dark curve of rocks, like the ginger cake with white vanilla icing we used to get at school. The fjord was shining silver, as though filled with mercury instead of water, and the cliff beneath Granhus looked like a hunk of pewter instead of rock. It was magical; the villages and homes dotted all along the banks of the fjord had their window lamps on—a Norwegian tradition for fisherman who are yet to return home—and so all the pockets of the fjord shimmered with gold lights. Like a glittery biscuit crumb, to continue the dessert analogy.

I felt awkward with Maren in the car, given that I'd just uncovered her slightly unhealthy fascination with her dead employer. And the collection of images of the murdered girl, Ingrid, was unnerving, too. I thought back to our conversation in Maren's bedroom on the night that Tom gave her a bollocking. Just as I was scratching around my brain for a decent conversation starter, I sensed she was feeling awkward, too.

"When we spoke before, I think I spoke out of anger," she said carefully, glancing in the rearview mirror at Gaia, who was scribbling in her art book.

I waited for Maren to explain which conversation she meant. The logbook? Whether honey was vegan or not? The chat we had about Tom?

"Things have not been the same, since . . ." she said with a meaningful stare. I've never been particularly talented at reading between the lines, but I deduced she meant *since Aurelia died*. "As you can imagine."

"Of course," I said.

"To be honest, I've been giving some serious thought to the future. I think that, once I've done what I need to do, I'll move on."

"Move on?" I said. I checked that Gaia was distracted before leaning closer to Maren. "Do you mean quit?"

"I mean move on," she said, flinching at the word "quit." "I'd intended to work for Aurelia for as long as she needed me. The rest of my life, if that was required."

I waited for something more, but it didn't come. "How did you begin working for Aurelia?" I asked.

She smiled sadly. "I had met Aurelia briefly seven years ago, back in London. She found out I was Norwegian and was over the moon. Her father's people were from Norway and she had fond memories of the place. A while afterward I found out she needed a housekeeper. I applied for the job. She hired me immediately." She smiled at the memory of it. "Sometimes these things . . . they just find you. You don't find them—they find *you*."

"Do you enjoy it?" I asked, thinking about the windowpanes furred with mold and the grime around the toilet.

She sighed. "I used to *love* it. I always wanted a big family home, full of kids and noise and *life*. But . . . it didn't work out. And when I was cleaning Aurelia's home in Hampstead I felt I was helping create that. Keeping order. But now . . . not so much."

"Derry said you were an artist," I said. "I was wondering why you gave up painting to become a housekeeper."

My mouth had rattled off again, asking questions my brain would otherwise have prohibited.

Maren pulled her lips into a tight grimace and stared at the road, which was a good thing, as she was driving along a particularly narrow stretch of road beside a sheer drop. "What else did Derry tell you?" she said in a low voice.

I struggled to think. "She told me about the seven chakras.

And I got some good feedback on my novel. I'm thinking of rewriting the whole thing in third person—"

"Not that," Maren snapped. "Why would she tell you I was an artist? And how did she know this information?"

I shrugged. "You'll have to ask her."

She hit the accelerator and overtook a lorry on a bend. "What does *she* do, huh? Mix paints? Choose wallpapers?" She gave a loud scoff. "Let her wash her *own* socks."

"It sounds like you were very talented," I observed. "And yet you gave it all up to . . ." I tried to say *clean the house*, but couldn't, so went for ". . . iron the tablecloths."

"Sometimes life turns on a dime," she said under her breath.

She sounded very sad when she said that, and when I asked what happened—albeit in a tiny voice—she didn't answer, but I noticed her knuckles whiten on the steering wheel as she gripped it.

"You said that Tom was manipulated into coming back to Norway," I said after a few minutes of awkward silence. "Who manipulated him?"

She threw me a look of horror. "I told you that?"

I felt a bit confused. "Yes. That night, in your room . . . And then you showed me the scale model of the first house . . ."

"You promise you won't say a word?"

"I promise."

She turned her eyes back to the road and visibly chewed over whether or not to divulge it. "Clive," she said quietly, checking the rear mirror to ensure Gaia was busy with her sketchpad. Then: "Perhaps 'manipulated' is the wrong word. He . . . persuaded him."

"Why do you think Clive would do that?"

"They're business partners. It was in Clive's interests to get Tom to finish the job."

That didn't strike me as nefarious as it had originally sounded.

"You can understand that it looks extremely bad," she continued. "For Tom, I mean. Not Clive. Everyone thinks it was Tom's idea. But as I said, housekeepers hear things that others don't." She threw me a smile. "How are you feeling these days? No more . . . dark thoughts? You're feeling happy, yes?"

"Yes," I said, realizing a few seconds after I replied that it was true. I *was* feeling happy. I was occasionally fearing for my life, and scared witless by Granhus's resident elks and ghostly women, but also happy.

She glanced at my forearms, where the scars still burned beneath the long black sleeves of my jumper.

"You get therapy for it?"

I shook my head.

"Well, out here is the best therapy. The views, the smells . . ." She took a deep breath as if to inhale the smell of the car's peach melba air freshener. "Good for the soul. And now you get to see Ålesund! Beautiful city. Norway's Venice, did you know?"

I told her I didn't. "Aurelia's grandparents came from this region. She would visit sometimes as a little girl," Maren said.

"Did Aurelia have any siblings?" I asked lightly, thinking of the girl in the newspaper clippings. "A sister, perhaps?"

Maren frowned. "No. She was an only child."

"Any cousins, then?"

She shrugged. "I don't know."

We reached the brow of a long, steep hill, a spectacular view of the city coming into view. "Ålesund!" Gaia shrieked, making Coco start. I reached back and popped her pacifier in her mouth and she quietened. "Can we go to the park?"

I told her yes, though in reality I had no idea where the park was, nor whether we could feasibly reach it. Ålesund was a beautiful archipelago of colorful buildings surrounded by twinkling blue fjords and dramatic, white-tipped mountains. I thought of

Aurelia coming here to visit her grandparents, perhaps when she had been as young as Gaia was. How excited she must have been to be building a home here, now.

So why did she kill herself?

I was perhaps the proudest nanny there ever was at Coco's choice of party theme—octopuses, which she pronounced "puss puss" with pouted lips while fervently clapping her hands. We were learning about them in our Montessori lessons. Well, actually we were learning about sea life, but both Coco and Gaia had developed a stealthy fascination with octopuses—all due to their having three hearts and blue blood—and so I improvised around that. I found some household items that had a sucker pad—a dish scrubber from Ikea, a soap dish, and a toilet plunger—and demonstrated the strength of an octopus's suckers along its arms. At least until Coco got her face stuck in the toilet plunger, and then Gaia tried to inject herself with biro ink to make her blood blue; thus we moved hastily to safer octopus facts, such as their tendency to chew off their arms when bored.

For the party, I managed to make octopus decorations out of balloons suspended from the ceiling with eight streamers attached to them. I drew faces on clementines and cut the peel to sit outward like tentacles. I even made an octopus cake topping by rolling purple icing into a ball, sticking some goggly eyes into it, and then rolling eight smaller tube shapes for arms. Finally, I made Coco a little octopus costume by repurposing an old green bedsheet and some of her old tights stuffed with foam for the legs. Tom had some round white stickers in his office, and I stuck them all along one side of the legs as suckers. Coco was over the moon, clapping her hands and trying to suction all her toys.

The party, however, was a little dreary. Once everyone had

given their gifts—which took all of two minutes—Gaia leaned over and whispered in my ear: "I think it's really sad that Coco doesn't have any baby friends at her party."

"We're her friends," I said.

"I'm not her friend." Gaia scowled. "I'm her *sister.*"

Gaia had a point: the party was a little staid. Tom looked miserable, studying his cup of organic apple juice. Clive and Derry sat in armchairs staring into the abyss of their phone screens. Maren made herself scarce—I don't think Coco minded too much—and while I had figured that my job was done after organizing the party and hand-sewing the octopus costume, it seemed that the other three adults were expecting me to play host, too. So, for the girls' sake, I put on a great show, getting everyone up to play Twister, which ended with Derry ramming her foot in Tom's eye. After that, we played pass the parcel, pin the tail on the donkey, and sleeping lions. By this point Coco was falling asleep, and I told Tom I'd take her up to bed while everyone else enjoyed the cake. She hadn't even blown out her candle.

As I gathered Coco up against my shoulder and made for her bedroom, Tom approached me.

"Sophie."

I braced myself for a lecture about the Epic Fail that was my attempt at an octopus cake, or a curt remark about the rubbish Twister game.

". . . I wanted to say that I really appreciate you making this birthday so special," he said. "I was dreading this, but Coco looked so happy in her costume and . . . thank you. Really."

He sounded so sincere, so *moved*, that I didn't know what to say. "It's a pleasure," I said.

He looked at Coco asleep on my shoulder. "Maybe I'll put the girls to bed tonight."

"Are you sure?" I said, and he nodded.

"Well." He cleared his throat. "I'll give it a go."

He took Coco from me and cradled her in his arms, before turning to reach out for Gaia's hand.

"What's Daddy doing?" she asked me.

"Daddy's putting you to bed," I explained.

"Come on, pudding," Tom rejoined. She looked from me to her father, gave a shrug, and took his hand.

I headed to my own room a little lifted after the gloomy party. Perhaps it hadn't been gloomy after all. Perhaps, in some small way, I had actually done something that mattered. I figured that Tom was probably thinking about how Aurelia would have loved to have shared this moment with him. Watching their little girl celebrate her first birthday, taking her first steps. It really was very sad.

But when I closed the door of my bedroom there was something different about the place. On the floor beside my bed was a book bound in red leather. I looked around. Had someone been in my room? Nothing appeared to be moved, but the book definitely hadn't been there earlier, and it didn't belong to me. Maybe it was the logbook Maren had said I was meant to fill out, about how the girls were getting on with their reading and so on.

I reached down and picked it up, noticing how soft the leather was. The letters *AF* were embossed in gold on the cover. AF? When I opened the book I realized quickly it wasn't a logbook. Someone had written inside in blue biro and occasionally black Sharpie, about twenty pages' worth. It was hasty, scribbled writing, but there were dates, and at a glance I could see this was fairly personal stuff . . . *why would she say that????* . . . *the look on his face* . . . *I'm feeling better these days* . . .

I shut the book quickly. It was a diary, clearly, and reading it made me feel unclean. I set the book on the bed beside me and gave it the side-eye, like it was a living object. It was taunting me. I had an itch to read it. I felt I was *meant* to read it, not in some cosmological, fate-of-the-gods kind of way, but because it most definitely hadn't been in my room earlier. It didn't walk in here of its own accord. Someone had obviously put it on the floor, in my room. Why else would they put it here unless I was meant to read it?

I had a little internal battle for a while, and then I spent a while imagining the two voices in my head as Revolutionaries and Royalists with bayonets, in white breeches and tricorn hats, charging across a muddy plain. Once that scene was done with, I looked down and jumped to see the diary was still there, red as a heart ripped fresh from someone's chest. I was certain it was staring at me. The gold letters on the front—*AF*—must be someone's initials. Maren's? No, her surname was Larsen. With a shudder, I realized Tom's wife was called Aurelia. Aurelia Faraday. Was this her diary? I was certain I'd seen the names *Gaia* and *Coco* in there when I flicked through.

I felt sick.

I got up, peered down the corridor, and then closed the door. Then I paced my room. I had decided quickly that taking the book to Tom or Maren and telling them I just found it on the floor of my bedroom was *not* a wise move. Maren already suspected me. She just didn't know *what* she suspected me of, but if I went to her and said that someone had popped the diary of Tom's dead wife in my bedroom, she'd never believe me. She'd suspect me of rooting around in Tom's office and stealing the diary.

So now I had to put it back somewhere. But what if I got caught? They only needed to see me with the diary in my hands and I'd be packed off on a plane back to England. And at the back of my mind, I knew that someone *had* to have put the diary in here. The only reason they'd do that is for me to read it.

So, with the Revolutionaries and Royalists still charging across the bloodied field of my mind, I went into my bathroom, locked the door, and began to read.

19

the lift

NOW

It's late. Tom is standing on the deck of Granhus smoking and looking out across the woods. He likes the thick black night that leans on the jagged silhouettes of the trees and the animal sounds that pierce the silence. Bats flitting and screeching, owls hooting, the dozen or so crows that constantly circle the house like a bad omen.

A few nights ago he heard a wolf howl. He stiffened at the sound, his senses primed to protect his household. He'd thought about reaching for his flashlight and rifle in case the thing came near, but then he'd remembered Erik mentioning that the wolf population in this region was all but obliterated. A lone wolf had been spotted once or twice, but it was likely one of few left, if not the only one, thanks to the government's culling program. If a wolf was howling, it was trying to find its pack.

Tom had felt sorry for that wolf. He finds himself listening now for it. His ear tuning to that same howl that echoes in his own head.

He stubs out his cigarette, goes to his office. It's difficult to switch off these days. Aurelia's Nest is constantly on his mind. He pours a glass of red, flicks on the office light, and stands before his easel. There's a note to himself written in pencil at the top corner and circled a number of times: *macrocosm*. A reminder to think about how the project fits into the bigger picture of Norway.

Right before Aurelia died he was feeling conflicted about Norway's eco-politics. He loves Norway, and not just because his wife's family were born here. It was the first country to ban deforestation. Given the very visible effects of climate change—colder summers, milder winters, and the landslide of consequential ecological effects—Norway made the Arctic its number one foreign policy priority as early as 2005. The Norwegian parliament pledged to make the country climate neutral by 2030. Yet there are many unfortunate countermeasures. The government's troubling mismanagement of natural resources, for instance. Whale hunting. The opening up of the Arctic for oil and gas extraction. The reckless culling of natural wildlife, particularly wolves.

A growing number of architects and construction companies are embedding activism into their practice, some of them engaged in building projects with the sole purpose of upending the hypocritical policies that are preventing Norway from taking a proper stand against climate change. The world is literally at stake; at this moment California is burning a slow but inevitable death. Last night, another tsunami took out an entire city on the other side of the world. Norway, a country formed by numerous ice ages, is on the verge of yet another.

The thought of this makes him think about the river. He could write a book. *How Damming a River Ruined My Life*. He chides himself for being so melodramatic. Be rational. It was an oversight on his part to think he could easily redirect something that had flowed naturally for hundreds of years. He read something recently about the role a single river, even a very small one, plays in

supporting ecosystems, and he felt very naïve. The engineer Ragnar had been right. He really should have foreseen the effects it
would have on the landscape, even on the animals.

"Knock, knock."

Clive comes in. Tom continues to draw on the easel. He's re-
thinking some of the elements of the build—he's never been one
to care too much about getting the design carved into stone, as it
were, preferring to remain fluid about the final product right up
until the last minute, and usually after.

Clive, though—he's a planner. He watches Tom make changes
to the plans, the plans they've already approved with the surveyor
and construction team, the plans for which they've got actual consent and to which they are legally obliged to adhere. He shakes his
head with a rueful sigh.

"So what you changing now, then?" he says, picking up Tom's
glass of wine and sipping from it, just like they did as postgrads at
Glasgow School of Art. Tom draws two lines down through the
cliff and adds a box. This famous lift they've been discussing for
all eternity. It's one thing to decide your new home is going to be
built on the side of a cliff, quite another to figure out how you're
going to get groceries down there. He's keen to see how Tom's going
to hold on to his principles with this one. His guess is—he won't.

"You've got to install a lift into the cliff in order to reach the
new house. How're you going to do *that* without explosives, hmm?
Unless you're planning on parachuting down there? Maybe a laundry chute?"

"The lift isn't going *into* the cliff," he tells Clive, tapping the
new addition on the easel. "It's going outside it. Fifteen feet from
the rock face, to be exact." He gets out his calculator, works out
the dimensions required. He has the exact measurements of the
cliff on his computer, but he can remember the important numbers off the top of his head.

"You'll still need explosives to secure the lift," Clive says.

"Explosives, explosives," Tom says, tutting. "You're just dying to blow things up, you are."

Clive grins, folds his arms. "It would make a good PR video for the YouTube campaign."

"If it's bad for the environment, it's bad for business, remember?"

"It would get the job done *fast*. Fast is what we need, Tom, not more delays . . ."

Tom doesn't answer. Clive drains the glass. "Seriously, though. How are you going to do this lift business? Because it strikes me this is extra time and money . . ."

"I was wondering when you were going to bring up your two best friends," Tom says. He turns, fixes Clive with a goading stare. "You know, I can't actually recall the last time we had a conversation where you didn't mention time and money."

Clive simmers, bites back the urge to pound Tom's thick skull. If Tom hadn't been recently widowed he'd dump this job. Screw the company. Some things aren't worth the hassle.

Instead, he says, "Since you brought it up—how *are* we doing for time and money, Tom? Are we on track? On budget?"

Tom clears his throat. "I thought that was your job."

Clive smiles. "Ah, yes. If only I had the power to create *time* and *money* out of thin air. But unfortunately, I don't, and since you keep messing with the plans and blowing our budget, I'm struggling to know where we stand. So—this lift. How're you doing it? Because if we need to order a digger I kind of need to know."

Tom mumbles his reply. "Hand drill."

Clive clearly hasn't heard him correctly. Tom can't have said they're going to install a lift using a hand drill.

"Come again?"

"He said he'd do it," Tom mutters. "It's not *really* a hand drill. It's one of those new ones on a frame. But it's manually operated."

Clive reels for a moment. He wants to belly laugh, but he might wake the kids, and he's had enough nights of shrieking babies for a lifetime. "Hold on. A *hand drill?* Who said he'd do what?"

"Dag," Tom says. "Probably a week's work. They're really efficient, these drills."

Clive claps his hands to his head and does a circle on the spot.

"What?" Tom says innocently, as though he hasn't just suggested that they attempt a highly technical construction project via the kind of tool you might use to remove a few flagstones from a garden path.

"This is insane," Clive says when he's regained the faculty of speech. "We're talking here about insurance policies being breached. We're not covered for this kind of labor . . ."

"He's volunteering," Tom counters.

"You're exploiting him."

Tom lifts his eyes. "You can talk."

"What?"

"About exploiting people."

"What the hell are you . . ."

Tom is right up into his face, kind of hoping Clive will hit him. "You underpaid those workers. *That's* why they walked off the site. Not because of some rumors about goblins and bumps in the night."

Clive raises his eyebrows all the way into his hairline. "How bloody dare you?! I paid those workers the agreed rate—"

"You lied to them about what the build involved, Clive."

"—the *agreed* rate that was *what we could afford,* Tom! I didn't expect you to start drafting in helicopters and using manual labor instead of explosives."

Tom falls silent. "You know why I won't use explosives."

"If you'd used explosives to deepen the foundations of the first house, right now you'd be sitting in your living room drinking a Scotch by the fire."

He watches as Tom seethes. Good. He's sick of tiptoeing around plain facts. What he'd love to say is that Tom is holding everyone hostage with these insane demands. The Norwegian surveyor was strict as a nun, but even *he* said explosives and digging were still playing by the rules, so long as they took certain precautions. Tearing up some trees was fine, too, so long as they were put to use.

He wonders if Tom's refusal to budge on these simple, rule-abiding methods is some kind of subconscious suicide mission that he's dragging everyone else into. For a moment he feels genuinely scared.

"Someone will get hurt, Tom," he says in a resigned voice. "Mark my words. You're going to kill someone if you keep going on like this."

aurelia's diary

I could barely move this morning. Tom threw me against the wall last night and I hurt my head and back pretty badly. Breastfeeding is difficult. Breathing is difficult. I imagine there's bruising, but I haven't looked. Still, I came off pretty lightly so I ought not to complain.

I went out for a stroll. Coco seems to like the baby carrier I bought. She enjoyed her legs being free and kicks and kicks. It's a little colder now, but today was mild, so I walked right to the end of the path—the one that Tom will turn into a road—and tried to imagine what it will be like when we're out here for the summer, picking up supplies every week from the village and smaller supplies from the "shop" in Herr Andersen's shed. I guess I wanted to see if I could walk to it. He does keep a wonderful supply of honey from his bees and Gaia loves the lavender sort.

The walk was tranquil and although I was still a little unsteady on my feet, I took it gently, stopping after an hour to feed Coco. It hurt, as always, but the

cool wind felt beautiful on my skin and on the bad
bruise on my back.

I reached Herr Andersen's place around lunchtime.
He was surprisingly glad to see me. He's such a
grumpy old sod and I hadn't called in advance, so I
expected him to shoo me away as usual. But
surprisingly enough he brought me inside and made
me tea and turned pretty gooey around Coco. She
does that to people, I find. She has such a cute smile
that she melts the hardest of hearts. I bet she'll be a
tremendous flirt when she's older. The only person she
doesn't seem to work her magic on is Tom,
unfortunately. But then, he didn't want her, so what
can I expect?

Herr Andersen is lonely, I think. His wife died a
long time ago and I don't think his kids or grandkids
visit very much—though given how obnoxious he is I
can't say I blame them. His house reeks of sour milk
and old cheese, and I noticed mice droppings. He
offered to show me his beehives, but I declined. I
didn't want to risk Coco getting stung.

He told me all about the history of the site we're
building on, and a little about the people who used to
live in Granhus. He didn't know their names, but he
said a family lived here for a long time. Apparently one
of them vanished. The mother. He wasn't sure what
happened to her, but the husband became an
alcoholic after that, the son left for Bergen, and the
daughter for America. And then the house sat in ruins
for years until another relative sold it off. To us. What
a sad tale!

I came away from his house with several jars of honey from his bees, a box of eggs for Maren (I hope she doesn't tell Tom!), fresh bread, and some chocolate. He had to give me one of his old rucksacks to carry it in. Not only had I forgotten to bring a bag, but I also had no money . . . He insisted I take it all anyway and I promised to pay him next time. I think he just enjoyed the chat. As did I.

When I got back Tom was waiting. More of the same. Maybe it'll get better once the house is built.

Won't it?

21

foreign agents

THEN

The days are creeping deeper into winter. It's a new year, a new start. In the mornings she sees fresh snow laying itself pale and sparkling across the leaves that carpet and skirt the trees. By lunchtime the sun has retreated, and she envelops the girls in their snowsuits and takes them for walks in the persistent night. It isn't just time and light that have different qualities out here—the dark is something else entirely. Here, the dark is a country, or an island that is revealed once the tide of daylight has retreated.

This morning, wind carries ice in its fist. The trees are black figures against weak light. Tom hands her a hard hat and her puffer jacket and leads her through the woods to show her the progress they've made on Basecamp. He wouldn't say much but told her to bring her camera, so she's excited—after weeks of delays, failed deliveries, and damaged materials, not to mention the craziness of attempting to build in the dark, perhaps they're back on schedule.

She looks back at Granhus and spies the gang of big black crows that hang out on the roof. A whole forest to choose from and they pick the roof as their home. They're like living pieces of the darkness. And what a racket they make! They keep waking Coco when she's just settled for a nap. She's had the pest control guy out five times now and it just seems to make them more determined to come back.

"You can open your eyes now," Tom says, but Aurelia's already opened them and is amazed. The house is erected on ten-foot-tall wooden pilings—tree trunks—with a winding set of stairs leading to the structure. With a gasp she takes the stairs quickly, where a huge set of glass windows throw back her reflection.

"Welcome to Basecamp," Tom says with a grin. How he has waited to say those words to her. He pulls back a flapping sheet of heavy plastic—marking out where the front door will be—and gestures for her to walk inside. She looks down at the floor, which is just plyboard marked with large black arrows and numbers. The underfloor heating and floorboards have yet to go down. Above her are thick oak joists marking out the next floor, and a smaller floor above that one for Tom's studio.

"Let me show you the living room," Tom tells her, leading her along the corridor. They step over tools and loose cables and enter a long open-plan room flooded with light. Aurelia brings her hands to her mouth, rendered speechless by the view that stretches out before her on the other side of the large seamless window: the fjord, set between the valley's green shoulders like a long black feather, bronze sky resting on distant forests, and a hairpin road winding in the distance like a mad scribble. And in a direct line from here, Ålesund, which, although she cannot see it, is positioned as though she can lift her arm and touch it with her mind. Her father's birthplace.

When she turns back to Tom her eyes are shining. "Thank you," she says.

He takes her from room to room, talking her through what will be where, how Derry plans to decorate, what pieces of furniture are currently being crafted from the tree he cut down. Each window is carefully positioned to frame another view of the landscape like a work of art. Gaia's bedroom features a beautiful round window, though no glass is yet inserted. Aurelia pushes the tarpaulin forward and glances out, taking in the cliff from this angle.

"What's that?" she asks, pointing at the splash of river slipping over the rock.

"It's the river," Tom says.

"It looks like oil," Aurelia says, and Tom steps forward to glance out. What he sees makes him dash out of the room and down the steps of the house.

Tom stands at the river, the new, suspiciously glossy river that trickles over the edge of the cliff, looking down at the furry bodies of forest animals nearby. He suspects they've died after drinking the water, though some appear to have had their throats ripped out. Mauled by predators, he suspects. Shortly after he diverted the river upstream, Clive suggested that they lay a culvert so the diverted water wouldn't seep into the soil. Tom had done his best to line the bed with rocks and natural solids, but Clive was right— the river had begun to slow down and make the land a little swampy. He left Clive to take care of it.

When he dips his hand in the river, he knows immediately what has caused the river to take on a greasy appearance and a sluggish pace, and what has likely killed the shrews and stoats— the foam compound they've lined the bed with has disintegrated and melted in parts, mixing with the water. In some sections, it has gone entirely, liquefied and now pouring dozens of foreign agents into the fjord.

He phones Clive.

"Tom, I did *exactly* as we discussed," Clive says. "I ordered the product from Oslo. Got the team to mix it and lay a new estuary in dry conditions. They did it all. I'll phone the company, ask for a refund . . ."

"Clive, Clive! I'm not worried about a refund, I'm worried about the *water*, for crying out loud! We can't exactly filter this stuff out . . ."

A long pause. "Tom, *you* insisted on the foam compound, not me."

"Derry suggested the compound . . ."

"You're blaming Derry for this? Look, I suggested a plastic piping and you said it wouldn't look right . . ."

"Read me the list of what the foam contains."

He hears rustling on the line as Clive digs through the office paperwork. "It just says it's a high-density polyethylene."

Tom hangs up. The water not only looks toxic, it smells it, too. He cups some of it in his palm and lifts it to his nose. It smells like plastic. Later, a Google search of the contents of the foam will tell him that he has just dumped a hundred pounds of butane, benzene, vinyl acetate, and other cancer-causing toxins into a river source that is certified as a Sustainable Destination by the Norwegian government and which nourishes thousands of plant, aquatic, and animal species.

To think he wanted this project to be eco-friendly.

When he rises from the river, something near the trees catches his eye. A woman. Not Maren, Derry, or Aurelia, either. Someone else. The same woman he saw before. But when he looks again she's gone.

"Hello?" he shouts, glancing through the trees. "Anyone there?"

He stares into the empty space where he's sure he saw her just before. His skin crawls.

As he walks back to Granhus he has the distinct feeling that he is being watched.

——

It's evening, and Aurelia's reading Gaia stories from her father's old journal of Norse folktales. Tonight Gaia has chosen the story about the man who transforms into a wolf, and despite her best efforts to direct Gaia to a less Gothic, child-friendlier story, Gaia won't be placated. "The *wolf* story, Mumma," she insists. Aurelia sighs and tries to scan the story for the passage she needs to rephrase.

> Once upon a time, there was a carpenter who suffered many losses. Many say his losses were caused by a curse put upon him by a witch; others declared his losses a consequence of his father's tyranny, for his father ruled over many lands.
>
> In time the carpenter took a wife, who bore him children, and he was happy. He would rise before the sun and venture into the fields, tending to his crops, feeding his flocks, and taking his ax and saw and crafting the treasures of the forest into thrones, cradles, and fine tables that villagers and sometimes princes came to buy. At night, he would return to his cottage long after the moon had risen high above the trees, where he would find his wife and children asleep in the beds he had made for them.
>
> One night, however, he returned home to find his wife and children—

"Find his wife and children *what*, Mumma?" Gaia asks, straining to see the words on the screen. The story has it that the poor guy returned home to find his wife and children mauled to death by a brown bear, their blood strewn across the walls and their faceless remains on the floor. She scrolls quickly past that part.

—to find his wife and children gone. He had no idea where they had gone, but he knew they would never return.

"But why, Mumma? Why would they leave him?" Gaia asks tearfully.

"It's just a story, darling," she answers.

The carpenter went to work the next day, and the day after that, but his heart was heavier than the moon. His tears flowed from his cheeks to the earth and turned into a glacier. His sorrow became a new wind that swept across the earth. And then, anger seized him, and because anger is twinned by no element, it changed his blood and bones. One day, he awoke to find his hands had become paws, his face had elongated into a long snout with pointed ears, and behind him swept a thick bushy tail. He had become a wolf.

No longer able to use his tools, the carpenter had to flee his home and roam the wilds of Scandinavia. It is said that, even now, on a full moon, he howls for his wife and children, wishing they might return home.

Once both girls are fast asleep, Aurelia heads outside to lay bowls of water near the river. When Tom told her about the dead animals that had drunk from the toxic river she was horrified. Tom had already looked into ways that they might undo any further damage to the wildlife, such as adding purifiers to the river to counter the effects of the foam compound, but there was little they could do immediately. The contractors had been notified, and a new culvert had been ordered—for now, she can only make these small supplications of water outside in the hope that some animals may be spared an agonizing death.

She groans when she notices yet more bodies heaped about the forest. Some are close to the river, winnowed now to a trickle through the undergrowth; the larger remains of foxes and badgers are farther away. She's uneasy about leaving them; perhaps they'll attract wolves.

She tilts her head up to the sky, allowing this thought to unfold: she never imagined that her dream of building a summer home in Norway would result in poisoning a river source that has existed since the last ice age. She's the sort of person who'll carry a spider to safety from the bathtub rather than kill it, and yet here she is, standing over the bodies of rabbits and squirrels, all dead because of her.

She bends over the remains of a bird, one she hasn't spotted before and yet one she recognizes. A corncrake. She knows it from the website Tom showed her of the critically endangered animals in the region. The little bronze streak on its face and underbelly. She closes her eyes, her stomach dropping. So now they're sacrificing endangered species on the altar of their dream house. This was not how things were supposed to go.

As she makes to pick it up she feels something tug around her ankles. She's stepped into a bindweed. She lifts a foot, but it won't let go. She reaches down to rip it away, but can't get a firm grasp, so she removes a glove. Her fingers do not meet a weed, but something that feels like a hand. She looks down and screams. Long fingers are grasping her ankles. She can't see who is pulling her, but the grip is so strong she falls over. On the ground she kicks and beats with her fists, and when she turns her head she sees two more bodies lying by the corncrake. They are not animals, but her daughters, Coco and Gaia, curled up as though asleep.

She screams again, a long shriek of horror that rings throughout the forest. She scrambles onto all fours, pawing around her for her girls. Finally she seizes them, gathering them in her arms and wailing in despair. It is some time before she realizes that she is holding not her daughters but the bodies of two more corncrakes.

Stunned by confusion, she drops the birds quickly and rises to her feet, staggering backward. A wind sweeps up the leaves, ruffling the corpses' stilled feathers. Only when she is certain that she imagined her daughters lying there does she turn and race back to Granhus, her heart beating in her throat.

You OK?" Tom asks, pouring her a much-needed glass of red.

She nods, says nothing, and drinks half the glass in one go.

"Whoa, there," he says. "Sip it."

She nods again, but looks at the glass as if it contains the elixir of life. He grins. "I suppose two glasses won't kill anyone. Are you all right?"

She nods fervently. "I checked on the girls. They're in their beds."

He tries to work out what this statement has to do with anything. "Let's sit down. Put some music on."

She follows him into the living room, still jumpy. He gestures at the velvet sofa—the one she likes—and makes her sit down. Then he rubs her foot, and she leans back with her eyes closed. When she returned from the woods she went straight to the girls' bedrooms and spent a good half hour with each, reassuring herself that they were alive. Then she took a shower, washing off the mud and tears. But her mind is yet a tempest of confusion. Why is she seeing things that aren't there? She knows exactly what Tom will say if she breathes a word of this. He'll give a look that insinuates she's crazy, or that she's overdoing it, and she'll feel even worse than she does now. For not only does she feel wracked with bewilderment, but she feels emotionally scattered. She recalls this silent effect of breastfeeding from the first time when she was eyes deep in oxytocin, the hormone that produces milk and also encourages maternal bonding. Forget bonding—she just wanted to blub all the time, like a tap turned on by remotely sad news stories or Facebook pics of kittens. It's back again, that sensation of being cut loose from her composure and having no control whatsoever over her emotions.

But she won't say any of this to Tom, who still looks perplexed when she explains that she feels extra angry and anxious right before her period. She keeps her eyes shut and makes the requisite noises that tell him his foot massage is hitting the spot.

She finishes her glass of wine, then another. She begins to feel better. Derry and Clive come down and announce they're off to have dinner in the city. They might stay over in a hotel for a night or two, and can Tom manage on his own for that long?

"No," Tom says. "It'll all be obliterated by the time you get back."

Clive points at Tom and draws a line across his neck with his finger.

"Have an *incredible* time, you two," Aurelia says, arms outstretched. "You *so* deserve it." She blows them both drunken kisses.

When they leave, Aurelia pours herself the rest of the bottle. Tom says nothing. She deserves it. If the shoe was on the other foot he couldn't cope. Nine months without wine? Forget it. Childbirth? Not without being knocked out first, and for about six months afterward.

"I wouldn't wish a marriage like theirs on my worst enemy," Aurelia says with a sneer.

Tom double-takes. "What, Clive and Derry?"

"Mm-hmm."

"Why's that?"

"Tom." She says his name flatly, as if he's missed a whole chapter. He pushes his glasses up his nose, in that way that signals he hasn't a clue what's going on.

"He's your friend, Tom. Surely you know . . ."

"Know what?"

She rolls her eyes and swirls the wine in her glass. "About his affairs? Apparently he's had loads of them. Derry always takes him back. Apparently she says it's just the way he's built, can you believe that?"

Tom looks genuinely confused. "*Clive* has affairs?"

She laughs, flicks her long buttery hair across her shoulder. "Oh, Tom."

His eyebrows lift in surprise. "He's never mentioned it."

He looks cute when he's befuddled. "*Never?*"

"No. I mean, guys don't tend to . . . share the way women do."

"Bollocks. He's got to have said something . . ."

". . . I mean, we'll pass comment on whether we find someone attractive, but that's hardly the same, is it?"

"You tell me."

He catches her eye and her meaning at once. "I didn't mean . . . Look, Clive has never mentioned anything like this to me. But some blokes do that, don't they?"

She's struggling to follow him. "Do what?"

"Affairs. Look at Matt and Imogen. He's had a few, hasn't he?"

"One, I think."

"What about Shrek and Fiona?"

"*Who?*"

He grins. "You know who I mean."

She laughs. "What, Chris and Anoushka?"

"Yeah."

"He so does not look like Shrek."

"Yes, he does. That's how you knew who I was talking about."

She covers her face with her hands. "Oh, blimey, I can't unsee that now. He has the ears and everything."

"Didn't he go off with one of her colleagues for a bit?"

"I think they're back together now . . ."

"They've had problems for years, though."

She imagines Anoushka as a cartoon character with the voice of Cameron Diaz. Tom's right—she looks exactly like Fiona.

Tom's trying to picture Clive cheating on Derry. They seem pretty happy, though he imagines Clive would be hell to live with. "Maybe it was a long time ago. I mean with Clive and Derry."

It's Aurelia's turn to look surprised. "Oh, OK. *That* makes it all right, does it? The passing of time . . ."

"Well. Perhaps they've put it behind them. They're trying for a baby now."

"Tom, are you saying that it's fine to screw around? Is that your stance on it?"

"I'm saying that every marriage is different. Some couples are fine with the odd indiscretion here and there . . ."

"Indiscretion?"

He falls silent, afraid to say anything else that will land him in hot water. He feels as though she's trying to trick him, that she's deliberately misinterpreting him. He's never been great with expressing himself. He often wonders if he's got some form of dyslexia, the kind that affects speech. For him, language is another form of measurement, not an art. Space, structure, light and shadow—architecture is both art *and* language. At dinner parties Aurelia occasionally likes to bring up the fact that Tom has never once written her a love letter. Not once. Even his text messages are dry, to the point, devoid of kisses, emojis, emotion. They're like chalk and cheese, she's said more than once. He can't deny it.

"You know I would never . . ." he begins, reaching out to take her hand. He can sense her insecurities rippling all over her. She feels hideous after the birth. She comments often on her "disgusting" stomach, surveying her body in the mirror with disdain. He doesn't understand it. She's compared herself to Derry, grabbing her love handles every time she gets undressed, announcing she's "got muffin top," like it's a virus. Why can't she see how sexy she is? He's not completely convinced that she doesn't. She *must* know she's gorgeous. Yes, her stomach resembles an enormous croissant, but she's just had a baby! The last time he said this aloud she burst into tears, and he's been afraid to compliment her ever since.

"I love you," he says. It's the simplest, safest way he can convey his feelings for her. A thousand words are wrapped up in those three. Apologies, promises, wishes, erotic utterances—they're all present in this simple phrase, a three-runged ladder to his heart.

She lifts her wet eyes to his.

"I love you, too."

That night she dreams of when the house is completely finished, of sitting by a roaring fire overlooking the sweeping vista of the fjord, the waterfalls, the city in the distance where her grandparents lived. Her mind leaps forward across all the summers that she'll bring the girls out here. She'll set up a telescope so they can spot snow geese chevroning the skies and sea eagles pivoting above prey. Gaia will have her own gallery wall for all her sketches and memory boxes of leaves and forest treasure, and perhaps she, too, will have a gallery. A studio, even, filled with new work.

But none of this will ever happen. In just seven weeks' time Aurelia will be dead, and the house they are building will be a carcass of splintered wood sprawling across the forest.

22

it didn't add up

Tom killed his wife. I was sure of it.

I spent the next couple of nights tentatively reading the diary, entry after entry, becoming more afraid with each one. During the day, I'd be counting aloud while the girls put a hundred raisins in a box, made octagons and rhomboids with straws, or transformed twigs into paintbrushes by tying pine needles to the end of them. By night, I'd be reading the poignant last words of their dead mother recounting how their father was beating her to a pulp.

When I finished all the entries I set down the diary with trembling hands. I got up and walked to my suitcase, which was leaning against the wardrobe, and took out my phone. I knew my number had been cut off some time ago—I probably owed the network a fortune in fines—but I was connected to the Wi-Fi, and sometimes I charged the phone just so I could search YouTube tutorials on Montessori activities for Gaia and Coco. And also Gaia liked to watch kids' programs on Netflix. Only a few programs worked over here, but I was still able to log in to David's Netflix account, and I'll admit to getting a little bit of satisfaction out of still being able to watch stuff that he was paying for. Gaia's TV was limited to weekends, but the cartoons she watched on Netflix were sweet, and often we had a good discussion about the story afterward, so I didn't see the harm. Anyway, the point was that I could still make calls via Wi-Fi. I could call Meg and ask her advice. *So I've just found out that my employer was beating his wife before she died. He probably murdered her. What should I do?*

I should probably just skip that part. I would ring Meg and calmly explain that I legit needed help. I had no way to get back to civilization, and now my life was in danger.

But then I remembered that Meg had yet to call to see how I was doing. I had no voice mails or missed calls. Nobody cared to see how I was, so even if I stated the trouble I was in, it was unlikely they'd do anything about it.

I pulled up my laptop and did some searching online. I typed "Tom Faraday Architect Murder" into the search bar. Fifty-three thousand links to Tom's architecture practice appeared. There were articles about buildings he'd designed, an alumni web page set up by Glasgow School of Art, and some photographs of him and Clive at black-tie events, grinning and holding a glass award. A Facebook memorial page had been set up for Aurelia. Photographs showed her at various stages of her life—as a child, wearing brown cord dungarees, her hair in pigtails. School photographs through her teens, travel photographs in San Francisco, Egypt, Peru, image after image of her with Tom and the girls.

It was striking how different he looked—he was twenty pounds heavier, his hair had less gray in it, and he looked so much happier. I scrolled through ten Google pages and came across some news reports about her death.

Tragic suicide of mum in Norway

Architect's wife found dead in fjord

I skimmed news reports and the comments on the memorial page, but there was nothing to suggest Tom was implicated in her death. The prevailing narrative was very much that she had suffered on and off with mental illness and had finally lost "her battle." Buried in Google Images were a couple of snapshots posted on social media of Tom at the funeral. I had to zoom in to check it was him. He looked absolutely crushed.

I glanced back at the diary. It lay open on my bed, the contents screaming out in blue biro. *He slammed my face into a wall . . . I'm still bleeding . . .*

I couldn't believe it. This man, who looked every bit the doting husband and devastated widower, had done these sickening things. He had strangled, kicked, and punched his wife, and he had done so straight after Coco's birth, by the sound of things. I looked at the images of her and Tom together and tried hard to see the fault lines. The woman on the pages was terrified. She was confiding in her diary because she had nowhere else to turn. And yet the woman in the photographs was happy, confident, loved.

It just didn't add up.

I remembered what Derry had said about Maren being obsessed with Aurelia. And the newspaper clippings I'd found about someone called Ingrid Olsen who looked identical to Aurelia. I typed "Ingrid Olsen" in the search bar. About a million results came up, but after a good long rummage I figured that none of them related to the murdered girl in the newspaper clippings. The clippings dated back to 1983—before I was born.

That didn't add up either, but the presence of the diary in my room reminded me of the most urgent issue—Tom was a violent, bullying man. Aurelia had feared for her life, and she had died. And really, I should have known better than to think Tom was all he seemed. I had the misfortune to know that, more often than not, relationships were institutions of abuse, betrayal, and occasionally torture, yet somehow I still held on to the hope that somewhere there existed a family who treated each other with actual kindness, respect, and love. I needed so badly to know it was possible, and it was crushing to consider that maybe it just wasn't.

Coco's screams brought me back to the present with a jolt. I had been so absorbed in the diary that I'd forgotten to sterilize the bottles. "All right, Coco," I murmured, letting her know her milk was on its way. "I'm here."

And as I said those words, I knew what I had to do.

I couldn't just leave. I had to protect Gaia and Coco.

As I tiptoed along the landing I saw a mouse dart across the floor, but I didn't care. As far as I was concerned it was earning its right to roam the house by not having already frozen to death. I raced toward the kitchen, reaching for the light switch. Nothing. The kitchen remained gray-dark, the windows all steamed up. I tried again, and again. And then movement by the window caught my eye.

A woman, standing with her back to me. Both arms by her sides. A long dress to her ankles.

Her feet weren't touching the ground.

I opened my mouth to scream.

She was hovering. *Hovering.*

No, no, no. I was hallucinating again. I had been doing so well! No hallucinations for weeks. *She is not there,* I told my brain, but my eyes and my wildly clanging heart said otherwise. She had long dark hair, flat and damp as though she'd just come in from the rain. She was wearing some kind of jacket in a rough material, like sackcloth, and beneath it I could see a dark gray dress to her ankles. Her feet were very swollen, like blue loaves. Maybe that was why she was hovering. It looked like it'd be quite painful to put any weight on feet as swollen as that.

But none of these details mattered, and my racing heartbeat didn't matter, because I was merely having a panic attack and my brain was compensating for the lack of a solid reason for said panic attack by configuring a scary image. Well, I would deal with this right now. Once, I had turned to the chest of drawers when it called me a slut and told it to shut up. And it did. It never spoke again. So I squeezed my eyes closed and stood there with my hands making fists and repeated my mantra.

"You are not there," I hissed. "You are not there. You are a figment of my imagination. When I open my eyes you will be gone."

I opened my eyes.

But she—or it—was right there, just inches from my face. I staggered backward, gasping, terror wringing all the air from my lungs. She was more creature than human. Her skin was purple and mottled, her hair was covered in slimy leaves and weeds, and I could see the black bodies of beetles wriggling in the tangles. Her teeth were black, piranha-like fangs in gray gums. But worst of all were her eyes—they were black and bulbous as a frog's, so dark they looked like holes.

I fell to the ground, shaking and sobbing. When I looked again the light was on, and the woman was gone. I was curled up in the fetal position and trembling all over, the sight of that horrible face emblazoned on my mind. Someone said, "Sophie," and I gave a loud shriek, jerking away from the hand that was stretched out to me. But then I saw a flash of blonde hair, and a small, worried face.

It was Gaia, and she was bent over me, asking if I was all right.

I tried to adult, but right then I was mired in deepest primal terror, so instead of dusting myself off with a beaming Mary Poppins smile and assuring my charge that I was quite fine, darling, and let us have some milk and cookies before bedtime, I pressed my face into my hands and sobbed my heart out.

Gaia wrapped her arms around me and kissed my head.

"It's OK," Gaia whispered. "I saw her, too."

23

someone else knows

NOW

I took Gaia straight up to my bed. I knew there was no way of getting her to sleep on her own after what had just happened, and to be honest, *I* didn't want to sleep alone. I tried to wake Coco, but she was fast asleep and determined to remain that way, so I turned on the video baby camera and brought the monitor into my room. Then I locked the door and barricaded it with the chest of drawers.

I was hyperalert and rigid with terror, my eyes locked on the shadows outside my bedroom window. I tried to wrestle the scene in the kitchen into some kind of sense. I had seen this woman a few times now, and if Gaia had seen her, too, then I wasn't hallucinating. But that didn't necessarily mean she was a shade from the Underworld, sent to torment us for the wrongs of our fathers. No, it meant that quite possibly she was some drifter who was sleeping underneath the house, along with the thousand or so insects and rodents that preferred the warm spots between the house and its foundations to the forest. I didn't blame them. And I'd overheard Tom go on about something called "right to roam," which was a big deal in Norway and meant that he couldn't stick a Private Property sign anywhere on the site. He got *really* annoyed about that.

Of course, none of this rationale explained the state of the woman's face, but it was dark—maybe I hadn't seen properly. Either way, I was going to protect these girls. That was my mission, and I had chosen to accept it.

All of this kind of reasoning helped me stop convulsing with fear, but didn't make me sleepy in the least, so I picked up my laptop and began to work on my novel.

"What are you doing?" Gaia said after a few moments, disturbed by the light of my screen.

I looked up from my laptop and tried to find an answer that would persuade her to go back to bed, fast. My brain wasn't working, so she took my openmouthed silence as a signal to skip across the room and peer into my laptop screen.

"Are you sending an e-mail?" she asked, "About the Sad Lady?"

Her face was fixed in an earnest, utterly fearless expression. She meant the woman we'd both seen.

A deep sigh. "Why do you think she likes our house so much?"

"Maybe it was her house," I said without thinking. Then, remembering that Gaia was only six and I should probably not scare her any further than she already was: "I think we've just been drawing too many scary pictures lately. There is no such thing as Sad Ladies or ghosts or anything like that, all right?",

Gaia gave me a flat stare. "You know full well she was there. In our kitchen. I've seen her *loads* of times."

My face fell. "You have?"

She nodded. "And Mumma saw her, too." A thought drifted into her head. "Do you think she scared Mumma so much that she ran away?"

I pulled her into a tight hug and rubbed her back. "I don't think so, Gaia. I think sometimes people die and it's just very sad."

She was crying now. "Why did Mumma die?"

"I don't know, darling. I'm just so sorry that she did."

Neither of us was able to sleep. The house groaned and whined with its usual restlessness, like someone tossing and turning to get comfortable. I listened rigidly for any sounds in the kitchen, though given that the Sad Lady hovered I doubted she'd make much noise.

My eyes fell on the red leather diary on the floor, peeking out from under the bed. Gaia had to have seen something. She had to have witnessed those atrocious scenes.

But how did I go about asking her if her father was beating up her mother without actually saying the words?

"Were Daddy and Mummy happy?" I said, as lightly as I could.

"What do you mean, happy? Happy like rainbows?"

"I mean . . . did Daddy ever hurt Mummy?" I held my breath as she took this in. Had I gone too far? *No,* I thought. This was important. The diary proved that there was violence in the home. Gaia would have seen *something.*

She looked confused. "*Hurt* Mumma? What do you mean?"

I opened my mouth to elaborate, but the look on her face made the words shrivel and die in my throat. She was so little, so innocent. And perhaps she *had* seen violent scenes, but had repressed them. I knew people did that. I had done it. And then one day they all came back like quicksand.

It would be a long while before I could fall to sleep. My mind churned with thoughts of the woman I'd seen. Of Tom, so crestfallen at Aurelia's funeral. Of the diary.

I came back to the fact that the diary didn't end up in my room by itself. Someone had put it there.

Someone wanted me to know that Tom had been beating Aurelia.

the drill

NOW

The real work begins today—the drill has arrived.

Two days ago Tom managed to resolve the issue pointed out by Clive about time and money in the same moment as he had faced an entirely new challenge. This one had the potential to stall the build for the foreseeable future, if not scupper his designs entirely: how to get the drill delivered. It was pretty hefty, coming as it did with a rig. The snow had cut off the road through the trees and a helicopter was out of their budget. In the end, it was Dag who saved the day—he had a friend with a boat out in Ålesund. He could pick up the drill and deliver it for a bit of petrol money. They'd still have to haul the drill up the cliff from the base of the fjord, but that was small potatoes compared to getting a helicopter. For the first time Tom feels excited about this build, as though he's stepping out of the black pit of mourning and into some lighter section of the tunnel. Dag and Erik are legends, the pair of them. They are invested in this house, know what it means to him. They *get* it.

The night the boat arrives, fog has enveloped the fjord. Tom stands on the shoreline of the fjord, shivering and clammy. He's only ten feet from the cliff and yet he can't see it. It's completely swallowed up by thick, pearly mist. The boat appears first as a single glow in the gloom, like a steamer arriving up the Thames in Victorian London.

"Good to see you, mate," he tells Dag, who's standing on the topside.

"G-good to see you, too. Now the f-fun begins."

It takes them three hours of solid graft to haul the drill up the cliff. On a clear night it would be a bit of a challenge; on a night as foggy as this one, when all their headlamps merely bounce off the mist and one man can't see another just two rungs above, it feels like the elements are combining against them. Tom is sweating buckets from sheer stress alone, never mind the exertion of hefting the drill up a frigging cliff. Clive has mysteriously made himself scarce for the night. Derry needed to be somewhere in the city, apparently. But he has Erik and Dag here, and a dozen of their friends who are giving of their time to help out a widower with his build.

He could cry when they reach the top. It's a victory in itself, even though there is so much more of the house to build. So much yet that could go wrong. But the new Tom, the one who's being forged in the flames of grief and single parenthood and a prevailing fear that he is screwing up his daughters, decides that the only reality is now. No more talk of *yet*. Celebrate the victories when they come.

And so, when the drill reaches the top he pulls twelve bottles of vintage Scotch from a case and hands one out to each of the men for their efforts.

Never has a man been more warmly thanked.

Dag starts early the following day. Despite the late night he's back on-site just after dawn, up and raring to go. He's excited about the drill, mostly because it's a pretty mean piece of equipment and he saw the look on Jakob's face when they collected it in Ålesund. And when he told Jakob what the drill was for, another look of respect. He, Dag Lykken, was going to be the one to personally drill the frame for the lift of this incredible house, designed by none other than Tom Faraday. He can't wait to tell his professors at university this news. He would be sure to take a few selfies with the drill for his Facebook profile, hoping Eva will see.

"Hey, hey, D-D-Dad?" he calls out to his father, who is busy hauling iron girders with two other workers toward the cliff edge for the second tier of the house. "Take a photo of me, will you?"

"Take it yourself," Erik grunts back.

Dag needs both hands to operate the drill. The photo can wait. He's making good progress. Another man, a Swedish guy named Nils, is checking to make sure Dag is drilling in the right spot. He's too much, this guy Nils. He keeps insisting on checking the spot every five seconds, even though they lined up the drill first thing and it's not like it can move easily. He's making Dag nervous. Eventually he gets called away to do another job and Dag breathes a sigh of relief.

Ten feet down. Another four feet to go and he can start on the next area. There are four in total. He glances around to check none of the men are looking before setting his camera on a slab of concrete and hitting the timer. He poses with the drill, giving a big cheesy grin. The photograph sucks. He'll do another. This time he doesn't look up but makes sure he flexes his muscles—the idea is that he's too serious about the job to look up for a picture, and he's been captured in the moment, not taking something as contrived as a selfie.

The photo is crap. It's kind of blurry, and is he really that thin? He needs to put on some weight, build some muscle.

He tries again. This time he lays the camera on the ground, angling it up so he looks bulkier. He waits. No sound from the camera. The timer must have been knocked off. He lets go of the drill handle. In the moment that he reaches down for the camera, the rod of the drill stalls deep in the rock, sending the handle shooting upward and zeroing in on the side of his head with enough force to lift him off his feet and into the air.

The last thing he knows once he's hit the ground is that the camera has gone off. Blood begins to swamp his ears and pool around his neck. Right before he passes out he wonders if this will make a cool shot or if it'll just be too gross.

The helicopter takes a long time to arrive. Twenty minutes from the call. Too long. Dag is unconscious and deathly white. He keeps fitting. He has lost a lot of blood. Erik is leaning over him, shouting and sobbing. Maren produces a first aid kit and bandages the head wound, but it's clear to all of them that this is a life-threatening injury.

Even when they arrive at the hospital, he has not woken up.

Tom sits in the hospital waiting area holding a cup of water that he has not touched in fifteen minutes. He feels as though he's in a trance. His clothes and hands are still covered in Dag's blood. Erik is pacing the corridor slowly, his hands in his pockets, a man resigned to the whims of fate. Dag is in surgery. Erik greets each doctor with the courtesy and patience of a man who expects his child to survive this, but Tom saw the nurses' faces when they pulled Dag from the helicopter. He doesn't expect Dag to last the night.

This is his fault. If he'd used explosives like Clive said, they wouldn't be in this predicament. In this purgatory. No. Wrong to think of oneself that way. His suffering is nothing. Dag is a boy. He deserves to be at a nightclub right now, checking out girls—or boys, whichever takes his preference—not lying on a table with someone sawing into his brain. His life hanging by a thread. Even if—*if*—he survives this, what if the injuries leave him with life-changing disabilities? Tom is in torment. He wonders what is worse—experiencing your own child going through something like this or watching another parent suffer, knowing that you alone have caused their child to go through this?

A nurse enters the corridor. Erik spins around, expecting news. They speak in low voices, and in Norwegian. Tom rises to his feet. If the news is bad, he has to be there for Erik. If the news is good, he wants to be there, too. He realizes his notion of what constitutes good and bad news has radically altered in the last twenty-four hours. He would sell his soul right now for Dag to make a full recovery. Literally sell his soul, like Faust. He takes a step toward the nurse, studies Erik's face. He looks crestfallen. Tom feels as though his feet are mired in concrete. *Please, God. Please . . . No . . .*

The nurse approaches. "He is still in surgery," she says. "Maybe an hour."

He swallows that down, staggers back to his seat. He wants to say something to Erik, but he has resumed his pacing, both arms behind his back, and occasionally he says something to himself. Tom suspects he is praying.

Tom thinks of his own father. How lucky Dag is to have a father like Erik. He can well imagine what his own father would be doing right now, if Tom were in Dag's place. He wouldn't even be in the hospital. Tom isn't an ethical vegan or a dedicated environmental architect because he wishes to atone for his father's sins. It's much more selfish than that. So terrified is he of being anything like his father, Giles Cornelius Faraday, that he has forced himself to become his opposite. Where Giles is avaricious, Tom is pointedly frugal. Giles is overbearing, so Tom is unimposing. Fashion sense, personal hygiene, even parenting styles have all been carefully observed and analyzed as to how they can be subverted, and yet the exercise has brought Tom shame. Tom recognizes that, ironically, this lifelong examination of his father in order to be nothing like him has defined him. Even now, at forty-three years old, Project Nothing Like Giles is too much a part of his life, an anxiety he should have long outgrown. But it is what it is.

Dag's injuries could have been avoided. No; *should* have been avoided. Tom knew, right when they were hauling that damn drill up the cliff in the densest fog he'd ever known, that the drill was a bad idea. Clive was right: he has taken his principles too far. Principles are great; people staying alive is much better.

He makes a pact, there and then, with Mother Nature, that he'll abandon the project entirely if she lets Dag live. He'll put down his tools and go home.

And just then, right as he's holding his head in his hands and whispering to Mother Nature, the doors open. A doctor appears, consults with Erik. A moment later Erik falls to his knees.

Tom rushes forward and catches him as he sinks to the ground, weeping.

the turning point

NOW

I told him he'd kill someone if he carried on like this. And what happened? He almost killed someone."

I watched as Clive poured himself a large whisky, and by *large* I mean half a pint.

"Drink, Sophie?" he said.

I shook my head. He was acting a little unhinged.

"I'll pour you one anyway," he said, pouring me my own half-pint. "We all need a drink after what happened today. Even the babies." He looked up. "I'm kidding."

I sat down beside Maren. She was trembling and openly smoking in the kitchen, which I'd never seen her do, but after what happened with Dag I could well understand.

"Are you all right?" I said. She nodded but didn't meet my eye.

"Is Dag going to be OK?" I asked in a mousy voice.

Clive rested his hands on the back of the chair, still too agitated to sit down. He gave a faint nod. "He made it through surgery. But I'd say he's light-years from OK."

The chaos of the afternoon had sent an electrical charge

through the house and through the woods. First the shouting, then everyone running in and out of the house. I came downstairs to find blood all over the kitchen floor. Then the helicopter came. Amidst all of this I'd been unable to prevent Gaia from seeing the blood smeared across the floor. I mopped it up and tried to convince her it was paint, but she still caught wind of Dag being taken to the hospital. She had met Dag. Apparently he had taught her a couple of tricks and she had a soft spot for him, as had Aurelia. Gaia was devastated to know he was injured and I had to lie to her and say he was fine, that it was just a cut.

Even though I hadn't witnessed the accident I couldn't stop shaking. I learned from Clive that Dag had had an accident with the drill. He had momentarily taken his hands off the handle and the thing had shot upward, hitting his head and knocking him into the air. The force was equivalent to being slammed by a small car. But apparently no one knew why the drill had done that. It had all kinds of safety devices to stop it from moving, and Clive had had a heated discussion down the phone with someone about faulty equipment.

"I'm suing, do you hear me?" he'd shouted, loud enough to be heard all the way in Oslo. "Suing!"

For my part, I couldn't stop thinking about what Maren had said about Mother Nature warning Tom. *He should have taken the hint. But he didn't, and Aurelia died.* I wouldn't say I'm ordinarily the sort of person who goes in for curses and folklore, but given that I'd recently seen someone floating in the air with holes for eyes before vanishing into thin air, the boundaries of my disbelief were being somewhat permeated. It seemed that here, in this house, anything was possible.

Tom came home the next day. He looked like a desert prophet, his clothes still covered in bloodstains, his hair dirty, and his breath foul.

"You should go to bed," I heard Maren tell him, but he shook his head.

"It's almost Christmas," he said, as if that explained why he couldn't go to bed.

He knocked on the door of my bedroom a while later, still bloodstained and filthy, and asked if he could have a word. I eyed the spot where I'd hidden the diary—beneath a loose floorboard— and said of course. The girls were asleep by this point and I'd been chipping away at my novel. Alexa was still being held hostage in the house in the woods but had discovered an ingenious way of digging an escape route without anyone noticing.

"I'm taking the girls away for Christmas," he said in a hoarse voice. "Oslo. Then a ferry to the Arctic Circle. Would you like to come?"

I nodded. I was thinking that I would *need* to come more than anything else, given how incapable he looked right then of caring for two small children. And there was the small matter of the contents of the diary, and the fact that I needed to protect the girls.

"Great," he said. A flicker of a smile. "We leave in two days."

The girls were excited, or at least Gaia was, and as ever Coco copied Gaia's excitement, clapping her hands and shouting "Slo! Slo! Ya-ya!"

Clive and Derry had decided to spend Christmas with friends in Ålesund. Maren said she would stay at Granhus, which I thought was kind of sad, and also scary—not only would she be spending Christmas alone, but she would be in Granhus, where floating women and trespassing elk seemed commonplace. But if there was anyone who had proved to be up to the task of dealing with the bizarre, it was Maren. I'd caught wind of how calm she'd remained when the drill struck Dag. "He had a hole in his skull the size of a fist," one of the men told Clive. "Pouring blood. I could see bone and brain. She put her bare hand on the flap of bone and pushed it back in place, wrapping the bandage around with the other." I worked up the courage to tell her about Dora, deflecting her initial shock by quickly asking if she would mind feeding her while we were gone. Astonishingly, Maren was quite sympathetic to the idea of a rescue bird concealed in the play-room, or perhaps she was just still in shock at my deviousness. Either way, she agreed to care for her, and off we went.

Oslo was magical. We visited the Viking museum, where I was delighted to find an actual ship from AD 800 sitting right there in the gallery. Gaia was fascinated to learn about the dead Viking queen being buried in the ship with cooking utensils and horses (also dead), and that she was buried not in a coffin but neatly tucked into her favorite bed. After that, we got on a train and headed to Bergen, where we caught the Hurtigruten ferry. It was more of a cruise ship than a ferry, with comfortable plush suites, viewing decks, and amazing food. The girls and I spent all our time staring out of the windows at the sea eagles we'd see drifting over the snowcapped mountains that lay on either side of the ship, waving at other boats as they passed by, or attending lectures about trolls and fjords. A few days later, we crossed the Arctic Circle and arrived at Tromsø, where Tom had rented an apartment.

I saw Tom relax the farther north we went. He had been on the phone to Erik and Clive every day, getting updates about Dag, who was now conscious, and the doctors were over the moon with how the surgery went. I was glad to hear this. For a while it looked as though he might not make it at all. But beyond these phone calls, I noticed Tom didn't seem so glued to his phone. He ignored calls if they weren't from Erik or Clive. He spent his evenings reading, or standing at the balcony with a cigarette, staring out at the mountains crowning the city. Occasionally he'd sit down with Gaia and help her improve her drawings. I found he had no notion of preparing Christmas dinner, so I improvised. What was intended to be a sophisticated mushroom and lentil nut roast with caramelized onion turned into an unguent compost with an aftertaste of peanuts. When Coco gagged after a few mouthfuls I replaced it hastily with bowls of cornflakes with almond milk.

"Merry Christmas," Tom said, pouring himself a beer to accompany said cornflakes.

"I feel like Tiny Tim," Gaia observed happily.

I was still wary of Tom, particularly about being alone with him. There was an awkward moment when someone on the train thought we were husband and wife. In Bergen, I spotted some police officers and the thought crossed my mind of rushing up to them and trying to tell them about what I'd read in the diary. But who would believe me? I was just the nanny, and a false one at that. Tom was a highly regarded, internationally recognized architect.

And something about his manner caught me off guard. For instance, on Christmas Eve, he took me aside and handed me an envelope. "Go get your family some presents," he said. I looked from the envelope to him with confusion. He seemed embarrassed. "It was very good of you to stay with the girls over Christmas. I appreciate it enormously. You're the best nanny we've ever had." His eyes were glistening with tears. A head cold, I thought, until his voice broke. "I really appreciate what you've done, and so I'd really like it if you'd accept this and go get some presents for your family. Please, I insist."

I went out to the shops with the envelope. I had no one to buy for. Not a single person. No one had e-mailed me to see how I was. No one had called. The only people I really wanted to buy for were the children I was with right then—well, not *right* then, but at that moment in my life. I saw a toy shop. They had sketchpads and an art set, and an orange octopus—not a real one, a soft toy—with a smiley face and surprisingly realistic tentacles. I bought them both and had them gift-wrapped for the girls.

On Christmas Day, Coco took her first steps. "Ma-ma Ya-ya!" she shouted—she had started to alternate between "Ma-ma" and "Ya-ya" despite my constant correction ("It's Soh . . . fee!")—holding her arms out to me and planting one little leg after the other. I held out my arms to her and she took six wobbly steps. I clapped my hands and turned to see Tom holding his head in his hands on the sofa. He was weeping at the sight of Coco walking, his shoulders legit going up and down. When she did it again he recovered his composure and got down on all fours, padding after her around the room until she collapsed into fits of giggles. After a few moments she squirmed out of his arms to practice walking some more, and he turned to me with a beaming smile. "Thank you," he said, as if I'd engineered the timing of her first steps just for him.

Later, when the girls had gone to bed, I noticed Tom was drunk. He staggered up to me, wineglass in hand, and said, "You're a great nanny, Sophie," with more warmth in his voice than I could remember encountering the whole time I'd worked for him. Also his words were very slurred, so all the warmth was just the wine. Still, he said: "Perhaps when we get back to London you can continue nannying for us. I mean, of course you might already have something lined up . . ."

"No, no!" I said hastily. "I would love that."

Another radiant, completely trashed smile. "I'll drink to that."

He tried to pour me a glass of wine and I hesitated—alcohol has always affected me more than the next person, and I'd seen it transform relatively sensible adults into fist-throwing Neander-thals more times than I cared to remember.

"I'll stick to water," I told him.

He shrugged. "'K."

I filled a glass, and we toasted.

"To . . . surviving," he said.

"To thriving," I said.

26

i saw her swimming

Gaia is dreaming about the last time she saw her mumma. It's a memory-fantasy mash-up, because there are characters from her favorite Netflix shows, and Coco is there, too, shouting "Ya-ya," and Maren keeps bursting out of a cupboard shouting Norwegian verbs that she has to repeat. *Kjenner! Leser! Løper!*

In the dream Gaia sees Mumma sitting on the edge of her bed, nodding off after reading a story. Poor Mumma, Gaia thinks. She's always so tired these days, and Gaia is tired, too, but she's glad she has company, as she hates this house. It has a bad feeling inside it, and although she's tried to tell Mumma this she suspects Mumma already knows. Maybe they'll go home soon. Daddy's new house got destroyed so that means they'll be going home soon.

And in the memory, she feels Mumma move off the bed. She opens her eyes just a little and sees Mumma stand up and look out of the window. It's must be morning, because Mumma's face is lit up and she looks worried. Gaia is still so sleepy. She mumbles something to Mumma, but she doesn't respond.

Next thing Gaia knows is her mumma is gone, and she knows from the look on her face and from the language without words that exists between them that her mumma has seen something outside, something very strange and concerning. Her mumma has gone out to check. Gaia's still floating in that warm dreamspace of sleepiness and it's much too early to get up because her clock hasn't even made the buzz noise that Mumma told her it has to make before she's allowed to come into her room. This is Mumma's effort to make Gaia sleep in her own bed, even though Gaia much prefers Mumma's bed, which feels as though it's made of swan's feathers and summer clouds. She hears footsteps on the landing and smiles—Mumma's coming back. But the footsteps don't sound like Mumma's, and she raises her head just enough to see someone else go past the bedroom door. It's Derry. Gaia hears the sound of the kitchen door swing shut, then the sound of Derry's feet jogging through the garden.

When Gaia wakes again, it's already morning. Proper morning, with the sun already up and the clock buzzing away. She taps the buzzer down and jumps out of bed. Mumma's not in her own bed. She's not in the playroom. Gaia heads to the kitchen and pulls a chair to the window by the sink. There's a strange mist rolling over the fjord. It looks like ghosts. And somehow, deep in her mind, she knows something is very wrong.

She's upset and frantic and tearful and has no idea why, but she feels like she's trapped in a huge spiderweb and has to break free of a thousand silken threads that bind her. She goes back to her bedroom for Louis and hugs him tight, then sobs and sobs because it's been ages since she saw Mumma, and she wants her back right now.

"Look," Louis says.

She looks down at the floor.

"What do you think it is?" she asks Louis.

250 c. j. cooke

She gets out of bed and looks at the markings. Two muddy curves, like two Cs facing each other, one a normal C and the other a back-to-front C.

"They're hoofprints," Louis tells her. Gaia stares at him, then inspects the hoofprints again. There are more of them in the room leading all the way to the door. She still feels tearful, but now she also feels curious. She remembers the story her mumma told her about the elk coming in the house.

Maybe it's a sign.

The hoofprints continue, big muddy clods all the way down to the kitchen.

"Come on!" she tells Louis as she pulls open the kitchen door.

"You should get a coat," he tells her, but she hasn't got time for that. Mumma wants her to follow her and she hasn't a minute to lose.

Sophie! Sophie! Wake up!"

I sat upright, mumbling about beetles, to find Maren stooped over me, her hair askew and her cardi inside out.

"What time is it?" I asked, checking my watch.

"Gaia's not in her bed," Maren said breathlessly. She'd obviously been running. She leaned on my bed frame, panting. The meaning of her words slowly sank into my brain.

"What do you mean she's not in bed?" I asked. "Where is she?"

"I don't know, I don't know . . ."

"Have you checked the basement?"

"She's not in the *house*. The kitchen door was open . . ."

I shot out of bed as if the mattress had suddenly filled with hot coals.

"Gaia!" I shouted. "Gaia! Come on, now! Where are you?"

Maren did the same. Tom staggered down the stairs, his face blanched. "What's going on?"

"Gaia's not in her room," Maren repeated. "I saw the kitchen door was open so I . . ."

Tom didn't let her finish. He bolted to Gaia's room, shouting her name, while Maren and I searched the rest of the house, just in case. It was snowing outside. I checked the playroom and found everything in place. Gaia's paints and crayons were still in the drawer, her sketchpad unopened.

Maren paused at the door to the basement, throwing me a look.

"Check it," I said, and she pulled back the lock and tugged the door open, flicking on the light before heading down.

"Any sign?" I called after her.

A few seconds later, an answer: "She's not here."

Tom raced outside into the snow. I heard him swear and ran after him. He glanced up at me. "She's been outside."

By his feet, another set of tracks. Small, Gaia-sized footprints, leading away from the house. She wasn't wearing any shoes.

Tom raced off, calling and calling for her. I grabbed my coat and boots and followed suit, tears streaming down my face.

She was gone, nowhere to be seen, and for every second that she spent outside the house, her life was in danger.

And it was entirely my fault.

27

aurelia's diary

Last night was the worst yet. My chest, stomach, and arms are in agony today. I know the bruising will be bad. He apologized over and over and pleaded with me not to leave. "Everything I do is for you," he said. "The house is all for you!" He said he was just under a lot of stress and that he sometimes gets jealous about the new baby. I can understand that. What I don't understand is how rage apparently gets the better of him and yet he manages not to touch my face. All the bruising is covered by clothing. He won't risk anyone asking questions. And yet, you just have to look into my eyes to see the sadness there. What this is doing to me.

He almost hit Gaia last night, which is how it all blew out of proportion. She had done something to his paperwork—drawn on it, I think—and he said he was going upstairs to talk to her about it. To the untrained eye he appeared calm, like any normal father going off to tell his six-year-old not to destroy Daddy's important documents. But I read the air around him, saw the look in his eye and the twitching muscle in his jaw that all indicate when he's about to explode. I can sense it in him, as though something builds and builds and needs release. I'd never seen it around the girls before, but as he started to walk out of the room I suddenly knew what was about to happen. I leaped out of the seat and grabbed his arm. He turned and looked at me as if I'd gone crazy.

"Don't," I said.

"Don't what?"

"You know what," I said. My eyes were blazing. I didn't care what he did to me, and suddenly it occurred to me that I would attack him if I had to. This thought has never crossed my mind because I figured he'd kill me, but protective instincts reared up in me at the thought of what he could do to Gaia, and I didn't care. I was prepared for whatever he meted out on me. I could take it.

"You don't touch her," I hissed in his face. His expression changed from amusement to anger, and I saw the rage in him shift direction, like a fire caught in a new wind. He looked down, then lifted a hand and clamped it around my throat.

And that's when it started.

Is it possible to feel terror and triumph in the same instant? I can tell you yes, it is possible, because with every blow of pain, I felt like I kept him away from Gaia a moment longer, each punch and kick allowing him to empty out all that fire onto me instead of her. I curled up in a ball afterward and wept.

I write everything here because I simply can't breathe a word of this to anyone. To everyone who knows us, we're the perfect couple, and Tom is the perfect husband.

Who would believe me?

28

the suspects

We spent what felt like centuries trawling through the forest, shouting for Gaia. Derry and Clive climbed down the ladder to the bottom of the cliff and starting wading through the fjord in case she had fallen in. When they shouted up I saw Tom's face—he went maggot-pale and seemed to stagger backward. And I knew instantly what he was thinking—that they'd found his daughter drowned in the fjord. Not a year after his wife was found drowned, too.

But they were shouting to signal that there was no sign of her. Maren called the police, and Derry ran up to the road in case she'd wandered that far. Tom and I stumbled through the forest.

"Gaia!" Tom shouted, his voice breaking. "Please, if you're here—answer me! I promise you're not in any trouble."

I spotted a shape that didn't seem to belong to the forest. It was at the base of one of the huge conifer trees. I raced to it, my heart beating so fast I didn't think my legs would make it.

It was Gaia, curled up in a ball at the bottom of the tree. She was unconscious. Her lips were blue, and no wonder—it was below freezing and she was barefoot, dressed only in a nightdress.

I called for Tom and he came racing. He took Gaia from my arms roughly, but I didn't mind. At that moment I thought she was going to die. I clasped my hands to my face and began to weep as he staggered back into the house with her, and when I fell to my knees in the snow I prayed to everything and anything that she would be all right.

The doctor came about an hour later. His bedside manner was cold, and I sensed he was displeased with our household of five adults who hadn't prevented a young child from venturing into the hostile wilderness for several hours. He said she could be treated at home, and prescribed warm compresses, hot soup, and blankets. We were not, he said firmly, to leave her under any circumstances.

Tom lit the fire in the living room, arranging logs and coal and stoking it until it was roaring hot. I said I would sleep next to Gaia on the floor while Tom looked after Coco. Gaia stirred around eight o'clock in the morning. I sat beside her, making sure she was tucked in properly and that she could focus on me. If she wasn't able to focus it was a sign that she was delirious or dehydrated.

"I've lost Louis," she said tearfully. "I don't know where he went. I took him outside and he must have run away." She burst into tears then. "Just like Mumma."

"Do you think you dropped him outside?"

She nodded.

"Well, I can go outside and have a look. He can't have gone far."

This appeased her. I dabbed her tears with a hankie and told her I'd go and look later on.

"You look very sad," she said, once she'd settled back down.

"Well, that might be because I was very worried about you," I said. "You gave me a fright. Do you want to tell me what you were doing running off like that? Hmm?"

"I think . . . I think I was having bad dreams again," she said.

"About what?"

"About Mumma going for a swim."

She had mentioned this swimming business before. It had to be significant. Maren had said that Aurelia killed herself by drowning. As far as I knew, nobody had told Gaia this—the party line was that Mummy had had an accident—but there had to be a connection. She was processing it. "OK. And why do you think Mumma went for a swim?"

She thought about it. "I don't know. She saw something out the window."

"What did she see?"

"I didn't have my glasses on."

Déjà vu. She'd said this before, I was sure. "And then she went out for a swim?"

She nodded.

"There was an elk print in the house, so I think she went outside to give him a bowl of porridge. And maybe he went into the water and she followed."

She was getting more animated and trying to sit up, so I told her to lie back down and keep warm. "You need to rest, Gaia."

She looked sad all of a sudden. "Where's Dora?"

"Dora's in her den, in the playroom," I said. "Shall I go get her?"

She gave a small nod. "Remember not to let Daddy know she's here, OK?"

It was a dangerous thing to still have the bird in the house. She'd grown into some sort of crow, or perhaps raven, with sleek navy-black feathers, round black eyes, and raptor-like claws. I figured it was cruel to keep her in a box all the time so I cordoned off a corner of the playroom with heavy curtains attached to the ceiling and held together with clothes pegs, both to keep her contained and to prevent Tom from seeing her. I propped a big branch against the wall for her to perch on and put bed pads on the floor for all the poop. She was very tame. She even responded to her name, which Gaia loved. She liked being held and stroked, particularly under her chin, and she'd cheekily decided that mashed-up chocolate biscuits were her favorite food. What was it Ibsen said? *A forest bird never wants a cage?* This one did. She had zero intention of flying away. I'd taken her out to the back porch and tried to fling her toward the forest a handful of times, but each time she merely hopped back and followed me into the house with her little gangsta waddle as if to say, *This my crib, yo.*

I went into the playroom, placed Dora in her box, and brought it through. Gaia sat upright and whispered for me to get her some pine nuts. Soft-hearted creature that I am, I obeyed. She put the nuts in her mouth, scooped Dora up in cupped hands, and let her peck the nuts from between her lips.

Side note: I'm aware that this was not very hygienic, and while I'd tried hard to think of a way I might circle this back to some kind of Montessori methodology, I was sure it would be perceived by both Tom and Maren as completely unsanitary, not to mention indulgent, because it was. I tried not to think of what would happen if Tom walked in. But Dora clearly made Gaia feel better. She laughed when she played with her, as did Coco—though Coco was always laughing—and her face looked brighter. In the grand scheme of things, I believed anything that brought a little sunshine back into Gaia's life was to be embraced.

"Look!" she said happily as Dora snuggled beneath Gaia's chin for a snooze. "She *loves* me. I love you, too, Dora girl."

I went out to the woods that night with a flashlight to look for Gaia's teddy, Louis, but there was no sign of him. It was still snowing on and off, great swirling flakes sugaring the branches and outbuildings. I spotted plenty of tracks and scat in the snow, which indicated that we were having quite a few visits from foxes and possibly wolverine. A toy like Louis—bathed as he was in Gaia's scent—would probably be snatched up by a predator and torn to pieces. Poor Gaia.

More and more my mind was trying to understand how the diary had ended up in my bedroom that night. Maren had promised me that my room was a private space and it wouldn't be entered without my permission, even for cleaning. Perhaps Coco had pulled the book off a bookshelf and toddled into the room with it, but this was unlikely, too, given I kept my door closed. Gaia would have told me if she left something in my room, and she wasn't prone to sleepwalking. It had to be one of the other adults. I could rule out Tom, for sure. Clive? I wasn't sure how a diary containing such information about his business partner made him a likely candidate, and Derry was pretty much on the same scale.

That put Maren in the prime spot on the list of suspects. Perhaps she had mistaken the diary for Gaia's logbook, which she had never mentioned since she'd first quizzed me about it. I doubted it—she surely would have recognized the gold lettering on the front, indicating Aurelia's initials. And if she *had* known it was Aurelia's diary, she would have read the contents. But when I spoke to her about Tom she said he was a good man, even though he had sometimes torn strips off her in public. She blamed Clive for persuading him into recommencing the build. So why would she put the diary in my room?

But remember, a voice in my head said—this one sounded like Laurence Olivier, replete with trilled r's—*remember that nobody is what they seem. Consider Tom. And Aurelia, who appears so joyous and grounded in all the photographs. And yet . . .*

I turned back to Google. I searched "Aurelia Faraday" and found an old interview she'd given about one of her photography exhibitions. She titled it *can't see the woods (for the trees)* and it was, she said, all about "perception, blindness, and how we often can't see the truth despite it staring us in the face." Interesting. This was two years before she died. The diary started just after Coco was born, but there were pages ripped out so it's likely she was writing before then. Come to think of it, why *were* there pages ripped out? Who had done that?

The link between the mystery murdered girl, Ingrid Olsen, and Aurelia had to have some kind of meaning, and Google was giving me nothing on that. Maren had said that Aurelia had no siblings, and a follow-up question to Gaia about her aunts and uncles confirmed that she had none on her mother's side. I would have to go into the attic, retrieve the newspaper clippings, and try to type the content into Google Translate. The problem was that if I got caught, I would need some kind of explanation. And I was fast running out of favor.

The next day Tom asked me calmly to have a meeting with him in his office. I felt sick. No one had ever, not ever, asked to have "a quiet word" or "a meeting" without it turning out very badly.

This time was no different.

"I'm not angry," he said calmly, once the door was shut. *Oh, good. Because anytime someone says that, I totally believe it.* "I'm disappointed."

I nodded and looked at the floor.

"Your job is to take care of the children, and that includes making sure they are safe."

I went to speak, but he cut me off.

"It's your responsibility to ensure they aren't able to get out of the house." He looked outside. "If anything like this happens again, I'm afraid I'll have no choice but to seek a replacement. Understood?"

I promised him there wouldn't be a next time. He nodded, stood up. We were done.

29

the discovery

C live was right: the diggers have saved an enormous amount of time. Tom wishes he'd done this sooner. He's even managed to avoid damaging the older trees, despite the roots spreading so wide. The diggers have some kind of new technology that allows the builders to work around the roots. It's impressive. They keep well away from the old site, where the river-infused earth gave way so easily, and from the resurrected river, which has returned to a triumphant zigzag down the hill through the trees and over the lip of the cliff.

Tom stands with a hand in his pocket, the other holding a cup of tea, as the diggers scoop up black clods of earth and dump it to one side. In an hour they've already dug a clean trench fifteen feet deep.

"Good day," a voice says.

He turns to find Erik standing there. He swallows hard. "Erik," he says, placing a hand on his shoulder. "You're here. I thought you'd be at home."

Erik cocks his head, gives a small, modest smile that says, *My job is here.* This is what Tom admires about Norwegians—they're made of the toughest human material. Built to endure both hard weather and hard times with grace. Even Dag has surprised Tom with his resilience. That blow he took should have knocked his head clean off his shoulders, or left him with horrific brain damage. One doctor said he should be a vegetable. Yet he's recovering at home, sending cocky text messages and photos of *his* house plans. The one he'll build for himself once he's well. Tom has promised he'll do all the drilling. It's even become a bit of banter.

"I see things have moved on a little since . . ." Erik says, looking over at the diggers.

"You might say I had a chance to rethink my methods," Tom says, following this up with an awkward laugh. Too soon, he thinks. He clears his throat and shifts his feet. "I see Dag's doing a lot better. His text messages say that, anyway."

Erik nods. "The doctors say he will not be able to go back to university this year."

Tom feels shame sweep across him once more. "That's . . . I'm so sorry. Perhaps . . . once Dag feels able to return, I'll happily pay for the rest of his tuition."

Erik shrugs. "We're in Norway. University is free."

"Right," Tom says, and Erik laughs. Tom joins him. The relief is immense. It's only laughter and yet it feels like winning the lottery. It signifies forgiveness. Erik slaps him on the back.

"Come on," he says. "We have work to do."

Over the next week, he works harder than he's ever worked in his life. His presence on-site wearing a number of hats, at least figuratively—architect, project manager, foreman, runner, concrete mixer, machinery operator—galvanizes his small team of workers. It becomes more of a team effort than ever, and he notices some of the men staying on long after their shift ends. Even Jakob, Dag's friend from Ålesund, shows up, ostensibly to take pictures of the build to send to Dag, but before long he's in a high-vis jacket and hard hat and is helping Erik heft joists down the cliff.

"Cup of tea?"

Tom looks up from the room in the cliff to see Clive standing on the hoist, holding out a flask.

He continues hammering. "Thought you'd gone back to London."

Clive steps inside, looks around. Aurelia's Nest is looking good. Quite spacious, too. They're in the natural rut of the cliff in which Tom has built a large open-plan living space and kitchen out of wood. Even the floor is down, and the frame for the next couple of stories is in place. He can see iron rods poking through the ceiling from where Dag drilled down. Poor kid. Good job he's not suing the company. Tom's a genius to lay on the pally-pal act, keep him sweet. Harder to sue friends.

"London?" he says, setting the flask on the floor. "Hardly. We're in the thick of things, aren't we?"

"Hello, boys," a voice calls. Derry. Tom looks up to see her climb out of the hoist, iPad in hand and black-framed glasses on. She's not wearing workout gear, either—jeans, Uggs, a white cashmere jumper beneath an unzipped padded coat. Her long dark hair is loose beneath the white hard hat. She's in interior designer mode. "Good gracious. This is incredible," she says, ignoring Tom and looking around. "Wowzers. The *size* of it. You'd never have thought it was this big, would you?"

"Certainly not as deep," Clive agrees. "We've made good progress, haven't we, babe?"

"We?" Tom says, his smile not quite concealing the bitterness in his voice. All week he has toiled and slaved to get the build on track. At nights he feels steamrollered, but secretly he's enjoying the physical exertion. Takes his mind off things. But Clive—

where has he been? On the phone, sending e-mails. It can't take a solid week to pay an invoice. Has he even visited Dag?

Clive ignores him. "You here to take measurements?" he asks Derry.

"I think I'll need to rethink my palette," she laughs, glancing around, hand on her hip. "There's much more light than I'd anticipated." She stands by the wooden frame that marks the window, looks up and down. "Is this where the windows are going?"

"That whole wall," Tom says.

"So it'll let in a ton of light into the *front* of the room," Derry says, heading to the back. "But it'll still be slightly darker here."

Tom shakes his head, points up. "We're putting in sun pipes. Count on it being every bit as light as the front of the space."

Derry taps on her iPad. "I'm thinking the walls in here will be mostly timber-clad, but at the back I want a sastrugi effect in a milky plaster over the concrete. Kind of a nod to the polar landscape."

"Sounds good," Tom says. On the iPad she shows him the palette of colors, textures, and key pieces she's put together—milky white, biscuity beige, and Arctic meltwater blue. Cottony textures, clean, unobtrusive furniture handmade by Oslo craftsmen, bespoke ceiling lights, and table lamps made of leftovers from the iron girders. He likes that idea. Anything that can be recycled is good.

After an hour Derry returns to Granhus to begin ordering her fabrics and wallpapers. She's not gone ten minutes when a commotion breaks out on top. Voices shouting. *What now?* Tom thinks. Probably the bloody moose again.

"I'll go check it out," Clive says, stepping onto the hoist. Tom steps out onto the scaffold and cranes his head up, only to duck back under as a stream of something milky pours down. It lands—

splat—on the wooden planks of the scaffolding. It's vomit. One of the workers actually puked over the side of the cliff.

"Clive, mate, send down the hoist!" he screams up, but just then his phone buzzes in his pocket.

"Yes?"

"You might want to come and have a look at this," Clive says.

the murder of ingrid olsen

NOW

I t had taken hours. Typing up the Norwegian newspaper clippings
into Google Translate required a substantial cutting and pasting
of Advanced Symbols for the extra vowels, å, ø, and æ, and for every
little circle I missed out above the letter *a* or line scored through
o, I ended up with a wonky translation. In the end, though, I got
the gist.

The woman in the newspaper cuttings with whom Maren was
so obsessed was Ingrid Olsen, a postgraduate marine biology stu-
dent at the University of Tromsø. On the evening of October 23,
1983, she had been walking home after a night out with friends
when she was dragged into an alley, raped, and murdered by a
single blow to the head. She was twenty-two years old. Having
prided itself on its excellent university, its extremely low crime
rate, and a reputation as "the Paris of the Arctic," the city of
Tromsø was left in shock. Her killer was Anders Dahl, a twenty-
year-old bartender from Bodø. The attack was random, and Anders was not known to have had any kind of relationship with
Ingrid prior to the attack. He was jailed for life.

In other words, all my work was for nothing. There was nothing in the tragic story of Ingrid Olsen to shed any light whatsoever on the diary or on Aurelia's death. Other than the fact that they looked like twins.

"Maren?" I knocked on her bedroom door.

"Yes?"

I walked in to find her by the window, looking down at whatever was outside.

"Is everything all right?" I asked.

"I'm not really sure," she said, her eyes still fixed on the scene at the building site. "There's been a lot of shouting about something or other, but I can't quite see what it is." She turned to me then, as though seeing me for the first time. "Shouldn't you be with Gaia?"

"Derry's with her just now, reading her a story. Coco's asleep. So I've only got a few minutes, but I wanted to ask you something, if that's all right."

She detected the nervousness in my voice. I *was* nervous. I was gearing up to tell her about the diary and ask if she had planted it in my room for me to read. Either way, we needed to do something. I wasn't sure what, but I knew that even if I managed to summon up the courage to call the police, I was going to have a stronger case if Maren spoke to them. She was Norwegian. And she was the housekeeper. She was bound to have seen something. Wasn't that what she had told me previously? That as a housekeeper she saw things she'd prefer not to have seen?

"Come in," Maren said, waving me toward her table. I noticed a new pile of laundry on her bed, and the house had definitely been cleaned over Christmas, so perhaps she was starting to feel a little better about being here, and around Derry. To my knowledge, they still hadn't spoken two words to each other, despite living under the same roof.

She sat down in the other chair and clasped her hands together, her face folded in concern. "Has something happened, Sophie?"

My throat had suddenly got very tight, and the room was swaying. Behind Maren was something I'd not noticed when I sat in this same chair previously, but now I saw what was definitely a framed photograph of Aurelia. *No,* I thought. *It's Ingrid.* Only the mouth gave her away. Smaller than Aurelia's. The woman in the newspaper clipping. The woman who'd been murdered. She looked like she was graduating.

Maren was staring at me. "What was it you wanted to talk to me about?"

I had prepared my line of questioning as a mental flowchart. *Ask her first about Tom and Aurelia. Did she see or hear anything of concern? If yes, proceed to step two. If no, she's probably lying and you need to proceed to step three, which is: ask why she blamed Clive for persuading Tom to come out here.*

But fear was scrambling it all up and rearranging the steps. "Did you rip the pages out of Aurelia's diary?" I asked. *Wrong question,* Laurence Olivier hollered, trilling his r. *That's step six. You've missed five whole steps!*

Maren frowned. "What diary?" she said. *She's lying,* Olivier said, and I started to panic. Why would she lie? If she planted the diary she obviously wanted me to know something. But perhaps she *knew* Tom was beating Aurelia. She had to have known. And either she was troubled by it—or she was guarding his secrets.

"That picture," I said, and she turned to glance at the photograph of Ingrid. *Now* she looked troubled. Horrified, even.

"What about it?" she snapped.

"She looks . . . very like Aurelia."

She got up slowly from the table and walked to the door. Then she opened it.

"Please leave my room," she said quietly.

I took a deep breath and summoned my nerve. "I saw inside the box, Maren. I saw the bracelet. It belonged to Aurelia, didn't it?" I fixed my eyes on her, watching as she took this in. She said nothing, but I saw a twitch of her hand. "What would Tom say if he knew you were stealing again?"

I was prepared to mention that Derry had said Maren was obsessed with Aurelia, but I didn't want to push it too far. It felt unkind.

"I always knew you were hiding something, Sophie," she said. "But I didn't peg you as someone who went snooping in other people's business."

"I didn't peg you as a thief," I threw back, and as soon as I said it, Laurence Olivier spoke in my head. *Superb comeback, old bean.*

But then she closed the door and turned a key in the lock. I watched as she walked slowly back toward the table. Why had she locked the door?

"The woman in the photograph is my sister. Ingrid," she said, glancing at the photograph. "Not Aurelia."

"Your sister?" I said.

"My older sister," she said, sitting down opposite me. She lit a cigarette and shook out the match. Her hand trembled as she withdrew the cigarette from her lips.

"Ingrid Olsen was your sister?"

"Yes."

"Tell me about her."

She looked me over with a little frown.

"We were sixteen months apart. Best friends. Could finish each other's sentences." She blew out a puff of smoke. "And she was murdered. But then, you'll probably already know that, since you've been trawling through my personal things."

"That must have been very hard for you," I said gently. "If you were so close. And she was—"

"She's gone," she said firmly. "Nothing I can do will ever change that. I realize that now."

I tried to figure out what she meant by this. *I realize that now.* Did this realization come from stealing Aurelia's things, or something else?

"It can't be coincidental that she looks so like Aurelia," I said.

She took a long drag on her cigarette and looked past me out the window. "Who knows?" she said. Her pale eyes slid to mine, and my mind raced. Maren could have put the diary in my room in order to make me suspect Tom of killing Aurelia, or driving her to suicide. But Ingrid's likeness to Aurelia could be no coincidence. Did Maren want to distract me from something by putting the diary in my room?

I stood up quickly in my seat to leave, and she stood up just as fast.

"You're not going anywhere," she said.

I sank back down into my seat, my heart pounding. Derry's words rang in my ears. *Maren's devious . . . I'd say Maren locked you in that basement.*

"Did you kill Aurelia?" I whispered.

31

an impossible task

Maren's face darkened. I thought she might actually lift the marble ashtray on the table next to her and hit me. After all, I'd just asked her if she'd murdered Aurelia. And as the silence stretched out in her cold, locked bedroom, I felt I already knew the answer: Maren's beloved sister Ingrid had been raped and murdered. Maren had discovered a look-alike in the form of Aurelia. Perhaps she was jealous that Aurelia was alive and her sister wasn't. Or perhaps her obsession spilled over into an ugly craving, and when it couldn't be satisfied—she snapped.

"Open the door or I'll scream," I said when she didn't answer.

"How dare you," she said then. "How *dare* you come in here and ask me such things! Of course I didn't kill Aurelia!"

She seemed genuinely wounded. "What about the diary?" I asked. "Why did you put it in my room?"

"What diary?" she said, lifting her hands in the air. "I have no idea what you're talking about."

We stared at each other. I was trying to work out whether she was telling the truth and she was looking at me as if I'd sprouted a second head.

"I'm sorry," I found myself saying while studying the shape of my knees. "It's just . . . I found all the newspaper clippings about Ingrid. And Aurelia's things that you'd been keeping in the attic. Derry said you'd been an artist."

She nodded tearfully. "I was."

"Then . . . how come you're working as a cleaner?"

She plucked a hankie from the shelf next to her and dabbed her eyes. "Many years after Ingy died, after the murder trial, I had a nervous breakdown. My marriage broke down. I had to give up my studio. I couldn't paint. I couldn't even stay in Norway. So I moved to London."

"Is that where you met Aurelia?"

She blew her nose. "Yes. I was stunned by the likeness. Completely stunned. And then when I found out her father was from Norway—ha! I was beside myself. It was uncanny. I kind of . . . stalked her for a while. When I found out she required a housekeeper I jumped at the chance." She tapped her cigarette ash into the ashtray and sighed. "I suppose I thought that by serving Aurelia, I was somehow continuing Ingrid's life. The life she should have had."

A tear rolled down her face. I suddenly felt rotten for accusing her of murdering Aurelia. She seemed to be telling the truth.

"And did you?"

"Did I what?"

"Continue Ingrid's life."

She looked at me in shock. "No," she said eventually. "No, I didn't. Couldn't. It was an impossible task."

"Then . . . why did you stay on as Aurelia's housekeeper?"

She thought about this for such a long time I thought she'd

gone into some kind of trance. "I suppose . . . that was for selfish reasons. At first I could pretend, in a way, that Aurelia was Ingrid. It felt good to be close to her. And then, after a while, it was simply good to be needed. It filled a hole, you see. But now you're here, I'm not needed . . ."

"Of course you're needed," I said. "Who would teach Gaia Norwegian? Who would keep the house together?" I probably sounded unconvincing when I mentioned this last bit, but Maren took the point.

She gave another long sigh and stubbed out her cigarette. "I've nowhere else to go. That's the other thing. I've drifted for so long now that I've no choice but to go where life's current takes me."

"You must know that's not true," I said. "You could start painting again."

She gave a hard laugh and clapped a hand to her cheek. "I've not lifted a paintbrush in over a decade. My technique must be horrendous by now." She glanced at one of the paintings above her bed of a naked woman sitting on a stool, one knee drawn up to her chin and her arms wrapped around her calf.

"Is that one of yours?" I asked.

She gave a small nod. "It's a self-portrait. That should give you an inkling of how old the painting is."

The painting was very accomplished. It looked expensive, like something in a museum.

"Can I ask you something?" I said, and she nodded. "Did you really not see any violence between Tom and Aurelia?"

"Violence?"

"I came across something that indicated he had beaten her."

Maren looked puzzled. "That doesn't sound like Tom."

"You're sure?" I said. "So . . . you didn't put the book in my room?"

"What book?" Maren said. She'd risen from her chair and drifted to the self-portrait above her bed, lifting a cloth to wipe off an invisible layer of dust.

"It doesn't matter. Can you unlock the door now?" I asked.

"Oh," she said, turning. "Of course."

32

the crossing

THEN

In six days' time, Aurelia will be dead, but now she sits in her bedroom writing in her diary.

> *I keep losing things and dreaming about where they*
> *are. My emerald earrings have vanished and I'm upset*
> *about it—Mum bought them for my twenty-first—and*
> *last night I dreamed that I knew they were buried in*
> *the ground just outside the house. I dug and dug until*
> *I hit what I thought was earrings, but when I pulled*
> *my hand out of the ground I had two eyeballs rolling*
> *around in my palm.*

"Evening, Aurelia," a voice says.

She looks up and sees Maren there, a bundle of dirty clothes held in her arms instead of in a laundry basket—one of Maren's many quirks. Tom's forever complaining about her. He has a point—she doesn't vacuum properly and often the windows look worse once she's cleaned them than before she started. But she's dedicated, polite, and fiercely loyal. Few housekeepers would have been prepared to come out to Norway like this.

"I didn't mean to disturb your writing," Maren says, turning to leave the room.

"No, no," Aurelia says, closing the red notebook. "It's just a diary. Of sorts. Just where I record some stuff." She smiles, looks down. Maren can see she's upset. "It helps me keep track of what's real and what's just in my head."

Maren turns. "Nothing is *just* in your head. It's all important."

Aurelia gives an "I know, I know" shrug, but Maren can see she's extremely bothered. She has dark marks beneath her eyes, and she's pale, but it's not the outward appearance of her that troubles Maren. After all, she's a new mother. Many women don't exactly look their best in these months. No, it's what Maren can see beneath the surface. She has worked for Aurelia for many years now, and during all that time she has been watching her carefully. Studying, admiring, wishing . . .

Maren sits down on the bed beside her. "Tell me," she says. "Tell me what's wrong."

Aurelia stares at a spot on the floor. Her eyes fill with tears, but she doesn't make to dab them, or to speak. She cannot explain what is happening. It feels as though her heart is breaking, and yet there is no reason for it. She shouldn't feel this way.

"I can hear things, sometimes," she finds herself saying. "In the house."

"What sort of things?" Maren asks gently.

"Voices."

"And what do they say?"

"Nothing that makes sense, really," she says. A tear slides down her cheek and hits the fabric of her skirt. "Sometimes I'll hear someone say my name." She smiles and shakes her head as though that is a ridiculous idea. "I feel different out here."

"Different?" Maren says, studying her. "You mean in Norway, or . . . ?"

"No, no. Just . . . in the woods. Here. In this house. It feels . . ." She shrugs, aware that she sounds daft. Then, in a small voice: "It feels like a different realm. Where boundaries between things are a little less . . . solid."

There's a long pause. Maren chooses her words carefully. "Maybe you need to go back to London for a while. It's not for everyone, Norway."

Aurelia feels herself bristle. Norway is the home of her ancestors, the place she associates with happiness and wild childhood abandon. It has already crossed her mind that she's not cut out for this environment, and she hates that thought.

"No," she snaps, rising to leave. "I'm staying here. Tom needs me . . ."

Maren nods. She can tell Aurelia is agitated, but isn't sure why. She proceeds with caution. "Tell me, is there any particular place in the house that you can hear these voices?"

Aurelia sighs and flicks her long blonde hair over one shoulder. "The basement."

"I see. The reason I ask is because this house . . . it has an extremely old ventilation system, as you'll know. I, too, have heard voices."

Aurelia turns her head, stares Maren straight in the eye. "You have?"

Maren nods, gives a reassuring smile. "Yes. Also in the basement. And sometimes in the kitchen. The vents make a noise. Do you think it could have been that?" She pauses, determined to keep her tone light, inoffensive. "Or something else?"

Aurelia draws a deep breath. Could it be that she's just been hearing the moans of old vents? No, she thinks. No. She has heard the voice of a woman, not the moan of a vent. Certainly the house is noisy. But she has seen things, too. Ghosts, she thinks. A woman in the kitchen, standing with her face to the window. A woman without eyes.

But she doesn't want to admit this. Not now. She feels like she's losing her mind. Ghosts. Ha! She *is* losing her mind.

"Yes," she says finally, not making eye contact. "It must have been the vents."

"You know, my sister had hair like yours," Maren says, reaching out to stroke it. "I used to plait it for her at night. It was to keep it from getting tangled, but the brushstrokes soothed her, helped her sleep." She looks at Aurelia with tenderness. "Would you like me to plait yours?"

Aurelia nods. She realizes how much she has missed her mother in the aftermath of giving birth. Not *her* mother, exactly, with her compulsion to turn every conversation into a tirade of complaints against Aurelia's father, but *a* mother. In the moment of becoming a mother she craved to be mothered, to be handled with tenderness. Her body feels so bruised and battered. As does her mind.

She sits in the chair, her hands folded in her lap and her shoulders rounded, as Maren picks up a flat brush and draws it down Aurelia's crown to the tips of her hair, which lie just beneath the strap of her maternity bra. Maren spends a long time brushing like this, smoothing out the kinks and the knots before beginning to divide the hair in three at the crown and braiding it carefully. Aurelia closes her eyes and enjoys the sensation of touch without anything being wanted in return. It's such an unusual feeling, these days, to be touched without expectation of milk, food, or love. Just to be held, to be cradled and soothed, is a temporary light in all her dark places.

Outside, a storm is breaking, rattling all the doors of Granhus. Rain overwhelms the drainpipes, gushing down the windows in torrents. Tom rushes outside to secure the tarp across Basecamp's incomplete roof, and even as he trudges through muddy flash floods funneling down the hill, he knows water damage is the least of his worries. The ground has turned to a swamp, right where Basecamp is built. A dramatic zigzag of lightning crackles across the sky, lighting up the trees and sending creatures scurrying for shelter. Tom is drenched to the skin, wind pummeling his ribs. His hands shake as his tries to turn on the flashlight on his phone to survey Basecamp's foundations. It is pitch-black, but what he sees makes his jaw drop—the river is rising directly beneath the house, bubbling up around the pilings.

He tries to tell himself that it will be fine, the house is on pilings, the river will pour down over the cliff. The storm will pass and they'll fix the damage. But by morning, Basecamp will be destroyed.

When Aurelia finally falls asleep she plunges into harrowing, vivid scenes that seem more than dreams.

She is standing at the foot of the fjord.

The tidewaters are a silver mirror; the sky is overcast. Mists marble and drift over the fjord. She turns and surveys the black cliffs that stretch all the way to the sky. Pretty white flowers are growing out of the cracks, but it's the stones that interest her enough to bend and collect them in her hands. Velvety blue stones, the color of jewels. An amalgam of stone and moss that forms a new species of pebble. She drops one into her pocket for Gaia. She'll love it. Like her mother, she takes pleasure in nature's gifts. She'll probably name it and create a special bed for it out of cereal boxes and tissue paper.

Just then, a noise makes her look up. A distant rumbling. She moves forward, her bare feet stepping into the cool water. Though the mists make it difficult to see, she knows that the sound is coming from the field directly opposite, a green slope that drifts down to the other side of the fjord. A splash. Her breath catches in her throat. She squints, tries to see through the fog, but she already knows what it is. The thundering hooves of reindeer.

As she wades into the water to get a closer look, the fog thins, and she sees the white and black bodies funneling down the slope toward the water, antlers rising from their heads like a tangle of tree branches against the moth-light.

Already several are in the water, and she wonders whether they've not seen the edge of the land and have fallen in. She glances behind her. Is Tom here? Maybe they can call someone. She's not sure what to do, or what she *can* do. She watches as the view clears, the mists divide, and buttery sunshine funnels through pearly clouds to reveal the scene in its tremendous, mythic spectacle: hundreds, maybe thousands of reindeer charging into the water. Aurelia would almost not believe her own eyes were it not for the ripples that are gathering now around her calves, sent from the cascading herd in front of her. The light strengthens and she lifts a hand to shield her eyes against the sun. Antlers and snouts bob ahead, about a quarter of the way across the fjord. They are swimming. She gives a shout, a laugh, to witness this. Reindeer migrating across bodies of water was something her grandfather Gunnar had told her about, but she'd thought he was making it up. She begins to wade out toward them, her clothes ballooning in the cold water. The meandering causeway of fuzzy, bloodied antlers and white faces, their long, strong legs striding through the water.

It's a long distance from one side of the fjord to the other. She swims out to a small island and wraps her arms around a black boulder, treading water as she watches the line of them zigzag across the fjord. For the most part they swim so close to one another she fears they'll hook antlers and drown each other. The formation begins to curve toward her so that she can make out the steam of their breath rising in the air, the snorts and grunts and splashing and the bobbing white tails, like rabbits. Most of the bulls are gray with black snouts, the females—cows, she remembers, not does—are pure, majestic white, unantlered, and there are calves, too, mostly swimming alongside the cows.

The heads of the herd are almost at the other side. She watches, breathless with a triumph for which she has no words, as the first bull reaches the shore, his tail twitching and his hooves stomping off the wet. The others gather behind, but he does not wait—the path is narrow and leads through the forest, and soon he disappears behind the pines.

The stragglers are cows with young calves. The distance between them and the herd grows by the second, and as she pushes off the boulder to swim closer, she hears a sound, a cry, that is at odds with the majesty of this scene. A child's cry.

Her heart hammering, she sweeps her arms through the water and kicks her legs until she is only feet away from the last of the herd, the two dozen or so calves and cows that stray behind the rest. As one of the cows moves forward she sees something that makes her cry out, that makes her heart almost punch through her chest: Gaia is swimming there, her small blonde head foreign among the animals, her pale face ducking above and beneath the water.

"Mumma!" she calls out. "Mumma, help!"

"Gaia!"

Aurelia's body floods with adrenaline as she surges forward. Already her mind is wheeling calculations. They're about a quarter of a mile from shore, and her energy is ebbing. The water is cold and Gaia will not last long. She'll take her back to the boulder, but when she glances behind to gauge the distance she is horrified to see that the boulder is no longer there. The waters have somehow deepened, and she is much farther from shore than she thought.

She powers forward toward Gaia, seizing her by the hair just as she begins to fall under. She wraps her arms around her and holds her, their wet faces pressed cheek to cheek, both bodies shaking with terror and cold.

"Mumma," Gaia says weakly, and Aurelia urges her to keep kicking her legs, to stay awake, not to fall asleep.

"Please, darling," she says. "I know you want to go to sleep so badly, but you have to try to stay awake, OK? I'll get you that dollhouse you wanted. You have to try, Gaia. Please!"

Gaia gives a faint murmur in response and wraps her arms around Aurelia's neck, but her grip loosens, and Aurelia is forced to swim with one arm, using the other to hook Gaia's face up out of the water. She sweeps and sweeps the water, dragging them to the shore, but the mist is thickening again and she can't see where she's going. She's trying desperately to draw on adrenaline and reserves of certainty. If she panics, her energy reserves won't last, and if that happens, it's over.

"Nearly there," she tells Gaia. "Nearly there."

But then, Gaia vanishes. Aurelia looks into the space between her arms, which are encircled in the water as though she's doing ballet. She's standing, too, her feet no longer adrift in the depths but on shale, the water reaching her chest.

"Gaia?" she shouts. Her cries echo off the cliffs. The reindeer are gone. She stares into the jaws of the fjord. "Gaia?"

But there is no Gaia. There is only Aurelia in the fjord. The mists all around watch on, a silent, waiting congregation. And when she wakes, they are in the room with her, portentous, watching, whispering their omen.

33

the discovery

NOW

Tom, Clive, and a handful of the workers stand around the pit of dark clay and look down at what the digger has revealed.

It's a body.

A few of the men cross themselves.

Clive and Tom share a look.

Tom finds he is ambushed by the memory of identifying Aurelia's body in the morgue. His knees buckle, but he manages to lean on the digger and hold it together.

Clive jumps down into the pit, his feet almost landing on the corpse.

"Clive," Tom finds himself saying. They ought not to touch it. More signs of the cross are made as Clive leans over the remains.

Clive can see the body has been in here a long time. The skull is most visible of all, leering up at the men, the jaw tilted forward and the teeth bared. There is some clothing, too, made of dark coarse fabric, stained in places from the earth. He swallows back a mouthful of vomit before taking out his phone to snap a few shots and climbing back up the bank of earth to approach Tom.

"This isn't good," he says. Tom is pale. He shakes his head in response. Clive looks over the workers. They are muttering among themselves in Norwegian.

"I think this is a good time for a lunch break," he calls out to everyone, signaling that they should disperse while he and Tom figure out the next steps. Tom seems to have lost all strength in his arms and legs, and is panting. After a good deal of wondering what's wrong with him, Clive remembers that Aurelia hasn't been dead a year, and that perhaps the sight of the body has proved too much for Tom. He wraps an arm around him and helps him to his feet.

"Let's go for a smoke," he says. It's the first acknowledgment he's made of Tom's filthy, environmentally toxic habit. Tom nods.

They smoke in the kitchen while Clive summons the words to say to Tom. "Look, I don't want to freak you out any further," he says, "But we need to act fast."

Tom nods, sucks at his cigarette. He already knows that, thanks. A dead body right in the center of a building site is worse than a landslide or quicksand. A body means they have to call in the gamut of environmental agencies, police, surveyors, and God knows who else. They'll have to exhume the body, obviously, but that alone can take ages. They'll have to scour the site for other bodies, and it won't matter that they're presently building a house here—if more bodies are found, they'll have to tear it down. Forensics teams will do their work. At a glance, he deduced that the body had been there a long time. It could well be from the Viking period. He has no clue about these things. But the historians might come along, and if turns out to be a protected burial ground or something of an archeological nature, they could have their building permit ripped up for good.

Clive watches Tom progress through the full spectrum of *oh, bollocks*. He lights another cigarette and speaks his next words carefully, and in a low voice.

"This will destroy all our work. You know that, don't you?"

Tom nods.

"I'm not sure I'm ready for another house to be destroyed. Are you?"

Tom shakes his head.

"So, what I'm going to propose isn't sensitive. It's not even ethical. But . . ."

"No," Tom says, not quite sure what Clive is going to suggest, but it probably involves dumping the body in the fjord. Again, Aurelia's corpse on the table washes up on his mind. Her swollen face, the missing toenails. He squeezes his eyes shut and pinches his nose, which has started to bleed.

Clive hands him a tissue in case he stands up to get one from the worktop and decides to run out of the house while he's at it.

"We need to tackle this quickly," he says. A noise at the door cuts him off. Erik walks in, his hard hat clutched by both hands in front of him like a man come to pay his last respects. "Forgive me," he begins.

"We're having a meeting," Clive says tersely, to which Tom lifts his head with the bloodied tissue poking out of his nose and signals for Erik to join them.

Erik feels awkward, but he's been petitioned by the other workers to speak up. "The men," he says. "They are worried."

"I'm sure they are," Clive says.

"In Norway, we honor the dead," he says simply. "We need to make sure the body is treated with care. Otherwise, it could be very bad . . ."

Clive sniffs the superstitious mumbo jumbo buried in that statement. "You're right, mate. This *could* be very bad."

"There are laws," Erik says, changing tack. "The body is protected by law."

Clive feels a tempest of frustration sweep across him. How hard is it to build a damn house? First storms, then an overenthusiastic moose, now a body protected by law.

Tom nods to show he has understood, but is not yet fully able to use actual words. His mind flicks rapidly to that morning in the land registry office in Ålesund, when the clerk showed him a screen of microfiche documents bearing the details of Granhus's previous owners. Only two: Henrik Skjærvik, who built the house in 1899, and then a man named Snorre something who did some renovations in 1980 before moving to Denmark. Henrik had apparently gone missing, and the clerk had made a big fuss about how the death date was unrecorded and there was no mention of a burial. It was likely that the body was his. Murdered, perhaps, given that he'd been buried without a coffin or headstone. Yes, forensics would be all over that.

"Tell the men to take the rest of the day off," Clive tells Erik, who flicks his eyes to Tom, not sure this is the answer he wanted. Tom still doesn't speak. Erik gets up, hard hat still in his hands, and nods.

Once the cars and vans begin to pull off the site, Clive gets up suddenly and stalks purposefully toward the door.

"What are you doing?" Tom calls after him. No reply.

Outside, Clive looks down at the pit. At the body lying there. For a moment he sees Aurelia. He tells himself to get a grip. Then he heaves the concrete mixer over, tips it on its side, and watches as the concrete pours down on top of the corpse.

"What are you doing?" Tom yells. He races for Clive, slamming into his chest with his shoulder, but Clive shoves him off. He finds the second mixer, pours it on its side. The body is covered now. Good. It'll dry by morning and they can cover it up with another layer of soil.

Tom sinks to his knees and stares down into the pit in horror. There's no way back from this. The body is desecrated. He looks up at Clive. "What have you done?"

Clive wipes his nose on his shirtsleeve. "I've saved the build." He winks and grins. "You're welcome."

Tom doesn't sleep all night. He hears Gaia calling him from her bedroom to read her a story, a habit he's kept to every night since Christmas. But tonight, he can't. He is tortured by a web page.

It informs him that the law for tampering with a dead body in Norway is seven years in prison. Also a fine, a huge amount of kroner—he hasn't the mental capacity to calculate the sterling equivalent—but that doesn't matter. It's the seven-years-in-prison part he is reading, over and over. It won't matter that Clive was the one who tipped the concrete into the pit. It's his build. He was present. The men saw the body. They'll inform the police. Any moment now, he'll see flashing lights at the window, be dragged from the house in handcuffs. His career over, the business ruined. His children raised by strangers. Seven years in prison.

"Daaa-ddeee!" Gaia sings from her bedroom. "Come heee-rrre! We need to read about Grete, remember?"

Grete. From Aurelia's old book of Norse lore. He gives a shiver at the name. That was the other thing. He recalls reading a story to Gaia about a woman who had a pet elk. That was fine. Then there was another story about Grete after she'd died. If the elk story wasn't weird enough, this one was about Grete in the afterlife being presented with a choice of Underworld tasks. She opted to become a *nøkk*, one of the supernatural beings whose purpose it was to stand guard at places of water. The *nøkken* were malicious, mischievous creatures—the picture depicts one as an amphibious female, more troll than mermaid—who warned and punished mortals when they were interfering with nature's course. Mankind was replaceable, the story stated. The planet wasn't.

Nøkken rings a bell . . . Where has he heard it before? Maren, he remembers. When he asked her if she'd seen a woman outside after the river gripped his hand . . . No, he thinks firmly, shaking the thought loose. These are just myths. *Myths.*

He thinks of the body.

He goes outside into the night, shines a flashlight on the pit. He finds he's frightened out here, the possibility of another realm taking root in his head. The concrete has begun to set already. It's not smooth, but the body is concealed. Of course, all it will take is for Erik's men to tell the police that a body is under there and they'll break up the concrete.

He lifts a shovel, begins to scoop up earth and throw it down, down on the concrete. Clive comes out of the house. With a grin, he lifts another shovel and joins him.

None of the workers show up the next day. Tom stands at the window of his bedroom, looking down at the roughly concealed pit. He's loath to go outside. The morning after, he calls Erik, who tells him he'll come to speak with him in person.

When Erik gets out of his van he looks over the site with a knot in his gut. It is not good that Tom has done this. He suspects Clive was the main culprit, but still—it is not good. He is having a hard time persuading the other men not to inform the authorities. *They're interlopers,* the men say. *Not even Norwegian. They don't understand our values.* Erik reminds them about Tom's wife, the lovely Aurelia. Some of them met her and were very charmed. They begin to back down.

Tom comes out of the house and greets Erik outside with a handshake and a wide grin. It is all a mask. "I wondered where you'd gone," Tom says brightly. "Were you sick yesterday?"

Erik shakes his head, looks at the ground. "No, not sick. Maybe a little anxious . . ."

Tom folds his arms. He's trying to keep the mood light, but he can read Erik's body language, and it doesn't bode well.

Both men are silent for a moment, filtering through the silence for the right thing to say. They stand unusually far apart from each other.

"The other men will not be returning," Erik says with a sad sigh. "They are nervous about the discovery. They say it is a bad sign. And I think the truth is they do not want to get into trouble."

Tom nods. "Understood."

Erik takes a breath. "I'm afraid that *I* won't be returning either." He slides his eyes to the pit. He can see a concrete mixer on its side, some gray puddles that have hardened. A layer of earth has been patted down. He knows instantly what strategy has been employed. "I'm sorry," he says.

Tom sucks in air, suddenly winded. "Right," he says. "I'll be sure to pay you for the rest of your time."

Erik shakes his head, holds up his hands. "No, no. Please. Just for work we have done."

"No, no," Tom says, "I'll pay you . . ." He can hear himself begin to sound like his father. Money as a defense mechanism. He swallows back the rest of his words.

"Keep in touch," he says, as Erik climbs back into his van. With a wave, Erik pulls off, driving much too fast.

no longer needed

NOW

"Can I have a story from the fairy-tale book tonight?" Gaia asked.

I was sitting on the edge of her bed with Coco on my lap, who was sucking greedily at a bottle of warm almond milk. "Which fairy-tale book?" I asked, glancing over at her bookshelf. We'd covered all of Julia Donaldson, Michael Rosen, Judith Kerr, Debi Gliori, some *Shakespeare for Kids* books. Only the C. S. Lewis box sets remained to be discovered. "Do you mean the one about Narnia?"

She shook her head and pulled back the bedcovers. "It's on Daddy's iPad," she said. "I'll ask him if we can borrow it."

I waited as she raced to the living room, then returned with the iPad and flicked expertly to a PDF file.

"There," she said, handing it to me and hopping back into bed. "I like the one about the elk. Can you read me that one, please?"

I scrolled through the file and found a story called "The *Nøkk* and the Elk."

Once upon a time, there was a farmer who forgot to pay the nøkk who lived at the bottom of the lake. The nøkk—whose name was Egil, after the lake—became incensed. He had allowed the farmer to bring his cattle to the lake day after day to drink. He had permitted the farmer's son to row his boat to the deep parts of his lake, filling bucket after bucket with fat silver fish. And he had often watched as the farmer's daughter, a beauty with long golden hair, had swum on hot days, often warning her away from the pikes by causing the wind to blow cold, or the reeds to tickle her ankles.

The nøkk was used to receiving payment for use of the lake, and yet the farmer had never left him so much as a winnow.

One summer's morning, the nøkk awoke to the sound of splashing from above. He swam to the surface and found himself face-to-face with a lamb caught fast in reeds. The lamb was bleating for its mother, and the nøkk could see the farmer trying to make his way to the lamb to save it. Both the nøkk and the farmer knew that he would never make it in time, for the lamb was young and weak, and the water was old and strong.

The nøkk approached the farmer, who fell to his knees in fright, as the nøkken are grotesque.

"I will save your lamb," the nøkk said. "And I will allow you to continue fishing and feeding your herd from my lake. But in return, you must give me your daughter to wed."

The farmer agreed, and informed his daughter, who produced a knife and swore to stab herself rather than receive such a fate. The farmer was sad, for he had many mouths to feed.

On the morning of the wedding, the daughter dressed as a bride, only she wore fish eggs instead of pearls, and pond weed instead of ivory lace, and upon her lips she smeared mud from the riverbed and garlanded her head with milfoil. She stepped into the lake until the water lapped at her chin, and it was then that she saw the nøkk. She gave a scream at the nøkk's appearance, for he had holes where his eyes should be, and his teeth were those of a wild beast.

"Call his name!" her father shouted, for he had learned that a nøkk can be banished by a human voice calling his name, and his daughter was yet alive. But the water reached her lips before the nøkk told her his name, and she drowned.

Despite the farmer's treachery, the nøkk accepted his sacrifice, and the farmer fed his other children for years to come.

Gaia was silent for a moment. "That's not the elk story," she said.

I scanned the story. "Oh, there's more," I said. "It's about how the *nøkken* sometimes turned into an elk. Is that the one?"

Gaia shook her head. "I've never heard that story before. Mumma never read it to me."

On hindsight, I could understand why—the story was pretty gross. I scrolled through and found another story about a woman called Grete and her elk, but Gaia seemed preoccupied with the *nøkk* story.

"Do you know how the daughter in the story was scared because the *nøkk*'s eyes looked like holes?" Gaia said then.

"Yes?"

She pushed her glasses up her nose. "That sounds like the Sad Lady, doesn't it?"

I thought back to that terrifying encounter in the kitchen with the floating woman with weird teeth. My skin crawled at the thought of it. I avoided the kitchen at nighttime now, and in the day it was so busy and light that you could almost forget that such a terrifying thing had happened. But Gaia had a point.

"Maybe if we said the Sad Lady's name, she'd go away," Gaia said. I tried to move on to a lighter, less terrifying subject, but she wasn't having it. "What would her name be?"

"Well, in the *story*," I said, emphasizing that it was, after all, fiction, "the *nøkk* was named Egil, after the lake. So if the fjord had a *nøkk*, it would be called Hjørund, as that's the name of the fjord." That was what Clive had told me, when he first drove me here from the airport.

Gaia considered this. "So the Sad Lady's called Hjørund?"

"If she was real, she'd be called Hjørund . . ."

"We both know the Sad Lady's real," Gaia said firmly.

I reached out and took her hand. "Well, now you know what to do to make her go away."

At this, Gaia stared at me for a long time, then took off her glasses and snuggled down into her bed without a single complaint.

Once the girls were both asleep, I headed downstairs to return the iPad to wherever Gaia had filched it from in the living room.

"Knock knock."

I looked up to see Clive standing in the doorway. I figured one of the girls had climbed out of bed and I was needed to put her back.

"You busy?" Clive asked.

"Not really," I said, swallowing hard. Something was wrong. Clive was usually a jokey kind of guy, by which I mean he was

withering and snarky, but right now he just looked kind of consti-
pated. Had he somehow found out who I was?

He asked me to sit down. I did, and he sat next to me. I could
see he'd been sweating profusely. Two damp circles at his armpits,
his brow moist. His eyes were kind of bloodshot.

"You might have . . . questions," he said in a voice that sounded
as though he was speaking to a six-year-old.

"Questions?"

"About what happened on Tuesday. And I'm here to answer
those questions."

I looked at him, owl-eyed. I had absolutely no clue what he was
talking about.

"I'm sorry," I said. "But I have absolutely no clue what you're
talking about."

He narrowed his eyes, as though studying me very closely. "Is
it money you're after?"

"*What?*"

He leaned back, rubbed his face as though he hadn't slept in
days. Come to think of it, I *had* seen him pacing one night when
I was up with Coco. She was still teething. I found that ice helped,
but going to the kitchen for it in the dead of night—and poten-
tially encountering floating women—wasn't worth it.

"Money?" I repeated. "Money for what?"

He looked at me as if I was hiding something. "So you didn't
see the . . ." He folded his lips into his mouth, as if whatever I'd
seen couldn't be uttered aloud.

"See the *what?*"

He glanced outside, then back at me. I followed his gaze. It was
pitch-black out there, but the expression on his face indicated that
he was seeing something. The Hanging Gardens of Babylon, perhaps, or a portal into the multiverse.

"Look, if the police come," he said, suddenly flustered, "stick to that story. OK? And I'll see that you're rewarded."

I was sure he was on heroin or something. He laid a hand on top of mine and left it there for a few seconds. Probably best just to let his train run out of steam.

But he was suddenly too close, and I wondered if I perhaps had something in my eye, or if my eyeliner was running again. I still hadn't quite mastered the art of makeup application, despite religiously attempting it every day.

"Are you sure you didn't see anything?" he asked again. Softer, this time, and closer to my face.

"See *what*?" I said, shifting slightly away from him and leaning back into the sofa.

He opened his mouth to speak, but someone behind him beat him to it.

"Clive?"

He yanked his hand away as if my hand had turned into raw flame. Derry was standing in the doorway, her thick fleece house robe pulled tight across her chest. She had this weird expression that put me on edge. She looked from me to Clive as though we'd just been sticking pins in a voodoo doll of her likeness, or hosting a druidic ceremony. *Everyone's gone mad tonight,* I thought.

Clive stood up quickly and wiped his hands on his trousers. They stared at each other wordlessly.

"Derry," I called out to her. "Are we doing our walk tomorrow morning?" I was keen to get back outside. I found it cleared my brain for the day ahead.

She ignored me and muttered something at Clive, who was protesting something and staggering toward her with his hands out. But she turned and stomped away. *This is why I couldn't do marriage,* I thought. *Too much reading between the lines.* But I was disappointed, too, because as Clive asked those bizarre questions,

I had wondered if I should ask *him* about the diary. It was possible he had planted it in my room. I made a mental note to ask him the day after.

That night, I was up again with Coco, rocking her back to sleep, when I heard Derry and Clive talking in their room.

"I saw the way you looked at her," Derry said. Then: "Did you want to?"

Was she talking about me?

35

you want this

THEN

Aurelia wakes with a gasp, the bedclothes swamping around her. She is panting, filmed with sweat, her heart jackhammering in her throat. She rises from the bed, the dimensions of the room all akimbo, and heads for Gaia's bedroom. She collapses on the shape of the bed and reaches her hand for where Gaia's face should be. The relief that hits her when she feels the familiar warm smoothness of her daughter's cheek and nose is overwhelming: she is still half inside the dream, can see each of the faces of the reindeer with unbelievable vividness. The glassy black eyes, the markings around their snouts, brown felt dangling in tatters from their antlers . . .

She squeezes her eyes shut and tries to breathe away the panic that mounts up again as she recalls seeing Gaia in the water, and that searing helplessness when she discovered Gaia was gone. The emptiness of her arms. An infinite emptiness.

But it was not real, and Gaia is here.

She sits up and covers her face with her hands, then sobs qui-

etly for a moment. Gaia does not stir. Aurelia doesn't want to go
back to bed. The thought of falling into nightmares again does not
appeal. She'll drink, that's what. She'll go downstairs and have a
nightcap, or four, so that she doesn't dream.

It's a mild night. Climate change has thrust schizophrenic
weather patterns upon Norway, so that the old concept of winter
clothes and summer clothes does not apply. She puts on her robe
and slippers and heads downstairs to the kitchen. She stands by
the window for a few moments, looking out at the trees, at their
almost-house. The sky is a strange color—navy streaked with yellow. The trees are usually troubled by wind, ruffled by its many
hands, but tonight they are still. As she cranes to get a better look
outside, there it is, a flicker of aurora borealis. The yellow streaks
deepen to a rich stripe of emerald green tinged with pink. It begins to sway, like a river in the sky, then splits into two separate
strands that bifurcate across the sky. She gives a gasp. Never has
she seen the northern lights. Not even as a child, when they went
north. She wants to run back upstairs and wake the children,
wake Tom, wake Clive and Derry, but then she catches sight of
the kitchen clock and considers that at this time of night, no one
is going to thank her for waking them up. And the thought of trying to get Gaia back to sleep after such excitement puts her right
off. So she stands there, relishing the experience of being the only
person for miles to see this sight, as though the heavens are dancing just for her.

"Nightcap?" a voice says. She jumps and turns around to see
Clive in the doorway. He doesn't look like he's even been to bed.

"You scared me," she says. "What are you still doing up? It's
three in the bloody morning."

"Bloody reading, that's what." He holds up the book that's
tucked under his arm. A Stephen King novel. *It.*

She laughs and stammers about the northern lights, but he ducks into the pantry, leaving her to watch the green glow fade back to sky. Once he's filched a bag of almonds and a bottle of gin he pulls a chair back from the dining table—she grimaces as it makes a loud scrape against the floor and hopes it doesn't wake Coco—then sits down and pours himself a glass.

"I think I'll join you," she says. "Do you mind?"

"Not at all. You'll need a . . ."

"Glass?" she says, plucking one from the cupboard. He grins, and she sits down opposite and allows him to pour her a generous shot.

"I'd never have taken you for a midnight drinker," Clive says once she's drained it.

"I'd never have taken you for a Stephen King fan."

He grins, shrugs. "Won't alcohol affect the . . ." His eyes fall to her chest before he can catch himself. He laughs and covers his eyes, embarrassed, with a hand. "Sorry."

Absentmindedly she presses a hand across her chest, even though she's wearing one of Tom's T-shirts and no cleavage is on display. "I'm not feeding her . . . myself . . . anymore," she says, tentatively, feeling shame sting her anew. "I breastfed Gaia until she was one, but it's been . . . difficult . . . this time round. Something called oversupply. It's when you get too much milk and your boobs swell up like footballs . . . Oh, Lord." She buries her face in her hands and they both laugh. "*Too* much information," she says. He fills her another glass.

"Here, this'll help." He fills his own, raises it in a toast. "Cheers."

"Cheers."

"How's Basecamp coming on?" she says after a moment's silence.

"Basecamp," he says wistfully. "Basecamp, Basecamp."

She notes a sense of something—ennui?—that has filled the room. "Sorry. I'm sure you *dream* about building, now."

He grins. She always did like his smile. It's the kind that reaches his eyes. She's always loved people with expressive eyes like Clive. "Well, we're at a tricky part just now, so it's kind of a touchy subject . . ."

"Hasn't every part of the build been tricky?"

He laughs. "Indeed. Well, when you've got Tom at the helm, it's never going to be straightforward, is it? I mean, rooms with trees *inside* them? Having to change the plans again and again to avoid damaging the bloody trees?" Another laugh, tinged with fatigue. "Well. I suppose we all now have a very healthy respect for trees, I'll give him that."

"I'm sorry," she says.

He frowns, shakes his head. "Oh, no, don't apologize. It's *your* house, isn't it? Got to make it right . . ."

"Yes, but you and Derry are . . . well, the longer it takes, the longer you both have to . . ."

He lifts the glass and pours her another shot, spilling some on the table.

"Whoops," she says, and realizes she's already drunk. He flicks his eyes at her, then pours his own glass. He lifts it to his chest, then leans back in his seat thoughtfully.

"I won't deny it, it's been difficult," he says. "Derry wants us to go back to London, but I need to be here."

She frowns. "Why? Can't Tom take care of things now?"

"It's better that I'm here. Derry understands. But obviously, she's pregnant now. So it changes things."

Her face drops. She raises a hand to her mouth and laughs too loudly. He shushes her with a finger to his lips. She laughs again and claps her hands together.

"Wow. Wow, Clive. I'm . . . that's amazing. Amazing. Is Derry . . . Is she OK? I mean, what about morning sickness?"

He nods, smiling, and she is pleased for him. Clive, a father.

"We'll be looking to you and Tom for parenting tips," he says. "I haven't a clue what to do with a baby."

"I'm probably not the best person to ask . . ." she says. She's always felt like she's a crap mum.

His eyes widen in disbelief and he leans forward, dropping his voice to a whisper. "Listen, I've seen you with those girls of yours, and you're *incredible*. Seriously. Nothing's as hard as parenting in my book. Nothing. Particularly when it comes to the mother."

She beams. This is a side to Clive she's never seen—tenderness. He's a hard-ass, dryly sarcastic at his warmest, and she's often wondered how he's earned himself a reputation as a Casanova. Now she's seeing it, she thinks. He can go from withering conde-scension to full-blown charm in the blink of an eye.

"I'm so pleased for you both. That's terrific news, Clive, really."

He grins. "Thanks. Not the best timing, obviously . . ."

"There's never a right time for a baby," she says, parroting the words her mother said to her when she confessed she was think-ing of trying for a baby with Tom but didn't think it was the right time. She was still getting commissions overseas in places like Durban and Pakistan.

"You're right," he says, still clearly elated. He runs his hands through his hair. She feels a twinge of something as she notes his flushed face and gleaming eyes, a man overjoyed to be having a baby. Tom's reaction to the news of Gaia wasn't exactly what she'd expected, or wanted. He'd fallen deathly silent. Couldn't form a sentence. You'd have thought she'd announced she had a terminal illness, or was leaving him. Later, he told her he was thrilled. He'd just needed a moment to compute the surprise.

"Well, it's certainly made me appreciate how much of a sacrifice it is for a woman to give over her body like that. And her career." He flicks his eyes up and down her body. "How did you manage it?" he says, refilling her glass. "When you had Gaia, I mean?"

Aurelia lifts her glass, considering this question. Did she manage it? She's not quite sure. It's always felt like utter chaos.

"You must have superpowers," Clive fills in, and she grins, but the smile soon wanes. She doesn't feel like she has superpowers. She feels like she's failing everyone around her every single day.

Clive notices the change in her expression. "Are you all right?"

She nods, clears her throat. "Fine, fine."

"Actually, I think I may have just spoken out of turn."

She looks up. He's smiling at her.

"It's not superpowers at all, is it? I mean, to manage two kids and a career, a husband, a house being built in the middle of nowhere. You must work crazy hard on so many levels, inside and out. And I bet nobody really sees what it takes out of you. How you suffer as a result."

She stares at him. His voice has grown so low it's as though it's inside her own head. He looks at her as though he can see everything about her—every thought, every wish, every desire. He clears his throat, looks away, suddenly embarrassed.

"Anyway . . ." She's not sure whether she says it or he does. How many glasses has she had? It's after four. They must have been talking for quite a while, and oh, Lord, she has one bare leg bent on the seat beside her, revealing a long white thigh to Clive and probably an eyeful of her crotch. Not that the view is particularly sexy—she's wearing cotton granny panties that sag down around her hips like boxer shorts. She lowers her leg and blinks hard, hoping he didn't see her crotch.

"Congratulations," she says again. "That's amazing, Clive. Amazing . . . I should . . ."

She presses both hands firmly on the table to raise herself to a standing position, but somewhere in between coordinating her legs and hands she knocks the glass to the floor with a loud clang. Clive moves to grab it, and suddenly she finds herself standing above him and staring in his eyes. His eyes are not smiling. But his hand . . . his hand is on her bare thigh, much too close to her crotch. It takes a long moment for her brain to connect with her mouth.

"What . . . are you doing?"

His fingers creep higher, slipping under the side of her knickers at her hip. "Why don't you sit down?" he whispers. Then, strangely, and with a smooth confidence that she'll recall with a shiver for days afterward, "You want this, Aurelia. *You want this.*"

In the haze of it all she finds she can't seem to speak and move at the same time, because for whatever reason Clive has reached up and caught the fabric of her panties between his fingers, so any movement is likely to end up with them askew, or pulled down, which would be embarrassing.

Without taking his hands from her underwear he rises and steps close to her. "Tell me you don't want this," he says. She finds she can't. It's not the gin. It's being wanted, and seen. It's the offer of respite from the nightmares that besiege her every night. And it's the message folded in his voice, in his touch, that tells her that he understands something about her. *Oh, yes*, she thinks. *I want all of this.*

He leans in and kisses her. She responds. His lips are tight and firm, his tongue quick and deep inside her mouth. A new sensation floods her, a gorgeous difference, a new mouth against hers. She feels his hands move and, as a voice calls out from somewhere, perhaps inside a dream, she realizes her knickers have pooled on the ground around her feet.

"Aurelia?"

She moves her head toward the sound, toward a blurred figure in the hallway. Familiarity sharpens her senses. The woman wrapped in an oversized robe, black hair to her shoulders, and a haunted expression, is Derry. Pregnant Derry, who is married to the man whose tongue has just been in her mouth.

Aurelia staggers backward. Clive has his hands in the air, surrendering. "Derry," he says, over and over. "Derry." No explanation or apology. Just her name.

Aurelia sinks back into a chair and watches as Derry's eyes move from her to Clive and back to Aurelia. She is not horrified, but sobered. Clive puts his hands on Derry's shoulders, rubs them as if she's just come in from the cold.

"Let's go to bed," she hears him tell Derry. "It's late. Please."

When Derry doesn't budge from the hallway, her eyes nailed to Aurelia's knickers on the floor, he takes her hand. Aurelia doesn't want to look, but can't not look at the scene in front of her. What was she doing just now? How the hell did she end up kissing Clive? Shame thumps down on her in hot waves.

"What's going on?" another voice says. She looks up and oh, God, it can't get any worse, but there is Tom, her husband, her utterly faithful husband standing in the hallway in his plaid pajamas staring at Clive and Derry. He sees her holding her head in her hands at the table, notes the shot glasses and the bottle of gin on the table and the spillage, sees she's drunk. He's worried. She can see he's worried.

"Rough night?" he asks tenderly. He turns and glances at Clive and Derry, who are heading quietly upstairs. This brings Aurelia some relief.

"Come back to bed," he says, cupping her face. "Don't worry

about getting up for the girls. I'll take a bottle to Coco, OK? Come on."

She starts to cry then, and even as she follows him upstairs and notices the pinkening sky, as Gaia calls out from her room and Tom races ahead to soothe her so Aurelia can rest, she knows what is done cannot be undone.

different storms

THEN

H igher, Daddy! Higher!"
Tom gives the swing a shove, so hard that it starts to
chink slightly each time Gaia swings to the apex.

"That's high enough," Aurelia tells him under her breath. He
relents until the swing moves like an exhale. Gaia squirms impa-
tiently.

"Higher! Higher!"

They're at a play park twenty miles east. He'd hoped the drive
would spark Aurelia back to life, bring back her smile, but if anything she's grown darker and more somber since they left the
house. He's got Coco in the baby carrier against his chest and she
has slept most of the morning. He wonders if it would have been
wiser to stay home, let Aurelia sleep instead of coming all the way
out here. He feels like he's walking on eggshells around her.

"Come on, pudding," he tells Gaia, bringing the swing to an
abrupt stop. "Let's try out the climbing frame, shall we?"

Once Gaia runs off to the climbing frame he motions to Aurelia to sit with him and Coco on a park bench nearby. It's a beautiful park, and a beautifully crisp day, for that matter. Cold, but not unbearable. Snow has whitened the hills in the distance and the trees at the park's periphery, but the equipment has been kept dry by children enveloped in snowsuits and set loose after many days of being stuck indoors.

Aurelia sits down. He notices she keeps her distance. She is wrapped in a beige cashmere shawl, beneath which are the jogging bottoms she slept in last night and a white T-shirt bearing several stains. No bra, no makeup. Her face is pinched with cold and her eyes are glassy and swollen from tears. It's like watching someone in freefall, but in slow motion, and with no actual falling—just the kind that seems to happen in all those interior spaces of the mind, the places he can't access.

"Great day, huh?" he says, smiling benignly at her. She looks ahead. He nods over at Gaia, who is playing with a couple of kids. "Glad we found this park, too. Looks like Gaia's made friends already. We could set up some playdates. Be good for her to get some Scandinavian friends."

Aurelia's lips move. She's speaking, but he can't hear. He leans closer. Closer. She doesn't flinch. All this time he's kept his distance because he thought she'd leap away from him if he touched her, and he couldn't handle being rejected. This thought winds up from the depths of his subconscious, and with it a memory of his father dropping him off at boarding school. Hands in his pockets. And how much that stung.

Very slowly, he puts an arm across her shoulders. She doesn't move. He breathes a long sigh of relief. Happiness stirs in him. Maybe it's not him that's making her so sad. Maybe it's something else.

"I feel . . ." she's saying. He tilts his head toward her lips. She's crying. Tears are sliding down her cheeks and she doesn't swipe them away.

"Aurelia . . ." he says. "It's OK."

She nods. Intellectually, she's aware everything is OK. OK, in the sense that right now they're sitting in a park, and she can hear one daughter laughing and her other daughter snoring against Tom's chest. But the reality is that everything is not OK, and certainly not today. Today she is not in a park but in a void that's midnight black. She is not a mother, not a wife, but a speck of nothingness floating in that vast, empty void. There is no horizon, no chink of light, no end to the nothingness. And she has no words to communicate this.

But when Tom slides his arm across her shoulders, the sudden human contact restores her words just long enough for her to frame the terror she's living inside.

"I feel like I want to die," she says.

Tom stares at her, mouth open. He doesn't know what to say.

"Mumma! Look! Look what I can do!"

They both watch as Gaia hooks her legs from a bar on the climbing frame and dangles upside down, laughing.

"That's great, pudding," Tom calls out, his voice breaking. "Careful you don't fall. That's enough now."

Coco jerks awake as he shouts, her pale eyes flinging open and glancing around in shock. She sees her mother, feels the *thump-thump* of her father's heartbeat beneath his sweater, and promptly falls back to sleep.

"Why did you do it, Tom?" Aurelia asks.

He starts. "Do what?"

"The build."

"Is *that* why you feel like this?"

She nods. Then, realizing this isn't the cause at all, shakes her head. "I don't know," she whispers. "I don't know what's wrong." A chink in the darkness to admit it. Within seconds the darkness engulfs her again in its smothering, measureless terror.

"How long have you felt like this?" Tom asks gently.

"Since . . . since you cut down the tree. And then all the animals dying after drinking from the river. It's just got worse every day. I can't bear it." Another tear rolls down her face. This time she wipes it away. "I can't bear being alive."

He nods, processing this. His wife is suicidal. In a park, while their older daughter laughs and plays with new friends, and their baby girl snoozes adorably against his chest. He figures he knows the real reason. Two days ago, Basecamp was destroyed during a storm. The storm was only half of it—the river was the real cause. When he'd redirected the river, it had actually dispersed through the site, turning the ground soggy and collapsing the foundations. The house they dreamed of, designed, built, and got into serious debt for, is destroyed, and he's not even sure they can claim anything on the insurance for it. Maybe fifty percent, but they'll still have a black hole in their finances and nothing to show for it.

Building a summer home out here was Aurelia's dream. But now it has become a nightmare. He pressed her to come straight after the baby was born, even though he knew she wasn't feeling up to it. *But we'll spend Christmas here,* he said. *It'll be magic.* It's his fault she feels suicidal. He has done this.

"I'm so, so sorry," he says, and she feels something in her heart give, a hot, tight knot come undone. She weeps freely, uncontrollably, and it takes all her resolve not to fall on her knees before him and tell him about what happened that night with Clive.

He tightens his grip on her, pulling her as close as he can with Coco strapped to his chest. He leans over and kisses Aurelia's forehead, whispers in her ear that everything will be OK, he promises. He'll build a new house. He'll beg, borrow, and steal if he has to. Sell his body. This gets a laugh from her, so he goes with it: he reckons he could get at least a couple of quid for his body, what does she think? Maybe he'll invest in a thong, shave his chest, pluck his eyebrows. And on the side he'll deliver pizzas. Anything to raise the cash. In his mind, a new design is already beginning to take shape. Not a house *on* the cliff, but *in* the cliff. Like a nest, unobtrusively settled into the nooks and crannies of the rock face, hovering over the water.

She smiles. "I like that," she says, wiping her nose on her sleeve. "It sounds beautiful."

She turns to him, her eyes wet, her smile wide, flooded with gratitude for him. Maybe she'll tell him someday about what happened with Clive. But she needs to understand herself first. She's reeling at what she did. She can't believe it. He cups his hand to her cheek and leans forward to kiss her. She responds with a chaste peck, but he holds her in that kiss, so glad of this sudden affection because it means she still loves him. In the warmth of his touch and the light in his eyes she feels the darkness slip away.

"You need to talk to someone," he tells her, brushing strands of unwashed hair from her face. She looks so delicate, she might shatter into pieces. "When we get back we're going to find you a therapist," he says, surprised by how confident he sounds. To his own ears he sounds like he knows what needs to happen. This idea barely brushed his mind before the words came out, but it sounds so very wise. Of *course* she should talk to someone! Why hadn't he seen it before? He's been so busy with the build. She's been crumbling before his very eyes and he hasn't once suggested she talk to someone.

"I promise I'll make this right," he tells her, holding her close. "I'll build your house, Aurelia. I promise."

"OK," she says, nodding and crying. "OK."

———

In the office at home Tom searches online for a therapist in Norway. He finds a number and pulls out his mobile phone to call them, but Aurelia won't have it.

"Let me contact my midwife," she says. "She asked me to get in touch if anything . . . you know."

"It's important we get you seen to, Aurelia . . ."

She gives him a look of *I promise*. He relents. "OK."

He watches as she sits down in front of the computer and begins to type an e-mail to her midwife. *Hi, Clare. How are you?* How to put this situation into words? *Hey, I had suicidal thoughts while watching my kid play on the swings in a park yesterday, can I get therapy, please?*

It's a hard thing to put into an e-mail, she thinks, covering her eyes with her hands. She hates asking for help. Always has. She can give help, no problem, but asking for it? For her it's the hardest thing on earth. Tom rubs her back, utterly relieved and heartbroken all at once.

"You can do this. We can put you on the next plane home."

She nods.

> Hi, Clare! Could we talk sometime? I'm feeling a bit low lately . . . I remember you said to get in touch if I was struggling and I'd like to find out if I can get some kind of support.
>
> Thanks,
> Aurelia Faraday

Satisfied, she hits send.

She rises from the leather office chair, heads to the kitchen, and puts the kettle on. While it's boiling she heads upstairs, pulls out the drawer of her bedside table, and retrieves her red diary, the one in which she writes down her dreams. Once she's made a cup of tea she sits back at the desk, watching the cursor blink on her screen, and reads through her dream diary.

I was pregnant again but with triplets and there was a doctor standing over me about to perform a C-section.

Tom tried to kill Coco.

Tom's dad was trying to kill me. He chased me through the house and then he was going to kill Gaia and Coco so I ran out of Granhus toward the cliff and he pushed me off and I fell into the fjord.

Tom and I discussed divorce and I pleaded with him not to leave and then he offered to make me pancakes and George Clooney was there fixing the radiator???

She's forgotten writing down most of these dreams. She pores over them now like a scholar deciphering ancient text, encountering the hasty cursive of her own hand as though they're stories written by someone else. Why would anyone dream such violent, chaotic things? Hormones, she thinks, but still—she always held that dreams originated from reality. If you dreamed about something like divorce, it was because somewhere in the depths of your brain you were contemplating it. She hasn't been contemplating divorce, at least not in any serious way. But yes, she has felt vulnerable after Coco's birth. Not just the addition of another child— the physical effects left her vulnerable. The construction of a brand-new home. Somehow, she understands that building their holiday home here in Norway has mirrored the building of a marriage. Their marriage. She's been surveying the construction of their own relationship, brick by brick, and with each setback she's felt as though they, too, might be as easily broken.

the note

THEN

He wakes at dawn. The space in the bed beside him is empty, but there is nothing unusual about it. He can hear Gaia murmuring next door, presumably chatting to her mother, who has probably spent another night on the floor beside Gaia's bed in an attempt to get her to sleep through.

Glorious sunlight fingers its way through the heavy curtains, and he sees the tall spines of the trees. Beyond that, clean blue sky. He sits up in bed and glances at his phone. Just after seven. He's surprised how much better he feels after talking with Aurelia. Yes, they have wandered together through the ruins of their dreams. Yes, the destruction of Basecamp is one of the worst things he has ever faced. But he feels closer to her than ever. Financially, he's ruined. His business will suffer. And there's the logistical matter of the cleanup. Glass, metal, and even plastic is scattered all over the site, probably floating in the fjord, too. So much for his painstaking efforts to save the environment. Cheers, Mother Nature. What a payback.

As he sits there in bed, that gorgeous, buttery light dancing across the floorboards, their new house begins to take shape in his head, his ideas gathering texture and color. Quickly he grabs his notebook and pencil and begins to draw: the long right angle of the cliff, then a strange orb thing that sits half in, half out of the rock. Kind of nest-like; yes, a kind of hive. He recalls Aurelia staring up at the cliff from the fjord with her binoculars and noticing the jut of black rock. *You could fit a house on there.* The concept coheres rapidly: a three-story house partially cantilevered over the fjord, and perhaps the rock itself forming the back walls of the house— ancient, million-year-old Norwegian cliff inside some of the rooms, still patterned with scratch marks from the glacier that formed it. It makes sense—he's wary of the land beyond Granhus, ruined by the river. But building on the rock—or in it—just might work.

How would he do it? He draws two lines that plunge down through the cliff to the bit that juts out. Then he stares at the drawing. He could hold the house in place with thirty-millimeter steel rods thrust down through the rock—thirty millimeters would be enough to bear the load if he drills deep, and it would also mean that the foundations don't interfere too much with the landscape . . . The house will have seamless, electrochromatic glass wrapped around the front façade, with the ability to change from clear to frost at the touch of an app, meaning that the house will, for the most part, blend into the rock. Nothing ostentatious, nothing to signal that the landscape has been imposed upon. Locally sourced wood will provide additional cladding and infrastructure—Siberian birch weathers to pewter gray fairly quickly, so he could use that to provide both insulation and camouflage. The house will simply blend into the rock.

This time, *this* time, he'll listen to his instinct. He won't interfere with the land.

He flips the page over and begins to draw the floorplan. Three stories, four en suite bedrooms, a large open-plan living space with a lift transferring them to the top of the cliff, even a rooftop garden. It's insanely ambitious, but there's freedom in hitting rock bottom. The destruction of Basecamp has wiped the slate clean, wiped out his finances, and obliterated his pride—and what he's left with is raw creative energy driven by a need to fulfill his promise to Aurelia. He's back to being a passionate, neurotic postgrad, wondering if he'll ever be paid to design so much as a garden shed. His father got to be right—Tom failed as he predicted, and he had to bail him out. Screw paying his dad back. Tom will go to the banks, or friends, for another loan, start again on the new house. The *real* nest. Aurelia's Nest. A place where she will feel safe, and happy. Like her old self.

When he finishes the sketches he gets up, gives a huge stretch and a few air punches. Then he heads downstairs to make coffee.

In the kitchen, Gaia is standing on a chair by the sink, hair wild as candy floss, looking out of the window at the trees.

"Good morning, pudding," he says, planting a kiss on top of her head. "Mummy still asleep?"

"Mumma ran away," she says.

"Have you had breakfast yet?" He rummages in the fridge. They're almost out of almond milk. He'll head into the village today and pick up some more.

"Mumma's gone," Gaia says. "I can't see her."

"Gone?" he says absentmindedly. "Where's Mummy gone?"

"She's gone. *Gone.*"

He pours oatmeal into a bowl, adds the last of the almond milk. Tosses it in the microwave. Life is great. He whistles happily and does a little dance, the idea of the house still buzzing brightly in his head. In a moment he'll go upstairs and check on Aurelia, see if she wants him to make her a cooked breakfast. Sod it, he'll just make it and surprise her. Then he'll tell her that he's going to build her house.

Several miles downstream, Aurelia's body floats facedown in the water, coming to rest against a bank of ferns and reeds. Her lips are parted; her blonde hair streams outward like pondweed. A fox starts, then dabs at her nightdress with a paw.

She will remain in this corner of the fjord for a week, currents tugging her beneath the water and hard against the rocks, rain beating down on the ballooning tent of her dress as though it might yet wake her up.

Can I get you anything?"

Derry's face swims up to him. She looks so concerned, and her question stalls the gears of his mind, which churn on an endless loop. He found the note. Just one word in Aurelia's handwriting, left on his bedside table.

Sorry

Had his wife not been missing for thirty-nine hours this note would have had little meaning. He'd assume she was sorry for spilling tea on a contract or shrinking one of his jumpers in the wash. And then he'd give her a kiss and get on with things.

Thirty-nine hours.

It has started to snow.

The police come. They take statements in clipped, cold English phrases, regard him with curiosity and suspicion. They put on plastic gloves and trawl through Aurelia's clothes, the house. He paces. Coco won't stop screaming. Gaia falls mute. She won't speak, won't eat.

Mumma ran away.

Sixty-seven hours. The phone rings. He dives for it.

"Aurelia?"

Not Aurelia. His stomach drops. It's the police.
We've found a body part.

She is buried in Highgate Cemetery in London, with its hideous
Gothic architecture and overbearing whiff of old money. Aurelia's
parents demanded that she be interred in the family plot, and he
has no energy to fight them, Gothic architecture notwithstanding.
It's a punishment on their part for whatever role they believe he
played in her death. But he saw her corpse, is still traumatized by
what death can do . . . So fine, bury her here, he thinks. Bury her
wherever you like. The body he identified was not his wife. It was
meat, destruction, death. Not Aurelia. A carcass. He will not
commemorate her here.

He returns to the house at Hampstead. The agony of its endless empty rooms. The children crying day and night for their
mother. Concerned relatives, mostly female, fussing over him,
bringing meals. One of them hires a nanny. Ellen. He almost
turns her away, then thinks better of it. She seems capable, and
he is not able to give these children what they need right now. He
can barely function. The world without Aurelia is absurd beyond
all credulity. Grief is not a mere *feeling*—it's an isotropic space.
He can't fathom living without her, that she is nowhere. *Nowhere.*

And one night, when he is astonishingly drunk, he comes
across the sketch he drew of the new house. He's written *Aurelia's
Nest* at the bottom.

He'll finish the house, he decides. Instead of imposing upon
nature, he'll give back to it. He decides that his original plan of
carbon neutrality isn't enough—energy-generating architecture is
the only way forward. He will *give back* to the land, instead of
taking from it. Aurelia's Nest will produce 100,000 kWh a year—
more than what ten average households consume. And when the

build is finished, he'll make the plans of the house available for free, so others can build their own energy-generating homes as far and wide as possible. Aurelia's Nest will be a "pod" that can be detached and put anywhere in the world, a kind of energy-positive crab shell. It doesn't have to be attached to the side of a cliff, either—it can be stood on a platform in a field, or a back garden. It can have five bedrooms or one. Energy-positive prefab homes.

He promised Aurelia that he would build her house. And that is exactly what he'll do.

curiosity and suspicion

NOW

It became plain that I had done something to upset Derry. Leaving without me in the mornings for her jog was understandable, given how slow I was, and perhaps my conversation was rambling. Perhaps I had failed to breathe properly on our breathing and bowing nights. After all, there was more to it than breathing and bowing—we rang a little bell, too, and sat with our legs crossed and occasionally *umm*ed and *aah*ed while attempting not to choke on incense smoke. My thoughts flicked to the night some weeks before when she had interrupted Clive during his unnerving interrogation about whether I had seen something. There had been a moment when he had leaned close to me . . . the air around him fizzed with expectancy. And then Derry had come in. Surely she didn't think I was trying it on with her husband? Clive was knocking on his fifties—pretty much old enough to be my dad. Even if he *was* trying it on, it was hardly my fault. Was it? Maybe Derry had connected his actions to something she had perceived. Perceptions, I had learned, were roughly ninety-nine percent to do with the mindset of the perceiver and the other one percent to do with actual fact. Even so, I felt sad. I had managed to build a semblance of a friendship with Derry and looked forward to our chats. I actually enjoyed the breathing and bowing sessions—they helped me feel a little less twitchy. Confident, even.

"Everyone! Come outside, please!" a voice called. Gaia stirred in my bed and sat upright.

"What time is it?" she said. I glanced at the clock. It was just past seven and still dark. "Why is Daddy shouting?"

"I don't know," I said, and we headed to the kitchen to see what was going on. Tom was there in his work gear. I realized I hadn't seen him come in the night before, so he must have spent all night on the build.

"It's done," he said, like a man possessed. "It's *alive!*"

Clive came in through the door behind him then, stamping his boots on the doormat. He was wearing work clothing, too. "Is Derry back?" he asked me. I told him I didn't know.

"Maren!" Tom shouted. A few minutes later she emerged, bleary-eyed in her nightie. He paid no heed. "We're all going to see the house."

Clearly we had no say in the matter, but it was exciting all the same. We all wrapped up in our coats and boots and headed out into the dark.

As we approached the cliff, it looked as though nothing had been built at all. The same chaos of diggers and concrete mixers and remnants of timber joists scattered all over the muddy outcrop. But then Tom shone a light straight ahead of him, and we all gasped—there was a glass lift right at the edge of the cliff.

"Like Willy Wonka, Daddy," Gaia observed.

"Yes, pudding. But better."

We all stepped into it. Tom hit a button and we all drew breath as the lift descended slowly down the side of the cliff. The sun was just beginning to rise, bleeding copper light into the fjord, and through the glass floor of the lift we could make out the shape of the house: three round tiers about halfway down, sitting out over the water, glowing gold in the new sun.

The lift descended into an opening within the confines of the house. He hit the button and the door slid cleanly open, allowing us to step inside the cold space.

"One, two, three." Tom switched on the lights, illuminating the house. It was still a shell, and there were bits of wood and metal lying everywhere, but it was finished. Completely sealed in. A spiral staircase spun up from the middle of the floor to the next levels like a giant metallic strand of DNA. Tom saw me staring at it.

"I know what you're thinking," he said. "Coco will have a field day trying to climb it."

I nodded. She was squirming in my arms, yanking on my clothes and hair to get down, but I wouldn't let her the place wasn't exactly Coco-proof. Tom ran a hand across the dusty silver banister, grinning at the staircase like it was a living object.

"Doubles up as a ventilation shaft," he told me, as though I might have a clue what this meant. "Thought we'd have to put in a mechanical ventilation system, but we improvised. Oh, but that's *nothing* compared to how we did the insulation."

He turned and walked toward one of the walls—I assumed he intended me to follow, so I did. This was a side of Tom I hadn't seen—he was as excited as a kid let loose in Santa's workshop on Christmas morning.

"Look," he said, nodding at a cross section in the wall. I looked inside. It was filled with plastic bottles.

"Great," I said, and he beamed.

"A ton of plastic bottles serving to insulate the house," he said proudly. "That's one less ton in the oceans, in the rivers, in our food. Imagine if every house was built this way. Hotels, office blocks." He clicked his tongue against his teeth, shook his head. I did the same.

"Look at this," Tom said, and I turned to see him pointing at the back wall of the living room. It was the actual cliff. Not dark wallpaper, as I'd thought, but solid granite, all the layers of sediment shown clearly. He and Clive had spent all night sealing the walls of the house to the granite.

Upstairs he led us through the bedrooms, all of which had light provided by sun pipes and energy-optimized windows. The front two bedrooms had views of the fjord, as did the rooms on the third level. The roof wasn't going to be a roof at all, he said, but would be covered in solar panels, a rainwater recycling system, energy wells, and a garden.

"We did it," Tom said to Clive, high-fiving him. Then he pulled out a hankie and started to cry.

39

she was mine

When we went back to Granhus I told Gaia to practice her spelling in the playroom. I placed Coco in her playpen with a wooden glockenspiel. Then I headed to my bedroom, locked the door, and fell to my knees.

Aurelia's Nest was completed. I wasn't needed anymore. I stuffed a pair of socks into my mouth to muffle the sounds that came flooding out without any bidding. I leaned forward to allow my tears to drip onto the rug, where they pooled for a moment before sinking into the white faux fur.

I was so incredibly selfish, I knew it. It was *good* that Tom had achieved what he came here to do, even if he was a murderer. It was good for his daughters. At the very least, they would have somewhere to live that would be ghost-free. But I would soon be back in England, and even though my salary had been accumulating in my bank account—enough for a rental deposit—I was once again untethered.

And I remembered sharply why I had attempted suicide that night. I looked over the scars on my arms. I felt exactly like I did when I pressed a broken shard of glass into my skin. Cut loose. Completely and utterly bewildered about what I was going to do with my life. Like an utter failure who didn't deserve to live.

At fourteen I was back in foster care—this time Mum had phoned the council while I was at school one day and said she hadn't enough money to feed me. To be honest I think she just got sick of me being around, now that she had a new boyfriend. So off to a foster family I went. I fell pregnant within a month of being there to one of the other foster kids. He was about sixteen, maybe seventeen, and the first boy I ever slept with. He had moved out before I even knew why I was puking into the toilet every time a smell—shampoo, bread, the wind—brushed past my nose.

Once I started to show, it was decided fairly quickly that the baby would be put up for adoption. I don't think this was my idea, but I didn't disagree—I had no ability whatsoever to care for a child. Losing my virginity had been horrible, and pregnancy was basically nine months of puking, so I had no romantic ideals about what motherhood might involve. Gemma—my foster mother— held my hand during the delivery and said I could spend a few hours with the baby until the social workers came.

I called her Mia. I knew it wouldn't go on the birth certificate, and the adoptive parents would choose her real name, but to me, she was Mia. *Mine*. She was so tiny—barely six pounds—but so beautiful and peaceful, and I was stunned, absolutely stunned that something so special could come from me. I had never imagined she would be so exquisite, that her little hands would be miniature copies of mine, that her skin would smell so gorgeous. She had a lick of shiny black hair on her crown and the longest eyelashes, curled up like a doll's. Somehow it felt like I had always known her, and that she knew me.

It broke my heart when they came for her. The only reason I let them take her away was because I knew she'd be much, much better off with a family.

On the day of her fourteenth birthday, I woke with a pain in my chest. It was a physical pain, but there was something beneath it. Terror. Mia had turned the age I was when I gave birth to her. About a year earlier, my mother had blurted out that Mia was never put up for adoption. She was put immediately into foster care. The horror of this burrowed deeper and deeper into me until I thought it would consume me. I fell pregnant because I was in foster care—I only slept with that boy because I wanted someone to like me, to hold me. And I had been beaten, shamed, starved, and abused while in foster care; this was doubtless the same fate that Mia had endured. When I had given her over to the social worker with big glasses and frizzy hair, I had done so in blind faith that Mia was headed for a much better life than I had had. And when it dawned on me that, no, her life was a repetition of mine, a horrible echo, a fate to which I had abandoned her, exactly like my own mother had abandoned me, I couldn't bear it.

That was the night I tried to kill myself. I had never told anyone about Mia. Not a soul.

And yet, I was glad I had survived. If I hadn't, I would never have met Gaia and Coco. And I would never have known the love of small children, those two smiley, utterly mental girls, who I had somehow managed to care for all these months.

Maybe I wasn't completely useless after all.

I was in the loo when the phone rang.

My phone, I mean. It was charging at the wall socket in the playroom after Gaia and I had been watching a YouTube video about how fjords were formed. I had popped out of the playroom for two minutes when the phone rang, shrill and loud throughout the playroom. Coco waddled over to it and bashed the phone with her little hand.

"Stop it, Coco!" Gaia yelled. "You'll break it!" Snatching the phone from Coco, she inadvertently answered the call.

"Hello?" a voice said through the mouthpiece.

Gaia pressed the phone to her ear, the way she'd seen her daddy hold it. "Hello? My name is Gaia. Who is speaking, please?"

"Gaia?" the speaker spat. "Put Lexi on. I want to talk to my *bitch* of a daughter."

It was my mother.

"I'm very sorry," Gaia said, "but swears are naughty and Father Christmas will be *very* cross."

"Gaia?" another voice called, this time from the doorway. Gaia looked across the room to see Maren standing there. She tried to conceal the phone, but it was too late—Maren had seen, and was perturbed. What was Gaia doing with a mobile phone?

"Give it to me," Maren said firmly, holding out her palm. Sheepishly, Gaia handed the phone over.

"Hello? Hello? Is anyone there? Answer me!" my mother yelled. Maren held the shrieking phone at arm's length and said, "Who is this? Why are you speaking to Gaia?"

"Who the bloody hell is Gaia?" my mother screeched. "I want *Lexi*!"

Maren told my mother that she had the wrong number. There was no Lexi at this number. She would have proceeded to hang up, and that would have been that. I would have arrived back into the room to a conversation about a madwoman yelling about a person who didn't exist, and nothing more would have been said or done about it.

As it was, right as Maren's thumb hovered over the button to end the call, my mother said, "Is Lexi still in Norway?"

"Norway?" Maren said.

"I heard she was taking some job as a nanny for some rich ponce," my mother said, and Maren explained that no, *Sophie* was their nanny. My mother insisted that she'd called my phone number, and proceeded to describe me. My mother informed Maren that she was holding me personally accountable for putting her through the hell of bad-quality weed that she'd had to source from a teenage neighbor. She also mentioned that I'd recently tried to kill myself, and what a misfortune it was to the world that I had not succeeded.

At this, the penny dropped. Maren knew I wasn't who I said I was.

"What's going on?" Tom said from the doorway. "Where's Sophie?"

"She's upstairs . . ." Maren started to say, because a half second after she realized I'd been lying the whole time about who I was, she made the honorable decision to cover for me.

"Sophie's not called Sophie," Gaia said loudly. "She's called *Lexi*, Daddy. Her mumma is on the phone. Do you want to say hello?"

Tom glanced at the phone in Maren's hand and read the expression on her face. Right then, Maren was still processing why on earth I might have pretended to be called Sophie, and the terrible thought that I might not be the same Sophie Hallerton as championed by Verity was slowly beginning to sink in. Her expression told this story.

"Give me the phone, please," Tom said. Maren reluctantly handed it over.

"Hello, Tom Faraday here," Tom said to my mother. "Who's speaking, please?"

And from there, all hell broke loose.

P*lease*, Daddy! *Please* don't send Sophie away!"

I could hear Gaia pleading with her father all the way from the kitchen.

"For the last time, she *isn't* called Sophie!" Tom yelled, loud enough for me to hear. "She's called Lexi! She's a *fraud*! I've a right mind to *call the police!*"

Tears dripped from my face as I packed my bags. I was going home. Tom was so outraged I thought I'd be dragged off to prison, but I think I managed to earn some sympathy by begging him to hear my side of things. I told him about overhearing the *real* Sophie Hallerton on the train. I told him I was only on the train in the first place because I was homeless, and that I had attempted suicide not long before that. I showed him the scars, and he seemed shocked. I promised him I loved his daughters, that I'd done everything in my power to be a proper nanny to them. To care for them as Aurelia would have wanted. He softened at this.

"Pack your things at once," he said, not looking at me. "I'll arrange for you to be transported to the airport this afternoon."

"But, Daddy!" Gaia shrieked at the top of her lungs. "What about Dora?"

"Dora?"

Tom clearly hadn't a clue what she was talking about, because he said, "What *on earth* are you talking about?" Then it dawned on him. He followed Gaia's guilty, petrified gaze to the corner of the room cordoned off with heavy curtains. Tom yanked one of them aside and looked at Dora in her den, perched on her tree branch.

He spun around and glared at me in disgust.

"You're kidding me. You've kept that bird in here all this time?"

"She's a little nervous about flying, Daddy," Gaia offered gingerly.

"But we're working on her courage. She likes pine nuts, but you have to mash them up and feed them to her with your mouth . . ."

"Get out," Tom spat at me. I turned on my heel and walked quickly out of the room.

I folded my clothes and placed them one by one in the suitcase. Then I quickly emptied the drawer of my bedside table of all the drawings and notes Gaia had done for me. A painting of unicorns dancing underneath a rainbow, with *I love you, Sophie* written in the corner. Another drawing of four figures walking hand in hand through trees. The four figures were Gaia, Coco, Aurelia, and me. A bird flew in the background. Dora.

As I looked over these pictures, I felt my heart break. An actual split in my chest, a physical snap that sent me to my knees. I began to cry. Deep sobs that came all the way from a place of tenderness, newly planted but so deep in my being that those tears felt like they carried part of me with them. I didn't care at all that I would be returning to nothing. I didn't care about being homeless, or about anything other than the fact that I would never see Gaia and Coco again. I loved those girls more than anything. I adored them. Right then, I knew I would do anything, absolutely anything, to remain a part of their lives forever.

But it wasn't possible. I was leaving, and I would never be allowed near them again. Tom would probably forbid me from even saying good-bye.

40

did you do it?

At Highgate Cemetery Clive feels the first drops of rain needle the shoulder of his suit jacket. Luckily the undertaker has a black golf umbrella to hand—they always check the weather forecast, just in case. The family never remembers to bring umbrellas.

Clive holds it over him and Derry with one hand, wraps the other arm around her narrow waist, hooking his thumb under the waistband of her skirt as usual—his sign of affection. They walk among the crowd through the Egyptian Avenue. The rain is growing heavier, forming muddy puddles in the path. Derry is wearing black Louboutins. When the rain begins to bounce off the ground she ducks into a vault to wait it out.

"How are you?" Clive asks her lightly, in the manner a husband might ask his wife on the day of her friend's funeral. He raises a hand to move a hair out of her eyes, but she flinches.

"Don't touch me."

He glances at the crowd of mourners ahead, shrouded now by black umbrellas. He can make out Tom, flanked by relatives, his head bowed. He looks like a man who has just emerged from a

POW camp. That thousand-yard stare. Rumor has it that Aurelia was found in pieces. He felt sick when he heard that.

"Look," he says. "I need to ask you something. About Aurelia."

Derry keeps her gaze on the space behind him. She looks unsettled. To the outside eye she appears every bit the grieving friend. But the morning Aurelia went missing, he knows Derry wasn't where she said she was. He wonders—hopes—his fears are wrong. Aurelia had been depressed. They all knew that.

"You said you were meditating. The morning she went missing."

He says it carefully. She arches an eyebrow.

"And?"

"Come on, Derry. We both know you were out running that morning. Your trainers were sopping wet. And your workout clothes."

She slides her eyes to his in defiance. She's been crying. Her nose is red, her eyes are puffed up. She knows what he's thinking, what he wants to ask.

"Why don't you just come out and say it?" she says through gritted teeth.

He rolls the words around his mouth, hesitant to say them aloud. How can he suspect his own wife of something so terrible as murder? And yet, something niggles at him. She lied. She lied about where she was that morning. Why would she lie?

"You had no part in what happened," he says adamantly. Then, less so: "Did you?"

Derry thinks back to the morning she came back from a run to find Aurelia climbing down the ladder from the top of the cliff to the small bank of shale at its base. It was barely sunrise, and Derry was astonished to see Aurelia there—in her nightdress, too. She looked punch-drunk, as though she was sleepwalking or hypnotized.

"Look!" Aurelia said, looking past Derry to the far side of the water. "It's a migration. Just like my dream."

Derry looked across the fjord. There was nothing there. Aurelia was shouting about reindeer crossing, but Derry couldn't see any.

Derry watched, transfixed, as Aurelia swam like a woman possessed, wheeling her arms through the glossy black water. It was freezing cold. Even a seasoned wild-swimmer wouldn't brave such temperatures.

Derry squinted at Aurelia in the distance. She was drenched and knackered, but she looked triumphant, as though she'd accomplished something.

"I saved it," she shouted at Derry, her teeth chattering. "I saved it."

Out in the water, Aurelia saw the herd cross to the other side. She was glad she'd managed to save the little calf that had been struggling in the water, but now that she was alone, the shore seemed tremendously far away. And the water had darkened. It appeared oily, and when she lifted her hand a trace of something remained. She thought of the quality of the dark out here. The water seemed like a liquid dark.

Some twenty feet away Aurelia could make out a figure treading water as she was. She felt a sweep of relief. It was a woman, her head slightly bowed, her hair damp, and her arms held by her sides beneath the water. Using the last of her strength Aurelia curved one arm through the water, then another.

"Help me," she said weakly to the woman when she was close enough, but when she looked up her breath caught in her throat and her blood froze.

The figure was neither female nor male, neither human nor animal. It was . . . a creature, or perhaps a monster, its hideous gray face dotted with horrifying black holes, and its eyes were bulbous and completely black, save a yellow light that glowed, small as a pinhead, right in the center of each pupil. Instead of hair, the head was draped with matted water weeds, the mouth open in a snarl, black fangs bared as though to bite her.

Aurelia opened her own mouth to scream, but the creature plunged under the water, and Aurelia's breath lodged in her throat. For one eternal, terrifying second, she scanned the air bubbles that dotted the surface.

Something grasped her ankle. A sharp, tight hold. Aurelia opened her mouth to shriek, but just then it pulled her under, easily as a feather.

Beneath the surface, Aurelia kicked and thrashed like something possessed. Her body was being held under by a tremendous force around her ankle that she couldn't fight off. Just when the shock of the plunge lifted, the fear that she might never see her girls' faces again ripped through her like a bolt of lightning. The terrible pressure around her ankle stood between her and holding Gaia in bed when she woke from a nightmare, telling her it was all right, Mumma was here and she had nothing to be afraid of. It stood between her and Coco, her soft, gorgeous girl who lit up every time she saw Aurelia, who was beginning to laugh these days, a sound that lifted Aurelia's mood a little higher every time. And when the burn of her lungs told her with harrowing certainty that she was never going to see her girls again, never going to witness their ascent to being women, that she would not be putting them to bed tonight or kissing their soft faces, the coldness of the water modulated to a strange but blissful warmth. She figured she'd broken the surface, that she was already home. That she'd been in the grip of a nightmare and, at long last, had woken up.

On the far side of the bank, curiosity drove Derry to slip off her trainers and swim toward the spot where she'd seen Aurelia treading water. Where had she gone? One minute she was there and the next . . . vanished. A fog rolled eerily across the water, and she shivered, sensing something sinister. It was the same feeling

she had sometimes when she went for a run. Like inhaling contaminated air. She had felt herself change out here in Norway. She
had had terrifying dreams about killing everyone in the house.
She had woken up sometimes not in bed but at the kitchen table,
a pen in one hand, a red journal in the other. She had never sleepwalked before—only at Granhus. And she was writing things in
her sleep. Vile things that emerged from that same darkness that
made her glad at the thought of Aurelia dying.

And she didn't seem capable of making it stop.

When she'd spotted Aurelia in the water, a thought had bubbled up in her mind that she should go and help. She was a strong
swimmer, much stronger than Aurelia. But another force had
gripped her and held her to the spot, a shadow instinct imposing
upon her own.

She waded out up to her knees, then lowered herself and swam
slowly toward the spot where she'd last seen Aurelia. She only
managed a couple of strokes before she spotted something ahead.
A white sheet, floating in the water. And then she screamed.

The white sheet was Aurelia's dress. Aurelia's body floated past
her, facedown, arms outstretched, her blonde hair streaming like
reeds across the surface.

Derry turned and swam for her life back to the riverbank. She
didn't look back, didn't stop moving until she had climbed the ladder to the top of the cliff. As she raced back to Granhus, the knowledge that she had let Aurelia drown crept beneath her skin. Why
had she done that? People would blame her, maybe accuse her of
killing her. She had to keep it to herself.

She returned to Granhus, still wet from the fjord. But it had
started to rain.

Gaia was standing on the chair by the kitchen window.

"Have you seen Mumma?" Gaia asked, and Derry's stomach
dropped.

"No," Derry answered, and it surprised her how quickly she regained her composure. "No, darling. I haven't."

That was two weeks ago. Aurelia's body was found, much to Derry's horror, but still she said nothing about what she'd witnessed. After all, Aurelia had been depressed. She had mentioned suicidal thoughts just days before she'd gone missing. Her midwife back in England reported an alarming e-mail, requesting therapy. And she left what seemed to be a suicide note.

From the shelter of the vault, Clive turns again to survey the crowd ahead.

"I did nothing," she tells Clive in a broken voice. "I just stood there and watched her drown. What sort of person does that make me?"

The other mourners are moving to the cars, about to head to the wake. Nothing that Derry is saying makes sense. He knows Derry was sore after that night she'd seen him and Aurelia kissing. He knows he's pushed her to the brink of her sanity at times with his philandering. But he also knows her well enough to know she wouldn't have killed Aurelia. He'd feared that his indiscretion had caused Derry to argue with Aurelia, and that this had contributed to her decision to kill herself. "Aurelia drowned," he says in a low voice. "It was suicide."

Derry shakes her head, covers her mouth with her hand. Back here, in London, she feels horrified at what she did. By how she'd *felt*. She is haunted by the sight of Aurelia in the fjord. By the way she'd just stood there, and watched, and waited.

As though she'd been someone else entirely.

41

the choice

I packed the last of my things into the suitcase, carefully sliding the precious pictures Gaia had done for me along with the handprints I'd done of Coco into the front pocket. I stared at my phone, at once hating myself for bringing it and wondering how on earth I'd managed to avoid taking a single photograph of the girls. It would be the only thing I'd have to remember them by. It occurred to me that perhaps I'd be better trying to forget them altogether. I would never see them again.

As I went to leave the room I spotted the diary beneath my bed. Aurelia's diary. I picked it up and held it for a moment, working out my options. I could use it to blackmail Tom. It was evidence that he had beaten her, and even if he hadn't killed her he might well have driven her to take her own life. I sat on the bed and thought hard about how I could use this to my advantage.

Think like an opportunist, I thought. *What would my mother do?*

I could threaten him, make some sort of deal. *Let me stay or I'll show this to the police.*

I don't know how I managed to pull my suitcase out of my room and along the landing. The realization that I was leaving Gaia and Coco forever had made my body almost completely limp. I felt as though I was having an out-of-body experience. In fact, it struck me that I felt worse than I did on the night I attempted suicide, or even when I gave up Mia. This was a scale of awfulness that surpassed everything I'd experienced. What life did I have without them? I loved them both more than I had loved anyone. I was homeless again, for sure, but I didn't care where I ended up, because there was simply nowhere that was ever going to feel OK without Gaia and Coco in my life.

As soon as I reached the kitchen Gaia came rushing up to me in floods of tears and wrapped her arms around my legs. Then she started to jam her feet into the ground in an attempt to stop me from moving forward, both arms pushing me backward.

"No!" she shouted. "You're not leaving!"

I tried to speak, but there was a fist-sized lump of infinite grief in my throat and it made talking and breathing very difficult.

"Gaia," Tom barked. "Go to your room."

"No!" she screamed, spinning around to face him. "*You* go to *your* room! I *hate* you!"

With that, she burst into hysterical tears and sank to the floor, drawing her knees to her chin. Coco staggered toward her, calling, "Ya-ya! Ya-ya!" It was then that I realized that "Ya-ya" was never Coco's name for me—it was her name for her sister. She said, "Awwww, Ya-ya," and wrapped her arms around Gaia to console her, and I thought my heart might break.

I pulled the diary from underneath my arm and held it out toward Tom. I thought very carefully about what I wanted to say to him. There were so many things I could have said. *You monster. How could you?*

But Gaia and Coco were within earshot. He might have been a cruel and villainous husband, but somehow he could also be a very good father, and he was all that Gaia and Coco had left. I had to do what I could to protect them.

So instead, I said quietly, "I want you to know I read this. And I've photographed the contents. If I hear that you're treating those girls anywhere *near* as badly as you treated Aurelia, I will send those photographs to the police. Understood?"

He widened his eyes and snatched the diary out of my hands, flicking through it briefly. Something twitched in his face. And yet he said nothing.

"What's all the screaming about?" a voice said. Derry came in through the kitchen door with Clive following behind. Both of them had been out for a stroll, and they looked at the scene with perplexed expressions. I hoped with all my might that Tom wouldn't start shouting again that I was a fraud.

Derry's eyes fell on the book in Tom's hands, then on me. "You've got your suitcase. Where are you going?"

I couldn't speak and I was using every ounce of willpower to keep from bawling my eyes out precisely as Gaia was doing. Tom shifted his feet and said, "She's got to go home. She's going now to the airport."

Derry took this in. She looked astonished, if not a little trans-fixed by the diary in Tom's hands. "I'll drive you," she said. "It would be a shame not to say a proper good-bye."

I was sobbing in the front seat of Derry's car as we pulled out of the drive and toward the dirt road that ran through the trees. Added to everything else was the knowledge that Tom was most likely going to toss Dora out into the wild, and I suspected she was still far too tame to survive on her own.

She'd die, cold and alone, because of me.

"Are you all right?" Derry asked. I could only nod and blow my nose loudly on a piece of loo roll that I'd stuffed up my sleeve.

"What happened?" she said.

I blew my nose again. "It's a long story . . ."

"Did Maren do something?"

"No. It was all my fault."

"Was it something to do with the diary you gave Tom?"

"Not exactly."

There was a weird feeling in the air, but I put it down to what had just happened.

"Well, what was it?"

"I screwed up again."

"How, exactly?"

I couldn't even begin to explain it all again. I was devastated, absolutely devastated.

We reached the end of the dirt road and turned left onto the main road that ran along the edge of the fjord. I looked down at the ruffled water and the trees swaying in the wind. It had started to rain heavily, and in the distance flashes of lightning lit up the sky.

The car had fallen silent, nothing but the drum of the rain on the roof and the groan of thunder filling the quiet. I tried to think of something to say to fill the space. I wanted to explain myself to someone, and above all I wanted to pretend this wasn't happening, that it wasn't real. But it was: I was being sent back to England. I was homeless. And I had nobody in the world to turn to.

"How is your writing going?" I said after a while. My voice sounded thin and broken.

Derry turned to me and narrowed her eyes as though I'd just asked if she'd gained ten pounds.

"Why did you ask that?"

I blinked. "No reason. Just . . . making conversation . . ."

She turned back to study the road. The car fell silent again. "The night I saw you with Clive," Derry said suddenly. "Did you sleep with him?"

I stared at her. "Did I sleep with who?"

She smiled, showing all her teeth. Her eyes glittered darkly. "You heard me. I saw the way you looked at him. You slept with Clive, didn't you?"

"No!" I said. What on earth was she saying? Perhaps she was playing some kind of prank, I thought, and my devastation at leaving was making me miss the punch line. Either way, it was kind of cruel, and I felt uneasy.

She cocked her head. "Did you want to?"

I noticed she was driving faster and faster. The speedometer read 145 kph, and the rain was making it difficult to see.

"Derry," I said, clutching on to my seat belt. "Do you think we can slow down?"

"Not until you answer my question," she said, and she pressed the accelerator, lurching us forward . . . 160 kph.

I went to shout for her to let me out, but just then the fog around my brain cleared and a question beamed bright: Derry had asked whether my leaving was something to do with the diary.

How did she know it was a diary?

"I swear I didn't sleep with Clive," I said. "I swear I didn't want to, either."

A muscle rippled in her jaw. When she turned to look at me, her eyes had a strange look about them. Even her skin appeared different. Sallow, and kind of gray.

"Derry," I said. "How did you know I gave Tom a diary?"

All the hardness seemed to melt out of her face, as though I'd flicked a switch.

"It was a dream diary," she said blankly. "Aurelia wrote down all her dreams. And then the pages got ripped out and the diary was rewritten."

The air had grown cold, and I suddenly felt very scared.

"Did you have something to do with that?"

"Yes," she said, as though she'd forgotten. "Yes. I think I did."

I'm not sure what happened next. I remember seeing a figure standing in the road, facing the car with their arms by the sides, as though waiting to be struck. Derry slammed on the brakes and swerved wildly to avoid hitting them, but she overcompensated and the car plunged through the roadside barrier onto the verge.

There was a moment when the car sailed into the air, lifting my feet off the floor. I must have been screaming, but I heard nothing, saw nothing, except the trees and the silent cliffs. Then the car smashed hard against rock, bonnet first, and an airbag exploded in my face. We rolled, once, twice, a dozen times, and I thought, This is it, this is how I die. How will Tom tell Gaia? How will she cope, losing her mother and me in the space of a year?

The thought made me angry. Even when we crashed into the fjord, I remember a flash of rage preventing me from blacking out.

I must have climbed or fallen out of the car window, because the next thing I knew I was in the fjord, looking up at the sky. I was floating on my back, moving downstream. My body sang with pain. Derry's car was crumpled at the side of the bank, its front end dipping into the water. I couldn't tell if Derry was inside or not, but I hadn't the strength to try to save her. With a terrific whine the car seesawed forward and plunged into the dark water.

The current beneath me moved fast, jostling me forward. I was powerless to do anything but let it carry me wherever it wanted. The water was freezing, and I was sure I had only a few minutes before I drowned, or died from hypothermia. Warm liquid crept down my face and into my eyes, and I suspected it was blood from a head wound.

I lifted my head to scope the direction of the current and saw a log in front of me. Perhaps I could grab hold of it, I thought, and stop myself from drowning. Or maybe I could roll myself toward the riverbank. But as the water swept me closer, the log turned. Lightning fell across a hideous face with black eyes and a mouth pulled back into a snarl.

It would have been a good moment for the transformation of an inanimate object into a monster to be a hallucination, but no. The Sad Lady was pulling me down the fjord. Only she wasn't a lady, or even human. It was the monster I'd seen in the kitchen.

Silently she dipped beneath the water, ripples moving outward across the surface. Terror turned me rigid. *Please, no,* I prayed. *Someone help!* The water slapped and curdled at my body, and I could hear a growl from beneath the water. After a minute or so I saw light ahead, and I recognized where I was—I was headed toward the end of the cliff beneath Aurelia's Nest. The light I could make out was from Granhus.

My feet hit the riverbank. The shape of the Sad Lady dipped back beneath the water, moving under the black surface like a large fish. I waited for her to attack, but she didn't. My fingers met reeds. Maybe, I thought, maybe I could pull myself out, somehow haul myself to safety. Maybe someone would find me.

But as I moved one arm, then the other, something tugged at my ankle. Gently, like you might tug a light cord—the Sad Lady, just letting me know she was there. I froze. So this was how I was going to die, I thought.

Just then, a tiny orb of light from the ladder that led down the cliff face, and a shout. "Sophie!"

It was Gaia. Her voice was small in the distance, but the wind carried it and I knew it was her. I lifted my head and squinted into the darkness. I could just make out the small white glow of a flashlight moving slowly down the ladder.

"Gaia!" I shouted, the sight of her firing me back to life. "I'm here! I'm here, Gaia!"

It was stupid of me to shout that, for in an instant the tugging at my ankle stopped. Beneath the water I felt the creature move, large and swift, then it broke the surface, the weird bulbous head moving quickly toward Gaia.

"Sophie!" Gaia shouted again. She was at the bottom of the cliff now, waving from the little beach at the top of the fjord, and I could see from the flashlight that she was starting to wade into the water. A dark mound on the surface moved closer to her with frightening speed.

"Gaia!" I shouted. "Go back!"

But my voice was too weak for her to hear. She was still shouting with excitement, and that thing was inching toward her.

It would kill her.

I thought of the story I'd read to Gaia about the *nøkk*, and the farmer who'd offered his daughter up as a sacrifice. The poor, nameless daughter, who didn't want to die. I didn't want to die either, I realized. Before I'd met Gaia, Coco, and Tom, I'd wanted to die. But now, I wanted to *live*.

I wanted to do so many things.

Gaia gave a scream. She'd spotted the thing in the water coming toward her. The creature was so strong, and so fast, that Gaia would never make it back up the ladder. She was trapped. I scrambled forward, knowing I could never make it in time.

My hand hit a rock. I seized it, pulled myself upright, and aimed at the dark shadow that was now rising up out of the water toward Gaia. Using all of my might I threw the rock and hit its head, hard. The *nøkk* turned, that yellow flame in its eyes flashing brightly. It dived back into the water and hurtled toward me at great speed.

"Sophie!" Gaia shouted.

I sank back against the reeds. I wanted to shout that I loved her, but I was so weak. My head was bleeding badly, and it seemed like sleep would be a great idea. I felt woozy and strangely warm. Yes, I thought. I'll just take a nap here in the fjord.

But as I was sliding down into a gorgeous slumber something clamped around my ankle, wrenching me back to consciousness. No gentle tug, this time. Teeth, I suspected, or claws, piercing my flesh to the bone. The pain made me cry out, a long, bloodcurdling wail. No quick death for me, I realized. The *nøkk* was going to chew me up, bit by bit.

"Shout her name!" Gaia called then, and I stopped yelling.

The name of the *nøkk*.

The words of the story shone bright in my mind. *A nøkk can be banished by a human voice calling its name.*

What was it Clive said the fjord was called? The problem with depression was that it tended to turn your working memory into Swiss cheese, and this was a very bad moment to be forgetful. At least Gaia might live. I hoped she had turned back. She might make it up the ladder to Granhus, to Tom and Maren. *Run, Gaia!*

The creature pulled me lower into the water. I felt reeds pushing up my top and against my neck, the icy slop of waves against my shoulders.

The name began with an H.

"Hjørund!" I said, no louder than a whisper, but just then a last, ferocious tug yanked me under.

And everything went still.

the guest

NOW

Once upon a time I thought that I'd be better off dead.
Seriously. I thought I got in people's way and that all the horrible things people had told me as I was growing up were actually true. That I'd be doing the world a massive favor if I just stepped off the planet. *Auf Wiedersehen*. Thanks for having me.

But when I woke up in the hospital to find that I was (*a*) alive and (*b*) holding Gaia's hand, I thought that perhaps I'd been wrong. Maybe living was a good idea. Maybe I would give it a go.

I survived the fall after the crash; Derry didn't. I probably *would* have died on the little bank at the bottom of the cliff, given that it was freezing cold and I had a chewed ankle and a pretty nasty head injury, but Gaia had been able to climb back up the bank to her dad and to raise the alarm. When they found me I was almost unconscious from hypothermia and a minute or so from being brain-dead. So I came back a second time. I guess I wasn't meant to go just yet.

Sometime later, Clive waded into the fjord to look for Derry, but sadly her body had already been tugged away by the current.

He swore blind that Derry had nothing to do with Aurelia's death. He said it was an accident and yes, Derry had witnessed Aurelia drown, but she'd frozen in fear instead of helping her. I don't think Tom believed him.

Nobody could work out why Derry had done this. She was friends with Aurelia. It didn't make sense. Clive said she had acted strangely ever since they moved to Norway. She had been sleepwalking, he said, suffering from bad dreams. I told them what Derry had told me—that Aurelia's diary hadn't been written by Aurelia at all. Derry apparently ripped out the pages and re-wrote what was essentially a bunch of lies. Maren suggested that Derry had been influenced by the *nøkk*. A *nøkk* could bewitch people, she said, stir up their baser natures. Some people were more susceptible to its influence than others, but if it had be-witched Derry, it could be why she had written the diary.

When I was able to leave the hospital, I returned not to England, and not to Granhus, but to Aurelia's Nest on the side of the cliff. It was almost finished, and the result was truly breathtaking. I wasn't even nervous about going inside, even though I'd almost died falling off the edge of said cliff. Tom had gone slightly off-piste when it came to the decorating and had abandoned Derry's plans, preferring instead to be guided by photographs of Aurelia's grandparents' house. The girls' bedrooms were super cute, with an entire art studio in Gaia's bedroom and a climbing wall in Coco's, replete with safety net and padded floor.

"I'll show you the guest room," Tom said, opening up the bedroom that sat at the front of the house. I gave a gasp. A deep copper bathtub was partly sunk into the wooden floor in one corner of the room. A large brass bed with a deep mattress, fluffy pillows, and a red Sherpa blanket was placed in the middle of the room, facing a roaring fire and a large velvet sofa in duck-egg blue. Tom pressed on one of the walls—showing me the wood cladding, I thought—and a cupboard slid forward very gently, revealing the "wall" to be a twenty-foot-long modular storage unit kitted out with a wardrobe, desk, bookcase, media center, and even a kitchenette. At the front of the room was a huge seamless wall of glass offering views all the way to the city.

"It's your room," Tom said, shoving his hands in his pockets and shifting from foot to foot. "Oh, but please don't feel you have to. I don't mean for you to stay as our nanny . . . As our guest. For as long as you like." He cleared his throat. "It's just an offer."

I told him I would love to.

For many days I stayed in bed reading and occasionally writing while Tom rebuilt his relationship with his daughters, taking them to parks during the day and, when the weather grew warmer, for long walks through the hills. We never saw the Sad Lady, or Hjørund, again. Maren ordered us all not to mess with the trees or the river, just to be on the safe side.

I finished my novel. In the end, Alexa broke free from the people holding her hostage, and went on to invent a mobile phone app that created tunnels—kind of the opposite of 3D printers. I was pleased with it, but the plot had grown a bit far-fetched. Alexa was always me. I knew that. I printed it off, quietly put it in a drawer, and looked out at Coco and Gaia painting in the playroom. There were other ways to write stories, I thought. I was writing my own story. And I was playing a big role in theirs.

I told Tom about Mia. He told me that when Mia turned eighteen I could reach out to her, if I wanted. He had a friend who might be able to help find her. Less than four years away. I had something major to look forward to. And I was in a much better place mentally to approach Mia than I had ever been before.

Today, Gaia, Coco, and I are taking Dora outside for our big Fly Away day. It's spring, so she really ought to be going off now to find her own nest.

"Do we have to let her go?" Gaia asks gloomily.

"I'm afraid so," I say. "The problem is that if we hold on to her for too long, she'll never be able to return to the wild. She'll be too inexperienced, and she won't be able to build her own nest."

Gaia looks on the verge of tears. "Sophie . . . I mean, *Lexi*," she says.

"Yes?"

"Can we visit Dora?"

"I don't know. Maybe she'll visit us."

She brightens at that.

We tip Dora's box carefully by a grove of fir trees, close to where I'd spotted other ravens making their nests.

"Out you go, Dora," I tell her. "There's a good girl."

Gaia pours a trail of pine nuts away from the box, and instead of immediately pecking them all up, Dora turns and looks from me to Gaia. It's almost as though she knows what we're doing.

Then we step back. I've prepared Gaia for what might happen next. Dora might follow us all the way back to the house, but we have to be firm for her own good.

Dora takes a few hops toward us. We wait. It takes about twenty minutes, but finally another raven swoops down and stands in front of Dora, ruffling its wings. They seem to have some sort of raven convo, bobbing their heads and walking around each other making little clucks. Then the other bird flies up to a branch, and Dora follows.

She doesn't fly back down.

acknowledgments

Thank you to my UK agent, Alice Lutyens, for believing in this book right from the moment I e-mailed a very sketchy paragraph, and to my US agent, Deborah Schneider—massive thanks for everything. Thank you so much to my editors, Kimberley Young at HarperCollins (UK) and Danielle Perez at Berkley/Penguin Random House (USA), for superb insights and for making me work as hard as possible on the edits to ensure I made this book the best it could possibly be. Huge thanks also to Sophie Burks, Felicity Denham, Sarah Harvey, Sophia MacAskill, Melissa Pimentel, Luke Speed, and Charlotte Webb.

Thank you to my students at the University of Glasgow, and to my colleagues Sophie Collins, Colin Herd, Elizabeth Reeder, Zoë Strachan, Louise Welsh, and Jane Goldman. To my friends and writing comrades, Leanne Pearce, Nuala Ellwood, Ruth Stacey, Peta Whitney, Shelley Day Sclater, Emma Heatherington, Kathryn Maris, C. L. Taylor, and many, many others—self-doubt is my biggest hurdle and so I value your encouragement so very much.

I had a feeling that a research trip or two to Norway would be a good idea, but I could never have imagined just how transformative my trips to those stark, awe-inspiring landscapes would be to the story. I spent some time on a ship in the depths of winter sailing in the Arctic Circle, absorbing the sights, sounds, tastes, languages, and textures of Norway. This was made possible by an Arts Council England grant, for which I'm incredibly grateful. I am also very grateful to John Arne Bjerknes at the Nordic Office of Architecture for giving of his time so generously to assist with the architectural elements in the book, and for doing a fact-checking read. Thanks also to Ben McPherson for an impromptu discussion about wolves, which refined my thinking about environmental ethics.

Thank you to my audio publishers and to the voice artists and actors who bring my work to life for listeners.

Thanks to my favorite person, Jared, who gave excellent feedback as I was shaping the plot, and who likes to say he basically wrote the book but settled for a cheese sandwich in lieu of a co-authorship credit. You're awesome, babe. Thanks for keeping the kids alive and scurvy-free while I traipsed off to Norway. Most of all, thank you for always, always believing in me. This book is dedicated to you, and to our beautiful boy, Phoenix, for inspiring the architectural element of the story. To our girls, Melody, Summer, and Willow: my jewels, my darlings, I love you all the way up to the moon and back a thousand times over.

I am so very grateful to all the many people who sell and champion my books. New Writing North has supported me since the very beginning of my writing career, in the form of a prize way back in 2008 and many other prizes and opportunities over the last twelve years. I am tremendously grateful, especially to NWN's chief executive, the amazing Claire Malcolm, for all you have done to help me realize my dreams. Thank you also to every bookseller, librarian, literature festival organizer, and arts officer who has played a role in placing my book into a reader's hands.

Finally, thank you so much to my readers, whose e-mails, messages, and reviews spur me on more than you can ever know. I'm thankful every single day to be able to share my love of storytelling with so many readers around the world, so thank you.

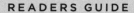

the nesting

c. j. cooke

questions for discussion

1. How did *The Nesting* make you feel? What did you think of Tom's decision to continue building Aurelia's Nest near the site where Aurelia died?

2. How did you feel about the way the story was told, including Lexi's point of view/voice and Aurelia's diary entries? Did you ever wish you had seen more of another character's perspective?

3. Which character did you relate to the most, and what was it about them that you connected with?

4. Were there any quotes, passages, or scenes you found particularly compelling or memorable?

5. What themes or symbolism did you pick up on throughout the story?

6. What did you think about the ending? How do you imagine the characters' lives after the end of the story, especially Lexi's?

7. What made the Norway setting unique? Why do you think it was so important to the story?

8. Did *The Nesting* change your perspective on veganism or the environment?

9. What changes or decisions would you make if you were turning the book into a movie? Who would you cast to play the main characters?

Photo by C. J. Cooke

C. J. Cooke is an award-winning poet and novelist published in twenty-three languages. She teaches creative writing at the University of Glasgow, where she also researches the impact of motherhood on women's writing and creative writing interventions for mental health.

CONNECT ONLINE
CarolynJessCooke.com
TheNestingBook.com
🐦 CJessCooke
📷 CJCooke_Author

Ready to find
your next great read?

Let us help.

Visit prh.com/nextread